The Spaceman

Also by Terry Deague

Where Pademelons Play

The Spaceman

Terry Deague

Contents

Prologue 1

Book the First: John Shepherd 3

Book the Second: Tania Chalmond 111

Book the Third: Marius Strangio 235

Acknowledgements 333

About the Author 334

The Demesne of Conroy

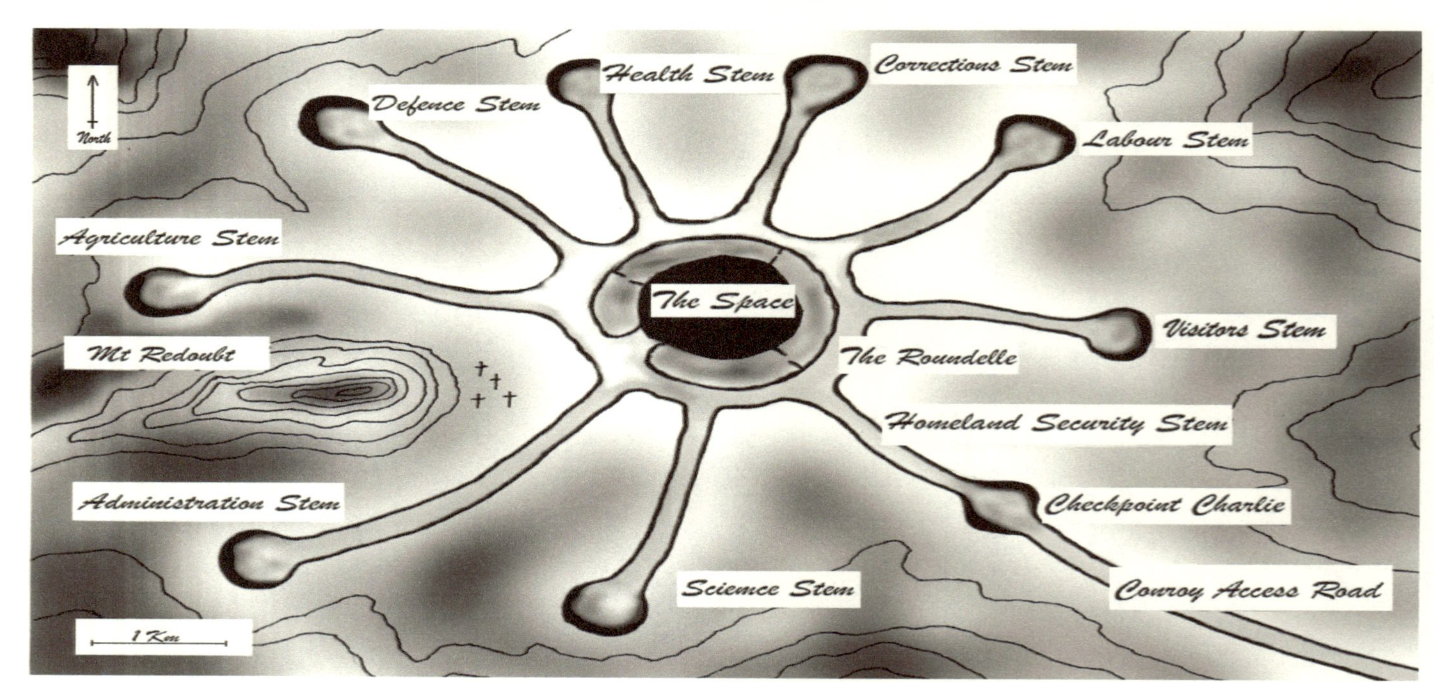

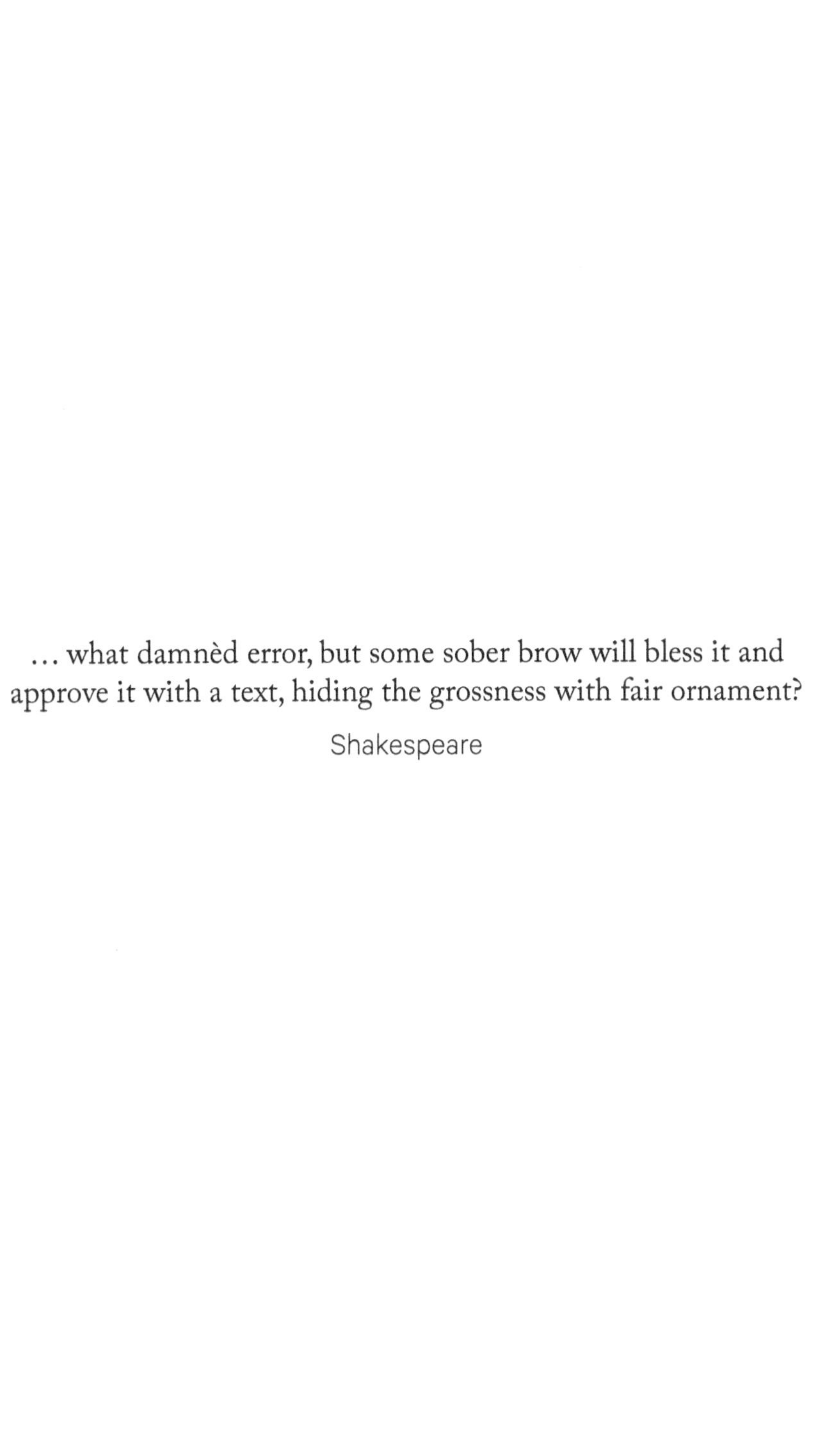

… what damnèd error, but some sober brow will bless it and approve it with a text, hiding the grossness with fair ornament?

Shakespeare

Prologue

Greetings.

You will likely know me. I'm the investigative journalist who was fortunate enough to be there on the ground when the extraordinary events forming the basis of this tale unfolded. And who acquired some renown as a consequence. By way of capitalizing on this renown, I decided to present the full story of The Spaceman for your pleasure and instruction in written form and to the best of my ability.

Having made this decision, I plundered my imagination for a ground plan for my project. Duly, I came up with one. I decided to tell the story from the unique viewpoints of several of the protagonists, rather like Akira Kurosawa - film director from the last century – chose to do in his singular movie *Rashomon*. Hence my account would be divided into three 'books' as told by three of my protagonists.

This meant I had to chase down these three people. Two were close by. Predictably, I found John Shepherd in Canberra. And I tracked Tania Chalmond down in country Victoria. The third was not so easy. I had to travel to Italy to find Marius Strangio. Once I'd snaffled them, and pressured them to participate in my project, I interviewed each at length and in depth, using the skills I'd acquired in fifteen years of investigative journalism. They were generous and forthcoming.

I can tell you I was chuffed by the result of my efforts.

Unlike the protagonists in *Rashomon*, my three players chose to stick to the objective truth as they understand it. I'm so very pleased they did. They made no attempt to put their own self-serving gloss on events. In this respect, I do *not* defer to Kurosawa. I insist on, and stand by, the essential honesty of my protagonists.

All that was left for me was to piece together the written and verbal transcripts I'd gleaned from them. And here I'd like to make a very important point apropos the editing process. I trust you will not count this point trivial. For me, it is not.

Their accounts are their very own, and I thank them for this. But the style in which their accounts are told is unapologetically mine. I've made no attempt to imagine and then to adopt the idiosyncratic styles in which *they* might have told the tale. My brief as I see it, in my capacity as an investigative journalist, is to report what they have to say, not to mimic them.

Allow me this concession. The content of the tale may be up to them, but the manner of its telling is mine to choose. In this presentation, it's *my* voice speaking to you, just as *their* voices once spoke to me.

Enjoy.

Gabrielle Zanders
Sydney, Australia
5 Nov 2033.

Book the First

as told by

John Shepherd

… and heard the Mountain's slumberous voice at
intervals thrill through those roofless halls.

Shelley

Directorate

Prowess is one part sense and nine parts pretence. I had ample qualifications for the position, but chutzpah was necessary to secure it.

The position was Director General of the Directorate intended as a response to what the Minister for Homeland Security termed 'an extraordinary state of emergency'. The tautology was the Minister's not mine. What state of emergency isn't extraordinary?

Shell-shocked by the viral pandemic that had only recently run out of steam, the Government now suffered an acute attack of the heebie-jeebies when faced with this new emergency. There was an irony here. This crew was more notable for its capacity to dismiss a crisis with elaborate spin than taking forthright action.

I was, of course, asked what my approach to this fraught situation would be. When giving my spiel, I noticed the all-male panel taking notes furiously, leading me to believe they had no idea how the problem should be tackled but were happy to pick my brains. So, when they finished asking *me* questions – most of them inane – *I* asked *them* a question: did they think *my* proposed approach was consistent with *their* idea of how things should be handled? *That* put the cat among the pigeons. Idea? What idea? They looked at each other with doomed hope. They coughed, spluttered, poured themselves multiple glasses of water, scraped chairs on the floor, and blitzed me with stammering and bureaucratese. One member asked to be excused – such was his pretext – to attend a call of nature. Finally, the Prime Minister of the day, that towering intellect, put an end to the debacle by announcing he thought my approach had merit.

I got the job.

Answerable only to the Department of the Prime Minister, I set about fast-tracking the construction of my Directorate from the ground up. The situation demanded haste. Several Commonwealth Departments vied for representation in it, as did a few State Departments. With the speed of light, I made my choices and arranged for the position of Administrator to be gazetted. This Administrator, responsible to me alone, was to act for the Directorate *in situ*. The *situ* I refer to was, of course, that critical piece of alpine turf at the centre of the whole damned brouhaha. I appointed Marius.

Hoping for a smooth ride, I crossed my fingers. Smooth it was not.

Redoubt

From multiple transcripts, and from conversations I had with Ray in the course of my duty, I understood his exodus from Melbourne, that great city in the south, was an act of voluntary retreat. Events in the big smoke were proving too difficult for him, so he did a runner. With bulging rucksack stowed in the boot, he set out one day at sparrow's fart, taking the road to the Alps. To reach his destination would require the best part of a day's drive, after which it would be shanks' pony.

He, the person who first stumbled on what is now our collective misfortune, had embarked on his fateful journey.

I found Ray Cromwell an amiable fellow. His line of business, I understood, was picture framing. He was little more than average height, but his build was solid, his head and hands huge. A mop of auburn hair flopped over his unwrinkled brow, restating the colour of his eyes. A well-trimmed beard, not yet streaked with grey, helped mollify the angular lines of his face. I am told he had a way with women. When he spoke in company, a downturn of the right side of his mouth, a full-lipped starboard yaw, signalled his fondness for human interaction. If pleased with himself, his eyebrows and eyelids retracted, leaving one to fear for the integrity of his eyeballs. The gaze he unveiled at such moments was honest and genial, indicative of hope that the pleasure he felt could be mutual.

The situation he landed himself in would, on the surface, have afforded him neither pleasure nor mutuality. Nor much hope.

Late afternoon saw him pull into a dozy town in the foothills. The town promoted itself as the gateway to the Alps. His cramped muscles thanked him as he relinquished the driver's seat of his vehicle to treat his body to a much-needed stretch. His innards showed gratitude also as he ate a lavish but solitary meal at the pub. He was aware he would, henceforth, only get to eat what he carried on his back, except for things he might, with luck, scrounge in the huts or from other hikers. Or forage. Or kill with bare hands.

It was summer. He wore a sloppy hat in jungle green, light water-resistant shirt, slacks in khaki, heavy ski socks in a ludicrous red, and a pair of infantryman's boots. He was seriously ready for a hike.

Before leaving town, he took a turn down the main drag. The vintage shopfronts were typical of Australian country towns, with rickety awnings shading the footpath, rectangles of plate-glass – faded and fly-flecked – from knee height to the full upwards reach of an arm, creaky insect-proof doors inclined to resist opening and then slamming shut on release, and interiors as drab and dusty as a sleeping wombat. The street, though mostly devoid of people, was graced by the occasional tethered horse, and replete with stray dogs. All in all, the town had a certain decrepit charm. He was aware he was soon about to relinquish nostalgic ambiences like this, but could never have imagined it would be forever.

He peered into a shop window displaying framed canvasses, and thought deprecatingly of the crude representations in garish acrylic he saw there. Typical was the cliché of multiple horses prancing, heads thrown back, through whitecaps at sunset. I can imagine his thoughts at this moment. Horses, he could accept, but where was surf to be found in these parts? Crass popular appeal must surely be the sole virtue of these pretentious pieces.

And the mitre joints in the frames were so very atrocious, so badly thrown together. An affront to his trade.

Thoughtful of tomorrow's breakfast, he bought some rashers of choice bacon at a nearby Italian deli, sliding this small white parcel into a side pocket of his rucksack.

Dusk saw him, low gear engaged, gaining altitude steadily. Remote bush, dominated by eucalypts, flashed by his side window while he listened to Bach. The bush, he reflected, would have seemed alien to Bach, and Bach to the bush. This was not Leipzig. It was not even Germany. It was not even Europe.

A year or so later, I asked Ray to explain his esoteric taste for Bach. He replied that when he was a dependent child, both his parents were crazy about country and western music. They assaulted the air with recordings of this piffle morning noon and night, watched with religious zeal live broadcasts of festivals from such places as Tamworth, and generally drove their son to murderous thoughts. 'He lied, she died, he cried', was his parodic take on the genre. So he searched the radio waves for something better, and found organ music by the peerless Johann Sebastian. He was sold.

The sun had set by the time he reached the trailhead, but a near-full moon in a clear sky served now to light his way. He parked the car in the flat grassy field used by prospective hikers for such purposes. His was the only vehicle.

He opened the boot and hoisted the rucksack onto his back. Ouch. So that was what 28 kilos felt like. Perhaps he should not have packed the apples and avocados. Even less, the bottle of shiraz. Perhaps he should have been content with instant noodles and rice crackers. Now he would have to endure this dead weight for the duration of the demanding hike he had in mind. Would he prove up to the challenge tomorrow?

He consulted his contour map by torchlight, confirming McAllister's hut was just a few kilometres down the track. Then he set off, with a rueful backwards glance at his vehicle. This part of the hike was easy. The track was broad and downhill. The beam from his torch ensured his ankles did not fall victim to its treacherous ruts and potholes. Tomorrow, he knew, things would be different. He would have daylight, but it would be many hard yards on a poorly defined trail. Mostly uphill.

The air was fresh, cool, and invigorating. His footfalls reverberated as he walked. He heard the Bach again, this time in his mind's ear. It was from the *Orgelbüchlein*. He felt gratified to be piped on his way by such magic.

He was relieved to see the turn-of-century log hut loom before him. Turn of the 19th into the 20th century. There would be bunks inside. On one of them, his choice, he would spread out his sleeping bag.

As he pushed it open, the door, on loose and shaky hinges, made a sound like a cork being withdrawn from a bottle. He used his torch to locate candles and matches in the hut. No need, then, to raid his rucksack. The flickering light set shadows dancing. The interior reminded him of pictures he had seen of Earnest Shackleton's celebrated hut in Antarctica. Ancient biscuit tins and empty green bottles inhabited fraying wooden shelves. Rude frames held up bunk beds doubtless reeking of mould.

Shackleton's hut would not, however, have supported resident spiders. Nor would it have housed a pink-eyed rat. This one did.

Needing to sleep off his enjoyable pub meal, he laid his sleeping bag on a low bunk, stripped, slipped his complaisant body between the stitched-up folds of down, and went quickly to sleep.

Upon waking, he went outside. He splashed his face with rainwater from the corrugated iron tank hugging one side of the hut. Back inside, he retrieved from his rucksack a canteen of utensils, a billy, a miniature stove, and the methylated spirits with which to fuel it. Now he set about cooking and eating his bacon treat.

The hut surprised him with leftover Weetbix, powdered milk, and sugar, all boasting acceptable 'Best Before' dates on their packets. For these treasures, he had a recent hiker to thank. He fuelled his body for the strenuous day ahead, then stashed some of the Weetbix and powdered milk into his rucksack for future use.

To complete his sustenance, he brewed some strong tea in his billy from teabags the house supplied.

Ablution facilities were outside, about a hundred metres away, in the form of a long-drop dunny. Dropping his daks, he enthroned himself, not bothering to latch the door behind him. Why should he? It swung free, throwing open his private moment to itinerant wallabies, and his gaze to the alpine wilderness.

Shazam.

His destination, Mount Redoubt, was before him, framed artistically in the doorjamb, a frame whose proportions approximated those of the golden ratio. The effect could only have been deliberate. Architects bent on taking advantage of serendipitous outlook may choose to design Guggenheim Museums or Freedom Towers. But why not long-drop dunnies? The architect of this unexpected delight had even lined the doorjamb with mitred strips of moulded wood. And, compared with what he had seen yesterday in the small-town art shop, this job looked competent.

The mountain, tipped by remnant snow, dominated the horizon. From where he sat, it was the largest peak visible, and the one with the most startling profile. Distance had rendered this profile as a deep blue silhouette standing out against the sky-blue beyond. Its north-east face fell away precipitously. Then – extremities choosing to flout each other – its line tapered off ever so gradually as it wended its way south-west. In combination, the effect was of the head and mane of a lion.

For a moment of madness, he imagined the mountain was speaking to him through an outsized megaphone. The frame, with its backward-sloping bevelled edges, had set this singular illusion stampeding in his mind. He was startled.

The peak had drawn his eye away from the fine detail and

deep green of the foreground. Now he let his eye wander over this foreground and beyond, through the series of solid but unremarkable undulations making up the middle distance. These undulations tended to blue the further they receded from him. This, he reflected with trepidation, was the terrain he planned to walk that day.

He set about realizing this daunting plan. He vacated the outdoor privy, washed his hands, packed his gear, and then left the hut behind him. He descended to a green but treeless riverbed, entered the icy cascade, forded it, then continued – uphill now with wet boots and socks – along a steep ridge. More than ever, he was aware of the weight of his rucksack.

As it rose before him, the ridge seemed without end. Knee-high blades of grass, going to seed and thick with black midges, lined both sides of the track. With every step, the rucksack tortured his shoulders. He heard groans, and realized they were his.

Immediately across the valley to his right, was a feature his contour map described as Mount Scornful. It was long, thin, and as smooth as a well-formed turd. Its resemblance to excrement was hardly grounds to justify the disdainful mien its name invoked. If his map were to be believed, access to it via any sort of negotiable trail was wishful thinking. Its prominence proved to be his constant companion for more than an hour, as he tackled the relentless slope running parallel to it, gazing down into the wooded gulch separating the ridge he trod from its supercilious companion.

He took time out to sit, rest, guzzle water, and munch on a muesli bar. Something – actually some *things* – on the near slope of Scornful caught his attention. Grey patches amongst the dominant green, their shapes were near-perfect circles, each several hundred metres across. The content of these patches appeared to be dead snow-gums. He counted the patches. He could make out ten. Likely, there were more out of view. Were they evidence of a past alien presence? Von Däniken circles? Or could this be what, in agricultural circles, is known, though not adequately explained, as dieback?

It was a phenomenon to whet curiosity. But not one inclined at present to surrender its mysteries to him.

He resumed his trek to the top of the ridge, turned, and looked back the way he had come. To his left was Scornful, its ominous grey circles pockmarks in green flesh. Down below was the icy river, miniaturized by altitude. His eye followed the twists of the trail he had taken from the river to where he was now. Nowhere was there a sign of human life. He was alone on this trail.

Turning to look at what was in store for him, he stifled a gasp at the sight of a series of intractable undulations, each spell of downhill followed by a longer stint of uphill. Beyond these undulations and, seemingly, not much closer than when framed earlier that day in the dunny door, was Redoubt. His legs buckled. Was he chasing a rainbow?

He trudged forward mindlessly, on automatic pilot. There was no longer any music in his head to pipe him on his way. The piper was on strike. A couple of hours later, he sat in a valley between two of the undulations, exhausted, demoralized, crestfallen, eating lunch: an avocado, water, two muesli bars, more water, an apple, and yet more water. He eyed the next uphill assault, trying desperately to psych himself up for it. Ruefully he told himself, *When the going gets tough ...*

A black spider, ugly brute, roughly the size of a small bird and about as friendly as a cornered cobra, half-crawled half-hopped across the trail in front of him. Arachne. Shelob. Aragog. It looked ready to inject poison into ambient blood. He was on his feet in an instant, backing away at a rate of knots. Was this the notorious and deadly funnel-web spider? In attack mode, he had heard, they could leap high into the air with fangs at the ready. From a safe distance, he watched it lope into the brush at the side of the trail, looking for some other unfortunate creature on which to vent its arachnid spleen. Heart pounding, he went back for his rucksack, slung it onto his back, and set off down the trail.

The spider seemed to have provided him with the adrenalin rush he so sorely needed. Fight not being a rational response, flight was his chosen ploy.

Late in the afternoon he finally reached a small saddle, giving access to the summit of Redoubt on one side, and to what his map said was Conroy's Hut on the other. He could see the hut about half a kilometre away. Its design was contemporary. Treated weatherboard did the job of logs. According to reports, it had replaced an older hut consumed by bushfire. It would serve to accommodate his tired bones tonight.

He turned to examine the mountain. He was amazed at how accessible it looked in the final analysis. The mane of the lion was at close quarters and, should that be scaled, a short saunter along the nape of the neck would lead to the head of the noble beast. The crown of this head was the highest point of the mountain.

He resisted the temptation for now. Instead, he made the short trek to the hut. And entered.

The scant detail I provide re the interior of Conroy's hut is reliant entirely on the perfunctory account Ray gave me. I have never been inside it. I believe few people *have* in recent days. *None* have since Ray settled in after which, of course, it became off limits to the world, excised from the habitable universe.

Like its outside, the interior design was contemporary. A slanting plasterboard ceiling presided over a single but compact room, open to the wider world through a single door and a couple of high-set windows. All accoutrements were built in: shelves, table, benches, and bunk beds. And that, I'm afraid, is all I know about it.

Once inside, Ray dropped his contentious rucksack, boiled the billy, and drank the most refreshing cup of tea of his life. Then, from his rucksack, he retrieved the bottle of shiraz, placing it unopened on one of the shelves, alongside some sweet biscuits resident there. Here, he reflected, was his new home for a time. Its single room with its minimal facilities had proved adequate to a generation of hikers for sleeping, sitting, cooking, eating, washing, recreating, and fornicating. *Sans* the fornication, it would serve the same purpose for him now.

He rested, his full length spread out along the lower of two bunk beds.

He did not lie there long. Suddenly, he felt refreshed, his mind alert and his body surging with new energy. He was possessed of a mission. He would climb the mountain before the day was done. Without the rucksack, this was achievable.

A tangle of low scraggly brush tumbled down the flanks of the putative mane. The path previous hikers had forged through this brush opened up before him. In no time he reached the spinal ridge, strewn with small rocks but clear of undergrowth. From here it was a stroll in the park. Guided by outcrops of pale granite, and by patches of still paler snow, he made his way to the mountain peak, the crown of the lion's head.

He feasted his eyes on a full circle of uninterrupted viewing. The vista from Mount Kilimanjaro, he had heard, embraced more surface area than any other on Earth. Surely, however, the vista he now enjoyed was a contender.

Away in the south was the main range of Alps, a high ridge capped in white, to which this peak might be regarded, if its name were to be believed, as a redoubt. To the north was a plain of soft green wilderness, annexed as National Park according to his map. Rust coloured slashes marked unsealed vehicular tracks.

Across this plain, an electrical storm was brewing. Distant lightning was terrorising the gap between sky and earth. Its forks were incessant in time, and pervasive in space. The muffled claps of thunder all but merged into a continuous roll. It might have been a battlefield down there.

He realized the storm was getting closer. The sky over his head was greying ominously. Mild panic gripped the primitive lobes of his brain as he pondered the prospect of being caught on top of the highest peak in the neighbourhood while nature wreaked its havoc. Off he went down the mountain at a gallop.

Dollops of water the size of grapes were pelting him as he approached the hut. Just before he reached safety inside, the sun put in a brief unexpected appearance, directing a shaft of sunlight through a gap in the clouds. He turned to see a sunny glint reflected from a huge embed of granite high on the mountainside, about where the eye of the supposed lion might have been. This embed was sheer. No topsoil – or anything else – clung to it.

It was as if the mountain had winked at him.

The heavy patter of raindrops on the metal roof entertained him as he prepared his evening meal of noodles, dehydrated veggies, and the remainder of the bacon. Thereafter, his entertainment, as he sat on one of the hard benches, consisted of patterns of light and shadow, bizarre and mobile, cast by flickering candlelight onto the ceiling and interior walls of the hut. When he had had enough of this magic, he took himself to bed. His sleep, instantly realized, was sweet and long.

Morning announced itself through the small window above the bunk beds. Summer had brought welcome warmth to the Alps, so he donned shorts and T-shirt, ate an adequate but unexciting breakfast, and ventured outside. The eye that had winked at him the previous evening now lacked life. It was not pretending to be other than a slab of granite embedded in a monolithic hunk of geologic anticline. It wasn't favoured by the early sun, as it had been by that of evening twilight.

He splashed his face with water, then made his way to the long-drop dunny situated about fifty metres away. Although he didn't bother shutting the door, his moment here of unavoidable delay was not on this occasion graced by an aesthetic view of the mountain. Nor of anything else except generic alpine scrub.

He strolled casually towards Redoubt, admiring the view. It

would be his until he no longer had a source of food. This would be his refuge from the problems life in the city had foisted on him.

Several hundred metres from the hut, he happened to glance down. There was an ugly black spider on the ground, half-hopping half-running, similar to the one he had encountered on the trail. For an instant, a delusion flashed across his mind. The spider was the same one. Arachne. Shelob. Or, nod to contemporary literature, Aragog. It had followed him here, intending to attack when the time was ripe. He backed off, and simultaneously checked himself. How silly. It could not possibly be the same one, coming all that distance just for him.

He watched it lurch away in the general direction of the mountain. Then it stopped. Its furry legs, all eight, curled themselves beneath its abdomen. Was the critter dead, or just playing dead?

He prodded carefully with a long twig. It was dead. Hmmm?

Close by, he noticed other small dead critters. A beetle. Dead. A butterfly. Dead. Ants. Dead. A witchetty grub. Dead. Death the common factor.

The corpses traced out a well-formed line. Odd, he thought.

He followed the line. A skink. Dead. A worm. Dead. A copperhead snake. Conveniently dead.

The line was concave, curving back on itself, determined (it would seem) to complete a full circle. When he had traced the curve for about fifty metres, a flock of currawongs passed overhead, signalling each other (and by accident any other sentient being within cooee) with their clunky calls. Then they fell from the sky a few metres beyond the curve, making a succession of thuds as they hit the ground heavily. They did not move.

Dead.

He froze. This line of critters, all slow movers while alive but now not moving at all, was a line of death. When anything crossed that line it died instantly. Fast-moving critters died too, the only difference being momentum carried their corpses a tad beyond the line. To wit, the currawongs.

That left him inside the line shaping up to be a full circle. Alive, but possibly inviting death, should he dare cross the line. A deadly trap. A circle of death. He was within its perimeter.

Spooked, he ran this perimeter clockwise, desperately, wildly, but careful to keep the line of corpses to his left. At the outset, his sweat was as chill as the panic he felt. In mere minutes of sprinting/scrambling, it had become warm and profuse. He crashed through scrub, vaulted fallen logs at a single stride, lacerated his shins and forearms on jagged foliage, freaked out at the sight of a dead wombat, another slow mover. It seemed ages before Redoubt was directly in front of him again, as it had been when he began his run.

There was the dead spider. Was it the same one? Yes, indeed, it was. Because, further ahead, he could make out the sorry corpses of the currawongs. He had gone full circle.

He fell to his knees, his torso tilting forward until his brow grazed the turf. For a few seconds he maintained this foetal position. Then he lifted his head skywards and let out − not an anguished howl but a mad laugh − shouting to the heavens:

Careful what you might wish for …

Herdsman

I should introduce myself. My name is John Franklin Shepherd. In this world lost sheep abound, just crying out to be shepherded. I am happy to assume both the name and the role. I am a herdsman *extraordinaire*, whose specialty is sheep, but not so much those of ovine lineage.

Herding such obtuse animals is pure bluff. Or pretence, as I have already signalled. The poor creatures haven't a clue which way is up, or maybe they couldn't be bothered to pursue the issue, so they are only too pleased to have someone like me tell them.

This is how I was able to rise so rapidly through the ranks of the public service to the point where I was offered a plum Directorate.

Don't jump to conclusions. I am, said and done, a colourless person. A statistical norm, let's say. I live in a leafy suburb in Canberra, have a wife and 2.3 children, and like to jog along the Lake every morning before breakfast. I have had a Christian upbringing of a mainstream stripe, but religion is no longer part of the baggage I tote. I like to think I have a rebellious streak that I mostly keep in check in the interests of advancing my career. My stand-out talent, a not insignificant one, is my ability to herd wayward sheep.

That's all you need to know about me, your narrator. Anything I might feel inclined to add would likely bore you silly. The tale I have to tell is far more interesting. It revolves around an event unique in human history.

Fasten seat belts.

Conroy

The name of the Directorate the Prime Minister asked me to head? Here it is: **D**irectorate of **E**nduring **T**errestrial **A**nomaly. Or DETA, in acronymic form. No, we're not talking perpetual earthquake here. The name, deliberately obscure of course, was designed by a committee. Its members, including me, had agreed that words like 'unidentified' or 'unexplained' weren't suitable, on grounds they might cause unrest, even panic. The English language offers so many opportunities for verbal obfuscation you could be forgiven for thinking it was designed for that purpose.

The particular 'anomaly' focusing the minds of the committee had a living breathing person trapped inside: the luckless Ray Cromwell. To the best of my knowledge, nothing as singular as this murderous 'bubble' had been seen before in the country or, indeed, on the planet. Our recent pandemic was a damp squib considered alongside the enormity of this mode of destruction. Early on, Ray had dubbed it a 'circle of death' but, consistent with the inexplicabilities of human preference, his turn of phrase was soon superseded, in the circles of those of us forced to live with the beast, by 'bubble of death'. A nod, perhaps, to the 3D nature of the phenomenon.

Much later, the phraseology was refined once more, this time to something our committee deemed would have less shock value. So 'The Space' became official terminology, which meant its sole inhabitant was soon, through the ingenuity of colloquial invention, dubbed 'The Spaceman'. Back then, it was still 'bubble', and Ray was just plain 'Ray'. But this guy was not your everyday Joe. His redoubtable talents were yet to emerge.

We only knew of a single bubble at the time, i.e. the one Ray had been obliged to call home. But, as the aphorism goes, misery likes company. Several more were soon found on a nearby feature known as Mount Scornful, complete with the scattered bones of dead critters and the skeletons of dead trees. Thanks be to all deities, these new bubbles gave every appearance of being extinct, of having petered out, of having done their dash. Nevertheless, their discovery had the effect of chilling a few thoughts and loosening a few bowels. How long ago, and for how long, had they been active? How many of these accursed bubbles – active and extinct – were at large in the country? Would the active ones proceed to eat people as appeared to be their intent? Could we afford to just wait and see how many people they would eat? Perhaps you can now understand why the Prime Minister of the day called a state of emergency, and authorized the Directorate.

The headquarters of the Directorate was in the national Capital, and from this centre of political jiggery-pokery I was expected to frame operational guidelines. But, inevitably, DETA acquired a significant physical presence in the brand-new special-purpose demesne of Conroy. At the behest of the committee, Conroy was built from the ground up, in virgin alpine territory, with the bubble at its epicentre. We chose to call it a 'demesne' rather than a township, not through elitist pretension, but to stifle at birth any notion the general public might get that it was a nice place to visit or (God forbid) live. Our preference would have been for the place to remain shrouded in mystery from the moment the first bulldozers moved in but, of course, that particular cat sprang from the bag within months of Ray taking up residence there in the shadow of Mount Redoubt.

My appointed representative in Conroy, was Marius Strangio, who boasted a solid background in administration, but perhaps not of such a place as Conroy. This particular nightmare was your prototypic *ultima Thule*, geographically and conceptually. Back of beyond, yes, and out of left field.

Conroy became a reality so quickly we barely had time to sneeze. A brass plaque set in stone, and located adjacent to the facility known these days as 'Checkpoint Charlie', commemorated its opening. Who opened it? A Minister of the Crown, naturally. Can you guess which Minister? Several had vied for this distinction but, when it came to the crunch, Homeland Security got the nod. Fully expected by all.

Services were installed: all the usual mod cons plus a sealed access road, a hospital, a police station, a primary school, shopping precincts, multiplex cinema, indoor sports centre, *et al* ... with a helipad and downhill ski runs in the planning stage. To the east was a huge solar farm providing power. There was no skimping on domestic accommodation whether permanent or temporary. Mostly it took the form – a stroke of genius on Marius' part – of the Quonset hut of World War fame, re-imagined and re-tooled for luxurious 21st century living.

Two Quonsets had been set aside for religious observance. One for Catholics and the other for O.D.s. Other denominations. In the main, only the ceremonial aspects of these two worthy belief systems – rites pertaining to birth, marriage, and death – held any interest for residents. Metaphysical or doctrinal aspects did not, generally speaking, grab them. This was in part because Conroy was perceived as having its own quasi-religious temple within its borders, viz. The Space. It may have been a *pagan* Space, but it had focussed the minds of most who lived in the demesne.

There was no provision for other faiths. Islamists, Buddhists, and the like could quietly go to hell. The Christian hell, of course.

Serious crime in Conroy was as rare as dandruff on dolphins. But vice of any and every description was another thing. Vice was as readily available in Conroy as in any other human precinct on the planet, and boasted a similar diversity. It was the glue ensuring the centre held. And it was immensely popular in all its forms.

So, overall, the upshot was that a whole new industry, unique even to the imagination, had evolved out of nothing. Focused on The Space, it had spawned its own demesne, and recruited its own workforce. Governments, both Federal and State, had been pleased with these developments. Happy to make a virtue out of necessity, they had indulged their addiction to spin by crowing 'jobs, jobs, jobs' to their constituents. For the Prime Minister and his cronies, what had once been a national emergency had now become an electoral asset. After all, the paramount duty of any elected official is to get him/herself re-elected.

As I have intimated, the fly in the ointment was Ray. He may have been the cause of us having jobs to do in the first place but, after that, he was widely regarded as a hindrance to everything needing to be put in place. An obstacle we had to work around. Mind you, I *can* see his point of view too, and am most sympathetic towards it. I happen to like the guy. The predicament in which he found himself was not of his making. He was a human being after all, and had his rights. The Directorate had a duty to respect these rights and uphold basic humanitarian principles.

Visitors

Brian Collyer, he said. Science. May I help you?

Frances Cromwell, she said. Just arrived. I'm obliged.

Welcome to Conroy. I'll take you to Visitors. Did you walk here with that?

It's not so heavy.

… I regret I was not on hand myself to greet Frances when she arrived. A most decorative woman, she was met by Brian who happened on the scene fortuitously. That was his story anyway. I knew neither of these young folk then, but I certainly came to know them afterwards. And since I was not actually present at their meeting and its immediate aftermath, I have no choice but to reconstruct these events from accounts they gave me later. I believe this reconstruction is more-or-less accurate …

Come from Checkpoint Charlie? he asked.

Yes.

Nobody helped you?

No.

That figures.

He threw her backpack in the rear of the Lecky, then opened the passenger door for her. She got in. He walked round and took the driver's seat.

The best you can expect around these parts, he said, is they'll look right through you.

The worst?

They'll rip your bloody arms off.

He inserted a small green card into a slot on the driver's side. There was no indication the vehicle had started, until he drove it off. These Leckies were spectacularly silent.

New to Conroy? he asked.

I was here three years ago.

Before my time. Was anything here back then?

Very little. Conroy's hut and a few odd Quonsets.

This must come as a shock to you.

It's unrecognizable.

I'll give you a Cook's tour. O.K.?

I'd be grateful.

The road we're travelling on is called The Roundelle. We're taking it clockwise. A four kilo circle from A back to A again.

He pointed off to his right.

Inside it is the main feature, he said. The infamous hut. Enclosed in what we call The Space these days. What's your business here?

To see my brother.

Holy moley. Your name. I should have guessed.

I imagine that makes me a celebrity of sorts.

You're not wrong. On the left is where I live. With all the other boffins. Science Stem.

Stem?

Stems are what we call roads around here. All nine of them. All *culs de sac* except for Homeland Security Stem. Beyond Checkpoint Charlie, that particular Stem becomes the Conroy Access Road. The road you came in on.

Each road a Government Department?

Not roads, sister. Stems. And, in all but three of them, the Conroy Divisions of six Government Departments have set up dubious shop. Get it straight. That's just the Conroy *Divisions*. Not the whole freaking Departments. Those beasties stay in Canberra, and Canberra's welcome to keep them.

Semantics, surely.

To an outsider, perhaps. But we insiders have to live with this bullcrap on a daily basis.

Sorry.

No need for an apology.

To make his next point, Brian lifted his hands momentarily from the steering wheel, allowing him to make a sweeping gesture.

The Stems radiate out from The Roundelle, he said. Like spokes in a wheel.

She pointed ahead and off to her left.

This one? she asked.

Administration Stem. The Admin Division lives here. Not the Division of a Government Department as such. Just a necessary evil. See the name on the signpost?

And where shall I be staying?

Visitors Stem. The last Stem before Homeland Security. They like to keep tabs on visitors. And lots else.

Big Brother.

You'd better believe it.

He pointed off to his left.

No Stems for a while, he said. The mountain has precedence.

Mount Redoubt.

Yes. Quite a sight. Agree?

She nodded.

There's the new cemetery, he said. Only two graves so far. Casualties of the construction phase. But room for plenty more.

You expecting more?

People die. You staying long?

Depends. A week perhaps.

He pointed ahead.

Agriculture Stem coming up, he said. A place where the choicest fruits and veggies indulge their wet dreams.

You've got them in the gun?

Don't get me wrong. Some of my best friends are in Aggie.

All these Departments. Do they get on with each other?

Now what would you suppose?

For a while they sat in silence punctuated by his verbal identification of more Stems off to his left as one by one they arose. Defence Stem … Health Stem … Corrections Stem … apropos of this last, he felt obliged to add a codicil.

State Government, he said. Their only foot in the door. All the rest are Commonwealth outfits.

A prominent billboard – just one of the many identical billboards around the shop she noticed – dominated the entrance to this Stem. In garish graphics, it spruiked a legal entity behind which perhaps a flesh and blood person lurked. **Eanis Estates.**

Who's Eanis? she asked.

Eanis the penis?

She rolled her eyes.

Harvey Eanis, he said. Runs all the real estate in town. And much else. Ninety-nine year leases, short term rental, his own unique take on time-share. Watch yourself when he's on the prowl. Didn't come by the nickname for nothing.

A blithe wallaby bounced across the road in front of them, unaware of the silent vehicle. He braked, then looked to both sides in case there were more.

A little problem, he said, we have at all times of day and night. That and brumbies. Oh, on our left is Labour Stem. The blue-collar folk hang out there. Trades and unskilled.

They treated well?

They cop it sweet here. They'd push shit uphill to get the same coin elsewhere.

Finally, the vehicle drew abreast of Visitors Stem. She glanced at the signpost.

No apostrophe? she said.

We're modern.

He pulled into the Stem. Slowing the vehicle to a crawl, he looked sideways at her, shaking his head in disbelief.

The dude's sister, he said. Fancy that.

She was indignant.

His name is Ray, she said.

Sorry, he said. No offence meant. Where are you staying?

Redoubtable Apartments.

Good choice. Got a keycard?

She found one in her handbag, and read from it.

24B, she said.

He stopped the vehicle opposite a miniature village of low-set units: Quonset huts in contemporary realization. Carrying her rucksack, he found 24B for her. She inserted the card in the slot and – *voila!* – the door opened for her.

I'll see you again soon? he asked.

If you'd like.

He presented her with a business card.

Phone, text, or email me. Tomorrow. Make my day.

He headed back towards the Lecky. Then he stopped in his tracks. He turned to face her again, shouting his message to her across the void between them.

Oh, he said, and get yourself a vehicle. They're free.

Thanks for the tour, was her shout in return.

He moved off toward his Lecky again, shouting a rejoinder over his shoulder.

More to come, he said.

Stems

One of my first tasks when developing a structure for the Directorate, and *ipso facto* for that of the demesne of Conroy, was to decide which Departments should be represented. Every Department in the country wanted a guernsey, that is to say a 'Stem' within which their proposed Conroy Division could be accommodated. I mean everybody. Even Education put in a claim. Now what possible conjunction exists, I ask you, between the situation at Conroy and the fingers-in-pie shenanigans characterizing national Education? B'Jesus. I promptly told those clowns what they could do with their shithouse claim.

We – me, Marius, DETA, and (by extension) the Australian populace – needed a Division of scientists to address this thorny issue. We saw scientific investigation of this in-your-face 'Terrestrial Anomaly' as a priority. How else could we uncover the nature of the beast, and force limits on its endurance? Such was the charter of DETA. We also reasoned that, as celebrated masters of the adventitious (and advantageous) art of spin-off, investigating scientists were well placed to stumble across a way to secure the release of the hapless Ray from his predicament and his prison. We felt for Ray. So Science got the first nod from me and their Division took possession of a Stem.

Defence put the case that there were military implications.

Assuming we got to understand the The Space, and learnt how to replicate it at the drop of a hat, perhaps that knowledge could then be used to contain the human component of a hostile invasion force intent on dominion of our wide brown land. Great Scott, said some in the Forces, with this ultimate defensive weapon at our disposal, we could contemplate a withdrawal from the US alliance. It would be sweet indeed to give those crazed Yanks the swift kick up the anus they so richly deserved. Defence was dreaming, of course, and drawing a few long bows in the process, but we decided in our wisdom they should be given a Stem. Their Division moved in gladly.

Then there was Health. From the moment news of The Space had first leaked to the general population, a disorderly queue had begun to form on its perimeter. Folk with infected arms, legs, genitals, and what-have-you were eager to expose their diseased parts to its supposedly benevolent karma. Upon executing a tentative insert-and-withdraw movement of their afflicted extremities across said perimeter, they found (praise be) the unwanted pathogens had vamoosed. Since even viruses were vulnerable to such treatment, this latter-day Lourdes had the edge on modern medicine. The healing experience of this multitude of the halt and the lame was significantly enhanced by Ray's omnipresence. Conveniently sporting a beard, he was most always on hand looking like Jesus. How could we not give Health a Stem? Their Division duly took up squatters' rights.

Along came Agriculture. The arguments they put forth were similar to those of Health, though not nearly so sexy. Whatever strange miasma The Space exuded, it could surely serve to replace ionizing radiation, to which immoderate influence agricultural produce is currently and routinely exposed. Take for example the humble tomato. Subject this popular salad vegetable to the simple in-and-out motion previously described and, Bob Brown's your uncle, all the bugs and microbes seething within it get zapped. Irradiated produce was well known to be among the *betes noires* of that pesky Green movement, but this clean and green alternative was, we felt, certain to allay even their radical concerns. So folk can go off and enjoy their salad with impunity. We gave Agriculture a Stem and their Division settled in.

Next cab off the rank was Corrections. A State responsibility, of course, and a euphemism if ever there was one. Imagine being able, they exhorted, to contain felons without resort to high walls or razor wire. Maybe a tiny problem exists, they admitted, when the moment comes to release said felons, i.e. after they have been 'corrected'. But that's a bridge to be crossed when the time arrives. At the very least, this form of incarceration can be reserved for offenders in the NTBR ('never to be released') category. We were dubious. Reluctantly, we gave them a Stem. They cobbled together a Division.

Finally, there was Homeland Security. They didn't *apply for* a Stem. No siree. That was not their way. They *demanded* one. Thumping the table, they insisted the national interest required we throw a heavy security blanket over the entire demesne, the whole kit and caboodle. For our military allies and trading partners to know we had taken emergency measures apropos of some unspecified 'anomaly' would be a national embarrassment or worse and, moreover, should this anomaly prove to be an asset in one way or another, the last thing we wanted would be foreign commercial interests sniffing around. Paranoid thought processes like these were stock in trade for Homeland Security. They lobbied our esteemed Prime Minister who, true to form, showed less backbone than a jellyfish. Of necessity, we gave Homeland Security a Stem.

Not only did they get a Stem, they got the pick of the litter. They insisted on the particular Stem that, at its southern extremity, morphed into the Conroy Access Road connecting the demesne with the outside world. So nobody could leave or enter Conroy without Homeland Security knowing about it. To this end, they set up Checkpoint Charlie, about a kilometre out from The Roundelle.

How in God's name and under Marius' watch, did they away with this lurk? My guess is it's the same way they got a Stem in the first place. Through putting pressure on the weakest link. Our Prime Minister.

And that wasn't the end of the story. Marius, who has a good nose for such things, made a disturbing discovery. In the process of bedding down their Division in the Stem of their choice, Homeland Security had managed to sneak in a contingent of spooks from the secretive Signals Directorate. Nobody should be deceived by the innocent ring their name has. The ingenuous might ask, If all they do is play around with semaphore and Morse code, what possible harm are they to anybody?

But some of us knew differently. It wasn't semaphore and Morse code they played around with. It was digital metadata. They were not at all the sort of people any halfway sane person would want in their backyard. Blatantly, their motto was 'Uncover their secrets, cover our own.' Need I say more?

Predictably, the scientists and the signallers did not see eye to eye. The signallers wanted the scientists' findings (and everybody else's) shrouded in tight security. The scientists wanted to shout their findings to the wider world.

This was only one example of the clashes of culture plaguing the Conroy project from its inception. Each Department allotted a Stem for their Conroy Division seemed determined to create an empire for the purposes of its own aggrandizement. Was such a motley crew capable of pursuing the common goal the state of emergency demanded?

How in hell was I to inspire them to unite behind a common purpose for the benefit and protection of all citizens of Oz?

Anchor

Welcome to the Program, Minister.

My pleasure, Gabrielle.

We have a living breathing *cause celebre* in Conroy. Why make life hard for him?

We're not.

… I missed this interview when it went to air. A worthy issue, aired in a public forum, and wedged to its detriment between alpha-male rock and feisty female hard place. Here for your benefit is a written transcript my secretary prepared from its video podcast …

Your slated legislation dictates to whom he can and can't talk, and doesn't allow him any appeal. Hardly fair to him.

Loose lips sink ships.

A wartime slogan, Minister. Are we at war?

Not at all, Gabrielle. It's in line with the government's policies of Ongoing Strategic Preparedness and the National Security Imperative for which, last time I looked, we have a mandate.

Preparedness for war?

Preparedness for eventualities beyond our control.

Our *cause celebre* knows a thing or two about eventualities beyond his control. Why are you not looking after *his* interests?

We are.

His right to free speech? To assembly?

As I understand his predicament, assembly is not an option for him.

I dispute that, Minister. Limited perhaps, problematic maybe, but far from out of the question.

Gabrielle, our primary aim is to protect him from exploitation.

By whom?

By forces uninclined to act in the national interest.

Like me?

Not at all, Gabrielle. Clearance shall always be available for journalists who play by the rules.

Like his friends, associates, legal team, romantic interests, politicians, the odd scientist around the traps, …?

Each case on its merits. National security must be a priority when so many malign interests are abroad.

What malign interests?

Gabrielle, may I ask you a question?

You haven't answered mine.

It's apparent that free speech is fine by you as long as it's your own. But when it's an opposing viewpoint like mine you're not so happy to have it aired.

Now will you answer my question?

Why won't you answer mine?

Because you're not the anchor and I'm not the Minister.

So, I'm not entitled to a viewpoint?

You have more than just a viewpoint. You have the means to enforce your viewpoint.

And you should not forget that.

Please answer my question? What is the source of these malign interests?

You shouldn't need to be told, Gabrielle.

Tell me anyway, in the interests of my viewers who *may* need to be told.

I won't be pressured by you, Gabrielle. There are malign interests out there and I swear by almighty God I intend to protect our citizens with the power invested in me.

Why won't you tell me what they are?

Why don't you ask those who voted us in? Ask my constituents. Ask the silent majority out there. They'll put you straight.

Thank you for your time, Minister.

Always my pleasure.

… apropos of the Minister for Homeland Security, I've only ever met him once or twice. He's an elusive character. Elusive, and doubly dangerous for it. Murky shadows are his preferred milieu. He made a rare public appearance to declare the demesne open a few years back. Since then, he's been virtually invisible.

Quite a *coup* for Gabrielle Zanders, I would think, having him on her program ...

Trades

I am endlessly fascinated by people so, when Ray Cromwell volunteered his backstory, I was all ears. It was on one of those occasions, more and more frequent these days, when I was obliged to put in an appearance at Conroy. Marius was having hassles with the Minister – Homeland Security, who else? – and I had to sort things out. I look forward to the day when Marius can deal with his own shit. After all, that's what he gets paid to do.

Anyway, for light relief, I dropped off at The Space for a chat with Ray. He's well set up these days. I believe the poor bugger has everything he wants. Broadband, a mobile connection, a pet parrot, his tools of trade, business continuity, a personal following, an audience, even a love interest I hear. He seems to be making out with this TV journalist. How they manage sex, given the physical constraints on their movements, is beyond me. There's bound to be a thing or two they could teach the Kama Sutra.

Ray was the son of a tradesman. A concreter, I believe. So when he started high school, his parents chose the trade stream for him.

... my father, Ray had told me, did the choosing and Mum just went along with it. Complicit just the same, I had said. Yes, he had replied, then had added, But she was, to give her due credit, reluctant ...

So, Ray did watered-down maths and science, a basic English without Shakespeare or any of that elite stuff, no French or any other foreign language, civics instead of history, and full-on woodwork, metalwork, and technical drawing. It was expected that, when he reached the seniors, he would become a part-time apprentice, and then slide seamlessly into a trade of his choice.

But Ray was cursed with two left hands. His first task in woodwork was to pencil a line on a ten centimetre piece of two-by-one, secure it in the vice, and then plane down to that line. He botched it. The woodwork instructor gave him another piece of two-by-one. He botched it. Then another and another. Months later, he was still trying to plane down to a line on a piece of two-by-one. The rest of class were working on ornamental teapot stands and the like. Taking pity on Ray, the woodwork instructor shook his head and moved him onto the next task: to make a dovetail joint in a piece of two-by-one.

Ray got the socket part of the dovetail right, but not the plug. The angles on the plug sloped the wrong way and wouldn't fit the socket. Feeling like a total klutz, Ray flung the embarrassing dog's breakfast behind a storage cabinet in the woodwork room and helped himself to another piece of two-by-one.

The woodwork instructor, true to the pedantic perambulations of his mind – 'a place for everything and everything in its place' – announced to the class the next day that a ten centimetre piece of two-by-one had gone missing. Did anybody know anything of its whereabouts? No response.

The next day, he upped the ante. The piece of two-by-one, he said, had been stolen. Would the culprit like to own up? Nil response.

A week of repeat announcements by this exemplar of anal retention failed to clarify the issue to his satisfaction. Then, on the first day of the following week, triumph writ large on his face, the woodwork instructor stood before the class holding up Ray's botched job. Who did this? he asked. An answer was unnecessary. All eyes turned to Ray. The jig was up.

… shit happens, was the way Ray had put it to me. Courtesy of Murphy, had been my affirmation …

Some months later – ambient shit having succumbed to time and/or biology – the principal summoned young Ray's parents to his school. He sat them down with cups of tea and addressed them bluntly.

Mr and Mrs Cromwell, he said, I want you to remove your son from my school.

Mrs Cromwell was shocked.

What's he done wrong? she asked.

Nothing to be alarmed about, said the principal.

He shuffled a few papers on his desk.

Let me share his latest results with you, he said. English, 94. Maths, 93. Science, 91, Civics, 96. Woodwork, 32. Metalwork, 28. The lad's in the wrong stream.

Time stood still while things sunk in. Mr Cromwell broke the silence.

You want us to take him out of trades? he asked.

That's my suggestion.

Well let me tell you something, principal. You do your job and I'll do mine. I pay my taxes, and I say the boy stays in trades.

Paul ..., said Mrs Cromwell.

Leave this to me, mother, said Mr Cromwell.

... were you present? I had asked Ray. No, Ray had replied. Mum filled me in many years later ...

So, Ray soldiered on in trades. Needless to say, when the time came for apprenticeship allocations to be made, Ray was not the pick of the crop. For a while, he looked like a stranded asset. Or the runt of the litter. Then, like the chance of life to a dying man, an offer came. Would he like to be apprenticed to a picture framer? Ray said, Yes. He was in no position to argue the toss.

His master, the picture framer, was Ray's salvation. In between framing pictures, running his small business, arguing with customers and banks, filing tax, and countless other peripheral and mostly joyless tasks, he taught Ray the basics of joinery, wood turning, glass cutting, canvas stretching, mat-board arrangement, techniques to combat foxing, and other arcane tricks of the trade. The master's gentle patience coaxed a latent diligence from his apprentice, who soon morphed into an assistant. They became a formidable team, culminating in a prosperous partnership.

Following in Ray's familial footsteps, so to speak, was his younger sister, Frances. By her brother's account a bright young woman, she had been watching with trepidation from the sidelines as her parents, and particularly her father, designed their son's future. As might be expected, her father also had plans for *her* future.

Social luddite that he was, he believed a young woman should leave school early so as to busy herself in routine secretarial work or other menial function of similar stripe until such time as she snared herself a husband. Should she not find a secretarial post, a stint of check-out chickery would serve instead, the purpose being merely to put bread on the table until her eventual spouse could do this for her. Her duty, once the desired goal of matrimony had been attained, would be provision of a conventional home environment for spouse and family, using her acquired secretarial or retail skills to supplement the family income if and when required.

… back then, Ray had said, Frances insisted on asking why. A plucky girl, I had thought …

Frances, it appeared, believed life should hold more promise than her father's plan offered. Was drudge – mere and endless – the only point of life? Her mother and brother, on the same page as she, were sure they knew the answer. Clandestinely, they supported her rebellion by, for example, employing diversionary tactics and laying false trails for the benefit of her recalcitrant father. Their ploy worked. One day, too late and to his chagrin, Mr Cromwell found his daughter had enrolled in medicine at a creditable (and geographically distant) university. He had been duped. His plan for her had been thwarted through treacherous family subterfuge, allowing her to exceed her station in life. He swore. He thumped the table. He punched holes in walls. For a week, he spoke only to those in his coterie of curmudgeons at the local pub.

Only a couple of years into her degree, Frances received news her mother had contracted terminal cancer. Empathetic soul that she was, she felt an obligation to put her degree on hold while she tended to her mother's condition and, ultimately, her palliated demise. She returned to the bosom of her family. Her father felt himself vindicated. He channelled brute wrath in her direction. He spat 'I told you so' at her, even though he had told her nothing of the sort. She went about her perceived new duties as carer with a composure that seemed instinctive. Ray and his mother were horrified, but had no option but to resign themselves to the hand dealt them by malevolent fate.

Let's return to Ray, accidental tradesman. This is *his* backstory I am telling. Not that of his unlucky sister.

When Ray's partner and mentor, worthy man, retired from picture framing, to indulge in what he supposed would be an idyll of golf and fishing, Ray took over the business and, in turn, took on apprentices of his own. One of these apprentices became *his* loyal assistant. A cycle as old as artisanship itself was hereby perpetuated. With one significant aberration, as those of the old school would insist. His assistant was female.

… Tania Chalmond, Ray had said. Of course, my response had been. Who else? …

Tania brought an aesthetic element to the business, some of which rubbed off on Ray. It showed up in her dress sense which, though mostly unobtrusive, always managed to include an aspect of startling originality. Her gear didn't shout conspicuous consumption, nor did it suggest slavishness to fashion, but something about the way her garments hung or the way accessories set them off invariably caught any eye that beheld. Some small bauble here, some cut of the cloth there would do the trick.

For example, take the humble work-apron she wore when involved in the down and dirty business of putting frames together and such like. While not in use, a pair of such aprons (a 'his' and a 'hers') hung from hooks in the workshop. It was obvious which was hers. She had taken the trouble to sew strips of scalloped brocade in bright red along the rims of its pockets. Red was her favourite colour.

She exemplified the adage 'as you dress so you are'.

Some might be inclined to apply to her person epithets such as 'plain', 'mousy', 'dumpy'. To some extent, her shape and colouring invited such an unkind judgment. But then, out of the blue, a haughty tilt of the nose, a cheeky flash of the eye, or a lyric note in her voice would make one think again. Where Tania was involved, it was best not to rush to judgment. She had something. *Je ne sais quoi?*

Then, without any deliberation on their part, the course of their lives – Ray's and Tania's – changed. The nature of the change meant they began to look less at the picture frames and more at the pictures. I should tell you how their new perspective on 'art' came about. Be aware I use the A-word here with a degree of slack that would inspire envy in the most indolent bludger.

One well-heeled client who collected period Japanese woodblock prints came to the firm seeking advice. The client planned to frame the prints in ornately patterned wood slathered in gold leaf. Tania threw up her hands. No, no, she protested. Ray, whose *modus operandi* was to play it safe by agreeing with the client's choice, felt on this occasion he had no option but to back Tania up. She had trumped him. Together they convinced the client his idea would traduce the simple delicacy of such prints. Only thin frames rendered in austere black were suitable for *ukiyo-e* and the like.

Chastised but impressed, the client invited them to his up-market home for advice *in situ*. They obliged. Soon they found themselves moving in elite circles. Their dreams of marbled halls had materialized. As word of mouth worked its magic within the esoteric and exclusive confines of their new-found social milieu, fortuitous developments began to crowd in on each other. Ray and Tania found their business had grown a new tentacle, capable of slithering its way into heretofore unknown crannies. Interior design became an important item in their inventory of expertise.

From here, it was a natural progression to the *Ray and Tania Show*, a regular slot on public radio. A website followed: rayandtania.com. The eponymous business partners were a hit. They had become interior design gurus.

I feel like a fake, said Ray. I'm no expert. Only a humble picture framer.

Do your clients have confidence in you? asked Tania.

Guess so.

Do you have confidence in yourself?

Guess so.

Then you *are* an expert. That's what it takes.

They were close, but there was no hanky-panky. Ray saw no need to add a sexual dimension to their business relationship, especially since he was in the process of discovering, with a heady mix of amazement and delight, that women by and large were attracted to him. Plenty of fish in the sea, he thought, I can afford to let one tiny tiddler off the hook.

What was Tania's reaction to his indifference? Ray seemed to think she was unfazed. By his reckoning, she had figured out – with that sixth sense to which he believed women have staked a claim – exactly where he was coming from, and was largely grateful to him. I have my doubts. Women, especially if young and insecure, like to have their feminine allure confirmed occasionally.

Matters of the heart aside, the upshot for the inept lad with two left hands was a hunky-dory future as he saw it. He had started out 'in trades' and had gone on to become a guru of sorts in the circles of well-heeled parvenus. How good is that?

Good times may not last forever.

First, his mother died. He grieved. So did Frances. Their father didn't grieve for the person *per se*. He grieved only for the loss of services his wife, and latterly Frances, provided – rightfully in his book – round his home.

… *His* home? I had asked Ray. Better believe the bastard, had been Ray's bitter reply …

For personal and (to some extent) administrative reasons, Frances ran into difficulties resuming her medical studies where she had left them off. Caring for her mother had exhausted her body and her soul. She felt she no longer had the mettle for formal studies. She stayed home, settling for a local job in nursing.

Then Ray became trapped in The Space. Tania began taking regular trips to and from Conroy, delivering him all the paraphernalia necessary for him to continue to ply his trade, and duly returning his wares to the wider world for sale. And by ensuring he had access to all the necessary infrastructure, Marius and I made it possible for him to continue to propagate his words of wisdom. He became Conroy's very own oracle.

Complete with cave.

Boffins

I made yet another trip to Conroy, this time to be briefed on how Science saw the current state of play at The Space. From my Canberra office, I had invited the Divisional Head, chief boffin Dr Steven Crisp, to brief us in Marius' office. Steve had asked if he could bring two of his sidekicks with him for support.

Having made all necessary arrangements, I duly took the drive to Conroy on a cold Monday in mid-June. Plans for a helipad were in the pipeline but, for the moment, the only access was via land. The Conroy Access Road existed to carry such transport.

I woke about eight the following Tuesday morning in the plush quarters Marius had arranged for me in Admin Stem. For a privileged few, a fourth-floor penthouse was the deal instead of Quonset 2.0. The light billowing through my east-facing window was so intense, I thought at first I had overslept. Then, when I looked out, I saw snow had been falling while I explored the land of nod. The lawn outside, covering the space between Admin Stem and my apartment block, was blanketed white to a depth of ten centimetres at least. The sun's rays it reflected were blinding. And light flakes were still falling as I watched.

By nine thirty, I was in my Lecky. Traffic was light as I turned left into The Roundelle. The snow plough had been through. The few vehicles I passed (and mine as well) had chains fitted to deal with the wintry conditions. First, I took a detour to the *Continental*, my favourite breakfast haunt in Health Stem, and spent a few precious moments getting my head together over French toast and a steaming long macchiato. From previous visits, I recognized the barista, a well-built woman in wire-frame spectacles and chef's *toque blanche*, but I don't believe she recognized me.

I was dressed not in my normal dark business suit, but in a khaki zip-up windcheater, salmon-pink cashmere jumper, pale blue woollen scarf, leather gloves, cream chinos, and two-tone blue and white runners. A potpourri of colour. Casual, one might say, and with a touch of deliberate crass. A business suit was mandatory for around the Capital, but outside those stultifying corridors I preferred to go informal and hence incognito. And warm. For no good reason I could think of, I was gratified I hadn't been recognized by anybody since arriving in Conroy, except at Checkpoint Charlie where of course I was required to present ID. The thought that, in theory anyway, the person with ultimate authority over the whole demesne could slink around unnoticed gave me a perverse pleasure. It was a point of pride for me. Here over my brekkie I was privileged to be a nobody.

Soon enough I was back on The Roundelle.

Just as I turned back into Admin Stem, I noticed the Lecky van, with the heraldic emblem of DETA on its driver's side panel, carrying the daily detachment from Labour Division to The Space. The workers inside were recognizable as such by their Hi-Vis vests. Their task once there, I figured, would be, among other duties, to clear away the accumulated ring of dead critters, grizzly product of the past twenty-four hours. Not an enviable task at the best of times, but especially not when sloshing through fresh snow up to your kneecaps.

I made my way to the centre of Admin operations, popularly dubbed – perhaps with a tinge of irony – The Depot. On the fourth floor, Marius' assistant, Max Baldock, ushered me into the Administrator's office. Max was both gatekeeper and gofer for Marius. And more besides, so the rumours went.

I greeted Marius. He was a tall man with attractive Italianate features including a Roman nose, a full head of black hair, cultivated dark stubble, and eyes like brown olive slices. His dress, which he perceived as mandatory, but which wouldn't have been my choice were I in his place, was a dark pin-striped suit, conservative necktie, and black shoes with uppers like mirrors. This man took his image seriously. I had found him sitting behind his desk in the space he called his own. Like all such offices in the synthetic precincts of Conroy, his looked and smelled spanking new. It was spacious, of course, as befitted the Administrator of the demesne.

On the panelled wall over his shoulder, behind Perspex and rendered with artistic panache, was a colourful mud-map, over a metre wide and in landscape aspect, of the layout of the demesne. It resembled an octopus, one (however) with nine tentacles. A nonapus mayhap. It was annotated in stylized cursive, each of the nine Stems (viz. the tentacles) identified by name. Also named in cursive were The Roundelle, The Space, Mt Redoubt, the Conroy Access Road, and Checkpoint Charlie. The sturdy but unobtrusive black frame I guessed was Ray's work. Or perhaps Tania's. I was impressed.

Forget the nonapus. Think big. These are surely the arms of our very own spiral galaxy which, I am informed, supports a black hole at its centre. And what is a black hole if not a lacuna in space that one may enter but never leave?

To my left (and to Marius' right) was a window looking out from the fourth floor office onto a scene in pallid grey, a scene washed out and as two dimensional as a cardboard cut-out. Light snow, still falling, nestled in the angles where branches met trunks in the scraggly snow-gums. The mountain would normally have dominated this outlook, but visibility at present was down to less than fifty metres. Redoubt was hiding.

Marius rose.

Take a seat, John, said Marius and, when I did, he asked, Coffee?

No thanks, I replied. Right for caffeine just now.

Marius rose, dropped a single coffee capsule into the machine, and waited beside it for his cup to fill. I indicated the map behind his desk.

A work of art, I said. How did you come by it?

Tania Chalmond did it. The Spaceman's offsider. She has a flair.

Plain to see.

Tania helps keep the fellow afloat. She's loyal to a fault.

I've noticed.

Have you noticed she's not the only one?

Who else?

The female reporter who's been getting up a few Honourable nostrils. She pays him clandestine visits, so they say. And then his sister's recently turned up.

He likes the women.

And they like him.

When Marius returned to his desk with coffee cup in hand, I decided the time was ripe to broach a contentious subject.

I never cease to be amazed, I said, at the brilliant job you've done getting Conroy up and running. It goes like clockwork.

You flatter me, John.

No, no. Nobody else could have done it as well or in such a short time frame.

I repeat. You flatter me.

Having any trouble with personnel?

None to speak of.

Or from higher up?

Whom do you mean?

Marius, we both know there are bullies around. So just remember this. You answer to me, and I answer to the Prime Minister. Nobody else is in the loop.

I know that, John. And I know you *know* I know.

So, stand your ground. I'll back you up. A promise.

There was a gentle knock on the door. We both rose. The boffins were about to arrive. And so they did, three of them. Dr Steve, whom we both knew, wore a neat unostentatious dark suit. I had not previously met his sidekicks: a man and a woman. In their mid-twenties, they were ten to fifteen years younger than the rest of us. They looked an attractive couple, though I don't mean to suggest for a moment they were an item. The style of their apparel was broadly similar to mine. Neat and casual. No power dressing. Perhaps my reputation for eschewing formality had preceded me. Or perhaps they were just behaving like no-nonsense scientists.

The man came with a laptop under his arm. The woman wore a deep shoulder-bag, made from *faux* leather, in light tan, and open at the top. Steve carried nothing with him.

John, said Steve, these are my colleagues. Dr Brian Collyer and Dr Li Wen. May I assume first names are in order?

You may.

There was a flurry of introductions accompanied by handshaking. As I shook hands with the woman, I asked her, Should I use Li or Wen?

Wen please, Mr Shepherd, she replied with no trace of the accent I expected.

And I'm John.

Marius indicated we should all sit. We did so in a broad arc in front of his desk, while he organized coffees. After he had seated himself again behind his desk, there was a minute or so of small talk over the brew before we got down to business. I addressed Steve. The others remained silent for the moment.

As you know, I said, I've called this meeting because I'd like to hear the scientific angle. Diagnosis and prognosis. So, let me put you on the spot. Cause and effect. How did The Space come to be?

We don't know, John, said Steve. And if any man or woman alive *does* happen to know, they can have my job.

How long is it likely to last? I mean The Space, not your job.

Steve raised his palms in the air and shrugged.

I was afraid that might be your answer, I said. So, tell me. What *do* you know?

Steve launched into what sounded like a prepared spiel.

We know, he said, that all life forms we have investigated die instantly when they cross the interface from The Space to the outside world. But not in the reverse direction. The effect is unidirectional. Anisotropic. This we know through mountains of experimental data painstakingly collected. We suspect the fatal outcome would apply to humans also, but we haven't the evidence for that.

No volunteers?

No.

O.K. But I've seen Ray's hands and legs cross the line. Why didn't …

Sorry to be pedantic, John. We don't call it a line. It's a bounding surface. Our preferred term is 'interface'. We live in a three dimensional world, you know.

You mean The Space goes up and down as well as side to side?

It does indeed. As many unfortunate birds and earthworms would confirm if they were able. Trouble is they don't talk. Especially when they're dead.

Point taken. But why didn't Ray's arms and legs go gangrenous when they crossed the interface?

Steve turned to Brian.

Can you enlighten him, Brian? he asked.

Right said Fred, said Brian.

Steve turned to me.

Brian's been doing experiments with mice, he said.

Those unlucky mice again, I said. Stuff them full of cosmetics. Use them to test every other damn human foible.

Yes, totally unfair, said Steve.

I plead guilty, said Brian.

He paused, and looked around expectantly.

Sorry for the frivolity, Brian, I said. Let's hear it.

Now it was time for Brian's prepared spiel.

We can, he said, interpolate the entire body of the critter into the critical zone. Back legs, front legs, abdomen, chest, everything but the head. The mouse still lives and breathes when it is withdrawn. Nothing nasty happens. Its legs don't fall off. The organs of the chest and abdomen keep doing their thing. It's the head that matters. The head crosses the interface and then comes back out, the mouse is dead before you have time to say cardio-pulmonary resuscitation.

So, it's the brain that's crucial? I asked.

We prefer to be more specific than that. We've narrowed it to the two regions of the brain known as amygdalae. One amygdala per hemisphere. Show you.

Brian played with his laptop. We waited. After a few seconds, he turned the screen to face me. On it, I saw a diagrammatic section of the brain, colour coded.

This is an amygdala, he said.

With his finger, he pointed to what looked like the kernel of a peach buried deep in its flesh. It was bright orange. I nodded. He turned the screen so it faced Marius.

The amygdalae are the brain's fear centres, said Steve.

So, the mice died of fright? I asked.

A simplistic conclusion.

Simple conclusion for a simple person.

There was a pause while the scientists let that one go through to the keeper. Brian broke the silence.

But the plot thickens, he said. Small less-complex life forms like bacteria, and even viruses we suspect, cash in their chips when they do their two-way shuffle across the interface. They don't even have brains, far less amygdalae. Did they die of fright?

Pass, I said.

Ditto.

Steve, doing his duty by smoothing the way for his protégées, turned to Wen.

Wen's done some ground-breaking work with bacteria, he said, so why don't we give her the floor?

Steve turned to Wen.

Wen? he said.

Wen turned to me.

We've developed a precise method for locating the interface, said Wen. I'll get you to imagine a culture of bacteria in gel wedged between two thin semi-porous films. We use *Lactobacillus bulgaricus*, a common and garden species. We impregnate the culture with a marker dye, so dead bacteria show up as a bright red stain. It's like the litmus test for acidity.

We call it a wentester, said Steve.

Wen blushed. She rummaged through her shoulder-bag, found a sample, and passed it across to me. I spent a few seconds turning it over. It matched her description.

Looks the real deal, I said.

So, if you're on the outside of The Space looking in, said Wen, and …

Always the best place to be, said Brian.

… you want to know exactly where the interface is, you slide the culture in and slowly drag it back out again. As it crosses the interface, a bright red line of dead bacteria shows up. *Voila*. You've found the interface.

It's deadly accurate, said Steve.

No pun intended? I quipped.

Decent response time, too, said Brian. Faster than sin on a skateboard.

How fast might that be? I asked.

Seconds. Fractions of seconds.

I passed Wen's sample back to her and caught her gaze.

Not waiting for the call from Stockholm? I asked.

There were discreet chuckles all round. Then the conversation slewed off on a tangent as Steve and Brian speculated on the dishonour the Nobel Prize would have suffered had Donald J Trump – President of the United States a decade or so prior – got his way and snaffled himself an Award. I had to call the guys back into line.

Gentlemen, I said. Could we attend to the business in hand?

Sorry, John, said Steve. Wentesters, wasn't it?

He paused for breath, and for a reset.

We've run them off in the thousands, he said. They've become an essential tool of trade for our researchers in the field.

Why thousands? I asked.

They're a single-use item I'm afraid. Our guys carry dozens at a time, along with sundry mounting jigs. In shoulder-bags just like Wen's. Known as wenkits.

So, with you boffins crawling all over his territory like flies, how does the unfortunate Ray feel? What price his privacy?

He digs us, said Brian. We don't hassle him 24/7. He helps us when we need it. We help him when he needs it. We tell him exactly what we're about, and he offers useful advice on a shitload of subjects. He sees us as his ticket to freedom. And himself as a sort of guru.

On interior decorating?

Or any topic you care to name. He's a polymath these days.

Mmm.

Silence now had its say, until I broke it.

So, I asked, armed with the wentester, what do you folk know about The Space you didn't know before?

We've mapped it, said Steve, from port to starboard, stem to stern, masthead to hull. Know thine enemy.

And its dimensions are … ?

We're dealing with a sphere of radius 436.13 metres.

Not point one four perchance?

Point one three.

I whistled to show my appreciation.

You scientists are something else, I said.

Suddenly I sensed Brian and Wen were engaged in a private confab. They were communicating *sotto voce*. I heard Wen's whisper, You propose to tell him? Then, realizing I was on their case, they went silent.

There's something you want to tell me? I asked.

Their silence incriminated them. The ball was in their court now. Wen played it.

We think The Space is shrinking, she said.

I drew a rapid breath. That was something I'm not sure I wanted to hear. The implications weren't pretty. Especially for Ray.

How quickly? I asked.

We need more data, said Wen. But if it's shrinking at all, it's doing so very slowly.

Brian interjected.

As slow as a snail on happy juice, he said.

I turned back to Wen.

How slow is slowly? I asked.

Using current data and assuming a linear rate, a couple of millimetres a month, she said.

In the silence ensuing, I tried to figure out how long Ray might have left. Four hundred odd metres divided by a couple of millimetres. Sounded like more than enough lifetimes. Perhaps the outlook for Ray wasn't so bad after all. The shrinkage seemed minuscule. Plenty of time there, I thought, for a solution to be found.

You'll continue to monitor this, of course? I asked.

Every minute of every day, said Steve.

So, in a worst case scenario, our Spaceman ensconced there in his Space might one day find himself with no space left?

Spaceless.

It occurred to me Marius had made no input so far to the discussion. I knew Marius' game. Unless invited, he would hold his tongue. If invited, he was apt to surprise with his ability to cut to the chase. He invariably had a contribution to make but his reticence infuriated me.

I invited him.

Marius, I asked, what's your take?

Marius scratched the stubble on his chin, flashed me a glance, then addressed the boffins.

I'm curious, he said, about what it is makes life. Why are rocks, icebergs, and planks of wood not living, while all plants and animals are? We, as living creatures, feel our life in every limb, but we don't know what life is. When we procreate, we don't know what it is we are procreating. When we use violent means to take life, even when the purpose is supposedly to sustain our own, we know in our heart of hearts it's a really big deal but don't know why.

He paused strategically before continuing.

So, where is the switch that turns life on and off? he asked.

You're talking about the cutting edge of biochemical research here, said Steve. We don't yet have an answer, but I'm sure one's in the pipeline.

The pipeline?

Yes.

Why wait for the plumber? I can give you a provisional answer right now.

The scientific team looked more than a little dubious. They appeared nonplussed by this brazen heresy. I imagined I could hear the thoughts rattling inside their egghead minds, thoughts along the lines of, What uncalled-for presumption is this from a mere member of the laity? A babe in the technological woods?

The downbeat tone of Steve's response betrayed his scepticism.

Let's hear it, he said.

Well, said Marius, whatever power it is controls The Space knows where the damn switch is, and can turn it off …

Power? What power?

… as fast as … sin on a skateboard.

The silence was profound, not at all what might have been expected given a killer cat was now on the loose among squawking pigeons. Marius egged on the cat.

Trouble is, he said, it doesn't know how to turn the switch back on again. Or could be it's just not inclined to cooperate.

Silence again. Egos were bruised. Steve's and Brian's eyes were glazed. Wen's were inscrutable. Since the lead balloon would not lift, I ventured a comment.

I have a hunch, I said. I know you scientists are suspicious of hunches by dint of training, but I'd like to share it with you anyway.

We won't burn you at the stake, said Steve.

This whole situation started with Ray. My hunch is it shall be Ray who finishes it.

Will he finish it, or will it finish him?

I raised my palms and shrugged.

Ask the man, I said.

Oracle

When I left The Depot, snow was falling more heavily. To keep my neck warm, I zipped my windcheater up as high as it would go.

As I slid into the driver's seat of my Lecky, it occurred to me I might follow my own directive, i.e. 'ask the man'. So, back on The Roundelle, heading clockwise, I took the short thoroughfare off to the right, opposite the cemetery. Nature, in the form of a thick expanse of snow-gums, had been required to make way for this road-metal track, in order that people could have ready access to The Space.

After only two hundred metres or so, I stopped in a small parking lot. Mine was the only vehicle there. To get from this point to my intended destination, legs were the recommended option. A narrow unsealed pedestrian trail, wide enough to allow a vehicle when necessary, continued for this purpose. New since my last visit, a flimsy hand-operated boom-gate – presently in the 'down' position – pretended to limit vehicular access. Marking the trailhead, one on each side of it, was a pair of prominent hazard signs. Adorned with black skull-and-crossbones insignias on vomit-yellow background, and with language designed to limit DETA's liability, they warned visitors of dire and irreversible consequences should they enter The Space.

A guard post stood nearby. Neither it nor the boom-gate had been here on my previous visits. These gestures to security were tokens if there ever was such. I could see the glow of a portable gas heater from inside the guard post.

The guard emerged as I stepped from my vehicle, presumably intending to check me out. His breath fogged the air. He was dressed for the weather in heavy overcoat, fur hat with ear flaps, woollen gloves, and snowshoes with bindings. A huge hulk of a man, he put me in mind of Frankenstein's monster.

He stood there for a moment as if uncertain. Then he lumbered towards me with hunched shoulders, stooped back, motionless arms, and legs as stiff as girders. I'll be buggered, I thought. Perhaps he really is a monster. Either that or a devotee of Cleese's funny walks.

I was forced to flash my ID and thereby blow my precious cover. He responded with an obsequious, Yes s-s-sir. It appeared the monster had a stammer.

My name's John, I said. What's yours?

J-J-John ... , he said.

The right choice of name if I may say so.

… C-C-Coffee.

I winked.

Don't mind if I do, I said.

The poor man was flummoxed, and I was forced to retract.

Please forgive me, I said. A bad joke.

He trudged back to his guard post with the same comical gait. Possibly he intended to phone ahead, reminding Ray he had a visitor. Ashamed of my failed attempt at humour, I gave him a pathetic wave which he failed to see. Then a twinge of guilt possessed me at the thought I was dragging Ray out into the weather.

Stands of snow-gums engulfing me on both sides, I set off down the trail. The worst of the fallen snow had been cleared from my path, possibly by Labour's work detail, the one I had seen earlier, in anticipation of traffic such as me. So, I was able to walk with relative comfort in my ludicrously inappropriate runners.

From previous visits, I knew what to expect. I walked only a hundred metres or so before bursting into a clear expanse *sans* snow-gums or any other vegetation. No more than fifteen metres across, its shape was that of a circular race track. If one ignored the covering of snow, one might imagine a peloton of sweaty cyclists wheeling round the bend at any moment. Ahead of me, across this expanse and enclosed by it, was The Space. Its perimeter was picketed by a circle of ski-poles spaced about fifteen centimetres apart, each painted red, and secured firmly in the earth beneath the layer of white.

I felt my heart leap. This was the place to which my destiny had led me. And, of more significance in the scheme of things, to which Ray's had led him.

Straight ahead of me, straddling a break of about a metre in the ring of ski-poles, was the 'conversation post', a feature familiar to me from previous visits. It nestled beneath a couple of straggly snow-gums. Protected from the weather in the manner of covered bridges *a la* Madison County, its roof – should one be able to peep beneath the snow settled thereon – was painted out of the same can that did the job for the ski-poles. One half was in and one out of The Space. The arrangement was not unlike that common to prisons, enabling inmates to entertain visitors, except that I faced a gilded picture frame instead of a steel grill. Ray was already seated waiting for me on the 'prisoner's side'. The frame was a new touch I hadn't seen before. Ray's work obviously. What kind of statement was he trying to make?

Some distance to the right of the conversation post was a pair of blue snowbound Porta Potties installed, and presumably serviced as necessary, for those occasions when throngs of visitors – bound sooner or later to be called by nature – descended on the precincts to pursue the science, seek treatment, consult the oracle, or simply enjoy the spectacle. Today's weather had put the kybosh on such a throng.

To the left of the conversation post, was a replica of the large sign with skull and crossbones bearing the warning yet again re dire personal consequences. To the left of this sign, and currently buried in snow, a narrow-gauge dolly-track straddled the interface at a metre-wide break in the circle of ski-poles. A shallow skip ran on its rails between The Space and the visitor's precinct. Presently, it sat idle inside The Space. I could see the lever that propelled it, and the rusty handrail that ran its perimeter, peeping out from beneath their cover of snow. From previous visits, I knew what its purpose was. Equipment or supplies too large to be hand delivered, would ride the rails from the outside world into The Space. Unwanted gear or waste would ride the rails in the reverse direction.

Behind the conversation post, and inside The Space, I caught a glimpse of that daddy of all *raisons d'être*, the place where all the trouble had started, Conroy's Hut. These days, of course, it was Ray's permanent domicile, standing a good hundred and fifty metres back from the conversation post. From within, I imagined

I could hear the throb of a pipe organ's bass notes. A recording of Bach, I presumed. Playing at prodigious volume.

Snow had accumulated at the threshold of the hut. Flakes danced in the air all around me. The partial white-out played havoc with my depth perception, lending to the scene an illusory flatness. I was reminded of postcard scenes of a white Christmas, cheery and benign, and wondered for a mad instant if all the fuss about a 'bubble of death' really had any truth to it. But, if that were the case, what the devil was I doing here?

About fifty metres to the right of the hut was an outdoor composting dunny, recently installed. Like all the other amenities attending the interior of The Space, Ray – in a solo effort – had installed it once it had been delivered by skip and dolly-track. Nobody was about to enter this Space to give him a hand. That was elementary.

Blessed be wires, leads, cables, pipes, and the like. Courtesy of such serpentine wonders, Ray had been able to connect electric power, hot and cold water, shower, bathroom, stove, white goods, TV, and internet to his personal advantage. Necessity makes handypersons of us all, and Ray had quickly learnt how to match the male and female ends of these sinuous conveniences, before burying them out of harm's way in underground trenches.

As I came close to Ray, I noticed – and not for the first time – a printed notice of A3 size, released from Marius' office, laminated and framed by Tania, and tacked to a pair of ski-poles. Since I was the one who had signed off on it, I was familiar with its contents. They were:

Demesne of Conroy
For the attention of all visitors:

Anti-infective treatment available Mon to Sat, 1130 hrs to 1300 hrs, strictly under supervision of authorized Health officials.
Oracular consultations available Mon to Sat, 1400 hrs to 1530 hrs.
For both these services, reservations are strongly advised.
Please show courtesy by adhering to these time-frames.

Clients not prepared to show such courtesy shall be physically removed and/or prosecuted. Even Delphi had its rules.
For further information or reservations contact
Marius Strangio
Administrator

I sat down on the visitor's side of the conversation post, facing Ray's head and shoulders in frame, an effectual portrait celebrating the golden ratio and the rule of thirds. Once again, my heart leapt.

This was *the interface* through which I gazed. The *invisible* interface. Ray's head, on the other side of it, was the source of an image comprised of reflected light. This image passed unruffled through the interface, impinging on my eyeballs, and ending up as an image inside *my* head. In like fashion, an image of *my* head passed, also unruffled, through the interface in the reverse direction, ending up as an image inside *his* head. Yet if it had been our respective heads, and not just images of them, passing through the interface – if we had swapped places let's say – there would have been lots of ruffle, to the extent things would have turned deadly for both of us. This was a weirdness that was beyond weird. I was in awe.

By contrast Ray seemed totally composed. He spoke first, indicating his alpine retreat with an ironic smile and a thumb-over-shoulder gesture.

I'd invite you in out of the cold, said Ray, but under the circumstances I doubt you'd accept.

Show me your bird, I said.

You think I keep a woman in there? said Ray.

He winked. We were old familiars by now. A long black scarf wrapped several times around his neck, a brown corduroy jacket sporting elbow patches, suede gloves, and the mandatory fur hat with protective ear flaps – of which I felt envious – kept him warm. A light dusting of snow coated his shoulders, and filled his beard.

Your fucking parrot, I said.

It's not a parrot. It's a gang-gang.

He paused for an instant, then corrected himself.

He's a gang-gang.

Have a name?

Jeremy.

And he just flew in one day, I'm told.

Who told?

A little bird.

Hmmph.

Dodged a bullet when you cornered him. Good news for you too. Company.

Jesus, mate. I'm never short of company. I've got company up the kazoo, and all of it so close I can feel the spit on my face while I read their fucking lips.

Science Division?

Mostly.

Many *of* them?

Swarms.

None here today.

Too cold for the pikers. A moral they'll be catching up on paper work, and quaffing oyster shooters round a log fire.

You resent that?

I'd be doing the same in their boots.

Anybody show up here, bar the boffins?

He rolled his eyes, and gestured with palms upturned at the weather. I amended my question.

When it's clear? I asked.

Far too often. I'd like some son-of-a-bitch to explain to me what those pretenders from other Divisions are doing round town. All those turkeys do is get under the feet of the only ones doing any real work. And they treat me like I'm resident gorilla at Conroy fucking zoo.

I'm not so happy about that. I'll look into it.

Appreciated, squire. It's not something I can do. I'm tied down so to speak.

As if to illustrate Ray's point, an itinerant sparrow traversed The Space, crossed the interface, and fell out of the sky just a few metres from us. It looked dead, and I'm sure it was. As the snow sucked the heat out of its poor body, it sunk slowly into its soft new bed. This was no novelty to me. I'd seen similar events before on previous visits. It was certainly no novelty to Ray.

We resumed our conversation as if nothing had happened.

I notice you've scored yourself a guard, I said.

Ray chuckled.

Priceless, isn't he? Wasted talent. Should be in stand-up comedy.

Who authorized him?

Well, it wasn't Marius.

Homeland Security?

That's what I hear. And that's not all I hear. Their plan is to increase security by stealth and in small steps. Long term they'd like a solid barrier. Topped with razor wire. And deadlocked. With guess-who holding the key.

Mmm.

It'll wreck my social life. And my view of the mountain.

Suddenly I became aware of what it was he would be looking at right now had I not happened to be in his line of sight. Weather permitting, he would, with me out of the way, enjoy a perfect view of the mountain. On impulse, but with trepidation, I thrust my fingers through the frame and into the infernal Space to feel the back side of the wooden moulding. *Voila.* Things were as I suspected. The frame was double-sided. I could feel the shaped wood and mitre joints at the back more or less as they were in front. All this time, it turns out, *I* had been in frame for *his* benefit, while *he* had been in frame for *mine.*

And, in the event of my absence or the absence of any other client, …

… the mountain would be in frame for his benefit, while he would be in frame for the mountain's.

Withdrawing my fingers, I put superstitious thoughts like this to one side, and picked up the conversation where it had been left off.

Ray, I said, I won't let this happen. I have the authority, not Homeland Security.

Man, he said, I can only hope you're right.

He took off his fur hat, shook the snow off, and put it back on. Then, brushing snow off his shoulders, he rose to his feet.

I'll get the bird, he said.

I watched as he shuffled in his snowshoes towards the hut, removed them at its threshold, and entered in thick red ski-socks. I was left to enjoy a pervasive silence inconceivable in my usual city environment. It was as if the white blanket of snow had muted all ambient sound as well as ambient colour. I could no longer detect the throb of bass notes – courtesy of J S Bach – and presumed Ray must, on entering, have switched off his sound system.

I was alone in the presence of this invisible soundless fiend, the evidence for which was the insidious interface just centimetres from my face, and at whose whim life itself was shown no mercy. A thought came to me as sharp and cold as an ice-pick to the brain.

What should be my plea to this phantom?

I heard a faint grunt off to my left. The figure of a person of indeterminate gender loomed out of the swirling snowflakes, plodding awkwardly towards me, careful to keep the ski-poles to his/her left. He/she had clearly avoided the guard post, and no doubt deliberately. Such a ploy would pose no problem. A single guard to protect a perimeter of almost three kilometres embedded in untamed alpine plain was obviously quite inadequate. Of said guard, it might be said he was on pointless duty.

The bulky clothing the approaching person wore – dark overcoat from neck to ankles, heavy woollen gloves, and purple knitted beanie pulled down to eyebrow level – was the reason I couldn't tell whether I was seeing an Arthur or a Martha. The person's footwear – white gumboots to the kneecaps – was the reason he/she was finding the going difficult. Sinking deep into the snow at every step is not the most efficient way to make tracks.

When the person drew adjacent to the dolly track, I figured he/she was within earshot, so I ventured an acknowledgement.

Great weather for it, I shouted.

The pitch of the reply reaching me gave the game away. Beneath the multiple layers of protective clothing, there resided perhaps a large child, or perhaps a counter-tenor, but most likely a woman.

Oh lordy, she said.

She seemed exhausted so, as she drew closer, I rose and offered her my seat. She all but fell into it. I stood at her right shoulder. Presumably as a mark of respect, she removed her beanie. Long tresses of lustrous auburn hair with no trace of grey now hung in front of her eyes. She swept these aside with a gloved hand and a flick of the head.

Come to see Ray? I asked.

Silly question, I thought. But, as it turned out, hers was sillier.

All the way from Wodonga, she said. He home?

For a bit of light amusement, try going via the guard post next time, I said.

Already have. What a pathetic clown.

We both turned our heads towards Conroy's hut, because Ray had just emerged. Having slipped back into his snowshoes, he was making his way in our direction dangling a bird-cage at his side. Inside – on its perch – was Jeremy, a fine example of a gang-gang. Scalloped slate-grey feathers decked out his torso. His bobbing head flaunted a feather-duster plumage in bright scarlet above a prototypic cockatoo beak.

Ray hung the cage carefully on the branch of a snow-gum overhanging his side of the conversation post. Indifferent to all human concerns, Jeremy proceeded – head down – to munch on a bowl of dead insects Ray had presumably raked up earlier from the active graveyard – a gift that kept on giving – asserting itself just outside his bubble. Ray sat facing the woman directly and me obliquely.

Jeremy, said Ray, meet my latest client. And that guy at her side is God.

Meet your maker, Jeremy, I said.

What can I do for you, *Madame*? asked Ray.

… I had the feeling Ray had asked this same question, with those same words, many times before …

I need your advice, sir, she said timidly.

You know the drill?

The drill?

Yes.

No, sir.

Ray's face took on a severe look as he caught the woman's eyes across the interface. His words to her were solemn, the more so because they were spoken at little more than a whisper. Suddenly, his manner became that of a religious zealot.

O.K., he said. *We must speak to each other only through this picture frame. Every word crossing such a portal must be the gospel truth. Whole and nothing but. Only in this way shall I realize within myself the powers of an oracle. Only in this way shall you realize within yourself the strength to receive my message to your heart. These are the terms and conditions. Do you agree to them?*

… I found myself incredulous in the face of the verbal tom-foolery Ray was trotting out before my very eyes …

Yes, sir, the woman said.

Then please proceed, Ray said.

I moved away discreetly, retrieved my cell phone from the pocket of my windcheater, and pretended to be absorbed in it. In truth, I could hear every word of their conversation, despite the *sotto voce* of its utterance. My ears are sharp.

I'm from Wodonga, the woman said. I'm enrolled in an IVF

program down in Melbourne because I don't seem to be able to get pregnant in the regular way.

In vitro fertilization?

She blushed.

Go on, please, said Ray.

We'd love a child of our own. Me and my partner both would. But IVF is hard work. It's painful. It's expensive. It's time consuming. It calls for great patience.

Ray nodded.

The patience of Job.

Ray nodded.

Sir, I've heard about your skills. That you can see into the future. I'd like to ask you, Is my IVF treatment going to be successful?

As might be expected of a guru, Ray stroked his beard.

I can't answer that question, he said. But I know who can.

Who?

Only the little people have the answer.

The little people?

Yes.

Like leprechauns?

Smaller than that.

Elves?

Oh, much smaller.

Where do I find these little people?

You don't. They'll find you.

The woman was perplexed. She stopped in her conversational track. Several seconds passed before she found voice.

When? she asked.

I can't be certain, said Ray. I suggest you go home and wait for them to come.

The woman's look was a mix of reverence and devastation. She had come a long way. She had crossed a state border. She had climbed to within cooee of nature's *literal* mountaintop. She had bared her all before wisdom's *metaphorical* pinnacle. All this in defiance of the inclement weather. And then, having proved her mettle in such manner, what was she told? She was told to take no action. To go home. To wait. It was, I figured, as if she had consulted a trusted doctor and come away without a prescription.

Ray reached through the frame, and squeezed her gloved hand gently.

Go home, he said. Carry on as before.

Her eyelids were heavy with resignation. She rose, gathered her hair together, and slid her beanie back on.

Thank you, sir, she said.

But her tone suggested serious disappointment. She turned. Back and shoulders hunched, she made her crestfallen way down the trail leading to the guard post. The guard would be inclined, I presumed, to let her pass when exit and not entrance was her intention. She would then make a forlorn trip back to her home in Wodonga and wait there for the little people to turn up, with only a skerrick of confidence she would be paid such a visit this side of doomsday.

Her departing torso was subsumed in the wintry wonderland.

I marvelled at Ray's talents. From framer of pictures, he had morphed into expert on interior decoration. And from expert on interior decoration, he had morphed into a guru on any subject under the freaking sun. It was all smoke and mirrors, I reflected, but he seemed to have mastered the black arts with consummate ease and, I assumed, some degree of cynicism. In an inexplicable way, it seemed his incarceration in The Space had brought to fruition some arcane latencies in his developmental journey.

From our right, a distant and unexpected snippet of music, something much more plebeian than J S Bach, impinged on our ears. Even Jeremy seemed alert to it. With enthusiasm, he launched a flotilla of high-pitched squeaks into the air, and staged a exposition of avian two-step on his perch. We swivelled our eyes in the direction of the music.

The musicians – maybe a dozen of them – emerged from the

pervasive whiteness, plodding through the deep snow in black gumboots, always mindful of the ski-poles. To all appearances, they too had by-passed the guard post. Troops of the Salvation Army, they flaunted traditional navy-blue uniforms. For the men: trousers, heavy jackets with epaulettes, scarves, gloves, and peaked caps. For the women: skirts, heavy stockings, overcoats, gloves, and domed hats with red-shield badges. Some played instruments: accordion, drum, and tambourine. All sang:

> Jesus bids us shine with a clear pure light
> like a little candle burning in the night.
> In this world of darkness, so we must shine,
> you in your small corner and I in mine.

I turned to Ray and shrugged.

Why this? I asked.

Every two-bit cause in the fucking universe, he said, is convinced I am their vindication. Their chosen one.

The Army lined up in two ranks adjacent to us, and proceeded to deliver three more verses, each of which ended with the refrain re small corners. Bemused, we listened. Delighted, Jeremy continued his dance. When the Salvos had finished their musical number, and precisely as we might have expected, the corpulent bandmaster, exponent of the accordion, passed around the plate. Not a plate at all, just a cheap plastic bowl. We each tossed in a gold coin.

That was it. Slim pickings for the day, but they could always blame it on the weather. In military formation, they left us to our own devices, taking the trail to the guard post. Showing the finger to Homeland Security in such flagrant manner was, I assumed, *de rigueur* in this neck of the woods. I could not imagine what our gormless guardian, John Coffee, was thinking, assuming he thought at all.

Apposite, I said.

What do you mean? asked Ray.

You in your small corner.

Ray stroked his beard, and inclined his head, his posture the caricature of a deep thinker.

I often wonder, he said, who's really in a corner.

I pursed my lips, and nodded my appreciation of the astute philosophical considerations behind this observation. But I had some reservations.

You certainly left that poor woman with no room to move, I said.

Oracles are never appreciated on their home turf.

No excuses. Who *are* these little people you'd have her wait at home for?

You mean you don't know?

I shook my head.

You can't guess?

I shook my head.

The technical term is 'gametes', he said. Microscopic critters. Sperm and ova.

I drew a sharp breath.

You tricky bastard, I said.

Ray tilted his head to the left and flashed me a wry smile.

And cruel, I said.

'Cruel' comes first, said Ray. 'Kind' may then follow.

I rose, angry with his inner charlatan.

Get your bird inside, Ray, I said. He's feeling the chill.

Swine

Late that afternoon, snow was still falling. After docking my Lecky at the charging station, I headed towards the lift, beanstalk to my digs. But I was stopped by the concierge who told me it would be necessary to change my plans. Conditions along the Access Road made travel unsafe, so it was imperative I stay in Conroy another night, daring to hope the weather would improve by morning. I muttered expletives, and put in a special plea to the relevant gods re the speedy commissioning of the promised helipad. Then I reflected ruefully that travel by chopper, if it ever *did* become available, was unlikely to be any less subject to weather conditions.

Upstairs, I rang my wife to explain the situation. Then I rang Marius to see if he was by chance available for dinner that night. He suggested a venue in Agriculture Stem known as *Pig's Ears*, which he said had a pleasant but unobtrusive ambience. All the best people eat there, he added. I was a little dubious about his suggestion of exclusivity but, since I was the dude from out-of-town, I was captive to his choice. Marius' taste, I told myself, was always spot on when it came to life's important peripherals.

I arrived at about seven. Ingeniously, the venue – from outside – actually looked like a pair of pig's ears. Two side-by-side Quonsets had been linked along their length by bespoke passageways of corrugated steel. Their semicircular facades had been painted, lending the assemblage a suitably swinish appearance, especially in respect of ears. The liberal covering of snow did its darnedest to enhance this impression. The entrance, to which a pathway had been cleared, was via the Quonset on the left. I took it.

Inside, the temperature was a congenial 22 degrees or thereabouts. No less welcoming, and unobtrusive into the bargain, was the silky-smooth piped music caressing the air, homage to modern jazz. An aural daub of delight, a nod to civility, a salve to sociability, this music was designed to facilitate table talk, not to drown it. Under its influence, I felt the tensions of the day release their grip on my frazzled neuronal network.

A false ceiling with concealed lighting, dim and soft, broke up the tell-tale lines of the Quonset. Tables, a single row meandering lengthwise, were spread with white linen. Chairs were of an ornamental high-backed variety, imitative of the British Raj. The venue was small (exclusive mayhap?), only about half the tables, say a dozen, being occupied. Judging from the back-and-forth scurry of waiters via low-set passages on my right, I assumed the companion Quonset to this one housed the kitchen and related facilities.

Brightly coloured children's drawings of rural scenes with an emphasis on pigs decorated the walls between long drapes emphasizing the vertical. I assumed the drawings had come from the local school and their frames from a local artisan of some note. This artisan a dazzling ray if you will pardon the bad pun. And the generally tasteful interior decor of the establishment made me wonder if Tania had, by any chance, been its instrument.

Ray and Tania. Tania and Ray. In so many instances, I fancied the synthetic ambience of Conroy – an ambience inevitable in a town that had grown like Topsy and grown (moreover) out of little more than thin air – had to an extent been mollified by the benevolent influence of this couple.

A flunky relieved me of my heavy tweed overcoat, thick scarf, and brimmed hat, revealing to the world the disguise – tribute to casual dressing – I wore underneath. But my incognito act was unlikely to fool the populace this time, I reflected, because anyone local to the demesne knew the Strangios. The Administrator of Conroy and his wife would hardly be dining here with a dogsbody. And there they were, the pair of them. Ensconced at a table with a picture-window view over the snowscape outside, they had preceded me to the piggery. Thanks to the strategic use of external lighting by management, this snowscape was visible despite the onset of darkness.

Her name was June. We had met before, of course. She was a vivacious woman, some would say flirty, her eyes with a propensity to dart around like small cheeky animals attempting to tease out all manner of secrets from those around her. But the line of her mouth was immobile as if it were stitched onto her face. Forewarned is forearmed, they say, and my prior experience of her was more than enough warning.

She embraced class distinction with enthusiasm. The way she allowed the sentences of her conversation to trail off at their conclusion told volumes about her position in society as she saw it. It said, for those hanging on her words, Mess with me if you dare. She was outspoken, believing it was the prerogative of her assumed class to eschew such niceties as tact and diplomacy. Watching Ps and Qs was for the lower orders.

Everything about her gear shouted exclusive, expensive, and fashion of the day. Hugging her form from neck to just below knee was a one-piece outfit in lustrous indigo with lacy full-length sleeves and hemline. Her shoes matched this colouring. A double strand of creamy cultured pearls dangled almost to her navel. She carried these trappings of high maintenance with nonchalance as if it were a trivial irritation.

Marius wore charcoal slacks, buttoned-up navy jacket, and loafers in pumice grey. What gives with this guy? I found myself asking. His garb was impeccable. That I grant. It just wasn't exciting. Its stuffiness was borderline antisocial. He was intelligent. He was creative. He was incisive. Why then so colourless? Conservative to a freaking fault. Where was the fire in his belly?

He made one concession only to vibrant colour. The careful folds of a cravat, in the identical shade of indigo his wife wore, drooped like wilting petals round his neck. His servility to her was as cringe-worthy as it was obvious.

I joined them at their table. Before we had even found the time for formal greetings, a waiter materialized at our table, as would a djinn from the bottle that housed our candlestick, which he proceeded to light. We asked him to come back in a few minutes, and then felt obliged to study the menu with silent diligence.

The house specialty, on offer as an entree, was *oreja de cerdo*, a.k.a. pig's ears done in the Spanish style. It was our all-round choice for starters. For mains, we followed up with mundane choices from what was essentially an international menu. A couple of bottles of cool-climate wine, of local origin broadly speaking, completed our order. Nothing was especially cheap, but the meal would be on the demesne should Marius pay, or on DETA should I.

Orders settled, the time was free for conversation. Knowing June, I suspected discourse would be challenging. I was not wrong.

How's the quango making out? she asked.

DETA? I asked in reply.

You have others?

I waited, hoping Marius would rise to the challenge. Predictably, his lips were sealed.

Judge for yourself, I said. Your husband has done a superb job. Housing, transport, utilities, you name it …

Severity and mild outrage inhabited June's voice as she spoke. It was all manufactured, of course, to put others in their place. The B-word had sometimes been used in respect of her, and right now she did her sobriquet proud.

The inquiry I pursue, she said, is *not* about the physical infrastructure of Conroy, with which I am fully conversant, but about …

The waiter arrived with wine bottle wrapped in a white napkin. Discreetly, June paused mid-sentence. The waiter poured a sample into Marius' glass, and stood upright like a soldier, waiting for him to taste it. The usual ritual ensued with, in the final analysis, Marius giving the nod. I was gratified to see Marius was good for something.

The waiter filled all three glasses, then departed. June, hell-bent on her inquiry, stuck to her guns, continuing to snipe.

What concerns me, she said, is the chain of command. From the bottom up.

Of Conroy or of DETA? I asked.

Both.

Simple.

Try me.

The good folk of Conroy answer to Marius, and Marius answers to me.

I kicked Marius under the table.

Are you democratically elected? June asked.

Who?

Either of you.

Not directly. You know that.

Nor *indirectly*, I believe. You are tin-pot dictators.

I raised my hands in the air, palms upwards.

Well *Presidente*, said June, how do you plan to play with your toy?

What toy?

Your fiefdom.

Mercifully, our entrees arrived at this juncture. I was off the hook. We all tucked in, agreeing afterwards the sautéed pig's ears were deliciously crunchy.

A figure emerged from the depths of the Quonset, setting his course for our table. His clothes were flashy. In fact, I would go further and say *beyond* flashy. They comprised powder-blue jacket, pink shirt, necktie with pink spots on white, flared white slacks (regurgitation of some long-gone decade?), and two-tone pumps in black and white. A stray thought crossed my mind. A putative pig of the Gadarene variety? I speculated. As events were to prove, this stray thought was not too wide of the mark.

On reaching our table, the visitor spoke with exaggerated bonhomie.

Bonsoir, Mr and Mrs Strangio, he said. Such an unexpected pleasure for me.

Hello, Harvey, said Marius. John, meet Harvey. Harvey, meet John.

We shook hands. Marius turned to me.

Harvey handles real estate for me, he said.

Harvey Eanis? I asked.

And you? Harvey asked.

I handle Marius.

The ambiguity confused Harvey for just the tiniest moment

before the penny dropped into some neuronal mechanism resident behind his brow.

John Shepherd? *The* John Shepherd? he asked.

Congratulations, said June. The high kai of twai from Canberra. Likes to travel under false colours.

Marius turned to me.

Harvey lives here, he said. Has his very own table.

Lives? In a bistro? I asked

I live everywhere, said Harvey. Privilege of a real estate man.

We have heard, said Marius.

Mate, said Harvey, there's one prime piece of real estate beyond my fucking reach, and I'd give my left testicle to have it.

Which one, Harvey? asked Marius.

I told you. The left one.

Which piece of real estate?

Central location. Direct access to The Roundelle.

He winked. Marius' reply was ironic.

Already taken, he said.

The piped music caressing our ears had, as if on cue, changed its tune. It was no longer modern jazz, lubricant for civilized conversation. It was music that invited dancing. Harvey turned to June, offering her his hand, and spoke smoothly.

But I don't believe *you*, Mrs Strangio, are already taken, he said. That being the case, it would be my pleasure.

June rose without hesitation. Hand in hand, the pair wended their way between tables, bound for a small area of uncluttered wooden floor set aside for performance in the far recesses of the Quonset. Soon we could see them in the middle distance whirling, swirling, twirling, lone dancers under the eyes of those there purely to feed their faces.

I looked at Marius. I couldn't read the look on his features. What I saw was not worry, concern, jealousy, anger, disgust, or anything at all one might expect to read. Portrait of a quandary? A quandary resolved? Sometimes Marius was inscrutable. But, though unreadable, his look as of right now was not benign. Of that I was certain. Something intractable – thought? memory? emotion? – had possessed his private moment.

The music to which the distant couple danced was wordless. But words could readily be added by anybody familiar with the era in which a blue-eyed person made these lyrics famous, and who might hope for a contemporary shot at their revival:

> That old black magic has me in its spell
> That old black magic that you weave so well
> Those icy fingers up and down my spine
> That same old witchcraft when your eye met mine …

Suddenly, a man in full-on formal wear popped up beside me, his black bow-tie almost in my face. With both hands he gripped the back of June's chair firmly, fingers in front and thumbs behind. I raised my eyes from the opal ring in brilliant blue on the fourth finger of his right hand to his genial face beneath a balding pate.

Welcome to *Pig's Ears*, Mr Strangio, he said. And Mr Shepherd.

… I was disappointed to find he knew who I was …

Marius turned to me.

This is Basil Shirley, he said. The manager.

I nodded to Basil.

Is everything to your liking, gentlemen? It is my commission to ensure our guests' needs are being met, and met well, he said.

As always, Basil, said Marius.

Then I'll leave you to it. It is always an honour to parade our humble services before such distinguished company.

Releasing his grip on the back of the chair, he left, presumably to take his obsequiousness elsewhere. I expected he might visit other tables, but instead he disappeared down the tunnel to the parallel Quonset.

Marius? I asked.

Yes, boss, said Marius.

If I may echo the words of your good lady, how would you plan to play with your toy?

Toy? Marius asked.

Your fiefdom. *Our* fiefdom.

It's a plaything?

Let's pretend. If the demesne was yours to play with what would you like to do with it?

What's wrong with what we're doing with it right now?

Our mains arrived. Two of them only. The waiter put them down in front of us. He must have caught the puzzled looks on our faces.

Madame has asked, he said, if we would hold hers.

Thank you, said Marius.

We attacked our food, taking a few bites each. Then I set my utensils down, picked up my wine glass, and caught Marius' eye. He kept on eating, avoiding mine. I spoke emphatically.

What we're doing now won't last forever, I said. Closure is our goal. Our mission statement says as much. So, when the present emergency is done with, when we've slain the giant, when DETA is wound up, when the future of the demesne hangs in the balance, what would you like to do with the freaking thing? Let your imagination run riot.

I took a sip of wine and waited expectantly. Marius shrugged.

The demesne? he asked.

The demesne.

Well, for starters, I'd drop that word. Demesne, for Christ's sake. Who chose that dreadful word?

I did.

Well, you're welcome to it.

O.K. Call it what you like. Call it a fucking town if you must. The town of Conroy. But remember this. *You're* the fucking mayor. And a despot to boot.

And who might you be? he asked. God almighty?

Try 'godfather'?

Marius put his utensils down.

You want me to spell out a future for our town? he asked.

That's the idea.

How about a ski resort?

Follow the money, man.

A casino?

Good boy. Now you're talking. And we want to make a killing, so what sort of client should we cultivate?

High rollers?

You're right on the lolly. We sit back. They rock and roll. We launder their shekels for them. At a price.

I paused.

Our price, I said.

Marius looked perplexed.

John, he said, what you're proposing is unethical. And possibly illegal.

Fuck the ethics.

The look on Marius' face was a picture. I could no longer contain myself. I burst into uproarious laughter, spilling wine all over the white tablecloth. The folk at the closest tables turned to see what the commotion was about.

Oh Marius, I said. Marius, you *are* a treasure. And a patsy. Can't you tell I've been taking the piss?

As if set in stone, the expression on Marius' face did not change. Nor did he speak. But tension was an invisible guest at our table.

You do know your wines though, I said. I'll say that for you. This one's excellent.

I read the air. Marius' silence was a toxic miasma enveloping me from across the table. I wondered if, perhaps, I had crossed a line into forbidden territory.

Marius, I said. Accept my apology. It was only a game, but I shouldn't have done it.

A game, Marius said.

A game. I enjoy playing them. A fetish of mine.

Marius' expression seemed to have lost some of its severity. He now looked merely bemused. He shook his head ever so slightly.

Marius, I said, one reason I hired you was your creative talents. And it paid off. Nobody but you would have come up with the infrastructure solutions Conroy enjoys. But creativity is not the only reason I hired you. You are scrupulously honest. Incorruptible. If you found fifty dollars in the street, you'd sweat blood to find the owner. Knowing you as I do, I'd trust you with my life.

I paused.

Do you trust me? I asked.

I'm not so sure about that, John, Marius replied. But *I* don't get to hire you.

I could see June returning, flushed from her gyrations on the dance floor. She had left Harvey at his lone table somewhere in the nether regions of the Quonset. A waiter bearing her main course followed close on her heels as she approached us.

When she reached our table, she stood at her chair, running a deft hand over its back, ostensibly waiting. Marius rose and moved the chair out for her. As she sat, he slid it back in under her rear end. A demonstration, by him, of old school etiquette, impeccable in its execution.

She opened her handbag, found a white lace handkerchief, and wiped her brow with it. Only then did she deign to greet us.

How's the home front holding up, pumpkins, she said.

Utopia

I have already described how Marius had organized, in timely fashion, the assembly of mass housing in Conroy using, as a prototype, a variation on the humble Quonset hut. This was just one example of how he came up with needy solutions.

Yet another stroke of creative genius had been his approach to transport within the demesne.

He had called for tenders for prompt delivery of a fleet of bespoke electric vehicles, whose speed and range were appropriately governed. The basic model, free for anybody's use at a moment's notice, was a two-seater with room for a modicum of luggage in the back. They wouldn't travel faster than 40 kph, and they didn't have sufficient range to leave the demesne (say, *en route* to Canberra) and then get back again. These vehicles were ubiquitous in Conroy.

Some – the petrol-heads mainly – had called them dodgems. But my advice to petrol-heads would be go eat your hearts out.

If the vehicles themselves were both bespoke and ubiquitous, so were the charging stations needed to keep them running. By design, the digital handshakes vehicle and charger were required to exchange were unique to Conroy. So, the Leckies of Conroy could not be charged outside Conroy. Nor could electric vehicles from outside Conroy be charged inside Conroy. Within the demesne, the latter were only a practical consideration should they have sufficient range to come, do their business, and return.

Private vehicles running on fossil fuels *were* permitted in Conroy, but their drivers were required, under pain of a hefty fine, to adhere to the blanket speed limit. The only fuelling station in the demesne for these vehicles was located on the Conroy Access Road just the other side of Checkpoint Charlie. Naturally, Homeland Security watched the comings and goings at this fuelling station assiduously.

Some, with a nose for such things, might have smelt an unspoken sentiment here: *go back to where you came from.* Truly, many Conroy citizens were quite content with their lot, even jealous of it, and disinclined to look kindly on outside influence, real or imagined. I'm not sure such xenophobia had been Marius' intention at all. Just another of those unintended consequences tending to stalk most human endeavour.

Marius' ideas were ahead of their time. Nevertheless, there had been disgruntled mutterings of 'nanny state' and 'social engineering' by sundry libertarians/anarchists around the traps, and attempts had been made by them to subvert or game the system. Internet forums had cropped up with the sole purpose of undoing the speed governors and/or the handshakes, but by and large Marius' canny system had prevailed.

Not only had the residents of Conroy been blessed with secure roofs over their heads, the mobility to work and play efficaciously, and the illusion of freedom from outside interference, but they also enjoyed the best utilities current technology could offer. Transmission towers for cell phones and fast broadband looked out over Conroy from a vantage point part way up the slopes of Redoubt. Social infrastructure – education, health, recreational facilities, and legal services – was the equal of any in the country. Processes were in place to ensure all this infrastructure was updated and/or supplemented as required.

The geographic spread of recreational infrastructure about the demesne was yet another example of Marius' ability to think laterally. Each Stem flaunted its own unique handful of social drawcards chosen by lot from the full range of facilities deemed by the populace to be important. My favourite food bar (the *Continental*) was in Health Stem. *Pig's Ears* was in Agriculture Stem. The two churches languished in Visitors Stem. Mulitplex cinema was allotted to Science Stem. The sports centre to Labour Stem. Poker machines to Admin Stem. A brothel to Defence Stem. There was even a gay men's bar (*The Tight Spot*) at the far end of Corrections Stem. And so on. No one Stem owned it all, which motivated people to move around. Cliques and cabals were off the table. Egalitarian society was the go. Scientists mixed with visitors. Tradies could mix with doctors and nurses. Marius' shrewd ploy was a social lubricant of the first water.

Some people weren't inclined to mix. Secrecy being its stock-in-trade, one Division in particular had been determined from the outset to keep its lackeys in their place. When, of necessity, these lackeys ventured outside their Stem, they felt pressured to go incognito. Which Division was this? Guess.

Now I happen to know a thing or two about 'incognito'. Incognito for me was a fetish. But for these people, incognito was

Divisional policy. And they were incognito in the same way angry gorillas aren't. Everybody could pick these spooks in a crowd.

Exceptions prove the rule, the rule here being that these innovations designed to enhance social fluidity had been a roaring success. Their success could be put down to Marius' creative instinct and practical nous. Here was a man who knew how to have an idea, *and* then how to implement that idea with panache.

Conroy. A utopian demesne. The ideal place for those who spin dreams to wear them.

Pity about The Space.

Dream

It is my habit to sleep naked. In the hermetic environment of my penthouse, nakedness is no problem, even when it is cold outside. Moreover, alone in the evening *sans* clothes, I feel I have permission to relax the firm grip on control I exert compulsively during the workday. It is a permission I give myself with considerable relief. Once I am naked.

So, *Pig's Ears* behind me, and bereft of clothing, I duly took myself to bed, ostensibly to work on my schedule for the rest of the week back in Canberra. But the schedule was no more than a ploy. A pretence *by* me, designed to *fool* me. I was both pretender and pretendee. Soon after I slipped my skin between the sheets, I felt my papers slip from my hands. My grip on control loosened as did my grip on my papers. They drifted to the floor as I drifted off into sweet sleep, somehow contriving to switch off the bedside light just before doing so. Control passed from me to the beast. Which beast?

The beast, purveyor of dreams, that stalks the night.

I was back again in the *Pig's Ears* with the Strangios. But not the *Pig's Ears* my memory knew. According to the beast's singular logic, its interior had been re-created as a massive domed void. The dome's ceiling, soaring above me, was slathered in children's drawings, bound in Ray's frames, each drawing having acquired a hint of adult surrealism. The soporific jazz had given way to a pervasive tinnitus, not a tinnitus of my individual headspace but of the void itself, a relentless high-pitched sound, the sound of impending doom. Perhaps the void was surrogate for my headspace. In any case, I was floating free in this void, looking down on the table where I was seated with Marius and June. Consistent once more with the beast's logic, I was in two places at once. 'Me' at the table, and 'me' floating.

Conversation at the table echoed eerily in the void. Floating abstractedly above, I could decipher little of it. Only some key words – such as 'quango', 'fiefdom', 'dictator' – stood out. Then Harvey arrived at the table to whisk June away. Soon after they left, Basil Shirley – manager of *Pig's Ears* – turned up. He gripped the back of June's chair.

The beast was treating me to a replay of my experiences just a few hours earlier, a replay with the essence of reality but with diabolic distortion.

The floating 'me' looked down on 'me' at the table and saw this latter 'me' looking at Basil's fingers, all eight of them, curling over the back of the chair. The fourth finger of the right hand boasted a brilliant blue opal ring. This 'me' at the table could see fingers only. No thumbs. They were out of sight behind the back of the chair.

But the floating 'me' *could* see the thumbs. They were working together furiously and surreptitiously, endeavouring to attach a small device to the frame of the chair. To my way of thinking, this device was electronic in nature. A bugging device, God forbid. Once his thumbs had secured it in place, Basil left.

The floating 'me' moved in close to the device, hovering over it. It resembled a small black-glass bead. It pulsed and throbbed both visually and aurally, in synchrony with the words being spoken by Marius and 'me' at the table. Indistinct words.

June returned. Her hands glided over the back of her chair as she waited for Marius to move it out for her. The floating 'me' moved in closer, and saw her right thumb and forefinger dislodge the device, and the other fingers of her hand close over it.

When Marius had finished seating her, June dropped the tiny bauble into her handbag, unseen by those at the table. The deed was done.

How's the home front holding up, pumpkins, she said.

All this distressed me so much I chose in my panic to re-take control. I used brute force to jolt myself from sleep to wake. Back in the real world, darkness was in play, and it was into this pitch I now plummeted. My bedside clock defied the general rule. It flashed 2:30 in relentless green, determined its mundane message would be received. Nothing was audible except remnant tinnitus, fragment from the world over which the beast presides. My heart pounded. I clutched my temples and found I was sweating. I flicked on the bedside light, fled to the mini-bar, and poured myself the first drink I was able to lay my hands on, neat white rum as it turned out. I skolled, letting it burn my throat. I poured myself another and tossed *it* back also.

Sitting down with a third drink in my hand, I felt I was ready to analyse my nocturnal experience. Did waking reality as it had happened earlier that evening, including especially the bits I had apparently failed to notice, match the beast's version? Had things actually transpired the way my dream suggested? If so, who was the malign intelligence behind the covert surveillance portrayed therein? And what was his/her/their motive?

Hold on, I told myself, this was a *dream*, nothing more. Reading too much into it would be an admission of paranoia. Perhaps the dream was just a friendly warning from my unconscious, telling me I should in future be more discreet when playing flippant mind games in public places.

I felt mollified. I downed my drink and felt even more mollified.

On my way back to bed, I gathered up the papers – my week's schedule – scattered beside it. I arranged them on my bedside table, slid my body between the sheets again, and was thankful for the dreamless sleep I was – in the final analysis – gifted. Perhaps, I reflected, it was the beast's turn to dream now.

Throng

I woke to find an unseasonal warm front had passed through Conroy in the wee hours. Outside my window the lawn, and Admin Stem beyond it, were mostly free of snow. Much of the white stuff had turned to transparent slush. Should a snap cold front follow through in the wake of this warm one, always a distinct possibility at this time of year, the slush would likely turn, in coming days, to black ice. Treacherous, but not my problem. I planned to be out of here before *this* day's end.

But I had something to do first. I felt I had been a tad abrupt with Ray when I left him yesterday so, before leaving, I planned on paying him a visit to make my peace with him.

Once outside, I said hello to a bright blue sky and a chill wind. Snowshoes and chains might not be *de rigueur* today, but windcheaters were a must.

At the *Continental*, glad to get in out of the lazy wind, I ordered scones and coffee from the well-built barista in the wire-frame spectacles. I was in for a shock. She replied, Yes, Mr Shepherd. Fuck, I thought, my cover is blown. But how did it happen so quickly? Only the day before, she hadn't known me from Adam. And yet today …

On the move again in my Lecky, I turned right into The Roundelle. A thrilling view of a snow-capped Redoubt confronted me briefly before I turned left into the track giving access to The Space. Parking was problematic, so John Coffee acted as my valet. Yesterday, my vehicle had been the only one here. Today, the parking lot was approaching full. Was this the throng I had been led to expect was the norm?

Thank you, John, I said.

My p-p-pleasure, said John.

I began to regret having ever poked fun at John Coffee. As I got to know him better, he came across as a quite decent human being. His ungainly stature and gait, his propensity to stutter, and the fact of his being to some extent a spare part, no longer struck me as sufficient reason to make cruel jokes about him. He could even prove useful, given appropriate grooming, as an informant from within Homeland Security, albeit one inhabiting the base, if not the basement, of the organizational pyramid.

Instantly, I felt ashamed of my last thought. John Coffee should neither be the butt of jokes, nor a patsy to be used cynically for political purposes. John Coffee should be left alone to be simple John Coffee.

Proceeding down the slushy trail, through the canyon of snow-gums, I was glad I had chosen more suitable footwear today. Sturdy hiking boots, overkill some would say. *These boots are made for walking.* They conveyed me with surety through the slurry of loam, sleet, and sundry botanical detritus, their firm grip on my ankles a wellspring of security for me.

The closer these boots brought me to The Space, the more it became obvious to me I was approaching a focus of activity. Noisy activity.

When I burst into the clearing, with the circle of ski-poles marking the no-man's-land behind it, I froze in place, staggered by what addressed my eyeballs. Here was an epic diorama, an expansive tableau, a stage-set in wide-angle tracing out a broad convex arc. The many elements of this outdoor stage – human and mechanical – embraced motion and exuded sound. The curtain was up, a performance was in progress, and I was privileged to be the audience.

As it turned out, this performance would have several acts.

Parked to the right of the conversation post, a huge cherry-picker dominated the scene. The performers at stage-right swarmed like upright bees, the cherry-picker their unlikely hive.

Most plentiful, with numbers of men and women in exemplary balance, were those wearing white-coats and light-tan shoulder-bags. Wenkits, I guessed. Almost as numerous, but with a shameless preponderance of men, were those in Hi-Vis carrying sundry tools of trade: trestles, ladders, and the like. The least numerous, a mere sprinkling, were all men in business suits. The white-coats would have been from Science Division, the Hi-Vis from Labour Division, and where the suits came from was anyone's guess. In all three cases, warmer garb would, of necessity, have lurked beneath visible over-garments.

Yet another white-coat stood in the basket of the cherry-picker, high over the heads of the others. He wore headphones, doubtless for the purpose of communication with those below.

I decided to watch for a while, remaining hidden as far as possible and for as long as possible, behind an obliging snow-gum. By my reckoning, I was party, when hidden in this way, to the unguarded behaviour of the putative performers. Wasn't it Heisenberg who warned the wide world that electrons changed their behaviour when they sensed the presence of an observer? Well, there were lots of hypersensitive 'electrons' out there, busy investigating The Space, who would not necessarily behave in the same way should I – the big I Am to their way of thinking – announce myself.

Brian Collyer, in white coat, stood at the base of the cherry-picker. Beside him stood a tall young woman I couldn't immediately identify. Her garb was pointedly civilian. In fact, she was the only person in the melee gathered round the cherry-picker who did not flaunt some sort of uniform. What she wore, in lieu of a uniform, was a heavy pale-blue overcoat, matching scarf dangling to her knees, skirt and top of a colour I couldn't quite make out, and thick black stockings meeting white gumboots at calf level.

Conroy was a small town so I tried to figure, by process of elimination, whom she might be. A possibility occurred to me. Could she be Ray's sister? Marius had told me she was in town. If my guess was right, then I felt I should, at a suitable moment, make myself known to her.

Having taken her under his wing, Brian was clearly out to impress her. He was the Science guy, in control of the situation, bent on explaining its arcane mechanics to a novice. His gestures were extravagant. His speech was loud and hyperbolic. I could tell this much even from my distance, though I couldn't make out any actual words. Nor could I judge whether or not she was inclined to be won over by his ways. Spare me, I thought, the vicissitudes of youthful mating rituals. They are painful to experience, and excruciating to watch.

I turned my attention to the high-flier in the basket of the cherry-picker.

He was mapping the interface between The Space and the outside world, using the eponymous wentesters for this purpose. That was my best guess anyway. He would secure one of Wen's devices in a mechanical jig, then use a screw to wind it out slowly. On his signal, the team of white-coats below would record its position using surveying equipment. Then he would let the used device fall to the floor of the basket before retrieving a fresh one from his wenkit. Every so often, on a signal to the driver/operator, he would order a change of position of basket and/or cherry-picker. This repetitive procedure looked mind-numbing. Soul-destroying. And, I figured, dangerous.

Should the basket accidentally penetrate The Space, where would that leave the guy doing the science? Or should he fall from the basket into The Space below, who would be on hand to attend to his broken body and nurse him to a lonely wellness?

So, I didn't envy him his job. This was science as it is practised not in the security of the lab but out in the unforgiving field, a.k.a. the immediate precincts of The Space, territory of forces unpredictable and infernal. *Abandon all hope, ye who enter here.*

I shuddered, and parked my gaze on points to the left of the cherry-picker and, in particular, on the conversation post. Stage-left, so to speak. Things were no less busy here. I invite you to imagine the scurry. Dozens of white-coats danced attendance on every quarter of the barrier of ski-poles. To my mind it seemed there was an element of competition here, such as might be seen in a bar at closing time, or on the floor of a stock exchange with bulls on the rampage.

The conversation post itself was currently unoccupied. The skip, lined inside with a tarpaulin, sat to its left at the visitor's end of the dolly track. Yes, the visitor's end. That's what I said. Yesterday, the skip had been *inside* The Space. Today, it was *outside*.

A small petrol-powered van with Victorian number plates was parked near the skip. From the rear of this van, Tania Chalmond was busy transferring from van to skip what looked like the makings of picture frames and other related equipment. She was dressed in her work-apron, the one with strips of red brocade on its pockets. People from Labour Division in their Hi-Vis were hanging around, but she was doing most of the work.

This procedure, I am informed, was a regular occurrence in this neck of the woods. To tell the truth, I had seen it once or twice on previous visits and had wondered then if such service rendered to Ray was not way beyond the call of Tania's duty. Such an astonishing degree of devotion and personal attention was something, I felt sure, deserved plaudits from all who breathed the sweet air of our troposphere.

One other person was on the scene. I could not guess her purpose. June.

She stood just a few metres back from the conversation post, seemingly oblivious to the activity around her, making a call on her cell phone. She wore, ludicrously I thought, jodhpurs with matching jacket and boots. Was this, I wondered, her take on power dressing?

After a minute or two on her phone, June moved to the conversation post, sat down on the visitor's side, and proceeded to gaze nonchalantly through the frame. She could have only one purpose. She was waiting for Ray. Tania saw her sit. She stopped work for a moment and moved across to her. I caught her words.

This is Ray's free time, she said. You need to come back at two.

Turning her head slightly, June gave her a withering glance.

I can't seem to remember, she said, having asked your opinion.

Tania must have resorted to some sort of body language at this stage. From my distance, I could not decipher it. Perhaps she rolled her eyes. Perhaps she showed June the finger. In any case, she got a response.

Do you know who I am? June asked.

Mrs Strangio, Tania replied.

And do you know who *Mr* Strangio is?

Administrator.

Case closed, darling.

Having cut Tania short to her satisfaction, June turned her attention back to the frame, confident she would have her way. And, sure enough, Ray came around the bend at just this moment. Dressed in windcheater, track-suit pants, and runners, he was jogging the perimeter of The Space, as was his habit each morning at this time.

Making his way towards the conversation post, he seated himself on the prisoner's side, facing June. From the distance and to my annoyance, I could not make out the whispers passing between them. I assume things got off to a start with Ray's solemn statement of his terms and conditions. *Every word crossing such a portal ...* and similar gobbledegook. From then on, I couldn't hazard a guess. But Tania was within earshot and looked as if she were drinking in every word. I made a mental note to have a chat with that young lady at some future moment.

I couldn't imagine what business someone like June, with her disruptive intelligence, would want with a pretend clairvoyant. Was she playing one of her spiteful games, did she have a desperate need, or were her latent superstitious tendencies coming to the fore? Perhaps all three. People are such strange cattle.

After a few short minutes, her audience with Ray apparently over to her satisfaction, June rose, and with deliberation made her exit. On the right, past the cherry-picker. I was thankful she chose this route because, had she taken the direct one as sanctioned by Homeland Security, I would have been sprung. Then, soon after me, she would have stumbled on John Coffee. Was she perhaps trying to avoid scrutiny? And, should the answer prove to be in the affirmative, here is an interesting follow-up question for you. Whose?

My attention returned to Tania. The skip being fully laden now with framing paraphernalia, she produced, from the passenger seat of the van, a packet of mail held together with a bulldog clip, a bottle of what looked like Scotch whiskey, and a bowl of fresh fruit hermetically sealed in cling-wrap. She transferred these personal items to a wicker-basket adorned with over-the-top floral motifs, which she then went to some trouble to wedge securely amongst the regular items in the skip.

With broom and shovel she cleared the rails of corpses in the vicinity of the interface. Then she worked the lever on the skip. Back and forth, back and forth. Noisily. It sounded like she was winding a spring which, in fact, was the case. When it was wound to her satisfaction, she pressed a release on the back of the skip and stood clear. The skip hurtled forward with sufficient energy to carry it across the interface and into The Space, where it shuddered to a halt. And before you heap scorn on this rattletrap from a bygone century, let me remind you that it did the job required, and did so moreover in such a way nobody was put in peril despite the hazardous nature of the precinct in which it operated.

Ray, on retreat to his hut now, turned, and gave her a nonchalant thumbs-up. Tania acknowledged him with a nod and a smile. At which point, she closed the back of her van and drove away. Right past me! There was a mix of amusement and surprise on her face as, from the driver's window, she caught me skulking behind my snow-gum. O.K., I thought, let her think what she likes. She may believe she has my number but, shit, don't I also have hers?

The vehicle having passed, I turned my attention back to the performance playing out in front of me. A performance I could continue to enjoy with the privilege of unseen observer.

Snooping? asked a female voice behind me.

I was so startled by this approach from my unguarded rear that I snagged my cheek on a sharp twig. Nursing the scratch, I turned, expecting to find Tania had returned. But it wasn't Tania. The woman I saw looked familiar, but I couldn't quite place her.

Another snoop, she said. The town is crawling with them.

It's a demesne, I said stupidly. And I'm no snoop.

Very much in my face was a woman short in stature, with blond hair, green eyes, teeth whiter than white, firm jaw, and confident manner. As my eyes scanned her garb at close range from top to bottom, I identified a hand-knitted beret in coarse wool, scarf in finer weave, weatherproof parka, and fashion slacks tucked into beige Sorels. All colours were muted, and all gear was expensive.

Then who *are* you? she asked.

John Shepherd.

Oh my God. Not the dude that runs the joint?

No. That's Marius Strangio.

And who is it tells Marius how high to jump?

O.K. Guilty as charged. Now tell me who *you* are.

Most of the time I answer to Gabrielle Zanders.

Of course. Television. You're … you're …

And, shit, I'd be chuffed to have you on my freaking show. Can I sign you up?

I'd be more than happy to oblige but you'll have to go through Marius.

Consider it done. Are you headed in the direction I'm headed? Maybe.

Then let's walk together.

I emerged from my hidey hole. And, as predicted, the electrons across the way changed their behaviour once they saw me. The frenetic activity and associated noise ceased abruptly. Everybody stopped in their tracks. Communication, such as it was, took the form of muffled whispering. The guy in the basket of the cherry-picker stopped his investigations just so he could gawk at Gabrielle and me as we approached. I offered up a prayer along the lines, God spare me all sycophancy and obsequiousness. I'm not fucking royalty, for Christ's sake.

Is it fear or respect these guys are showing you? Gabrielle asked as we walked.

She had touched a raw nerve here, so I tried to dodge her question by asking her one of my own.

I imagine a person like you would be wedded to your studio. What brings you to Conroy?

My question first, she said bluntly.

I'd hate to think it was fear. I don't regard myself as a bully.

Bullies never do.

O.K. My question?

I do a lot of my own investigative work. Conroy is a quirky place with a really big story behind it. Sooner or later something's going to blow. I want to be here on the ground when that happens. So, I try to be around as often as I can afford.

I believe you've been seeing a bit of the Spaceman.

She winked.

And, she said, you've been listening to a wee bit of gossip.

She stopped in her tracks, forcing me to stop also. Then she faced me.

You know who those snoops are down there?

The ones in suits?

That's the dudes.

You tell me.

They're the skeleton staff. From Defence mainly. Some from Corrections. Some from Agriculture. Waiting to see if the boffins discover something of significance to their Division. If Science *does* uncover something the other tribes deem to be of interest, they'll descend in swarms. They'll blow in like the beer was free.

How do you know this?

My job, squire. Take a walk down Defence Stem sometime. Check out the living quarters. Dig the occupancy. Hardly a soul to be found. The few you might stumble across keep themselves busy writing reports nobody reads. And snooping.

I'm impressed. You know your job.

Some of us do. Harvey Eanis would be another example.

Not the real estate guy?

That's the critter. He rakes in the shekels and uses the vacant premises for his own nefarious purposes.

What purposes might *they* be?

Assignations. There are a lot of bored wives in town.

I took a deep breath.

You know, I asked, who ultimately cops the blame if this sort of thing gets out?

You, I'm guessing.

So, you planning to drop me in the shit?

She winked again.

What's it worth not to?

We started walking again. Well, I thought, here is another person who loves to play verbal games. I pray to all deities that there's nothing more to it than 'game'.

In no time at all, we had reached the base of the cherry-picker. Gabrielle made straight for the woman I assumed was Ray's sister. I followed. On reaching her quarry, she opened conversation as she would with a familiar.

Greets, Frances, she said. Meet John Shepherd. Head of DETA.

Frances blinked. She flipped the dangling end of her scarf over a shoulder. Her reply was cautious.

Hello, she said.

I held out my hand to her. She took it.

And who are you? I asked.

Frances Cromwell. Ray's sister.

I thought as much, I said. Welcome to Conroy.

Thank you.

So, how would you say Ray is holding up?

Quite frankly I'm staggered, she replied. Sometimes I think if he'd chosen it himself, he couldn't have found a situation more to his liking.

Are you planning to stay around?

Brian Collyer, close by but on the outer, was shifting his weight from one foot to the other. This, I guessed, was a display of frustration. His thunder had been stolen. I acknowledged him with a short wave.

If I'm at all able, was Frances' reply to me. I'm very close to my brother.

What she means, said Gabrielle, is she needs a job here to support herself.

And an agent it would appear, I replied, …

… then I asked Frances, What are your qualifications?

Nursing, she replied.

I must have seemed dubious, because she lowered her expectations.

Care worker, she said.

Take it up with Marius. I believe the hospital is short staffed at the moment.

I turned slightly as if intending to slip away.

Now, I said, I gather you two have some private business to transact.

No secrets around here, was Gabrielle's response, …

… then she asked Frances, Shout you an early lunch?

Watch your words carefully, young lady, I said to Frances. When journos say 'no secrets', it's *your* secrets they're talking about.

Up yours, champ, said Gabrielle.

At this point, I *did* manage to slip away, heading towards the conversation post, where I hoped to be able to offer my *mea culpa* to Ray.

A changing of the guard (of sorts) was happening. No bells

rang, no sirens sounded, no whistles shrieked. But, as if on an invisible inaudible cue, the brigade of white-coats began to disperse. The Hi-Viz driver of the cherry-picker lowered the basket, so the high-flyer inside could struggle out, lugging with him a wenkit replete with used wentesters. He followed the other white-coats as they made their exit. Via the authorized route. They had nothing to hide.

Taking their place was a brigade of blue-coats from Health Division. I knew what this meant. Scheduled anti-infective treatment was about to begin. In anticipation, a knot of prospective patients looking suitably gutted by life had begun to coalesce around the conversation post, together with their carers and a contingent of paparazzi toting cameras and microphones.

I assumed the latter were hoping to report a medical miracle or two of biblical stripe. Whether their report was slated for publication in a mainstream outlet or destined for click-bait in some sleazy online forum is anybody's guess. One thing was certain: they were waiting for Jesus to appear.

And Jesus, aka Ray, didn't disappoint. Heralded by uplifting organ music, he emerged from his hut, wrapped in a greatcoat with slacks and runners beneath. Jeremy, caged, was with him. He moved towards the conversation post, bird-cage swinging, with a slow steady gait, an upright posture, a serene yet solemn manner, and an elevated sense of occasion. The real Jesus would have approved. With a little imagination, an observer might have seen white flowing robes in place of ponderous greatcoat, and a hand raised as if to bestow a blessing.

On reaching the ski-poles, Ray hung up the bird, and set about dismantling the conversation post. Yes, that's what I said. The schmuck began to dismantle it.

Clearly, he was an old hand at this job. It was a daily routine causing him no sweat. Of course, he made sure at all times to keep his nose strictly on his side of the interface. Otherwise, Jesus might have swapped roles with Lazarus.

The structure came apart about as easily as would flat-pack furniture. First, Ray lifted off the detachable roof, exposing a support scaffold with four wooden legs slotting into plastic pipes driven firmly into the topsoil. Then he unhooked the double-sided picture frame from its central position in the scaffold. Finally, he lifted the whole scaffold from its anchorage in the ground. After this operation, all that was left intact were two bench seats facing each other. And four derelict embeds of plastic pipe. And the interface, transparent yet inscrutable.

As an encore, Ray slid a pair of polished hardwood planks into position so they straddled the two seats. The planks slotted one into the other via tongue and groove. The end result was a sliding bench ready for the business in hand, viz. the business of healing the sick. Ray seated himself in a conveniently placed director's chair, crossed his legs, tugged his beard, softened his eyes, and proceeded to look messianic.

As opposed to the last time I had encountered him – man to bird – Jeremy was still and silent throughout this double act of disassembly and re-assembly. Perhaps, like me, he felt intimidated by the theatre in evidence on all quarters around him and had decided at this juncture to abandon his preferred role of performer and assume instead the less familiar role of spectator.

A section of the multitude – none of whom I suspect had made appointments – seemed determined to heal themselves. Solo. Using the elbow where necessary, each punter took up a position anywhere they could find a vacant gap in the ring of ski-poles. Then they poked their offending (and presumably infected) appendage through said gap. Stern-looking folk from the blue-coat brigade, stood around to keep order and to make sure these self-starters, who had been known at times to show scant regard for their own safety, didn't overreach the mark. I mean overreach *literally*. Should one of them seem ready to thrust a nose, ear, mouth, eye, fevered brow, or anything else attached to their head or face across the interface, the blue-coats would descend on the offender like the proverbial ton of bricks. Prudes that they were, the blue-coats didn't abide genitals either.

But the main game was indubitably happening back where the conversation post had once been. Here snoops in suits stopped to gawk. Here the paparazzi mimicked a feeding frenzy. Here patients, strictly by appointment, lined up, some in wheelchairs, to have their whole body scanned by The Space. A select team of blue-coats would lay the patient out on the bench, feet first, and strap him/her down. The same blue-coats would then slide the bench forward until the patient's body – as far as the chin but strictly no further – was inside The Space. To avoid mishaps with existential consequences, wentesters acquired from Science were used to pin-point the interface accurately. After a few seconds, the blue-coat team would withdraw bench and patient.

Then, wasting no time, they would release the patient and strap down the next.

I was mesmerized by what I saw. As spectacle went, this was epic. As entertainment went, this was high church. As theatre went, it was in the grandest style with a cast of hundreds, with outdoor ambience, and with musical accompaniment by an old master. What's not to like?

From the other side of the divide, I caught Ray's eye. Or did he catch mine? In any case, with a jerk of the thumb and that knowing smile I had come to expect of him, he indicated I should join him to the right of where most of the anti-infective action was taking place. Rising from his director's chair he made a move in that direction. Taking his cue, I moved too.

Jeremy, left behind, squeaked with displeasure.

We settled on a spot where we could speak in relative privacy through a gap between ski-poles, a gap that would take our voices but deny passage to their instrument. At our feet, the daily ration of small dead creatures was starting to accumulate. A beetle here, a skink there, … In this neck of the woods, healing was one side of the coin. Death the other.

I'd like to apologize, I said, for my brusque manner yesterday.
You were brusque? he asked.
I thought so.
Forget it. *I* have. And besides …
Accept my apology anyway.
… nothing you or anybody else does makes a speck of difference to me while I am in here.
Why not?
In here, I can do what I like. Even commit murder. And there's not a fucking thing anybody out there can do about it.
You think you are above the law?
I *know* I am.
Is there someone you'd like to murder?
Is there nobody *you'd* like to murder?
Touché.
Put it this way, squire. In here, myself for company, my freedom is absolute. Even Napoleon rotting away on St Helena, Cool Hand Luke doing time on his chain gang, Hans Castorp holed up in his sanatorium, couldn't …
I didn't know you were literary.
In here, I've all the time in the world to read stuff. And television's pure crap.
I won't dispute that.
Ray tossed his head back and surprised me with a big-throated laugh. He also surprised the crew in the vicinity of the healing bench. After his laugh had subsided, a jaunty tone infected his voice.
The way I see it, he said, you people outside The Space are the ones trapped. Not me. I do what I frigging like in here, but you lot out there …
All eight billion of us.
… knuckle under at every turn of the treadmill.
So, you see yourself as an *Übermensch*?
I do. And for every *Über* there's a shit-load of *Unter*.

We being the *Unter*, I'm guessing?

If the cap fits ...

What if we cut off your food and water?

Be my guest. Just leave me my shiraz, will you?

A sharp cry from the direction of the healing bench caused us both to turn our heads. It had come from a patient, buckled up on the bench. In joyful expectation of a medical miracle, she was waiting to commit her body (but no further than her chin) to the mercy of the purportedly benevolent forces in play on Ray's side of the ski-poles. She was not expecting to be whacked full in the face by a dead currawong falling from the sky, even though kamikazes like this were not uncommon around these parts.

The poor bird, ignorance its alibi, was judged guilty of trespass, a capital offence in the diabolic court always in session here.

I turned back to Ray, and held out my hand.

I must go, I said.

We shook.

The treadmill calls? he asked.

I nodded.

Remember, I said, to spare a thought for those of us less fortunate. I shall return.

Do call in.

Bank on it.

I turned, walked a few steps, and found myself face to face with Redoubt.

I froze. This was the second time that day the mountain had made its presence known to me. But this time it held me body and soul in its thrall. *That old black magic has me in its spell.* A shaft from the sun glanced off the granite embed, the putative eye of the lion, and sought me out. More than mere illumination reached my eye. It was a wink, I swear. A powerful non-verbal communication from a sentiency that challenged human comprehension. I have met people who had less life in them than this mountain.

I stood and gaped. *How should I respond to that wink?*

Spots

The next time I saw that mountain was in photographic representation. Captive within a generic frame, definitely not one of Ray's, it hung above my desk in my Canberra office. In such guise, robbed of any semblance of depth, Redoubt had been rendered sterile and devoid of life. This was in keeping with all the other accoutrements of my contemporary working space. Within the confines of my elite office, the only living thing was me, and I was beginning to have doubts about *that*.

It was September. All issues for me these days were reduced to paperwork, phone calls, and pettiness. Such was the Canberra *zeitgeist* during this crucial chapter in the affairs of the nation. If ever a muscular response was called for, it was in the here and now, given the existential drama playing out, potentially to destruction, in the demesne of Conroy and its vicinity. But bureaucratic paralysis sucked all nourishment from muscles. Memos were written in response to circulars, and more circulars followed in the wake of these memos. The name of action was lost.

To make matters worse, I couldn't escape – when back in the Capital – the smorgasbord of conspiracy theories regarding The Space spread virus-like among the populace. Our ideological adversaries offshore to our north – the usual suspects – had fostered many of them, e.g. the one claiming deranged scientists had let it loose from clandestine labs. Green fanatics, not to be outdone, claimed it was Nature's way of reasserting herself. Religious nutters – quoting Ezekiel – claimed it was God's punishment for our iniquities. The list was endless.

Consequently, the prospect of a somewhat tangential conference in Melbourne seemed an attractive diversion to me. Sponsored by the Department of Defence, its banner was *Contemporary Defence Ambitions and Commitments*. In line with the importance this Department attached to the events transpiring in Conroy, I was to be a keynote speaker.

The conference turned out, predictably, to be a self-serving non-event, and my contribution was buried under heaps of the usual blurt and bumf.

True to my earlier resolve, I sought out Tania Chalmond while I was in that most liveable city in the south. I phoned her at the Ray and Tania shop, and made an arrangement to meet her *in situ*. I was curious to know details of what had transpired between Ray and June during the consultation June had insisted on during my last visit to Conroy. I had not been within earshot on that occasion, but felt certain Tania had been. That's why I wanted to talk to her.

The shop fitted my expectations of premises set up to flog picture frames and ancillaries. Its name was *In The Frame*. It was situated in a shopping strip in the suburb of Elsternwick, frequented by an upmarket consuming class. There were artworks to suit tastes resident behind brows of all altitudes, framed in a style recognizably that of Ray and Tania. Some of it was doubtless wrought by Ray himself in the seclusion of Conroy's hut. There were coffee-table books on art and interior decoration with glossy multi-coloured illustrations. There were books purporting to teach the novice how to draw, paint, sculpt, and decorate interiors. And there were sundry artists' supplies: paints in oil and acrylic, blank canvasses, French curves, crayons, graphite sticks, and so on.

A pimply young man, whose name I learnt was Graham, lurked behind the front counter. He was the stand-in for Tania when she was not on deck, e.g. when she was taking the long drive to Conroy and back. Tania told me he lacked trade skills but could play shop assistant tolerably well.

She showed me the workshop out back. The smell here was the first thing that struck me. It was a piquant mix of raw canvas, paint, glue, and wood shavings. Jobs in progress cluttered benches willy-nilly. Completed items piled up awaiting collection by clients. A roller-door at the extreme rear gave access to a public laneway through which bulky supplies and equipment could be received or despatched.

The grand tour over, Tania drove me in her van to a small eatery nearby, where we ordered lunch. She was dressed with a degree of care in a blouse and belted skirt, items conforming to yesterday's fashion, the skirt celebrating colours at the red end of the spectrum. She had applied only the minimum of make-up to her face, which nevertheless sparkled. The elevation of her heels was only matchbox thick, but nonetheless her hips managed to sway as she walked. The effect, as a whole, worked well for her. In dress and in carriage, she seemed to my eyes young, fresh, jaunty, and virginal. I guessed there was method in her madness.

While we ate, I put my request to her with appropriate caution. Caution was unnecessary. She was only too happy to comply.

So, I'll pass on her recollection of what Ray and June had said to each other across that precarious interface at the perimeter of The Space on that wintry morning earlier in the year. This is my voice aping her voice. You'll be aware it is hearsay of the second order and would never pass muster in a court of law.

O.K., I say she said Ray had said. *We must speak to each other only through this picture frame. Every word crossing such a portal …*

… but I believe you know the spiel. The incantation. Ray's terms and conditions. And you can anticipate June had agreed to them. And Ray had then invited her to proceed. We can take all that as given and move on from there …

What do you know about Harvey? June had asked.

Harvey who? Ray had asked.

To the best of my knowledge there's only one Harvey in town.

Harvey Eanis?

That's the critter.

I hear he's got designs on my piece of real estate. Location, location, location. So please let him know he's welcome any time to inspect the property. I'll sit him down to a pot of tea inside my humble dwelling. Or whatever else might be his beverage of choice.

I'll pass the word on.

I wait.

I hear he's a bit of a tom cat.

Ri-i-ight.

Well is he?

… at this point Tania told me Ray had stroked his beard and had proceeded to look the epitome of a guru. And b'Jesus, I can just picture it, the devious devil …

He's a *big* cat, Ray had said. That much I *do* know.

Care to expand on that? June had asked.

Well what sort of big cat would you like?

… at which point Tania told me June had been at a loss for words, and this I find hard to imagine. Ray, I am told, had been forced to re-phrase his question …

Would you prefer spots or stripes? he had asked.

Is this some sort of mind game? June had asked by way of reply.

Spots or stripes?

O.K. I'll play along. Spots.

Good choice.

I could change it.

Your prerogative. But not his.

Come again.

He won't change his spots. They never change their spots.

Give me a break, Charlie.

I guess he could have them surgically removed.

What?

Surgically removed.

You taking the piss?

An oracle worth his salt would never take the piss.

… and here, Tania told me, June had risen abruptly and angrily from her seat. This I have *no* difficulty imagining. On turning to go, she had delivered her parting shot …

Thanks for zilch, sport, she had said.

… and as June had spun on her heels so to speak, Ray had turned to Tania with a wink and a final remark …

Who'd be an oracle? he had asked rhetorically.

This was the juncture at which Tania concluded her account to me. Now there was a pause, during which we sat sipping our coffees.

That's it? I asked.

That's it, she replied.

What do you make of it?

I was about to ask *you* that question.

You think he was just playing games?

Games are not the whole story.

What makes you say that?

I know the guy.

That being the case, perhaps you could tell me why he suddenly left a decent life in the city to take refuge in Conroy's hut.

What makes you think I've got the answer?

You're his business partner. Maybe more than that.

Tania dropped her eyes and reddened slightly.

Nothing more, she said.

Do you like him?

She raised her eyes again. The strength of her affirmation took me by surprise.

Very much, she said.

As a matter of fact, I said, so do I. But I don't make the arduous journey from here to Conroy and back with a van-load full of shit. On a weekly basis. A full day's drive each way.

Perhaps I like driving.

I'll wager that's not why *he* made the one-way journey a couple of years back.

No.

Then why?

I don't know the details.

Family problems?

That's would be my guess. Only a guess.

There was a natural pause. As I read the air between us, I decided I'd pushed her about as far as discretion would allow. For the moment.

O.K., Ms Chalmond, I said. I'll let you …

Call me Tania.

… off the hook. You've been most forthcoming and I appreciate it. I only wish you'd left me with more answers than questions.

So do I, Mr Shepherd.

Call me John.

Skylark

It was late spring before I made my next trip to Conroy. And, *voila*, journey by wide-bodied helicopter was now an option. A skylark was possible, and naturally I was up for it.

The weather, perfect for an inaugural flight, was fine and clear. With a goodly handful of others, I boarded at about 10 a.m., taking the co-pilot's seat as was my prerogative as Head of the Directorate. The pilot, a rugged fellow, laconic but taciturn, handed me noise-cancelling headphones with attached microphone, through which we could enjoy two-way communication in the course of the journey.

The flight, HWB1 from Canberra to Conroy, was forerunner to a much-awaited regular scheduled service. Behind me, the other people on board included public service types in suits, together with a sprinkling of residents of the demesne, whose dress was often, but not always, more casual. Steve Crisp, Head of Science, suited, fell into both categories, and to him I ventured a quick wave of acknowledgment. I made a mental note to seek him out upon landing, to press him for a verbal progress report.

Welcome aboard, expeditioners, said the pilot over the headphones. Please make sure your seatbelts are fastened.

We were soon in the air above the inner suburbs. I picked out

Parliament House, of course, then the Lake, then – in the distance – the Black Mountain tower. I imagined I could see the roof of my own house among the sprawl of terra cotta and Colorbond we passed over. Soon the unrelenting suburbs allowed intrusions of patchy green. More suburban monochrome pushed back, keeping the green at bay. Finally, a pervasive green won the battle as we left the city behind.

Obligingly, our pilot pointed out features of significance: the Murrumbidgee River, the Namadgi National Park, the border between the Australian Capital Territory and the State of New South Wales, the iconic Kosciuszko National Park, and the Snowy Mountains highway. The terrain below put me in mind of an emerald layer of shaggy carpet, snagged in places by gentle curves of road-metal blue or gravel red, and spread out over an undulating floor. I was mesmerized. Bird's eye views such as this tend to have this effect on me.

When the gentle undulations began to morph to major uplifts, I realized the Alps were making a statement. The gap between chopper and earth seemed now to be closing. I was not sure whether this meant we were descending or if the earth were rising to meet us.

Are we descending? I asked the pilot.

We are, he replied.

Then he pointed.

Brumbies, he said.

Following the line of his finger, I looked down. Crawling across the carpet like a swarm of brown grubs were the first living things we had seen since leaving Canberra. Funnelled by a long deep gulch, they were headed in the same direction we were. At speed. The pilot's voice barked into his microphone.

Hotel Whiskey Bravo to Conroy, he said. Over.

Alpha Tango Charlie receiving, came the reply.

Wild horses below, heading your way.

Fuck. Not again. Excuse the French.

Sorry, mate.

Not your fault. I'll sound the alarm. Best you don't land till they've passed. Out.

Our pilot now found it necessary to inform his passengers of his intentions. His exasperated voice filled our ears.

Ladies and gents, he said. We are approaching Conroy, but we'll be obliged to circle for a bit before landing, to avoid collision with a herd of brumbies. Best not to mess with these beasties. I'm told they're an occupational hazard in Conroy. We can expect to land in about thirty. Thank you.

What are they doing in a National Park? I asked.

Keeping the frigging grass down, I expect.

The chopper banked. In the distance, I glimpsed the contentious mountain, Redoubt, with its unmistakeable lion's head shape. From this altitude, its presence seemed oddly diminished. Could this really be the same prominence many had come to conclude was implicated in diabolic collusion with supernatural forces?

As the trajectory of the banking chopper continued to follow a tight circle, a different mountain loomed into my view. The pilot confirmed my guess that it was Mt Scornful. On its smooth green flanks, I could make out those strange grey circles, presumed to be extinct Spaces. Maybe a dozen of such. Mysteries resided here, clues to yet more diabolic collusion. Mysteries long dead now, and so unable to tell their story.

No Spacepersons inhabited them, I am told, unless as a pile of bleached bones.

Layers

For an insane moment, I imagined John Coffee had been promoted. There he was at Checkpoint Charlie, greeting passengers as they disembarked.

W-w-welcome to C-C-Conroy, sir, he said to me as I flashed my credentials.

Then reality re-asserted itself. It was not John Coffee. There was no stammer. It was just one of the regular Johnnies from Homeland Security. I asked him if they'd seen any brumbies down here.

They did the town over, mate, he replied. Traffic in chaos. Prangs on Defence Stem. And one geegee, I hear, ended up in The Space.

No.

That's what I'm told.

This news worried me. Just another thing to check out before leaving. I put this unexpected concern aside for the moment, determined to pursue my earlier resolve to get a briefing from Science. Steve had passed through Checkpoint Charlie ahead of me, so I hastened to catch him up.

As I drew level with him, I launched my assault.

Steve, I said, a word with you, please. Could we share a Lecky?

I let him drive. We decided on brunch at the *Continental*. As we headed off to Health Stem, Steve ventured another disturbing fact.

Did you know the Minister for Homeland Security was on that flight? he asked.

You sure? I asked in reply.

No show without Punch.

I think I would have recognized him.

Perhaps he didn't want to be recognized.

Where was he?

Right at the back. In hat and sunglasses. He and his aide got off first and then skipped Checkpoint Charlie altogether. They were on their way before you could say Ongoing Strategic Preparedness.

Well, well. I must catch up with him.

Best of British.

We arrived at the *Continental*. Steve left the vehicle at the charging station, while I found a table. The woman with the wire-frame spectacles, there as usual, gave me a knowing smile. I sat myself down to mull over the developing situation. I had hoped this trip would be largely a pleasure jaunt, but it was not turning out that way at all. Another problem had arrived out of the blue. I was beginning to think my shepherding skills were deserting me. A sheep or two appeared to be going their own way.

Steve joined me. So did pizza slices and coffee. We masticated silently for a while. Steve spoke first.

What did you want to talk to me about? he asked.

The wilt on the tilt of the quilt, I replied.

I thought it was kilt.

Whatever floats your boat.

Following these moments of *non sequiter*, I attacked Steve's eyeballs with my chisel gaze before voicing my real concern.

Is it shrinking? I asked.

The Space?

Yes.

The short answer is yes.

The long one?

It might get technical.

Try me.

O.K.

He paused, gathering his thoughts.

We used to compare The Space to an onion, he said.

I fail to see …

An onion has layers. As you peel back these layers one by one, the object shrinks in size.

O.K.

Same with The Space. Think of it in terms of layers.

I'm with you so far.

In the case of an onion, successive layers all have the same thickness.

That's how it is with The Space?

No.

I was afraid you'd say that.

If The Space *did* behave like an onion, Ray would have no problems. He'd be dead of natural causes well before his space ran out.

So, if The Space doesn't shrink like an onion how *does* it shrink?

The story my team tells me is that successive layers have equal volume, not equal thickness.

That makes a difference?

All the difference in the world. To maintain equal volumes as you strip them off, successive layers need to increase in thickness. They start out thinner than a hair's breadth, but then increase over time. Soon we're talking hare's breadth. H-A-R-E. The increase is relentless. In the end the interface just collapses in on itself and The Space is no more.

Exponential?

Worse. Our mathematicians call it hyperbolic.

Is that bad?

You'd better believe it.

So how long has Ray got?

We think five years. Maybe six.

How can you be sure so sure?

Simple maths.

I drew a sharp breath, exhaled, took a sip of coffee, and mulled this over. The power of numbers had delivered a grim ultimatum.

Cat got your tongue? asked Steve.

The cat's busy with the pigeons.

The conversation had reached a moment of mandated pause. My coffee seemed to have developed a bad taste. Steve broke the silence.

Well, not a pretty story, John. In the final days, it'll happen very quickly. All over in a flash. The Space will be here today and gone the next.

Without warning?

Oh, we'll get warning of a kind.

Tell me.

At the finish, our guys tell me, you'd be able to see the interface moving. If only it wasn't frigging invisible.

So, what *will* our eyes tell us?

Who knows exactly? Trouble is while they're busy blinking, it'll be all over bar the shouting.

There was silence, after which Steve did his best to emulate my chisel gaze. But chisel gazes, I fancied, were *my* bag, and I hasten to insist *his* bag had holes in the bottom.

Let me remind you, he said, of the position you took when last we met.

Position?

On how the problem would be resolved.

How did I say it would happen?

Ray would find the answer to the problem.

I said that?

You did.

I put my powers of recall to the test. And, yes, it did seem I had let slip some remark in this ballpark. A foolish remark, spur of the moment, somewhat outside my area of expertise. A bit of a throwaway line really. Now I was being held to it.

O.K., I said. I expect Ray *will* deliver the goods.

Steve nodded.

It's either Ray, I said, or …

Or?

… your team will need to put on its dancing shoes.

Book the Second

as told by

Tania Chalmond

There is love of course. And then there's life, its enemy.

Anouilh

Custodian of two X chromosomes, I challenge the world

Since you are bound to want to know, human curiosity being what it is, I'll tell you now about my life prior to becoming a dogsbody dancing attendance on The Space, and a semi-permanent resident of Conroy. My backstory.

In my judgment, an era began when the Minister for Homeland Security declared the demesne of Conroy officially open, an occasion commemorated by that brass plaque near Checkpoint Charlie. This makes the years preceding this seminal event Before Conroy. Or, in short, BC. By which reckoning I, Tania Chalmond, was born in 21 BC.

My backstory begins then.

I duly drew my first breath. From that moment I found myself in the company of a mother, a father, and two older brothers in a small town – which shall remain nameless – in country Victoria. My father had no time for me. I was only a girl. He was a man. He said little. When his lips *did* move, I knew it meant trouble for me. So, I avoided him when I could. Some said *he* also avoided *me* but, in reality, he simply wished me out of existence.

He was a market gardener who produced free-range eggs on the side. I can't remember seeing him without grime beneath his fingernails and sweat on his brow. As a child, I spent much time after school collecting, washing, and stacking eggs under his disapproving eye. My brothers were allotted more responsible duties in our greenhouses and veggie beds, as befitted the heir to the estate and the heir in reserve.

My mother spent her days on the 'finer things' my father had no time for. She was religious, but not fanatically so. She attended church each Sunday, on her own mostly, except on those occasions when she chose to drag her kids along for company. There we perched ourselves on hard benches, still and stiff-backed like four fossilized yokels, celebrating this other-worldly space by singing other-worldly hymns, champions of plodding rhythms we couldn't abide and turgid meanings we couldn't decipher. The experience always gave me an odd and slightly uncomfortable feeling, as if my brain were being stiffened in starch and then flattened in a mangle. When I returned home after such treatment, it took some time before my brain was ready to function again in the real world.

I got the same odd feeling when I looked at the framed picture hanging above her piano. It was a stock print of a bearded Christ at night-time, the moon a halo for his head, one hand dangling a lantern at his side and the other – outstretched – grasping a door knocker. The wall supporting the door, ominous in the darkness, was smothered in a tangle of spindly creepers. I learnt, later in my wanderings, the picture was by W Holman Hunt, and was called *Light of the World*. The Christ figure, I was led to believe, was acting out the words Behold I Stand at the Door and Knock …

It has haunted me for life.

My mother played that piano. I loved hearing her play. I owe my fondness for classical music to her modest talent, and to the fact she played for herself only. If she'd known I was listening, I know she would have stopped. So I derived guilty pleasure from my hidden presence at her recitals. I was spying on her private moment. I particularly liked stuff with plenty of dash, like Robert Schumann's *Carnival* (from almost two centuries earlier which fact I struggled to get my head around) and quite unlike those dreary hymns passing my lips on the occasional wretched Sunday.

As if part of the curriculum, puberty arrived for me at the same time I entered high school. Breasts pressed their case, insisting my function in society would be a nurturing one. I had mixed feelings about this. But the boobs looked quite handsome in the mirror, and I guessed they were part and parcel of being female, so I signed off on them.

The changes to my body and bodily functions were only the tip of the iceberg. Suddenly it seemed a demon life had hijacked me, body and soul, inclining me in all sorts of wayward directions.

Desires and urges, hardly known to me previously, came at me from who knows where. Some were delightful, others perverse, and all scared the living daylights out of me.

In the delightful category was the fantasy that took hold of me one particular Sunday, in church of all places. I just couldn't keep my eyes off a beautiful young boy in the front row of the choir. As he sang, his dense curly locks cascaded onto his brow. Such a noble brow. With brown eyes beneath to pierce my soul, and a visage to brand my brain. So, when I got home he was still there seared into my synapses. That night, I dreamt of him. I was a nurse, tending him in some unspecified illness. He was helpless before me. The culmination of my nurse's duties came when I slipped into the hospital bed beside him. The dream became vague at this point, and perhaps this was just as well.

Oh, the lovely boy! The lovely, lovely boy! I would marry him. I would be his bride. He would own me. I would own him. We would stay together for life.

In reality, I never even learnt his name.

I was neither sporty nor scholastic nor particularly good-looking. In short, a dud. School and its multiple agendas left me cold. Except perhaps for art, but nobody took that subject seriously. I stumbled my way through to Year 10, achieved a bare pass, and then left without regrets. Left school, and left home too. Here's how the latter came about.

One day, approaching summer and aged fifteen, I was searching for stray eggs in one of our greenhouses. The younger of my brothers, aged seventeen, was there among the raspberry canes, sprawled in a discarded tilt-back lounge-chair, laptop on lap. He didn't see me enter. As I approached, I saw what engrossed him on the screen. It was a porn site. Drawing level with him, I could see his fingers moving feverishly, not on the keyboard, but under it. That's when he spun around and saw me.

I stared. He looked guilty, and snapped the laptop shut. We said nothing. I went back to my quest for eggs.

After that day, I saw him many times indulging his furtive pastime. But no longer was there a guilty look on his face. Instead, there was a broad grin, almost a leer. Hello sis, he would say, feel like a bit? And I imagined what that leer said was, I see all this carnal magic in photographic representation on my screen, but my sister owns the real McCoy. Ripe for the taking.

I thought about this later. The demon life of post-puberty seemed to have possessed him also. Perhaps it possesses all of humanity. The more I thought about this, the more I was alarmed. And alert. I fancied the older of my brothers, aged nineteen, would have inducted his junior number into this clandestine practice. And no doubt the older brother would, in his turn, have entertained the same thoughts as regards me. Ripe for the taking.

There were just too many places around the farm where such 'taking' could be accomplished with ease. Of course, I stayed clear of the greenhouses. But still I imagined I saw the brotherly partners-in-crime conspiring in corners with snide looks on their faces. I fancied the subject of their conspiracy was me.

My very own brothers, for pity's sake! Over so many years, their role in respect of their little sister had been that of protector. And I had been so grateful for the protection on offer. Two big powerful brothers showing their concern by looking after vulnerable little sister. But now, with the demon rampaging inside their persons, the protectors had morphed into predators.

It was time to do a runner. I had always dreamed of the big city anyway.

I counted up my savings. It looked good. I guess I had known it would someday come to this. My booty was pocket-money from the harvesting of eggs supplemented with wages gleaned after school at the Woolies check-out. There was enough there for my fare and some more besides. Moreover, I had a plan. Christine, a former friend of mine from school, had left for Melbourne a year ago. I knew where she hung out and intended to land on her doorstep. I felt sure she would take me in. I left a note for Mum, promising I would write when I was settled to let her know things were fine. Then, afflicted by fits of trembling, but excited as all get-out, I jumped ship.

The group house, where Christine lived with four other girls of similar age and circumstance, took me in. The house was in the inner western suburbs. It had three bedrooms, one of them little more than a cupboard. I bunked down in the kitchen. None of us had private space to speak of, and all of us lived on a shoestring. None had real jobs, and everyone subsisted hand to mouth. But, in retrospect, these were some of the happiest days of my life.

In retrospect also, I can only wonder how we managed to escape infection during the pandemic raging at the time. We lived at such close quarters there was no way we could practice meaningful social distancing. But, against the odds, we survived. More than that, we thrived.

I quickly learnt how to recycle clothes. Garments that had already been recycled at least once prior through op-shops. My mother had taught me how to sew and mend, but my ability to match colour, cut, and style was unteachable, something you either had or didn't. I had it. The other girls took advantage of my special talent. The *quid pro quo* was I got the pick of their hand-me-downs.

My appetite for independent living, and my sating of it, nourished my self-confidence. My self-confidence in turn sharpened my appetite. I was on a roll. I owned me. Nobody else did. And finally I knew it.

Oh … and I lost my virginity around this time. Frankly, I don't know why such a loss is even worth a mention. Popular lore has it this event is seminal in a person's life. But I looked at myself in the mirror the next day and saw the same person I had always seen. I spied on my own headspace, and concluded the thoughts and feelings swirling around in there were compatible with those I had always thought and felt. So why the big deal?

All of us in the house had on-and-off boyfriends. At the time, mine was a daggy guy called Bobby. We enjoyed kisses and cuddles (I called them kiddles) whenever we could, often in the back of his car. But, on the occasion to which I here refer, the occasion on which we willingly went a shade further than mere kiddling (that is to say all the way), it wasn't the car.

We had expected to have the house all to ourselves for the day. Neither of us were happy when Bobby arrived only to find, as I already had, that one of my housemates, a vacuous twerp called Sally with less ability than a goanna to read the air, had decided after all to stay around. Several hours later she *did* actually deign to leave, by which time Bobby and I, twiddling thumbs up till this point, had had more than enough sweaty time to dwell seriously on what we might have been doing all this while, and to be very very ready and eager to get down to it. The rest is history.

Afterwards, Bobby was over the moon. He figured that, once he had spudded the well so to speak, he had the right to stay around forever to draw it down. He had another thing coming. 'Forever' was a privilege I had in reserve for my curly-haired choir boy when he eventually came to town. Bobby, sad to say, was not he.

Which is not to say I didn't enjoy my first full-on sexual experience. It was quite another thing. It wasn't sleazy. It wasn't painful. It was the gratification of an instinctive urge, a throwback (I presumed) to human prehistory, a mysterious delight embedded in our evolutionary development. Its rewards bordered on the transcendental, especially the post-coital glow. I wanted more of it. I *craved* more of it. Just not with Bobby thank you.

I tell a tiny lie. Circumstances, by all reports, had trashed my innocence, if you'll forgive me using this word in such prissy fashion. Yet, despite my former denial, there *were* some differences in my behaviour before and after the carnal event. These differences were small. Hardly worth mentioning. But nonetheless I feel obliged to set the record straight by owning them.

On the very next day, I took a 'morning-after' pill and, on every day thereafter, a 'before' pill. This was a regime I would never have dreamed of – much less found to be necessary – whilst I was 'intact'. I could afford this elective medicine because my mother, bless her cotton socks, had been sending me the pocket money I would have received had I still been managing the egg situation on the farm back home and, doubtless, the needs of my randy brothers. What the male members of the family thought of my mother's largesse, assuming they knew about it at all, really doesn't bear contemplation.

Still, my straitened circumstances, and lack of a real future to which I could relate, began to get my goat. I was tired of flitting from one McJob to the next. So one day, with no firm plan in mind, I took a train to the CBD, and then a tram, any tram. The rattler took me into unknown territory, somewhere in the near south-eastern suburbs. I alighted in a strip of shops, restaurants, and other small businesses seeming to go on forever. It looked interesting. I explored on foot.

My attention was drawn to a shop purporting to sell and frame artworks. Called *In The Frame*, it seemed like my bag. I entered. Inside was a good-looking clean-shaven man in his mid-thirties putting the elements of a frame together on the front counter. He didn't look up. He seemed totally absorbed in what he was doing. As if browsing, I ambled round the premises before approaching him. Then I stood directly in front of him until he looked up, a question on his face. He had features that soothed, eyes that engaged, and chubby hands that loved to make a point. I was immediately taken with him.

I bit the bullet. All caution thrown to the wind, I asked him for a job. I expected him to be taken aback, but he wasn't, or else he didn't show it.

What are your credentials? he asked.

None really, I replied. Just that I know I'd enjoy this sort of work.

What sort of work?

The work that goes on here.

What sort of work do you presume that is?

Framing pictures.

He was silent, as if deep in thought. Then, with his face smiling as if a foil to the import of his words, he popped what I guessed was a pivotal question.

What do you suppose is the purpose of a picture frame?

It was my turn to think now. I mulled his question for just a few seconds. It was a challenging question, a good one, but I felt I was up to it. I thought about my erstwhile family home, about Light of the World, and then summoned up the necessary confidence.

To let the picture speak, I said. The frame slopes inwards like the cone of a loudspeaker. Or megaphone perhaps. So the picture gets to deliver the full value of its message to the viewer. Loud and clear.

I knew my answer was unconventional, daring even, crazy perhaps, the response of a person with little to lose. After all, pictures are inanimate objects not living beings. And I could tell he was impressed by my response but reluctant to show he was impressed. Once again, he paused for thought. I waited.

Miss Flibbertigibbit, he said, it's not my usual practice to …

I could see things slipping away so, in a panic, I interjected.

I'd do it for free, I said.

… hire somebody off the street. And I don't do slavery.

My lower lip trembled and my gaze hit the floor. He continued.

But, he said, I *am* looking for an apprentice as it turns out, and I'm prepared to take a gamble with you. It's a gut feel. I trust you won't make a mug out of me.

… what price my emotions? Down the rollercoaster, up the rollercoaster. Was this really happening? I asked myself …

When can you start? he asked.

I started the very next day. Some people may have regarded my commute, involving a tedious train journey, a strap-holding lurch on a connecting tram, and walks at start of, at finish of, and in between varieties of rolling stock, as unthinkable. Sure, I had to get up early and get home late. But I was young and the teeming city life was seductive. I loved every minute of it.

My partnership with Ray worked out better even than expected. I didn't make a mug out of him. Instead, I took to the trade well. Ray was a great teacher. Soon, I could throw a frame together as well as the next person. My work drew no complaints, not from Ray and not from customers. And, in my time off, I loved strolling down the main drag (known as Glenhuntly Rd), peeping in at coffee shops, gelato bars, bookstores, fashion houses, and restaurants of all stripes. Nothing approaching this existed down on the farm.

After a few months of this, Ray surprised me with a follow-up offer. He wanted a live-in person for security purposes, so he offered me accommodation at a nominal rent in a unit above the shop, a unit he once occupied himself, now currently vacant. Accessed via a staircase tucked in behind one of the benches in the workshop, it consisted of a dream bedroom, a sweet kitchenette, and a darling bathroom. The bedroom was larger than anything I had slept in at any time of my life. It had a double bed and a window overlooking Glenhuntly Road. Several stock photographs of iconic Australian landscapes, of Uluru and the like, adorned the walls in frames I was pretty certain were put together by Ray. By now, I could identify his work, or fancied I could.

I could scarcely believe my ears when Ray made me this offer. Was I dreaming? I was earning money now, and the rent was only a fraction more than what it would cost me to commute from my shared house. The unit was a real step up in the standard of my accommodation. And it was in a prestigious suburb where 'real' people lived.

If you truly mean it …, I said.

His eyes sparkled and frowned simultaneously, redolent of good-natured chagrin.

You doubting me? he asked.

… I'll take it.

Good choice, he said. Now, I don't keep cash on the premises, so I can't see anybody breaking in. But promise me that, in the event, you won't tackle the intruder. I'll give you the numbers to ring, and then you bloody well stay hidden. Deal?

Deal.

That night, I said my goodbyes to Christine, Sally, and the others. They were incredulous. Even a tad envious, I'm sure. But we parted on good terms and, over the years, I maintained contact with Chrissie.

For the first few days after assuming occupancy of my new living quarters I was on cloud nine. At the finish of each working day, treasures in themselves, I would sit at the window of my bedroom feeding my face with crisps and Coke, mesmerized by what I was seeing and hearing down there on the street. The vehicular traffic, cars, trams, and most anything on wheels, was balm to my eyes, music to my ears. And on the footpaths people swarmed, sophisticated people, going about businesses not involving egg washing or veggie growing.

When the sun had a mind to set, allowing evening to add its romance to the daylight ambience, I would find myself still sitting there, unable to tear myself away from my box seat. Headlight beams down below, celebrating their luminous materiality, crossed each other like Star Wars weaponry. People intent on pleasure and dressed for the purpose, wound their way through pools of kaleidoscopic colour, pausing briefly to make contact with each other as would ants on a trail. Restaurants and other night spots, honey pots for these ants, washed the precinct with hues borrowed from a palette Renoir might have assembled.

This was my scene now. I was part of it.

Circumstances compel me to put my

backstory on hold

My apologies. Frances has just informed me a brumby has strayed into The Space and has injured itself critically. I feel I must check this out. I promise to resume my backstory once I have attended to this matter. I assume, with scant justification, there might be some assistance I can give.

Please preserve yourself in patience. I shall be back with you in two shakes.

A horse suffers, I shed tears, and find love

It was a terrible time for me, and for some others, not least the poor animal, whose cries compounded the agony as they rent the air. But the air didn't listen, just passed the news to sentient ears. My ears. Our ears. The air had said simply, I can't deal with this one. You deal with it.

How to describe the cries? I would have called it a shudder, a high-pitched shudder assuming this is no contradiction in terms, a shudder penetrating all forms of matter. Earth air fire water. Animal vegetable mineral. It had been his petition, his plea, to all such natural agencies, for a return to the normal course of events, a course that included his rightful dominion of the alpine plains and his unbridled romps on them with creatures of his kind.

It *was* a 'he'. This much was announced by scientists, with a confidence clinical but not empathetic.

Romps, for him, were not to be. The unfortunate animal was now in the company of two-legged devils he would prefer not to know. Who were they? One, I confess, was me. And the Cromwell siblings, one inside and one outside The Space. Then there were the scientists, one of whom was that know-all Brian Collyer. And also John Shepherd, the high kai of twai of the whole kit and caboodle, in gratuitous denial of his exalted status.

Ray, Frances, and the scientists, I am told, were on hand to witness the moment the brumby burst into The Space. I arrived soon after, alerted by a text message from Frances. John Shepherd shortly after me. So, both his and my first view of proceedings had the horse down on its flank, writhing on its bed of pain inside The Space, and flooding the precinct with those high-pitched shudders. The show on Mr Shepherd's face as he apprehended the scene was one of annoyance mingled with concern about the implications for Conroy. He waved to me and, perfunctorily, I waved back.

The horse had shattered both front fetlocks in an argument with ski-poles set firmly in the ground, ski-poles now in pieces, ski-poles that had no right at all to be there. The scientists had acted in a timely fashion. I entered to see them administer a tranquilizer dart. Soon the poor creature, drugged to the eyeballs, lay sprawled on a tarpaulin, mostly inside The Space. Ray had manoeuvred him onto the tarp. Small whimpers were all the animal could now manage. Life was ebbing slowly from him, as it would from a plucked parsnip, a root wrenched from its nurturing loam.

Yes. Whimpers had replaced the shudders. But the memory of the shudders would terrorize my headspace for eternity.

Why was such travesty visited on this noble beast by creatures not worthy to lift their feckless eyes to his proud mane? Was it in preparation for euthanasia? A quick and decisive bullet to the brain, a brain whose sensations in these final moments would, I dared to hope, be the sweetest of equine dreams? No. This was not to be.

He was lined up for rigorous scientific experimentation.

Holding back tears, I objected. Likewise Frances. No, please, no, we shouted. But the boffins, in the thrall of their witchcraft, would have none of it. The opportunity was a one-off. And the horse was going to die anyway. A death in the cause of scientific inquiry. A death in the manner of disinterested investigation.

And, to their shame, neither Ray nor John Shepherd raised their voice against these latter-day necromancers in defence of the horse.

How was the investigation accomplished? Having removed four or five strategic ski-poles, the boffins tugged on their end of the tarp, until the horse's head was within their grasp. They shaved it, smeared it with a clear silicone grease, and attached multiple electrodes. Continuing to pull on the tarp, they eased the head by minuscule degrees across what they called 'the interface', taking readings on their arcane equipment as they went. Throughout, Brian was wearing a stethoscope, presumably to monitor the animal's heartbeat.

Then Brian removed the stethoscope. He bent his ear low over the animal's head, taking care of course that his own head did not stray into The Space.

Looking up, he announced, Cashed in his chips.

I'm not sure if it was the death itself or the crass euphemism, but I could no longer hold back the tears which burst forth, adding wetness to my involuntary sobs. That most august of earthly creatures had suffered demise without dignity. And I found myself cradled in Frances' bosom, as she wiped my tears away on her blouse. Her bosom was soft, warm as a wombat, sweet smelling, and an intense comfort to me. I looked up into her hazel eyes, while she looked down, with lips slightly parted, into the blue ones I'd been born with.

Possum, she said. I love you.

She lowered her head onto mine and kissed me on the lips. It was oh so very soft as the most passionate kisses must always be. I felt the blood surge southbound through my body all the way to the quick beneath my toenails. Some incipient centre in my brain, primed by evolution to harbour animal sensations, flared into life. More tears flowed, as I flung my arms around her.

Over her shoulder, I saw Brian looking in our direction. He was detaching electrodes from the head of the deceased animal.

As our gazes met he froze, electrodes and their leads dangling from his thumb and forefinger like the Devil's worry beads. The show on his face conveyed disappointment, personal pain, and perplexity.

Averting my eyes, I returned Frances' kiss, and found myself wishing for a privacy in which kisses could last forever.

I find my mission in the demesne of Conroy

The matter of the stray brumby, unlucky animal, is behind me, so now I can return to you with the rest of my backstory. My apologies once again.

Where I left off, it was about 4 BC. Before Conroy. Before cartographers put a dot on the map to show where the hell the godforsaken demesne was. Before the Minister of Homeland Security took the opportunity, as he is prone, to big-note himself. Before the commemorative brass plaque was bolted onto rock near Checkpoint Charlie.

Recounting then: I had taken up the position of apprentice with Ray Cromwell. I now worked in his shop, putting frames around pictures among other things. The shop, giving the game away, was called *In The Frame*. I lived above the premises in a tidy little unit. I adored the job and the neighbourhood.

I learnt a lot about art too. Ray left books lying round the shop, books about art and architecture, with glossy pictures in full colour. Sometimes he talked to me about them. I wished I had had the opportunity to enrol in fine arts at a university. No matter, I told myself. Like so much else that was happening inside my brain, I could teach myself.

I like to think I was instrumental in expanding the horizons of the firm to include interior design. And since, in all modesty, this *was* a flair I could fairly boast, I proved able to give something back to Ray in return for all he had given me. I derived great pleasure from being in a position to do so. I found myself, a little farm girl, giving *him* advice. Our radio show, *Ray and Tania*, added to our repute and was a real hoot for me. We were now gurus. I was on the path to stardom. My burgeoning self-confidence knew no bounds.

I wished I could have said the same of Ray. There was a darkness inside him I was unable to penetrate and which I'm sure sapped his self-esteem. I knew quite a bit about the man, even details of his love life. But not when it came to family. On that subject, he would not be drawn. I told him everything about *my* family, including the issues I had had with my father and brothers but, when I invited him to reciprocate, he chose not to. He clammed up, steering our talk in the direction of flippancy. All I was able to glean from him was he had a mother, a father, and a sister. Beyond this, I knew not a bean. I was hoping one or other of them might one day come to visit him at the shop but they never did.

The only visitors he had at the shop, apart from customers, were his bimbos as he called them, though certainly not to their face. You would *never* mistake them for customers. They were good lookers in a flashy sort of way, dressed to kill but you certainly wouldn't shoot them for their brains. His practice was to churn them over at a rate of knots and, frankly, I'm not sure how he managed to keep the supply going. He always seemed embarrassed should one turn up at the shop. When such a mischance happened, he contrived to whisk the gal in question away quick smart.

I was put out by these dalliances. I had begun to think of Ray as *my* territory. Mine to work on. Mine to nurture. Mine to own. Yes, I confess, I was beginning to fancy him. And I'm sure he noticed as much.

One day, after he had closed up shop, Ray invited me to his home, which I understood was a small terrace house in a nearby suburb. He had to drive me in the van because I had no wheels yet and was still in the process of getting my license. I was not sure what his motive was in inviting me, and this made me more than a little edgy.

His house was cute, one-hundred-years-old cute. It was single-story and small, with solid party walls on both sides. The rooms inside were arranged one behind the other like compartments in a tram. I guessed when he had occasion to spirit his bimbo paramours away from unwanted scrutiny, this is where they ended up.

Behind an antique front door, solid as a vault, was a passageway with a couple of bedrooms opening onto it. Their doors were closed, so I didn't get to see inside them. Beyond the bedrooms was a large general-purpose room, probably formed from two smaller rooms by knocking out a dividing wall. The brickwork on one of the walls had been artfully exposed. Windows opened onto a light-well from one of the others.

Beyond this room were the kitchen and bathroom facilities.

He sat me down on a teak-framed couch, part of a determinedly bland lounge suite in the big room, while he went to the kitchen to prepare the meal. At the other end of the room, the end furthest from me, was a solid dining table in imitation antique with settings for two and an opened bottle of red wine. He had obviously planned this tryst in advance. I began to feel edgy again.

On the coffee table in front of me was a book of Hiroshige reproductions. I guess Ray expected I might like to browse through it, and I *did* turn a few pages before redirecting my attention to the wider environment. Lining the walls of the room were framed landscapes in water colour, competently executed, but nothing of any great consequence. I compared them in my mind to the photographic reproductions hanging in my unit and put the difference down to the way his tastes had changed over time, interpretation having triumphed over exactitude.

He entered from the kitchen with two steaming bowls. Our meals. That was quick. He knew I liked Italian and so had decided on spaghetti Bolognese. Good Bolognese is prepared well in advance, and this smelt good. Once again I got an edgy feel. What did he have in store for me tonight?

He poured the wine, and we tucked in. Twirling pasta on my fork, I decided to speak first, making mention of his wall hangings. But he pipped me at the post.

O.K., Tinker Bell, he said. What's with the cow eyes?

Cow eyes? I asked as if I didn't know what he was talking about.

Look, was his response, I'm flattered to know you have feelings for me. But there's no future in it for a smart cookie like you. You deserve better. Why do you think I take up with bimbos?

Why do you?

The fork-full of twisted pasta was now balancing on the edge of my bowl.

Because I can't offer anybody a future, that's why. And my bimbos don't expect it.

Why not?

Why don't they expect it?

Why can't you offer anybody a future?

He paused. I lowered my eyes. Eyes lowered and crest fallen.

Can we just take it as given? he replied.

I could feel a quiver in my lower lip and fought hard to avert tears.

Is it because of our age difference? I asked.

Princess, he said, that's the least of it.

Involuntarily, as if some other person had taken possession of my body, I rose, pushing my chair back forcefully. Tears streaming down my face, I fled down the corridor and out the front door. Without a clue as to where I was or where I might go, I paced the dark unfamiliar streets until his van pulled up beside me. The passenger door opened.

I got in.

Neither of us said anything until we pulled up outside the shop. Then, as I went to get out, he twisted in his seat, pulled me towards him, and kissed me on the lips. It felt good, really good, everything I had been hoping for, but I wasn't about to concede this.

I'm truly sorry, he said.

I flung myself out of the van, let myself into my unit, and cried myself to sleep.

Next morning, neither of us acknowledged to the other that anything had happened. In the shop, we talked shop. The unspoken was a living presence we skirted around. Things went on like this for several days. Then he made the announcement that was to change our lives forever, and whose unintended consequences were to echo round the globe.

I'm going away for a few days, he said. I'm leaving a young fellow to handle the front desk so you'll be free to manage the workshop. Graham Groves is his name.

Ray never came back, of course. He became trapped in The Space.

The first time I went to see him, Conroy didn't even have its name. It was nothing but the bush hut (his domicile now), a couple of Quonsets, and the odd high-clearance 4WD vehicle. The Quonsets housed teams that, among other things, kept Ray supplied with the essentials of life and ensured the precincts were kept clear of rotting carcasses. A rough vehicular access road had been pushed through the unturned earth where there had been only a walking trail before. The little van I drove had suffered a real thumping on my way in, and I had had to go to great pains to pad, with whatever soft items I could find, the sheet glass needed for framing.

Ray had grown a beard since I had last seen him, a neat well-trimmed job of an auburn complexion. We spoke across the devilish boundary which didn't have ski-poles yet, and which, I have to say, spooked me completely. Honestly, I had been inclined to disbelieve reports of his peril at first, to deny the potency of the quandary he was in, until I had chanced to look down at my feet to see the circle of dead creatures. Uggghhh. That was the moment the awful truth about the invisible barrier had dawned on me, moving me to recoil from it as if it were a trellis laden with triffids or the like. This was something new to the planet, and not likely (I would think) to be well disposed towards its inhabitants.

Why are you here? he asked.

To see things for myself, I replied.

Two back-facing forefingers stabbed the air. He was pointing at his face.

Then why don't you take a good fucking look, he said.

So *that* was the score. I had driven his van all that way just so he could clobber me with a handful of rueful words. I knew when I wasn't wanted. Stuff him. I would leave him to his bimbos. Just let him see what use he could put them to now.

But on the drive home, as tears welled up again, I realized things were not that simple. Ray was part of me, and if I ripped that part of me out and flung it in the trash, I would be an incomplete person. As hollow as the bimbos I disparaged. I *couldn't* just write him off. It would be an offence against nature and humanity.

I felt myself to be in a Space of my own. Not a physical Space, more a Space in concept only, but one with a similar capability for entrapment. How should I put it? I was fond of him but, if involvement with him had seemed unlikely before, it now seemed impossible. How could I contemplate an intimate relationship – even one with about as much likelihood of coming to fruition as had Onan's disavowed seed – when the object of my desire lived in one world and I in another? *And never the twain shall meet.*

There was also the business relationship to consider. How could the old firm continue to function as before, including our commercial partnership? On the surface, this was an easier problem to solve. Only the theatre of operations needed changing, and that only in part, the part requiring Ray's physical presence. It would be necessary, of course, for me to make this tedious drive on a regular basis, ferrying the makings of framed pictures to him, and the completed items back. But I could manage that. Driving was still a novelty to me. I had only recently come by my licence.

I arrived home in the wee hours. I didn't even bother trying to sleep, because I knew my mind was churning over at a dizzy rate. I spent the next day in the workshop, functioning on automatic pilot. When night came again, I slept because my body demanded it, but I knew my mind would insist on busying itself round the clock in some sort of background mode, trying to find a solution to my issues. Things played out like this for a few more days and nights before I felt a sudden calm overtake me, as if the world and all its shenanigans had slipped out of time itself. I knew my unconscious processes had come up with the solution I needed.

I would do the drive as and when required.

But I began to feel an overwhelming need for physical sex. Bobby, the guy who had robbed me of my virtue so to speak, had given me a taste for it. Confound him. Now I wanted Ray. It was unfair that, before The Space had claimed him, Ray had chosen to fuck his bimbos rather than me. Inside The Space he was off limits to me, and undoubtedly (I imagined) his bimbos as well. Was I now to lead a celibate life? I thought of seeking out Bobby again. The flesh is weak. But I quickly dispelled that idea and focused on my new-found mission in the demesne of Conroy. Bobby, as accessible as breath, was a flake. Ray, as inaccessible as alchemy, was my guy.

I made my next visit to Ray a few days later and, after that, repeated the exercise weekly. For the first few visits, frames and framing paraphernalia had passed between us across the deadly boundary, but no words. The bemused look on his face at such moments had sent me a silent message along the lines, Girl, you are stark raving. The look on my face, my silent reply, had said, So be it.

I was aware, of course, of his appreciation of good food. He liked to cook, he liked to eat, and he liked to wash the victuals down with fine wine. Moreover, I couldn't help noticing that the weekly basket of provisions Admin supplied him consisted of staples only. So, on my own account and from time to time, I supplemented this measure with delicacies I knew he liked. I imagined he appreciated this gesture, but he never formally thanked me.

On my visits, I couldn't help but notice Mt Redoubt. Reports that it had the head and mane of a lion, were accurate. Even when white weather obscured its profile, I could feel its leonine presence. On days with clear blue sky and the odd fleecy cloud, it stamped its pantheistic authority on all the surrounding territory. On days with greasy grey cloud portending snowstorm, it announced its serious displeasure with gods and mortals alike. On days with really heavy clouds, harbingers of torrential rain and the attendant sound and light show, it threatened death itself. I did not like that mountain. Its staring granite eye spooked me.

I had the good fortune to meet Ray's sister, Frances, on a couple of my visits. I took an immediate liking to her. She was an elegant woman, a smart dresser, possessed of a beauty I would have killed for. She was a couple of years older than me, with the same colouring as her sibling, and about a hand breadth taller than him. That made her *several* hand breadths taller than me.

If there was some intractable dysfunction within the Cromwell family, she was not the cause of it. She was evidently devoted to Ray, horrified by the situation he found himself in, and determined by whatever means to see him through the crisis. Like me, she was committed to multiple visits.

Unlike her brother, she *did* talk to me in a civil manner.

I'm not sure what drives you, she said, but that's not an issue. The bottom line is the support you give him. And for that, I can't thank you enough.

What drives me …, I started to say.

But, placing a gentle hand on my shoulder, she cut me short.

No need, she said.

I …

No need, pet.

Things were moving quickly. Each time I visited, there were more Quonsets. A system of roads – the so-called Stems – began to materialize. And, praise be, the access road had acquired a road-metal surface. These were clear indications the authorities were taking the situation seriously. Why? I wondered. I was not a political animal, but I had my own, possibly jaundiced, view of the current crop of pollies. Always on the make, they were. So, what interest could The Space hold for them, either individually or collectively? What might conceivably be in it for them?

But, Halifax, *something* was in it for them because, at this stage of proceedings, two government appointees materialized. Marius Strangio, an interesting and mysterious man, whom I suspected might be gay, took on the job of Administrator of Conroy. John Shepherd, a dyed-in-the-wool career public servant to whom Marius answered, took charge of the broader issues of concern to our political masters.

Mr Shepherd, whom I understand was the author of that absurd handle, 'demesne', lived and worked in Canberra, making only occasional forays to Conroy. But Marius ensconced himself among us as a permanent fixture, even bringing a wife with him. I didn't like her. Bitch. Had tickets on herself.

When word got around that I was 'Tania' of the *Ray and Tania Show*, I began to score a few commissions round the traps from bars, bistros, and other commercial venues bent on servicing the local clientele. My first commission was the interior design of a small cafe in Science Stem. From then, word of mouth ensured the offers just kept coming. Of course, I found this a most welcome development. I was being seen as a necessary fixture in Conroy. Whenever I ventured into town, people would recognize and acknowledge me. My trips had acquired an alternative justification, one moreover that would, I hoped, serve to nullify the conceit of people such as Ray.

There were signs Ray was settling into his new domicile. I

noticed it, and so did Frances. It was not just resignation on his part. He seemed relieved, almost contented. It appeared to me a great burden had been lifted from him. The dark place within him, the place I had been unable to penetrate, was as if it had never been.

Then, one day, as I was passing material to him across the boundary, he deigned to speak to me. He had a bird for company by this stage, a gang-gang he told me later. It was a pretty bird, enclosed, for its own protection from the deadly forces in play, in a large cage. He – for he was indeed male – was quite vocal at times, supplementing his squawks with a toss or two of a head full of scarlet feathers. Ray liked to keep the bird by him even when outside the hut. So, on the occasion when he, Ray, deigned to break his silence, the cage, with bird inside, hung on a nearby branch.

Jeremy, he said apropos of the bird.

Nice name, I said.

Ray took a deep breath, cocked his head to one side as if mimicking Jeremy, and looked me straight in the eye.

Every week without fail, he said. A bloody long drive in anybody's book. Why do you do it, girl?

You really want to know?

That's why I asked.

To keep you in the loop.

Why should I be kept in the loop?

In The Frame is your business, Ray.

You could carry on without me.

I could. But then it wouldn't be Ray and Tania anymore.

It would be just Tania. And that would work fine.

No, Ray. It would be dead in the water.

I turned my head. A kookaburra had inadvertently traversed The Space, falling dead a metre or so behind me, a reminder of how lethal this boundary was. It took no prisoners. We were unfazed, having seen it before, me a couple of times, and Ray much more frequently. But it set Jeremy off. The noise he made was like that of a door on creaky hinges being opened and shut continuously as in the Jacques Tati film.

I was thankful to Jeremy for his intervention. He had successfully brought our conversation to a halt at an opportune moment for me. I had made my point forcibly and, moreover, I had had the last word.

Around this time, Frances swapped the role of occasional visitor to Conroy (like me) for that of permanent resident (unlike me). I asked myself, Why? Perhaps the same dark forces that had haunted Ray, were a problem for her also, to the extent she felt obliged, like Ray, to flee her city life. To support herself in Conroy, she had taken up a position as nurse in the hospital in Health Stem. By all reports, she was proficient in this arena.

One day, having done my routine pick-up and delivery to Ray, I offered to sketch for him the layout of the demesne, so he could appreciate to some degree the recent developments outside The Space. He, of course, had no way of seeing these things first hand. Stroking his beard, he pretended he couldn't understand why I would bother going to such trouble, then added he had no objection if it pleased me. So I set to work *in situ*, i.e. within his view, with him pretending total indifference. It was a pencil sketch on a large white card set up on an easel. From memory, and from things I had been told by those in the know, I drew The Roundelle, and the nine Stems radiating out from it, all of which had sealed surfaces by now. I marked on it some recent features, such as the school, the hospital, recreational facilities, etc.

Let me set one thing straight. This was never going to outdo Google Maps. This was a humble mud-map courtesy of Tania Chalmond, flibbertigibert. In the case of certain of the Stems, I had neither the spare time nor the opportunity to explore the geography at first hand. For example, I was taking it purely on trust, on hearsay, that each Stem terminated in a *cul-de-sac*. I had ventured to the end of only a handful of them to check this out.

While I was putting the finishing touches to it, Marius chanced on the scene, dressed in his trademark dark suit. Looking over my shoulder, he expressed his astonishment.

For Ray? he asked.

If he'll deign to accept it, I replied.

He turned to Ray.

Why wouldn't you accept it? he asked.

Ray, put on the spot, shrugged.

Don't you have any interest in what's happening out there?

Ray shrugged again.

Don't be a turkey. This young lady, both thoughtful and beautiful, is doing you a special favour. If you won't accept her gift, I shall.

I'm happy to do one for you too, I said.

At this juncture, Ray saw fit to speak …

What makes you think, he said, I don't sneak out in the dead of night and take a peek?

Peek at what? asked Marius.

Conroy, for Christ's sake.

Because, said Marius, if you could do that, Conroy would doubtless just vanish in a puff of smoke.

Both Ray and I looked at him blankly. Sometimes Marius could come across as just a shade obtuse. Moreover, I'm sure that was his intention.

Put it another way, said Marius. It's because you're *not* able to get out and take a peek that we're here in the first place.

He rested his hand on my easel.

Finished? he asked me.

For now, I replied.

Signed?

I scribbled my chicken tracks in the bottom right corner. After which Marius took my sketch down from the easel and turned it round for Ray to see.

Like what you see? he asked Ray.

Fine by me, was Ray's perfunctory reply.

Now Marius handed the sketch across the boundary to Ray who took it.

Make a frame for it, Ray, said Marius, and hang it in pride of place. It deserves no less.

He turned to me.

I'd like to accept the offer you made, he said, if that's O.K.

What offer? I asked.

To make another sketch. Just for me.

When I came back a week later, I had it ready for him, framed and all. Like Ray's, it was on stiff card but, unlike Ray's, it was done in bright acrylic colours, not a mere pencil sketch. Chuffed, Marius thanked me profusely. But it was the least I could do. When Ray had acted in a curmudgeonly manner towards me, it had been Marius who had pulled him up short and persuaded him to accept my gift. Marius was a gentleman.

With the BC years drawing to a close, and with a shitload of trips to Conroy behind me, the situation for Ray, our very own Spaceman and the object of my affections, was becoming more and more comfortable. Labour had put in place a circle of ski-poles and, to go with it, an unknown agency had soon after authorized and installed a token guard post, manned by a weirdo called J-j-john C-c-coffee. The circle of ski-poles had gaps for a conversation post, and for a mechanical dolly. The latter device, straight out of the 19th century, enabled back-and-forth transfer of gear across the contentious boundary. Load up the skip, press the button, and Bob's your uncle. And, courtesy of the 21st century, Ray had access to the very latest technologies, ranging from superfast broadband to equipment for playing Bach fugues to maximum effect. What's not to like? And, believe me, he *did* like it.

The largesse was not all given to Ray. By the time 1 AD came about (the first year of our Lord, and I'll leave you to speculate who the Lord might be) the demesne of Conroy was, by a country mile, the most developed conurbation in the nation, if not in the world of nations. The brand-new infrastructure it boasted was second to none, and some of the innovations put into practice were breathtaking in their daring, most notably perhaps the fleet of Leckies free for individual use within Conroy. Ray, himself, may have had no conceivable use for a Lecky, but all the rest of us were happy they were available.

So, Ray was not daunted by his circumstances. On the contrary, he was a pig in mud. The way he relished the power he had acquired, first as a bearded guru and then, with the passage of time, as a fully-fledged oracle, was really quite shocking to behold. For his own pleasure, he had become a trickster, a Hermes, a Jacob (son of Isaac), a Brer Rabbit.

To conclude my backstory, let me give you an example of his artful behaviour. The occasion was one fine day at The Space, while I was loading the skip with supplies for him. He and that preposterous bird were at the conversation post, on The Space side of course. He was speaking to an elderly man across the boundary, through that double-sided frame he had built. I'm not sure who the man was. A visitor to Conroy certainly. A client perhaps. Somebody needing their Rembrandt mounted perhaps. But I heard every word of their conversation.

What's the name of your shop? the man had asked.

In The Frame, Ray had said.

Where is it?

In Melbourne.

Yes, but what suburb?

La Bum Fuse.

The man was bewildered.

Bum Fuse? he had asked.

La Bum Fuse, Ray had replied.

I thought I knew Melbourne. Where exactly is that?

My apologies, Ray had said. I've given you the French.

What has France got to do with it?

In the original Spanish, we would say Elsternwick.

Ray, the crafty devil, *did* enjoy taking the piss.

I buy bed linen for a pair of seasoned debauchers

It was a spring Sunday. The gentle purr of the van as I headed towards the South Coast was proxy for my exalted mood. My inner engine was humming as was that of the van. I was in thrall, I believed, to the most magical moment of my life so far, a moment bent on serenading the world whether the world was up for it or not. All I, and the moment, cared about, dreamt about, wanted, was Frances, Frances, Frances.

Was Frances a consolation prize? For some time now, it had been Ray I wanted. But he seemed indifferent. He was pushing forty whereas I, at twenty-three, was a mere slip of a girl (or a flibbertigibbet, as he had once called me), aching to pluck from the inscrutable air the ornaments of fully-fledged womanhood. For me, the age gap was a secondary consideration. Now though, I had his sister, who was from my own cohort I guessed, give or take a year or two. And, yes I confess, from my own gender as well. Tut, tut. So the cookie crumbles. So the cards fall. It was Frances, Frances, Frances, and I was in love, love, love.

The road from Canberra to the Coast, mostly downhill, twisted and turned in front of me like a snake writhing in a bushfire. As a matter of fact, there had been bad bushfires here not so many years back. They had spared Conroy and The Space, which was just as well for Ray, who would have found himself faced with an invidious choice, unable to leave and unable to stay.

As the van, guided by my hands, negotiated the undulations of the road, I felt as if swept up in the rhythm of a grand waltz, a balletic celebration of my ecstasy. I had come from Conroy that day on a mission. Actually, two missions. I had frames to deliver to a client. And I had decided to see if I could spruce up my apartment with goodies gleaned from the Sunday markets.

But these matters were of little moment. As I drove, my thoughts kept returning to Frances. With her help, I had made a discovery. Appreciation of the beauty of a woman's body, I had found, is not the exclusive preserve of men. It can and will be shared by women. Indeed, why should anybody ever have considered it otherwise?

There is the prosaic world we mostly live in. And then there is a world apart, a world only occasionally accessible to our senses, a world that burns bright as magnesium. Last night I was privileged to know that world in all its fiery intensity. Frances and I had pleasured each other till the wee hours and beyond. We had been the intoxicant of choice for each other. We had each slathered indiscriminate kisses on the other. We had each explored the other's body over and over, never tiring, never relenting, never apologizing. And now, driving alone, I still felt the remanence of that world stirring my flesh.

We had shared these precious moments only last night in the privacy of Frances' digs in Visitors. Her one-dimensional quarters reminded me of Ray's terrace house back in the big city. The tram. Just like me, she could lay claim to one half of a Quonset hut in Redoubtable Apartments, that being the way, courtesy of Harvey Eanis, most singles and couples lived in Conroy. Families, by contrast, might qualify for an entire Quonset. To live otherwise, namely in more than one dimension, had become a status symbol in Conroy. People like Marius could be expected to have acquired such a privilege.

… apropos of Frances' quarters, I was sure I could help out with decor should she ever consent. Her digs needed an overhaul in the worst possible way. Oddly, for one who dressed so elegantly, she really didn't seem to have much of a flair for interiors. Everything surrounding her was neat and tidy, I'd say that for her, but as plain as tapioca pudding. It needed the cherry on top …

Words had been unnecessary on that auspicious night when we consummated our love physically. Nevertheless, Frances and I *had* talked to each other. Mostly incoherent lovers' speak, words and fragments of words caught up in the maelstrom of passion, sweet nothings as they are sometimes called. But, in the interludes between such fervid moments, between climaxes so to speak, she had asked me what my plans were for the following day, and I had told her.

Are you after something specific? Frances had asked.

Short answer or long answer? I had asked in reply.

Long answer, but keep it short.

She had asked for it, so I had pummelled her playfully under the sheet, the occasion of lots of giggles.

You know Harvey Eanis? I had asked.

Who doesn't?

O.K. Well, I've made a deal with him.

Are you mad?

Let me explain. I rent my digs from him, but I only use them two nights a week. Three maximum. He wants the other nights and he's prepared to pay for them.

For what purpose?

Guess. No prize.

Assignations with women?

None of my business, but I imagine so.

Any particular woman?

You'd be better placed to answer that question.

I can think of a few who would be up for it.

No prizes there either?

So, what takes you to the Coast tomorrow?

Choose bed linen for the love birds.

And a shake or two of itching powder as a bonus?

Naughty.

Want something more friendly? How about a cuddly boa constrictor?

This inconsequential exchange had provoked, by way of response, something much more consequential. Giggles and touchy-feely shenanigans brought an abrupt end to coherent conversation. The dynamics of our mutual passion had taken over, fracturing sentences into unrelated words and words into animalistic syllables. We had become otherwise occupied. This cherished moment and the others like it had become, for us, pearls of great price.

Over the next rise the coast came into my view. A categorical horizon separated two shades of blue. One, the lower, looked as if it had been chiselled out of onyx. The other, uppermost, caressed the eye and stole the breath with a pale steadfast infinity. These liquescent hues were only ever to be found on the palettes of deities plying their trade south of the equator.

I turned north and, as arranged, delivered my frames to an art shop in Ulladulla, whose business model was plain to see, namely to snare poseurs on holiday from the big cities. Afterwards, free now to pursue my own devices, I headed back south again and soon found myself pressed on both sides by multiple ranks of makeshift stalls. Mostly they were open tents, with goods for sale displayed on trestle tables and vans parked beside or behind them.

I parked my vehicle as close as I could manage and proceeded on foot through the thick of the punters and stallholders.

I entered the fairytale world of alternative consumerism. It was replete with new-age jewellery, pet rocks, healing crystals, organic fruit and veggies, home-processed chutneys jams and pickles, sweet smelling candles and soaps, books and vinyl records showing signs of significant handling, hand-knitted toilet roll holders, reconstituted children's toys, etc., etc. It was very much what you might expect of a Sunday market.

I penetrated the maze without finding anything much to grab my interest except for some perfumed soap. This was a disappointment. Had I come all this way for nothing? Then I emerged onto a backstreet, where three regular bricks-and-mortar shops had opened their doors out of regular hours, presumably to take advantage of the serendipitous after-hours foot traffic. There was a stationer cum newsagent, a hardware store, and a store selling home ware. I made for the latter, and was rewarded.

Within, I found the bed linen I was looking for. The sheets and pillow slips I admired were of fine cotton, white, with a repeating pattern of bright crimson love-hearts. Cool, I thought. Just the ticket. Why not pander to the ardent lovers apropos of their moment in the sun?

Pleased with myself, I headed back to the van.

On my return journey to Conroy via Canberra, with thick stands of eucalypts whipping past the driver's window like benevolent phantoms, my thoughts turned for a moment to Harvey Eanis. I remembered the comment on which I had eavesdropped, when Ray was playing oracle to that bitch, June Strangio. Ray's contention was that Harvey coveted his patch of turf, to wit The Space, for its real estate value.

This raised the question in my mind: assuming Ray was to be believed, then was Harvey serious or was he joking? Persuasive evidence decreed The Space was a no-go zone with potentially fatal consequences should anyone venture there. If Harvey had been serious, it could only mean he was in denial of this evidence. Plenty of deniers had sprouted over time in the garden-beds of conjecture, most of them doubting The Space was in any way lethal. Often their scepticism was fuelled by a conspiracy theory, plenty of which flourished in social media, along the lines that the government was up to another of its tricks. Predictably, these maverick deniers were not generally prepared to test their premise by putting their bodies on the line.

So: was Harvey Eanis one of these deniers? If such were the case, I suspected his denialism would likely be driven more by greed than by scurrilous on-line conspiracy theories. And, if so, would his greed drive him to put his denialism to the ultimate test? Would he dare to cross the interface in defiance of whatever demons presided over The Space?

Arriving back at Conroy, I looked for Frances. She was not to be found at her quarters in Redoubtable Apartments. Perhaps she had been offered an emergency shift?

… I had sometimes wondered why, once she had snared her job, she had not moved house to Health Stem. It would have been closer to the hospital. I liked to think it was because she'd decided she would rather stay close to me …

Pity about her absence but our love would keep. Reflecting on my day, I decided it had been both enjoyable and profitable. I made up the spare bedroom in my apartment using the bed linen I had purchased, then stepped back to admire my work. The love-hearts showing on the pillows and turned-down sheet were testimony, I concluded, to my taste and forethought.

Gabby and I probe the core mystery with limited success

Five days later in the early morning I was back in Conroy having driven through the night. I felt no fatigue, just adrenalin surging in my veins. Excitement born of expectation. Wasn't I about to resume my tryst, my dalliance with the most precious person in my life?

The first thing I did was reclaim occupancy of my apartment. To my surprise, I found the spare room had not been used. The bed with the love-hearts had not been disturbed. Well, I thought, that's of no concern to me. As long as Harvey pays me for the use of the room, why should I worry?

The next thing I did was make my usual exchange of goods with Ray. He sensed something was afoot, some new circumstance, but was unable to put his finger on it. I saw the quizzical look as his eyes searched my face but could not yet bring myself to tell him it was his own sister I now fancied. Perhaps I would leave this chore to her.

Then I realized I had not even bothered to contact Frances to let her know I was in town. Shouldn't this have been my top priority? Wasn't it true I was pining big time to engage with my beloved again, physically, cerebrally, emotionally, holistically? Why, then, did I visit my apartment first? It was not about to run away. And why did I deliver goods to Ray immediately following that? Delivery was something that would keep, to be done at any old time.

That's when it dawned on me I was *afraid* to renew contact with Frances. With feet as cold as winter sleet, I was deliberately putting off till some indefinite future timeslot my moment of bliss, the moment I had really come here for. What was I afraid of?

I'll tell you. I was afraid of what she might have been thinking over the last five days. Would analysis have prevailed over passion? Would five days of her mulling things over in the clear light of day have persuaded her to step back from this relationship with a mere flibbertigibbet of her own gender? Was our bright moment only ever a flash in the pan?

There was only one way to find out but I was terrified to put the issue to the test. Better not to know the answer than have to confront an unbearable reality. The seedlings of hope were safe in the furrows of ambiguity whereas the blaze of certainty might blight them fatally.

With beating heart, I steeled myself and called her number. I counted those doom-laden ringtones: one, two, three, four, …

… then, when she answered, it was as if she had been awaiting my call.

Oh, came her voice over the phone, you've no idea how glad I am to hear from you. Where are you?

… I might have been overjoyed at her enthusiasm, had it not been for what followed on its heels …

Here in Conroy, I answered.

Get over here a.s.a.p. I need your help.

What's wrong?

Tell you when you get here.

On my way.

She hung up. Were my worst fears to be realized? A cry for help from her did not sound like any sort of promise our grand passion was about to resume where it had left off. But I made tracks. At the door of her apartment she greeted me with nothing more than a peck on the cheek, then ushered me down the passage to the room in which she received guests. She was dressed and groomed casually but immaculately. Not a hair was out of place. Not an eyelash.

The layout of her apartment, based on the half-Quonset model, was familiar to me because it mirrored my own. I have made earlier mention of its pedestrian decor. Perhaps I should now elaborate.

Sparse, minimalist, characterless. Those are apt descriptors of the room where Frances now kept me waiting. The bare floor was crying out for a little relief in the form of rugs or the like. Redundant wall-space by the yard was everywhere, crying out to be filled. Cloth-covered lounge chairs out of quotidian beige, in one of which I now reclined, faced a coffee table with transparent top, host to an untidy scatter of pulp paperbacks and women's magazines. At eye level were several innocuous wall-hangings. There were prints of French impressionists, the usual suspects, done to death in countless suburban living rooms the world over. There were a couple of small inept home-spun tapestries, the work of her mother I ventured to guess. And, most gauche of all, there were framed certificates announcing her professional qualifications. A large window without drapes was set into the unrelenting curve of the Quonset wall, revealing a stark exterior view of neighbouring apartments.

The worst of it was the interior of her quarters revealed very little of the hopes and dreams of its occupant. What I already knew about her, brief and bright though our relationship had been to this point, was so much more than what was revealed to me by this wretched room.

I needed to have a word or two with her.

She emerged from the depths of her quarters, from where I surmised the kitchen must be, carrying a decanter of water and three … yes, three! … glasses on a tray. As she poured for me, she started the conversational ball rolling, summoning a voice in which I sensed fragility. She seemed on edge, and I longed to put her at ease.

Do you know Gabrielle Zanders? she asked.

Not personally.

You know *who* she is?

The TV journalist.

Frances sat herself down in a lounge chair facing me, her long legs sprawling.

You know, she said, she's set up shop here in Conroy to milk the situation for what it's worth?

I've seen her about.

Well, she's on her way over here to interview me. I want to ask you to be by my side to give moral support.

Why? Does Gabby pose a problem?

I don't enjoy getting the third degree.

Why should she do that to you?

She's done it before.

I held my breath for a moment while I ruminated on possible motives, consequences, and other intangibles. Was Gabby within her rights? Was Frances being overly precious?

Let me speculate, I said. Conroy is not exactly a prime tourist destination. I'd say she wants to know what motivated you, and your brother before you, to come here in the first place.

I'm sure you're right. But how is it you imagine you can read Gabby's mind?

Because it's something *anybody* 'd be most interested in knowing. Including me.

Frances bit her lip. She looked disconcerted. I'd hit a nerve. If my assertion seemed to me as harmless as trickling water, then its effect, apparent on her features, was akin to a monsoonal deluge. Had I been too upfront?

Her next words were hammer hard.

No, she said. You would not.

Why not?

Now her words quivered like a marquee in a gale.

Believe me, is what she said, you really wouldn't want to know the truth. It's altogether too …

Try me.

… ugly for your pretty ears.

I rose from my seat, approached her, and placed a gentle arm across her shoulder. She turned her head and, holding back tears, kissed the back of my hand.

I'm sorry, I said.

The quiver was still there in her voice as she spoke.

Don't be, she said. You're not to blame. I'll tell you when I'm able. Just not now please.

I sat on the arm of her lounge chair and put a hand on her thigh. Flinging an arm round my shoulder, she pulled my head down as she lifted hers up. The resulting tableau must have resembled Rodin's *Kiss*, except for the out-thrust of her gangly legs. The kiss, our kiss, following so naturally from our embrace, was especially delicate and delicious. There had been no need for my earlier anxiety. The clear light of day – to be precise of five of them – had not cooled her passion. I was glad. So very glad.

Her anxiety, on the other hand, needed prompt attention. And who better to give it than me?

At this moment, as Murphy might have decreed, the doorbell rang. Gabrielle Zanders had arrived. We disentangled ourselves. Frances went to the door, from where I heard greetings exchanged.

Frances introduced us, which was unnecessary because we already knew each other from a distance. Gabby's neat plain business skirt and top announced clearly that she saw herself as being on duty. Not altogether surprised to see me here, she gave me a knowing look. As she sat with us round the coffee table, I asked myself, She couldn't know about us, could she? No, I told myself by way of reply, How the fuck *could* she know?

Terror invaded my breast. Celebrities, even a *minor* one like Gabby, tended to have this effect on me. Irrationally perhaps, I felt myself inferior to their kind, so much so that speech deserted me in their presence. What could I say of any importance to a person of her stature in the scheme of things? In such a scheme, I was a nobody.

Rummaging in a handbag draped over her left shoulder, Gabby extracted a notebook and pencil. You don't mind if I take notes? she asked. The question was rhetorical. She had already taken our consent for granted.

We had anticipated Gabby had come to heavy Frances about her and Ray's motives for turning up in this neck of the woods. After all, she was an investigative journalist and this was generally supposed to be a significant puzzle, central to the whole history of Conroy. So she surprised us both by taking a different tack. Ignoring my existence, for which I was thankful, she addressed herself to Frances.

Do you know, she asked Frances, that a person going by the name of Cromwell has recently made his presence felt in Conroy?

You mean Ray? asked Frances.

I said recently.

Who?

Calls himself Paul Cromwell. Recently hired by Labour. A concreter. Old guy.

Frances' face turned deathly.

First day on the job, Gabby continued, the dude fell face-first into a concrete pour. They pulled him out and hosed him down. Opinion seems to be he's blind as a bat. How the hell did Marius give a work permit to somebody like that?

Have you …

Have I told anybody else? Sure. I told Ray.

While I poured a glass of water for Frances, Gabby flipped open her notebook. Frances' hand shook as she took the glass from me. She spoke.

Did Ray ...

Did Ray say anything? You know Ray. I know Ray. Ray talks in riddles.

Frances, eyes wide and unblinking, sipped water with trembling lips. I said nothing. Gabby bided her time, then asked a straight question.

Who is he, Frances?

Time stood still. Frances was distraught. For a mad moment, I thought she was about to bolt from the room.

Is he your father?

Frances' entire face was quaking now. Behind the involuntary camouflage this display lent her features, I thought I detected a slight nod. Gabby made an entry in her notebook, poured herself a glass of water and snapped the notebook shut.

O.K., she said. Enough for now. Time to cool it.

Evidently Gabby had sensed she had pushed Frances about as far as she could. For the moment. I rose, stood behind Frances, and placed my hands on her shoulders. I could feel the tension there, tension (I felt sure) afflicting every muscle in her frame. Tiny paroxysms rippled through her upper arms, and I realized she was sobbing.

So, I thought, this is what our romance of a week or so back had come to, our consensual union of body, mind, and soul in thrilling rapture. Rapture now scuttled well and truly by events in the real world. A contractor, a vision-impaired old fart, possibly Frances' father, had turned up to suck the life out of our dreams. What right had this interloper to do this to us?

While I massaged the shoulders of my distraught lover, Gabby caught me with her purposeful gaze.

You know nothing about this? she asked.

I was startled.

Not a thing, I replied.

Of course not. Silly of me. How could you know? This supposed father only turned up day before yesterday.

The gaze of her green eyes suddenly became as intent as that of a domestic cat about to pounce on helpless prey.

It's like they say. You two *are* an item.

An item?

She nodded.

How … could anybody know?

Small town. Funny. Given your undying devotion to his welfare, I'd have picked you and Ray as the item.

Her eyes softened. I suspected this did not mean they were any less dangerous.

Look, she said. *Mea culpa.* I don't like being cast as the villain. We're a minority of women in a town ruled by men. All of us are significant players in the ongoing story that surrounds Conroy. We should stick together. Compare notes.

As I felt Frances' flesh flinch beneath my fingertips, my outrage out-finessed my timidity.

You, I asked, with your pad, pencil, power dressing, and inquisitorial manner?

Give me a break, girl. All of us feel the call of duty in one way or another given the situation we find ourselves in. That doesn't mean we can't have our off-duty moments.

I'll put it to the present company if she ever gets her shit together.

I could tell Frances' eyes were cast down, not yet prepared to meet her interrogator's toxic gaze. She raised an arm from her lap, wrapping her fingers around mine as they caressed her taut shoulder. As she squeezed my hand, I felt the love skulking behind her action. Not for the first time, I felt a rush of blood to all parts of my body.

But, feeling there was something I needed to do, I lifted my hands from Frances' shoulders.

Shall I walk you to the door? I asked Gabby.

My remark had been pointed. She nodded. Perhaps she, the minor celebrity, felt intimidated now. At Frances' front door, and out of her earshot, she turned to me.

Ms Chalmond, she said, I think we both …

Tania.

O.K. Tania. I think we both have an interest in getting to the bottom of the mystery. The core mystery.

What core? What mystery?

The mystery of why Ray bothered coming to Conroy in the first instance when it was nothing but a hut. The mystery of why the Cromwell family is now here in spades. The mystery underlying the existence of the demesne as we see it today. Is that enough fucking mystery for you?

I guess.

Are you on board?

Only …

Yes?

… if it doesn't hurt Frances.

Later, when evening had put a benign stamp on events, I found myself between the sheets in Frances' bed. With Frances there beside me. I was enjoying – and I'm sure she was also – our delicious proximity to each other. She had calmed down to a degree. While reckless lovemaking was not on our agenda, we both relished the comfort – quiet and snug – of the other's body, the brush – soft and salty – of extramural lips, the stirrings – gentle and mutual – of deep regard one for the other. In this context, my youthful inexperience found voice in my head. I asked myself, Could this be another more tranquil variety of love?

At one point in proceedings, she turned to me, kissed me with warmth on the lips, and whispered, Thanks.

What for? I asked.

Nothing in particular. Just everything.

Then she surprised me. She followed up with a fey line of doggerel:

> I love you, my darling.
> I love you. I do.
> But don't get excited.
> I love my goose too.

What gives with the Cromwell family, I asked myself, that inclines them to take the piss, if ever so gently? Had I uncovered a family trait? A Cromwell meme?

Revelation was of the essence. I had begun the day believing my passion for her was on shaky ground, dangerously susceptible to the cruel judgment of her reason, reason abetted by the clear light of day. Now I realised *she*, whom I had feared, was the more vulnerable party. Frances was the one whom events could most likely bring undone.

Revelation was followed swiftly by resolve. I resolved I would not be party to grievous games. In fact, I would set myself in opposition to them. I resolved I would do whatever was within my power to head off any events designed to do her injury. If we were in fact an item, as the world at large seemed to acknowledge, then I undertook in this moment to keep that item as intact as the fixity of stars in the firmament.

I sealed my resolve with a gentle kiss to my loved one's right breast.

I shout myself a tour of Conroy, admiring its art

Frances was on nursing duty the following day so I found myself at a loose end. I made a snap decision to spend some of my enforced time alone shouting myself a self-guided tour of Conroy by Lecky. I planned to combine this with a visit to Marius in Admin, who had invited me to view *in situ* the schematic I had made for him of the layout of Conroy, the mud-map he had requested of me. It was a Sunday, but he had promised he would be there in his office to greet me.

I began with breakfast at *One Fine Day*, aptly named as it turned out, because the day was glorious. Cotton-ball clouds wafted across a blue as deep as infinity. Swarms of yellow butterflies were practising their stagger-dance, wings scissoring the air. Currawongs, sleek and black as tar, flaunted their aerial skills, in the process betraying flashes of a raffish white beneath unfurled feathers. Nature was turning it on for me.

The small and friendly cafe in Science where I now breakfasted was the site of my very first commission in Conroy. A mural, depicting a beaming face in rainbow colours, greeted me on the facade of the Quonset the business occupied. No great shakes as a work of art, it nevertheless promised a satisfactory culinary experience (which was then duly delivered) to the punters it enticed inside. The mural was not my work. I did interiors.

Over my pancakes and coffee I contemplated, with guilty satisfaction, the decor for which I had been responsible. My aim had been to break up the allusive lines of the Quonset through the use of false ceilings, vertical constructs, and the like. Where, despite my best efforts, I had been unable to realize this aim, I had done my darndest to make a feature out of the relentless curved surfaces. I believe the end result had been a success.

Replete, and back in my Lecky, I began to feel excited at the prospect before me. I was ready for adventure. Up until today, my experience of Conroy had been piecemeal as, for example, when I discharged a commission or made a delivery. Now, today, I was free to discover Conroy in overview without restraint by commitments I felt obliged to fulfil. To get beneath its skin. To breathe its essence.

I was up for it.

From *One Fine Day*, I drove the length of Science Stem, reversing direction on reaching the court at the end of the *cul-de-*

sac. Facilities in this Stem – living quarters, labs, and community resources – were housed almost entirely in Quonsets. Given the gentle undulations and meanderings of the Stem, and the tricks perspective played on the mind, the Quonsets *en masse* resembled a cloudburst of blue-grey bubbles, drenching the straggles of green-grey alpine flora. Given the blue overhead, and the majesty of the mountain behind, it was a picture-perfect scene. Contrary to what might be common expectation, its visage wasn't anything like that of a military barracks. To my mind, it lacked the necessary degree of coherence, discipline, and order for such a comparison to be in any way apt.

In this neighbourhood, the only concessions made to the dominance of the Quonset model were for the supermarket, multiplex cinema, and school, all of which took on the inevitable box shape, ubiquitous inside and outside of Conroy.

The facades of many of the Quonsets were decorated with wanabee art, often quite colourful, often lacking chic. For example, the frontages of labs invariably depicted stock situations, such as grinning boffins wearing white coats, eyes only for their test-tubes or Petri dishes. But some frontages, particularly those adorning living quarters and recreational amenities, *did* boast more variety and originality. I was particularly intrigued by the evidence I saw, in more than one location, of a local Banksy at work.

I give you one example of several I found that day in Science. The mural on the semi-circular facade of an entertainment venue calling itself *Play the Game* comprised a pair of Cosette look-alikes, with bare feet, grimy faces, and tattered hemlines, playing knucklebones in the dust. It looked vaguely familiar, but it took some time before the penny dropped in the tardy mechanism of my head. The depiction was a clever parody of a fragment in the fine detail of a canvas by Bruegel. I had seen in it one of Ray's art books. This local artist knew his stuff. I reflected ruefully, he/she could probably claim to have won many more commissions than I had.

Then I noticed an additional detail in the mural, a detail not necessarily obvious at first glance, a detail indicating a certain impishness on the part of the artist. One of the urchins had a cell phone protruding from a pocket in her smock.

Please don't come away with the impression Science was a purely static locality, a set without actors, a world without action. Not so. Things were jumping there. The spectacle before me was a flurry of family-friendly fun. People – men, women, and children – spilled out of the Quonsets onto the walkways and pavements, where they gesticulated in groups with vigour, joy, and passion. Or else, dropped in somewhere nearby for coffee to do likewise. Or else, set off in Leckies or on bicycles to more distant destinations for such purpose. Some wore white coats, but most were in civvies. It *was* Sunday.

I loved to spy on people interacting at a distance from me, pondering what mischief they might be up to. My imagination given free rein in this way, I could conceive of arguments evolving, deals done, plots hatched, relationships formed. Unheard discourse of unverifiable motive proceeded for my amusement while I, safely ensconced in my moving Lecky, was free to play my guessing game. Safely ensconced, that is, provided I kept a wary eye out for the pedestrian and vehicular traffic milling chaotically around me, throwing themselves in my path at times. They were kamikazes.

An incongruity occurred to me. From my vantage point, I could point to, and thereby identify in some sense, any number of these pavement strutters without having a clue as to what was going on in their heads. Yet I was party to the headspace of a certain local artist I had recently come to admire, without being able to identify the culprit in any sense at all.

I passed a Lecky bus just as a contingent of Science personnel, sporting white coats and wenkits, were boarding it. No doubt they were bound for a routine shift at The Space. The logo on the driver's side door took the form of a heraldic shield crossed by diagonal green and yellow bars. Australian colours. I had, of course, seen this logo before. Many times. It was the DETA logo. It decorated, among other things, the driver's door on every common-and-garden Lecky, including the one I was driving. But now, for the first time, as if I were blessed today by a heightened sensibility, I intuited some sort of conflict in its design. Precisely what feature was the source of this conflict? The question nagged me for quite a few moments, until the nature of the discord dawned on me. It was a subtle feature indeed. Contrary to the usual convention, the bars on the shield connected the upper right corner with lower left. Bend sinister. Forward slash instead of backslash.

A suite of questions now assailed my mind. Such a design was presumed by some to be a signifier of illegitimate birth. Who was it had decided such a signifier should be promulgated here and now in Conroy? I could not imagine such a thing happening purely by accident. And was the promulgator's intention to suggest DETA was the bastard child of Oz? And, assuming Oz to be the mother of this child – mother country and all that – who could be the father? And had this father successfully sown wild oats in places other than Conroy? I intended, should the opportunity arise, to bring this whole perplexing issue up with Marius when I met him later in the day, together with the question of who the aspiring Banksy was. I felt Marius would know the answers.

Done with Science, I headed back to The Roundelle, where I turned left. By Conroy's modest standards, the traffic in this circle was heavy. Since I was taking it in the clockwise direction, Admin Stem was next up. I decided to skip this Stem for the moment since I was committed to return here later on my visit to Marius. Its treasures would keep.

So the next feature of interest to me was the cemetery on the lower slopes of the mountain. I parked my Lecky there and let myself out. There were only two headstones, and I was not sure if they marked the location of ashes or of coffined bodies. The emoticon for 'sad' flashed before my mind's eye. The inscribed names, determinedly Anglo-Saxon, meant nothing to me, but I had been told the deaths of these unlucky souls were the consequence of building accidents. One thing was for sure. They would not be lonely here for long. An adroit killer, with a unique *modus operandi*, was on the loose in the precincts of The Space. It had not yet claimed any human victims but my guess was this was only a matter of time. I wondered who the first victim of such unsourced malevolence might be.

The next Stem was Agriculture. Like in Science, I found oodles of festive activity here. Things were swinging. But, unlike in Science, little of the activity I saw involved the people who actually lived here. In fact, the living quarters *per se* seemed largely deserted. I had been told by a number of people in the know – Frances, Ray, Marius – there was little work for paid personnel to do here as things stood, not in Agriculture nor Defence nor Corrections, so the flunkies from these Divisions were mostly cooling their heels in places like Canberra, held in reserve so to speak, waiting for news of a major breakthrough from Science.

So, on this auspicious Sunday, most of the activity in Agriculture involved off-duty residents from Stems like Science, Health, Labour, and Admin, Stems whose Divisions *were* able to find an immediate use for personnel. Today, released from workaday cares, they were out and about in their Leckies, bent on whatever enjoyment they could glean.

As well as the more prosaic efforts made to decorate Quonset facades, there were quite a few with artistic merit, often done I reckoned by the indigenous Banksy, whose style I fancied I could pick by now. The mural, a fairly recent addition, on the double-fronted *Pig's Ears* restaurant, was one of these. I parked in front of it with the intention of scrutinizing it more closely. There was more than a hint of irony in the way the pigs were anthropomorphized in this mural. I was looking for a signature, but the only identifier I could find anywhere on it was an inconspicuous letter 'B' in cursive, tucked away in the bottom right corner, trying hard not to be noticed. My God, I thought. Could it be the *real* Banksy had come half way round the world to delight us in Conroy?

Good afternoon, was the sudden voice from behind me.

Startled, I turned to face a man whose formal dress suggested he might be the *maitre d'* of the establishment.

Oh, good afternoon, I said. You startled me.

My sincere apologies, Miss Chalmond. May I be of assistance?

I must have looked confused, because he felt obliged to identify himself.

My name is Basil Shirley, he said. We *have* met.

I felt foolish. Of course we had. Some time ago, I had done the interiors for *Pig's Ears*, so I would have entered into negotiations with him at some point. For the life of me, I couldn't remember having done so. I decided against inviting him to call me Tania. There was something about this man, his obsequious manner perhaps, that got up my nostrils. I pointed to the mural.

Do you know who is responsible for the art work? I asked.

I do.

Who?

I'm so sorry, *madame*. I am sworn to secrecy

Secrecy?

Put it down to artistic temperament.

Well, well. Our very own Banksy. True to form.

As I turned to go, his voice followed me.

You are always most welcome at our table, Miss Chalmond, he said. Bring your friend.

I may do, I replied.

… friend? I thought. But how could he know? …

Perv that I was, I simply *had* to visit Defence to see the brothel. Its frontage boasted its name, *Space Odyssey*, in red lettering, and a burlesque in graphics of curvaceous women in body-hugging space-suits. It was executed once again in that consummate style I had seen so often today, and signed off, in low-key fashion, with the letter 'B'. I felt peeved by the reclusive behaviour of this artist.

I didn't even know his/her gender. I found myself wishing we could get together sometime to compare notes, he/she the doyen of exteriors and me, of interiors.

The innovative facade seemed somewhat wasted on the clientele of the brothel whom, I am told, always used a back entrance. Judging by the number of Leckies parked toward the rear, I gathered it was patronized right this very moment by clients enjoying a matinee. Seeking a tad of interior sunshine to match that favouring those of us who chose outdoor recreation.

I saw the sprawling hospital in Health Stem, and imagined Frances slaving away inside, administering injections and emptying bed-pans. I saw the well-patronized gay bar, *The Tight Spot*, in Corrections, the mock brickwork arches on its dual-Quonset facade an obvious nod to the iconic Stonewall Inn. I saw the sports centre in Labour Stem, a massive cuboid structure in which healthy living could be worshipped and/or pursued desperately.

And so to Visitors, haunt of overnighters and the like, come here from all over Australia – nay, the world – to consult the oracle or have their infections treated. Frances and I were among the more regular residents of this Stem. Moving on past our respective apartments, I came upon two forlorn churches, side-by-side Quonsets sporting crosses. Patronage was light, despite this being the day of rest for most Christians.

From here, my next stop-over was Homeland Security Stem, which might have been another planet.

As if by decree, none of the Quonset huts here sported decorative facades. Nor was anybody paying a visit for the purposes of entertainment or recreation, because there was no such frivolity to be had. Little foot traffic dared venture out. The only vehicles I saw were those in transit to and from the outside world, the sort of thing I did on a more-or-less regular weekly basis. A conference centre dominated the Stem, taking the form of a nondescript cuboid monolith, a grey windowless eminence, but even here there was no sign of current activity to be found.

Searching for something from the history books to which this might compare, I thought of East Germany before the wall came down. Complete with Checkpoint Charlie.

Was some sort of curfew in force in Homeland Security? I wondered. I found myself constantly checking my rear vision for signs I was being tailed.

I was glad to quit this creepy Stem. This marked the end of my free-wheeling tour of Conroy. All that remained now for me was to pay my respects to Marius and, with this in mind, I hung a left into Admin Stem.

The sun was low on the horizon as I did so. Colours were soft and sumptuous in this magical light. Outlines, smudgy and lacking their noonday severity, were not inclined at this hour to jar the machinery of eye and mind. Even the mountain to my right, apparently under the spell of this light, had contrived to seem less forbidding. The eye of the lion looked down on the world below with apparent benevolence. Such was my personal take on things. Maybe this was a case of self delusion or wishful thinking on my part.

On the corner the Stem made with The Roundelle was another supermarket and, next to this, a large complex housing pokies, hugely popular today. Ignoring these, I found myself in a thicket of cuboid administration buildings, embracing both sides of the Stem. After my open-air experience of the day past, I felt cocooned by this environment. Passing the law courts and the police precincts, I arrived at The Depot. I parked my Lecky in a charging station nearby.

The Depot was, fittingly, the most prominent of the buildings in Admin. It was a four-story job out of concrete and glass, characterless both outside and (as I knew from previous visits) inside.

Taking the lift to the fourth floor, I found myself assailed by a clinical environment, sucked dry of any human imprint. I might have been in an office block in any modern city anywhere in the world. I knocked and entered where I saw *Marius Strangio* and underneath *Administrator of Conroy* etched onto a tinted-glass door. Inside, ensconced in his ante-room, was Max – Marius' minder – who, expecting me, ushered me through to Marius' office. Marius' greeting, as he sat me down on the other side of his desk, was genial. Genuinely so. He was glad to see me.

Coffee? he asked.

Please.

He dropped a capsule into the mechanism of the machine and stood by.

We should talk turkey more often, he said. As befits people who really run the show.

Me? I asked.

Why not? Sure, you have no formal status here but you're a key player. Without you the place would not be the same at all. I'm grateful to you in so many ways.

He pointed to the wall behind his desk.

There's one of them, he said.

So it happened my attention was drawn to my creation. The octopus. Or nonapus perhaps? The spiral galaxy. The full catastrophe. I found myself admiring it, ashamed of the outrageous vanity of my thoughts.

Passing me coffee and a glass of water poured from a decanter, he sat behind his desk, choosing water only for himself.

Take a good look while you can, he said. I'm afraid I'm going to have to take it down.

Why?

Orders are orders.

Whose orders?

He did not answer me directly. Instead, he intercepted my gaze with a knowing look saying, Guess.

For what reason?

Security protocols.

Marius paused. He settled back in his chair, folding his hands behind his head. He caught my gaze with his. Only then did he launch into his spiel.

During World War Two, I am told, the city fathers of some of the principal municipalities in Australia decided in their wisdom to take down all the street signs. They figured this would confound the Japanese invasion force when it arrived.

But mine is only a mud-map. It's not about to give the game away to the Japanese. Or to anyone else.

It's not me you have to convince, darling.

What sort of paranoid response is dictating this?

Marius' face betrayed a sad smile. He took his hands from behind his head and held them palms up with fingers splayed. Then he let them fall to his sides.

Your effort won't go to waste, he said. I promise you it shall occupy pride of place in my living quarters. I'll need to find something else to take its place here. I fear I shan't be able to match it for quality or fitness for purpose.

I liked the man. I was impressed with his discretion, the precision of his language and of his manners. His speech contained only the barest trace of an accent I presumed to be Italian.

My eyes scanned the glossy surface in front of me. Normally, one might expect to see an upright photo of wife and children there, a constant reminder to him of his nearest and dearest. I wasn't aware Marius had any children, but I knew the bitch who was his wife. Her image did not grace his desk, nor any other image. This man kept himself to himself.

May I venture a personal opinion? he asked.

Please do.

When the hysterical researchers report their findings …

You mean 'historical'?

Should you insist. When the ink has dried on their accounts of Conroy's rise and fall, a handful only of select people shall find their names there. Yours will be among them.

But I'm a nobody.

Don't demean yourself. You're part of the A-team.

What makes you think that?

Let me ask *you* a question? Who is the most significant player in Conroy's brief history to date? Without whom Conroy would this day be nothing more than a bush hut.

Ray, obviously.

And you, Ms Chalmond, are the one who's always by his side. As much as anybody else around the traps, even including those pesky boffins, you understand the problems The Space poses for its Spaceman. And, what's more, you have a stake in solving them.

I have a stake?

Nothing less than your life, I believe.

My life? Get real. You exaggerate my commitment.

I don't believe I do. And as for the future, …

… and here he set his hands talking, adding to the drama he felt the moment deserved, fingers piercing the air, paws slicing it, fists squeezing it …

… because the stakes are so high for you, you shall force a solution.

I play voyeur at The Space and learn some new tricks

Dusk. A gusty breeze was getting up.

As I retrieved my Lecky from the charging station, I happened to notice Gabby, doing precisely the same thing. Unnoticed by her, I decided to stay within cooee and see what she was up to. I *had* heard she was one of the privileged few able to snare a coveted apartment in Admin Stem, as opposed to us plebs down in Visitors, who had to be satisfied with what we were allocated. If the celebrated TV anchor and investigative journalist were just now stepping out, perhaps she was following up an interesting lead. I was curious.

She turned left into The Roundelle with me hot on her tail.

A moon, all but full, was making its debut in the east. Then she did something I was not expecting. She hung a right into the designated road giving access to The Space, an access monitored in daylight hours, and sometimes beyond, by John Coffee. What business had she with Ray at this hour? Like everybody else in Conroy, I had heard some rumours, rumours on which I wasn't especially keen to dwell.

I didn't follow her. Maintaining my course in The Roundelle, I put my foot down. More or less opposite Defence Stem, I chucked a screaming U-turn and parked adjacent to an informal and well-trod foot track leading from that point to The Space. Scurrying down this track, I reached the annular clearing, within which The Space sufficed as the hole in the doughnut, just in time to see (on my right) Gabby ensconced already at the conversation post, and Ray heading towards it from his hut.

And – would you credit it? – I saw something now I hadn't been aware of before. The ring of ski-poles shimmered a ghostly green in the equivocal moonlight. To satisfy safety regulations, I assumed. Bright red in the daytime and luminescent green at night. Out of what can did this unlikely paint come?

I looked out over a charmed circle. By day, territory fit for scientific research and similar no-nonsense activity. By night, a realm fit for the frolic of little people. At all times, day or night, in these rare precincts, there are new lessons to learn, new experiences to enjoy, and new secrets to unearth.

Now I had no option but to take a chance. Bending double, I made a mad dash for the circle of ski-poles. Once there, I pressed my back against the poles and, panting, edged my way slowly towards my quarry. Snow-gums, inside The Space but hanging over the ski-poles, provided cover from the treacherous moonlight. Ray had made it to his side of the conversation post, but I doubted either one of them had seen me. So far, so good.

Reaching the skip, I vaulted up and over the handrail round its edge, and toppled head-first into it. Clunk. Ouch. I quickly righted myself, and shot a glance through the gap between the handrail and the superstructure of the skip. It was like peering through a letter slot. Shit. Both heads were turned towards me. They had heard my fall. But, a second or two later, their heads turned away again. Perhaps they assumed they had heard yet another poor critter – an owl perhaps – on its death dive from its sanctuary in the sky to its final resting place on mother earth. Or, as fate would have it, into the skip resident there.

I rubbed my sore head. I was now in position to play spy with impunity. Provided, that is, some wayward gremlin didn't decide to press the release button on the skip, sending it – with me as passenger *sans* choice in the matter – hurtling into The Space.

Continuing to peep through my letter slot, I watched the pair of them silhouetted in the moonlight and sitting across from each other at the interface. Ray was frying something over a portable gas burner resting on a small table within his reach nearby. Owing to the inadequate light, I couldn't be absolutely certain of what was cooking. Perhaps it was blinnies. My mouth watered. After topping them with what might have been sour cream and salmon roe – ingredients with which, on rueful reflection, I had provided him – he set about sharing the feast with Gabby, a feast accompanied by – courtesy of yours truly once again – a bottle of good wine.

I was party to snippets of their conversation, delivered to me between tasty mouthfuls, and only when the gusts of wind favoured my direction. Snippets such as:

Gabby:	… game you think the wacko is playing? …
Ray:	… aversion to sound medical advice …
Gabby:	… doesn't leave her in a very nice place …
Ray:	… always thus. Left surgery too late given …
Gabby:	… deserves a life of her own …
Ray:	… you to tell that to the old goat …
Gabby:	… well then shall we? …
Ray:	… sounds like a plan …

I imagined they touched hands briefly through the double-sided frame. Then they rose. Ray turned off the gas burner. After this they – in cooperation – went about dismantling the conversation post, piece by piece. They laid the hardwood planks across their seats, as if setting things up for the daily anti-infective program. Then they proceeded to take off their clothes. In no time, except for Ray's beard, they were buck naked.

The feeling this evoked in me was a cocktail of shock, resentment, embarrassment, disgust, and a sense of having been cheated on. Why? Hadn't I ditched Ray? Wasn't he now a free agent? Did I have any right to feel jealousy? Wasn't it his right to get his rocks off with the floozy of his choice? Feeling dizzy, I laid myself down in the base of the skip. I really thought I might pass out on the spot.

I sat up, put my head between my knees, took a couple of deep breaths, counted to ten silently, and recited the alphabet backwards and soundlessly. When I had managed finally to tame my nausea and check my beating heart, I realized something shameful about myself. I desperately wanted to see what would happen next.

Back at my letter-slot, I found Gabby still there, nonchalant, naked, seated on the planks, one curvaceous thigh crossed over the other. Waiting for Ray. Yes, waiting. To my surprise, Ray had disappeared.

Not for long. He emerged from his hut, starkers, with a blanket over his arm. His madness had method. The weather had been balmy today but, with evening now pressing its claim, there was a nip in the alpine air.

In point of fact, their nakedness was not so very much in-your-face. The glow of the moon, through which all visuals swam, flattered the human form without exposing precise detail. The figures of the expectant lovers hung bright in this languid light but, except perhaps in my prurient imagination, I could not make out their naughty-bits, which must necessarily have been there just the same, and no doubt ready for action. The amorous pair had been transformed into glimmering wraiths, the congealed light itself serving to clothe their nakedness. I imagined they would pass as principals of a *corps de ballet*, the discreet lunar glow their leotards, the magical ambience of the evening their supernatural sheen.

He laid himself flat on the wooden mattress with his head studiously inside The Space. She lay on top of him, contrariwise, with her head determinedly *outside*. After that came what might best be described as a horizontal *pas de deux*. Their movements were *that* graceful. Despite the blanket. Perhaps because of the blanket. I, unseen voyeur, was entranced.

There was a sound-track to this performance, a vocal accompaniment conforming, I would think, to involuntary impulse, to popular experience and expectation.

They had more tricks up their sleeve. He slipped out from under while she supported herself on knees and elbows, the idea being (I must presume with a blush) that she could be entered from behind. After they had exploited this position for what it was worth, he laid himself back down again and she sat on top, both of them relishing (and here again I must presume) the eye contact available now for their enjoyment.

What followed from this point was a succession of outrageous positions, notable for their ever increasing ingenuity and gymnastic prowess. Halifax. Just to watch was exhausting.

I felt sure they must eventually tire and, sure enough, they did. They slumped side-by-side in a palpitating heap, re-visiting the head-to-toe position with respect to each other, happy now to enjoy the post-coital bliss they had earned. His head was inside The Space and hers was outside, as had been the case throughout the course of the more vigorous phase of their antics. Mind you, I talk here about potentially *lethal* antics. They diced with death in much the same way as one would do swimming with sharks.

When I was sure there was nothing more of interest to be seen, I quit my post and lay back in the skip, my hands a cradle for my head. I looked up. The mountain was there, brought closer than ever by the absence of perspective consequent on the uncertain light, light dimly tracing the outline of the summit but ever reluctant to fill in detail. I could not make out the eye of the lion. I knew it was there, but my fancy had to paint it in.

At a much greater remove, way up above me, loomed our galaxy, and the entire universe of stars far beyond. Stirring me, as it had stirred generations of humankind over the aeons, was that mosaic of immeasurable time, incalculable distance, and unfathomable meaning. I surrendered myself to its hypnotism, its propensity to stall time, its ability to blindside the imagination.

Compared with what I was seeing now in the night sky above, the moment of jealousy I had experienced earlier was no more than a puny atom of deranged thought mattering not a tad in comparison with the vast pulsating macrocosm out there. It mattered less than the merest fleck of cosmic dust drifting without purpose through a realm of boundless unconcern. Why ever had I bothered? Jealousy was an emotion whose point, or lack thereof, had no bearing at all on the greater universe.

But the grand passion that had drawn my attention just minutes before was another thing. It had a majestic force, so it seemed to me, capable of throwing out a challenge to whatever panorama the seething immensity above might turn on for my benefit. Passion drove human life like supernovae drove celestial machinations.

What I had seen, over the lip of the skip, so to speak, may seem no big deal to those with a track record in this sport but, to an innocent like me, it was an epiphany of such power I had not previously experienced or even imagined. On a more mundane level, it was an object lesson in what could be achieved through human invention even within the stringent constraints The Space imposed. Hallelujah. The cat could be skinned in more ways than one. The missionary position was not the only show in town.

I owed this lesson to the unwitting pair, lying in a state of euphoric exhaustion just metres away from me, sipping the dregs of the heady draught they had up to now guzzled so greedily. I had taken this lesson on board at the expense of the privacy they had every right to expect, privacy I had stolen from them. Suddenly, my shame was rampant.

Why was I doing this?

Lying there, struggling with this shame, I realized I was cold. I wanted now to quit the scene, but felt unable to do so without serious risk of being observed. I assumed I would have to stay put until Gabby decided to go home, and Ray chose to retreat to his hut. Shivering, I groaned inwardly. *They* had a blanket.

That's when I heard the snores. Snores in two different sonorities. First one, deep and resonant, then its tremulous echo, high-pitched and paper-thin. Animal oblivion consequent on animal indulgence.

Here was my chance. Sitting up, I manoeuvred my belly over the handrail and let myself fall to the soft turf outside the skip. In my mind, I traced out the path of my intended retreat through my moonlit ambit, confirmed the snores were still current, and then went for it. I dashed. Back in my Lecky, I felt pleased with myself, and not a little guilty.

The next morning, quite early, I dropped by to check out the scene. I was in my van. Not a Lecky, because I intended to continue to Melbourne afterwards. Nobody was about, not even John Coffee. He had not yet come on duty. I took the liberty of operating the boom-gate for myself.

Good fairies, it seemed, had restored the conversation post. It was now ready for daily oracular consultations. Ray, expert on everything, steward of the future, would be ready, when the time came later that day, to share his clairvoyance with the masses.

I grapple with competing versions of hell breaking loose

All hell has broken loose, said Frances.

What exactly? I asked.

Get over here girl and see for yourself.

I terminated the call and was in my van again bound for Conroy. Prematurely. It was still only mid-week.

In late afternoon I arrived within cooee of Conroy. I could tell at Checkpoint Charlie that something was afoot because I received more than the usual scrutiny. Then, on the Stems themselves, and even on The Roundelle, I believed I could smell the outrage. The air itself seemed in revolt. I made my way to the hospital on Health Stem, where Frances was on duty. Her ashen face matched her white garb. She greeted me with a firm hand on my shoulder, a hand that directed me with determination into the depths of the wards. Now I *was* worried.

You know June Strangio? she asked.

… we were walking side-by-side down one of the hospital corridors …

Of course.

We're going to see her.

Why?

We reached a room on the left. Frances opened the door, revealing a private room with its bed curtained off. We approached. She pulled aside the curtain. June was in the bed, propped up, dressed in white hospital bedclothes. She was not her usual picture of composure and control. She looked distraught, and strangely human for a change. Then, when she saw me, blind rage filled her face.

The little floozy herself, she said. How dare you.

At a loss for words, I could utter only stammering monosyllables.

I'm … I'm not sure …, were the syllables.

June raised her hands, pointing two index fingers at her face. Had they been pistols, she might have blown her brains out with them. It was only then I saw what her problem was.

Her cheeks and brow bore red blotches in the form of love hearts. Such dubious cosmetic frippery rang a bell with me. How could it not? It matched the repeating pattern on the sheets I had smoothed down on the bed in the spare room of my apartment. The bed I had set aside for lovebirds.

They can't be removed, you little witch, were June's furious words. And they're all over my fucking body.

To prove her point, she ripped the bodice of her gown apart, revealing breasts and belly covered in yet more hearts. I could only assume they extended all the way down to the tips of her toes, but she refrained from demonstrating this.

We're doing our best, said Frances, to get rid of them, Mrs Strangio. But so far they refuse to budge.

June's words might have shattered glass.

Refuse to budge? she screamed. They're fucking indelible.

Please calm down, Mrs Strangio, said Frances. We'll set things right, I promise.

June's hysteria morphed to bitter irony.

Yes, she said. I guess if it comes to it, they can always be removed surgically.

... at this, she saw my startled eyes and, delighted with the reaction she had provoked, resumed her harangue ...

Yes, you little harpy, she said. You, in cahoots with that phony prophet, plotted my downfall, and now you have blood on your hands.

... I was beginning to resent the slurs she was hurling willy-nilly in my direction, especially since each of them was preceded by 'little' ...

And at this latest slur, Frances' features hardened. She pursed her lips. Her eyes narrowed. Her brow darkened. I was afraid for a moment of the injury she might do June. Instead, all she did was impale her on a barbed remark.

And you, madam, have a scarlet letter branded on your forehead, she said.

She gripped my elbow, spun me round forcibly, and bundled me out the door. Once outside, she led me to a waiting room, sat me down, made me a cup of spoon coffee, and – gentleness in her eyes now – sought to allay my confusion and sooth my rioting emotions. Through the window, I saw the day was darkening.

I began to realize there was much more to this tragi-comedy than I knew. My face would have shown it. My bowels certainly testified to it.

Another party was involved ..., said Frances.

I guess there would have been, I said.

... and he's now dead.

Dead?

The first human casualty of The Space.

Who? I asked.

Guess.

Not Harvey Eanis?

She nodded.

How? I asked.

If it wasn't so bloody tragic, it'd be a real hoot. Picture the copulating couple there in your spare bed stirring from their dalliance to find themselves covered from head to frigging toe with love hearts. Leached from the sheets you bought. By the agency ...

I stifled a giggle.

... of their own sweat. You could call it an STD. Serves them right I guess for not being careful.

My giggle proved irrepressible.

By all reports, she continued, when Harvey saw the rash he had acquired, he lost it completely. He made for The Space, mad as hell, and charged inside. I imagine him still pulling on his underdaks as he did so. We don't know exactly what happened inside, but soon he was out again.

How ...?

We're not sure whether he jumped or was pushed.

You don't suspect Ray?

I don't want to. He's my brother. But the facts worry me.

What facts?

Harvey came out in the skip. Dead on arrival.

I paused to let my mind churn over the ramifications of this 'fact'. It was Frances who spoke next while I ruminated.

A consignment of dead meat, she said. Gift from The Space to the world outside.

Gift gratefully received? I asked.

Not in all quarters.

But …, I said, … I believe Harvey was prone to deny The Space was lethal. And you said yourself he'd lost the plot.

Your point being …?

Maybe it was reckless misadventure on his part. Or suicide even.

So, he climbed into the skip unaided, and pressed the button himself?

I just can't believe Ray did it.

Nor can I. But then who *was* the culprit?

I rose with an urgent determination.

We need to speak to him, I said.

Frances, gripping my wrist, forced me to resume my seat.

This is not the time, she said. Save it for tomorrow. Right now, he'll be enjoying physical consolation.

While my mind churned over the implications of *this* one, Marius peeped in at the door of the waiting room. Seeing us, he came on over. His face was a mask.

Interesting times, he said.

Here to see your wife? Frances asked.

He nodded.

She's going to need all the support she can get, he said.

Your wife thinks it was Ray. With Tania acting as his accomplice.

We shall see what we shall see. It's no time to be casting nasturtiums. John Shepherd has flown in to oversee the investigations. My guess is he'll call both of you in due course. *Ciao.*

An abrupt retreat, I thought. Leaving us to deal with our rioting thoughts as best we could. When he was right out the door, I spoke.

Mr and Mrs, were my words, have one doozy of a relationship going.

Horses for courses, said Frances. I imagine it's a marriage of convenience. Doubtless both of them have love interests elsewhere.

Frances, I said, I'm *so* glad we've got us.

Seconded.

She glanced at her watch, then rose.

Now, she said, I must finish my shift. See you later tonight?

My place or yours?

Yours?

She bent over me and gave me one of those kisses that started out on the lips but then took my whole body hostage.

Back in my apartment, the first thing I noticed was somebody had stripped the bed in the spare room. The bedclothes bearing the lurid love hearts were gone. So, my apartment was now a crime scene. I shivered at the thought of the sneak-thieves who had, in the pursuit of justice and in my absence, violated my privacy with such impunity.

That night, in bed with Frances, I could not settle. Nor could she. I resented the fact that events in our life could scuttle the choicest moments of our relationship. I so much wanted for love to be our refuge. But love did not appear to have the upper hand in this tussle.

First thing next morning, John Shepherd called me. Frances was snoozing. I left her with a note and headed out.

In Marius' office, I found John and Marius waiting for me. John Shepherd, determined as always to dress casually, wore open-necked shirt and pale-blue cashmere jumper. Marius, in the chair, had chosen the same pin-striped suit he had worn in the hospital the previous evening, and possibly all week. I was glad he was there. I was on edge. I felt I would get more sympathy from him than I would from the boss of DETA.

Once I had been seated, the fireworks began. John and I, both facing the chair initially, found it necessary to swivel in our seats so as to face each other.

Tania, John said, …

… this first-name form of address lulled me, as it was doubtless intended to do, into a false sense of security …

… I'd like you, he continued, to hark back to the last time we talked. When I visited your shop in Melbourne. Remember?

Of course, I replied.

We had a very pleasant chat. I enjoyed it.

So did I.

You mentioned a leopard unable to change its spots.

Yes.

Is this the fate you and Ray were plotting to inflict on the late Harvey Eanis?

I gasped. He had caught me off guard. He was effectively accusing me of murder or, at least, of being an accessory to such. All I had done was report in all honesty a remark Ray had made to me. I had not expected such an aggressive stance from this man. Especially not after the kindly tone of his introductory words. This Charlie was playing both good cop *and* bad cop.

No, I replied. No way.

A coincidence then?

It was Ray, not me, who mentioned spots. Using his crystal ball.

Predicting the future?

That's his forte.

Well, he was spot on.

I was not about to say anything, so silence prevailed for quite a few seconds. John Shepherd broke it.

Have you spoken to Ray yet since you arrived? he asked.

No. I plan to soon as I leave here.

I *have* spoken to him.

For a dreadful moment, I feared Ray might have thrown me to the wolves. This proved to be an unworthy thought.

Yes? I asked.

The future may be his forte, but the past is a domain he likes to steer well clear of. Or such is the impression he leaves me with.

I felt like saying, That's my boy, but kept my silence.

I never expected, he said, our fledgling law enforcement squad here in Conroy would be investigating murder any time soon, but that does appear to be the strength of it. They have my blessing. You'll be staying round for a while?

We may need you, said Marius, for further questioning.

I have a business to run back in Melbourne, I said.

Both men looked dubious.

Well, I guess we know where to contact you, said Marius. Don't do a runner.

Am I a suspect?

I believe the preferred expression is person of interest.

My mind reeled. I felt as if nailed to my seat. Nobody said a word for endless seconds. Time, as if spun both visually and audibly by the wall clock, was the only show in town.

Now I noticed for the first time that the map I had painted for Marius, the map of Conroy and its Stems, was – as he had foretold – no longer hanging behind him. In its place was what appeared to be a 19th century caricature by a French artist, whose signature, Lavrate or some such, was scrawled along the bottom. Its title, printed immediately below the signature, I *could* decipher. It read *Les Gros Bonnets Du Village*. It depicted a tableau of minor dignitaries, all of them men, from a small French parish strutting their stuff, their chests puffed with pomposity, their leering faces challenging the world, their hats serving to identify them. They included the mayor, the fire chief, the baker, the priest, the town jester, etc. In their midst, and without a hat, was a goose.

The work was enclosed in a mock-antique frame of a neutral

complexion. Not one of ours. It was in landscape aspect, and less than half a metre wide. Consequently, it was dwarfed by the space around it, the large wall behind Marius' desk. My mud-map, much larger in extent, would have been the better match for this space, had it been a consideration.

Gros Bonnets apparently held some special significance for Marius, and I wondered what that might be.

You're free to go, said Marius.

I stood up. Then, deciding to throw caution to the wind, I directed a question to my grand inquisitor.

What will you do, I asked John, if your crew finds Ray guilty of murder?

A wry smile crossed John's lips.

Why, he said, we'll wait for him to emerge, of course.

I gaped. Then, somehow managing to put on foot in front of the other, I left. Outside The Depot, I imagined I detected a scowl on the leonine face of the mountain. Did *it* have something to say on this matter?

I phoned Ray. I needed clarification in the worst possible way.

You know where I live, he said.

I wasted no time getting from Admin Stem to The Space. He was there at the conversation post waiting for me. I was 'fit to can', as my mother used to say on those occasions when she found herself at her wits' end, usually because of us kids. But Ray was relaxed. There was mirth in his hazel eyes.

What's your problem, princess? he asked.

… princess! I could have swatted him …

I want the truth, I replied.

Nothing to it. I had a visitor, but he didn't stay.

Precisely how did he leave?

He took the skip. Way to go.

And now he's dead. Foul play is indicated. You're the prime suspect.

Do I give a flying fuck? What can anybody do to me? I'm

out of the loop. I invite the punters out there to believe whatever frigging version of the truth they'd like. There's plenty they can choose from.

Including the one that has me as your accomplice.

That I'll deny.

Thanks. May I ask why you'd even bother?

Because I need you.

You ... need *me?*

That's what I said.

What for?

To look after my sister.

Frances?

I've only the one sister.

Game, set, and match to him. He'd turned the subject right around, thereby stopping my interrogation in its tracks. He was good at this. Managing the cut and thrust, the twists and turns of repartee was second nature to him. I believe, if required, he could steer a conversation through the gates of hell.

He leaned his torso forward, his brow almost touching the picture frame. My eyeballs were butterflies he now captured, his gaze a net from which their escape was impossible.

You *will* look after her, won't you? he asked.

... so, he knew about us ...

Of course, I replied.

... and didn't add, but should have, those magic words so often said and sometimes meant: I love her ...

His gaze intensified. He reached out through the interface for my hand.

We must speak to each other only through this picture frame, he said. *Every word crossing such a portal ...*

Cut the crap, Ray. I'm not one of your supplicants.

But you are. If only you knew.

His hand on mine was warm and gentle. I was not about to

withdraw mine. I managed a glare, but didn't move and said nothing.

Frances, he said, is about to hit a brick wall. She is very vulnerable. I don't know if she'll survive the impact.

What brick wall? What impact?

He said nothing.

Her father? I asked.

Hers and mine.

What's his problem?

He's one big problem. A living breathing Gorgon's head of problems. But he doesn't believe in keeping them to himself. He insists on sharing them round, …

The problems?

… or better still unloading them onto the unwary.

Such as …?

Frances for one.

Look, Ray. I promise to protect Frances. But, please, won't you be more forthcoming? If you want my help, I'd first like to know more about what gives in your family. What *is* going on here?

Can I take a raincheck?

Raincheck? Stuff your shit useless rainchecks. You'll pave the road to hell with the fuckers.

Shuffles, coughs, and whispers blitzed my ears from behind. All sorts of people were gathering round the conversation post. I realized I had startled them with my last angry retort. I realized also why they were gathering. It was that time of day. They were waiting for Ray to foretell their future. His groupies had arrived.

Suddenly, I let go of Ray's hand, rose to my feet and left in tears.

As if my day had not been sufficient of a trial to me, a call from Gabby was waiting on my phone when − back in my apartment again − I scanned it for messages. No show without Punch, I thought. With trepidation, I called her back.

My hat off to you, squire, came her voice over the phone. That was a pretty neat trick you pulled with the bed-sheets.

Gabby, was my rejoinder, spare me your smart-arse comments.

No need to get your knickers in a twist, girl.

Just tell me straight, and be quick about it. What is it you want from me?

To see the look on your face when I tell you the news.

What news?

Ray. I've loosened his tongue. He opened up to me.

About what?

About what really happened on that day. Why don't you invite me over and I'll tell you?

Soon, large as life, she was seated in my apartment, in the room where I entertained visitors. On the odd occasion when I had them. Her casual gear signalled she was off duty. Casual it may have been, but it must have cost her a pretty penny, which is consistent with the sort of image she just loved to flaunt. It was name brand. Top of the range. Conspicuously consumed. Colour coordinated to within an inch of its life. Perversely, I imagined her lounging there in her birthday suit. She couldn't know I had recent experience to draw on when conjuring up that mental picture.

Have I described my Conroy apartment to you? I don't believe I have. So let me take that opportunity now. My digs are a source of pride to me. I'll confine my description mostly to this room, the entertaining room. All the other rooms in my apartment are fashioned in the same style.

Ever mindful of the need to stay warm in the alpine winter, I had covered all my floors with colourful patterned rugs of fine weave. For example, the rug dominating this room in which Gabby and I now sat, was a splendid Asian specimen in soft pastel hues, for which I had paid – and was still paying – a packet. The windows and some of the wall space were hung with thick drapes in ruby red. Above me, I had dared to settle on deepest indigo for the curved ceiling, to disguise the lines of the Quonset and to confer a feeling, should anybody perchance look up, of great depth, like in the sky at night. The light fittings dangling from this ceiling, each commanding its own unique altitude, were like slender firebrands on stalks. Where wall space was available for the purpose, prints pressed from 21ˢᵗ C woodblocks – carved copies in cherry-wood of the *ukiyo-e* classics from centuries past – hung in plain black frames. I couldn't afford antique prints made from antique blocks, so these modern ones were the next best thing.

And, as for the accoutrements scattered about the room – low-set table, lounge chairs, a *chaise longue*, bookcases, and the like – these had the colours of autumn woodlands, the sturdy and slender character of silver birch trees, and the comfort of cocoon nest or womb.

I liked to think my apartment epitomized snug and that Gabby too was getting precisely that vibe. Her first remarks were my vindication.

Cosy digs, she said.

O.K., I said. Give me your version of events. I've heard so many recently.

Mine's the real deal, said Gabby. I had him singing like a canary.

Let's hear his song.

You shall.

She paused briefly for effect.

In the early morning of the day in question, she said, so Ray tells me, Harvey appears like an unwanted apparition. Clad only in his jocks. Not even shoes on his feet. His body's covered in red blotches, strangely reminiscent of love hearts from the bed-sheets in your spare room. And he's as mad as a cut snake. I only wish I'd been there with a camera crew.

So far, your story scans, I said.

Ray's story, she said. Then he leaps over the conversation post as if it were a country stile and, bingo, he's in The Space. He tears strips off Ray. Fills the air with obscenities. Some story about a leopard whose spots can't be removed.

Go on please, I said.

Ray is aghast, she said. He tries to calm the guy and asks him if he knows what he's just done. Harvey replies that he doesn't believe that crap about dropping dead when you leave The Space and says he's buggered if he's going to let a real estate opportunity like this go to waste.

Still in his jocks? I asked.

Still in his jocks.

As he tries to close a real estate deal?

As you would.

Again, Gabby paused theatrically.

After a time, said Gabby, he makes as if to leave via the gap the skip passes through, but stops short when he gets to the boundary.

The interface, I believe they like to call it, I said.

Whatever, she said. Anyway, it appears Harvey's having doubts. Ray is amused. He challenges Harvey. He says if Harvey gets across safely, he'll be only too happy to follow. Harvey makes several more shots at crossing the line, but always pulls back at the crucial moment. So, Ray, sick of this stupid game, retires to his hut. I imagine the word 'wanker' crosses his lips.

Understandable, I said.

Harvey, she said, tail between his legs now, but riled up, knocks on the door of the hut. When Ray comes out, Harvey puts a proposal to him. His plan is to climb into the skip after which he wants Ray to press the release button. 'You're asking me to assist your suicide,' Ray says. 'You're a bullshit artist,' Harvey says.

Takes one to know one, I said.

So, Harvey, she said, moves across to the skip, parked in The Space as it turns out. Ready for use. Ray approaches him with a heavy broom. 'What's that for?' asks Harvey. 'Sweep the rails clear of dead critters,' says Ray. 'Wouldn't want your transport derailed, mate.' So, Ray passes the broom to Harvey, and Harvey pokes around with the broom on the other side of the line, managing to clear the rails of the corpses of the larger animals that had breathed their last there.

You'd have thought that would have been a light-bulb moment for the silly bugger, I said.

You'd have thought wrong, she said. Satisfied with his job, and cocksure, he climbs into the skip. 'You sure you want me to do this?' Ray asks. At which, apparently, Harvey calls him all sorts of names, not nice ones, among which Ray remembers 'motherfucker'.

So, Ray pressed the button? I asked.

Ray presses the button, she said. The skip does its thing. And Ray watches to see if Harvey climbs out on the other side. Which he doesn't.

And then? I asked.

Ray gets on his phone, she said. Calls Marius. Soon after that, all hell breaks loose. When they extract the body from the skip, there's not a mark on it. Bar those tell-tale love hearts from head to toe.

She gestured at me, palms upward.

End of story, she said.

It rings true, I said.

It *is* true she said.

She engineered another of those pauses.

Women have ways, she said, of drawing the truth out of a man. Or perhaps you're too green to have figured that yet.

I bring solace to Frances in her moment of need

My gaping mouth proclaiming my astonishment, I stood in the doorway watching the old curmudgeon who had turned on his pouffe to face us. Not happy about my presence, he reacted in the first instance by denying my existence. That was easier said than done. My presence was blatantly corporeal and, as such, was never going to be a cinch to dismiss. So, his next reaction was scornful retreat. An *apologetic* retreat would have been in order had he been man enough. Who gave him permission to deem me out of existence?

Moreover, he had startled the living daylights out of me. The dribble of food down the wall beside me – food he had flung with vehemence – resembled the slime trail of some oversized mollusc. This was the food he had dubbed *the slop you have the gall to serve me up* soon after Frances had entered the living area with me on her tail.

Having made his point to his satisfaction, he turned his back on us to face the TV again, his face only centimetres from the screen. Some might have complained he was hogging it. But, really, who else would want to watch the rubbish he was watching? Some oft-repeated British sitcom complete with canned laughter. Indeed, who could stand being in the same room as that accursed box? The program to which it was tuned wasn't the only problem. It was emitting decibels of such clout as would awaken dead pharaohs.

He was clad in a frayed chenille dressing gown, secured at the waist with its tasselled cord, mercifully sparing us a view, perchance he turned again, of his private parts. His calloused feet were bare. His hair, yellow with age, was dishevelled and unruly and, though sparse in front, hung down the back of his bent neck as far as the shoulder blades.

A few moments before, front-on then to me and Frances, his fury in full throat and his food in flight, I had imagined I saw family resemblances there in his features. But the Cromwell attributes I had come to know and love, attributes exuding bonhomie and an eagerness to engage, were transmuted out of all reason in this bitter old churl's face. His eyes were cloudy with bags beneath, his brow deeply furrowed, his cheeks jowly, his lips an unhealthy purple, his neck and chin blotchy and peppered with coarse stubble. Hairs sprouted from his ears and nostrils. His voice was cracked and trembling. One could scarcely believe that beneath this grotesque mask there lived a creditable specimen of humanity.

As of the present moment, though, his face was turned towards, and almost touching, the boob tube. Did he imagine he could, like Orpheus, pass through to a presumed netherworld on the other side? And thereby escape the reality of this, his assumed emoh ruo? Here was a man used to getting his own way but presently unable to. I was sure I was a part of that problem. I was *here*. But how might he have treated his daughter if I hadn't been here? It didn't bear thinking about.

This dysfunctional moment was playing out in the living area of Frances' apartment. A living space I knew well and have previously described as bland. Bland was the least of its problems right now. Right now, it was a dog's breakfast. And that was an insult to dogs and breakfasts.

The unadorned mock-timber floor of this half-Quonset sported stale food scraps, greasy pizza boxes, crumpled beer cans, dirty eating utensils, unopened mail, orphaned pages of newsprint, etc. Discarded men's clothing – dirty socks, shirts, and underwear – were scattered all over the shop. Feet belonging to the unwary were as likely as not to land on half-squeezed tubes of shaving-cream, shards of broken glass, scraps of rotting fruit, and – not to be denied their moment – banana skins. Flies and worse had gathered to feast on the detritus. The air was putrid. No windows were open.

How had this come to pass? Frances, I have said before, hadn't a clue when it came to imaginative decor. But her habits were immaculate. How had she allowed an unspeakable shambles like this to develop on her watch?

A flight of fancy took me on wing. I was looking not at Orpheus but at an unlovely goblin hunched over an infernal (and noisy) machine spinning gold from the dross and charnel spread around him. I know. I know. In the ubiquitous tale you and I heard as a child, it was a beautiful peasant girl spinning the gold.

The fairest of maidens egged on by the goblin. But tales like this do have a mind to evolve over time.

At this point, allow me to digress so as to add some context to this contentious tale. The shambolic picture I have painted for you so far was only half of it. To give you the full story, I need to leave the goblin to his devices for now and wind back the clock to the moment when, earlier this fine, but fading afternoon and with a spring in my step, I had turned up bursting to pay respects and more to my beloved. Nine or ten days had elapsed since my last visit to Conroy. I was eager.

In the Stems on the way to her apartment, I had sensed tension still stalking the air but had divined no reason to suppose John Shepherd's precious Keystone Cops had made any progress in their investigations. Equally, I had no reason to suppose I was in the clear but, hey, nobody was about to pin me down and apply the handcuffs. Most people I had come across had given me a friendly wave of recognition.

Confident now my feelings towards Frances were returned, and there was no chance she would reject me, I hadn't hesitated to head straight for her apartment. I had deliveries to make to Ray, but they could wait. No need this time round for any craven excuses for delay. It was to be a moment of great joy.

So, it transpired that, full of delicious expectation, I rang the buzzer at the front door of her apartment.

But when Frances opened the door to me, she seemed disinclined to invite me in. Her body, a plucked chicken out of which the stuffing had been knocked, was barring my way. Her eyes, unblinking, stared at nothing in particular. The corners of her mouth were drawn down, and her parted lips gasped and gulped as if she was short of air. I had not seen her in such acute distress before. I was shocked into silence.

My father's here, she said between a gasp and a gulp.

I reached out instinctively to comfort her.

Should I go? I asked.

For a moment she seemed frozen in place. Then suddenly, dissembling, she gathered herself. The cornered animal within had sensed I might provide her with an opportunity for escape. Embracing action, but joylessly, she brushed my hand aside.

No, she said. I want you to stay. High time you saw the full catastrophe.

With a hand on my shoulder, she ushered me down the corridor. The door at its far end, the door leading to the living area, was closed. Behind it, I could hear the blare of TV at high volume. We stopped short of this cacophony, beside the door to the second bedroom. Which Frances then opened.

The visual chaos inside took my breath away. The entire space was consumed by an unstable pyramid of junk. Totally buried beneath it was, I assumed, a bed. Of what was the pyramid comprised? Men's clothing, enough for an army, the washed mixed with the unwashed. Stacks of old newspapers and magazines, bound with twine, the bundles poised to topple. Cardboard cartons, some bursting, whose contents were useless and legion. And, most shocking of all, the smashed-up remains of Frances' framed credentials that had formerly hung on the walls of her living area. Testament to Frances' pride in herself, and to her unseemly vanity. Pride and vanity now also smashed.

How did he get all this stuff here? I asked.

A removal van the size of a barn.

And brought into the premises by a front-end loader?

Tania, it's no joking matter.

I tried to placate her with a gentle touch to the arm.

Sorry, I said. But why?

Why what?

Why the God-awful mess?

He's a pack rat.

But if, as you say, he's practically blind, why does he need the old newspapers?

They're his. That's why. He paid good money for them.

For a moment she hesitated, presumably to let me take it all in. Then she opened the door to the en-suite wedged between the two bedrooms and servicing them both, inviting me to view yet more despoliation. Inside, another pyramid of junk buried the bathtub. The merest hint of a porcelain rim, peeping out from beneath the pile of debris, was the sole reminder to me the bathtub was actually there. I was loath to believe what I was seeing, and it must have shown.

Out in the corridor again, on our way to the living area to beard the lion now, she stopped me with a hand to my shoulder, muttering some words, a hint of desperation hiding amid the chatter of syllables.

I've got to get out of here, she said. Can we go to your place?

Sure, I replied.

I'll make the excuse I've got a shift at the hospital.

Sure.

That's when she opened the door to the living area, exposing us directly to a solid wall of sound, and to a back view of her father sitting on the pouffe facing the full blare of the TV. He had not stirred as we entered. Not surprisingly, he hadn't heard us.

Frances moved across to him, laid a hand on his shoulder, and spoke a single word to him over and over with ever-increasing volume until he finally responded.

Father … father … father … (etc.), is what she said.

He turned, and that's the moment the food he was eating took wing, to become stuck on the wall near my head. The moment I received my first impression of the man. The moment the first utterance I was to hear from him was uttered. A moment I'll never forget.

… *the slop you have the gall to serve me up*, were the words as I remember them. The food may or may not have been directed at me, but the words were certainly directed at his daughter. Having spat out this bile, he turned his back on us and his front to the TV. With me desperately trying to regain poise, and Frances appalled.

And that brings my story to the moment where, in an effort to bring you up to speed, I had wound the clock back. The moment that had me watching the goblin spin gold.

… now read on …

Frances put a hand on his shoulder again.

Father, she said.

Angrily, he turned from his entertainment to face her.

Read this to me, he said to Frances.

He offered her a food-stained copy of a daily tabloid and a jumbo-sized magnifying glass. She declined to accept them.

Dad, Frances said, I'd like to introduce …

Read this to me, he said again.

… my friend, Tania.

He looked at me blankly, but said nothing. *Persona non grata* looked back.

Tania, Frances said, this is Paul, my father.

Hello, I said.

Ignoring me, he continued to thrust the newspaper under Frances' nose. Frances refused to respond.

I've been called to the hospital, she said. Emergency.

Hospital?

I'm a nurse, Dad.

How's a man to keep up with affairs if his very own daughter refuses point blank to do her duty by him?

Dad. It'll keep.

Grim-faced and wordless, she turned and shepherded me with haste out through the two doors we had come in by. From behind us, expletives sprayed like bullets. When we emerged into the fresh outside air, she exhaled deeply and audibly, as if she had just surfaced from a dive of some fathoms.

I'll explain, she said.

No need, was my reply.

She seemed to stumble slightly, and then came the tears. A flood of them. I had to help her walk the few hundred metres to my apartment. The spectacle would have seemed ludicrous, I guess, to passers-by. They would have seen one gangly woman, to all appearances inebriated, supported by a much shorter woman. But, mercifully, few people were about and none intervened.

As my left arm circled her waist, her right came down to meet it. The fingers of her hand played there with the fingers of mine. I felt chuffed by the intimacy, and by the inkling I had that I could and should give emotional support. The two of us together was more than the sum of us separated. This, I believe, is called synergy. It is a beautiful thing.

The pose we struck, moments later, as we sat sideways on the *chaise longue* in the guest area of my apartment, entwined intimately, and enjoying wicked drinks in long glasses, might – I imagine – have served as a prototype for ardent lovers. Breast against throbbing breast, we enjoyed long-tongued alcoholic kisses. Our hands scurried across willing planches of flesh both convex and concave. There was no attribute with which we were endowed by nature that we didn't yield to the other.

O, holiest of holies! There is such inimitable solace consequent on physical lovemaking. No mental strife can withstand its palliation. Frances had forgotten her tears and was ready, I hoped, to square off with the events causing them. Lying back in the *chaise,* in close contact with each other and still panting, we reached a moment of satiation after which discourse was not only possible but something we both desired. We faced each other cautiously for some moments before Frances ventured the first words germane to the case, a case nobody by preference would want to own, but with which it appeared she was now prepared to deal.

So, she said, now you've met my father.

… and, as I have said, her eyes were dry …

I have, was my cautious reply.

That was his best behaviour you saw. Had you not been there, he would likely have resorted to physical violence.

Against you?

Not these days. I'm far too nimble on my feet. He takes it out on the walls and furniture. Right now, as we speak, he'll most likely be trashing the joint.

What's his gripe?

The world.

Can't you turf him out?

He's my father.

I kept my silence. No rejoinder was possible. How should I respond to the bellow of a sacred cow? The sacred cow of family. Family, the other F-word. In its extended form, father, mother, brother, sister.

I looked after my mother when she was dying, she said, and now he expects the same treatment.

From you?

I'm his first port of call.

Sensing in these words of hers some unpleasant implications for Ray, I pondered for the moment what consequences such writings on the wall might entail for our Spaceman. Then I pulled myself up. Halifax, I thought. Predicting the future is Ray's bag, not mine.

She interrupted my musings along these lines.

Poor old codger, she said. He's his own worst enemy. He won't take advice. When the doctors told him he had cataracts, he took no notice. Now they're inoperable. And he's practically blind.

Deaf as well.

And, I suspect, a touch of dementia.

So you have to be a martyr?

What choice do I have?

Look. Marius was the turkey who let him in, so surely Marius should find a way to get him off your case. You can't go on like this.

Marius *is* working on a plan. But it won't be easy to dislodge the old stager. He'll stick like a limpet. And I'm the frigging rock.

At this, the tears returned. I placed a hand on each of her cheeks and raised her lips to mine. Her tears tasted salty. Suddenly, she flung her arms round me, drawing me close. I responded with more kisses and with tears of my own. It appeared some of her grief had transferred itself to me. I realised this was yet another aspect of our love. We knew how to share the best and the worst with each other.

Shall I fix us a bite to eat? I asked.

If you'd like.

Comfort food. Then we can go to bed.

Her reply, a single whimpered word, was, Yes.

I was seeking a blueprint for love. But, in such matters, I was a greenhorn. They say blue with green should never be seen. I was to learn that, despite my best intentions, the heaviest burdens were not able to be shared.

A dream, a rethink, a *tete-a-tete*, and a skipping girl

Next morning, I was in the shower. It was a hand-held telephone shower. I was directing the water from the rose at my left armpit. Suddenly, I was surprised to hear a voice coming from it. It was my mother's voice. When I held the rose up to my face, I could actually see her image in there. For me, it was like being on FaceTime in a rainstorm, but I couldn't be exactly sure what she might be seeing at her end.

… dutiful daughter that I was, I had been in regular contact with my mum over the years. She had been glad to hear of my success in the picture framing trade, but not so glad to hear my business partner was the notorious Spaceman who had been so much in the news. When she heard I was making regular drop-offs to and pick-ups from him, she was beside herself. As mums would be. She thought I should show him the finger forthwith but, as I had told her, I was not prepared to do that …

Hello Tania, came my mum's voice from the shower rose.

Hello Mum, I said. I'm in the shower.

Can't you multitask?

I'm dripping wet. How are the folks at home?

I've got your two lovely nieces here with me. Like to talk to them?

Sure.

I peered into the rose, and saw two white eggs sitting in a nest of twigs. One of the eggs cracked, then the other, and two pretty baby girls emerged. They made baby noises. Then suddenly they developed wings, and flew up, using their wings to hover above the nest. They were not baby girls anymore. They had become butcher-birds, in sleek black-and-white vests. They began to squawk in the way butcher-birds do when sounding a warning. Then they flew off.

Mum was seated at the piano now. I could see her in the shower rose. The Holman-Hunt print loomed above her. Its vibes felt less than friendly.

Like a tune? she said.

Before I could reply, she began tickling the ivories. It was a waltz from *Carnaval* that always put me in mind of a train clattering over railway tracks. Da-dum-da-*dum*. Da-dum-da-*dum*. Da-dum-da-*dum*. And then, naturally enough, I was on that train.

I was in the front of the train, where I could see through glass to the driver. It was my father. And all the passengers except for me were men or boys. No women or girls at all. My two brothers. The choir boy of my pubescent dreams. Bobby, my first lover. Ray. Marius. John Shepherd. All the significant men and boys in my life so far, one might say.

We were all strap-hanging, despite the ready availability of seats. Nobody paid any attention to me. Perhaps they were engrossed in secret men's business.

Then we were all on the floor. The train had braked fiercely and without warning. We picked ourselves up and, as you would, jumped down from the bogie to confront the outside world. We all gravitated to the front of the train to see what the problem had been. And there was Frances, sprawled across the tracks, sliced into three pieces.

She shouldn't have been lying there, said my elder brother.

Aggghhh. Aggghhh. Aggghhh. I woke, coming up for air. I assume the tremendous shock delivered to my psyche had catapulted me from dream to wakefulness. I was now back in bed in my half-Quonset apartment. Alone.

That was the way my day started, and it was not about to get better any time soon.

Frances had left early, having had a shift to work, a real shift not a pretend one. So, I was left to my own thoughts. Predictably, they were bleak. It was as if, when Frances went out via the front door, demons had slipped in through it.

First, I showered, not daring to look into the rose. Then I had my usual breakfast of fruit, cereal, and coffee. Everything I ate or drank tasted shit.

Out the window, the weather seemed gloomy but there was no rain or snow. A grey day. I was reminded of another day not so long ago when Frances, duty calling, had left me – just like now – to my own devices. The weather, then, had been scintillating. And I had been bent on adventure, in the form of a tour of the demesne. My mood had been one of eager anticipation.

This present day was different. When I thought now about the Stems I had explored on that earlier day – byways which for the most part had kept me enthralled – I found nothing at all of joy left in my heart. The pleasure I had experienced back then was now gone from my soul. How could it be otherwise, it occurred to me now, when those Stems had at their core something as evil as The Space? And when, from on high, they were overseen by something as malevolent as that mountain?

The thought processes I entertained in these moments of

dismal introspection could best be described as a cerebral stock-take. Otherwise known as a rethink. And this rethink changed Conroy in my head from a great place to live, to the circles of Hades itself.

I pottered around all morning, even though I knew I had a call to make on Ray. Given my agoraphobic mood, I was reluctant to venture outside. Then, in an attempt to improve my mood, I put on a CD of *Carnaval*. Bad choice. What was I thinking? Immediately, I found myself back on that train.

I realised now I had to get out for the sake of my sanity. I rang Ray and suggested I pick up an early lunch for him. He asked me to bring him a spinach and ricotta roll from the place where I had ordered it on previous occasions. I knew (but how could he?) that the place he meant was *One Fine Day*.

Oh, he said, and a milkshake.

I believe the word you're searching for is 'please', I said.

Please.

… I felt quite chuffed I had had this chance to snooker him …

Soon, with my regular load to deliver, I fronted up in my van to those gaps in the ring of ski-poles hosting the dolly track and the conversation post. Since it was Sunday, Ray had no scheduled duties, neither oracular nor therapeutic. Scientists, ignoring the day of rest, were milling outside The Space. Ray was waiting inside it. Jeremy was in his cage, hanging nearby from the obliging tree. Having delivered Ray his lunch, I proceeded to unload my delivery into the skip. Sitting alone at the conversation post, Ray munched on his spinach roll, leaving reminders of it in his beard.

After I had wound the spring and pressed the button, sending the skip on its merry way, Ray beckoned me over. I sat down at the conversation post, staring at him through the framed interface which most days − today being no exception − gave me an attack of the willies. He nodded in the direction of the scientists.

They plan to relocate the ski-poles, he said.

Why? I asked.

They say The Space is shrinking.
I was alarmed and showed it.
You joke, I said.
No joke.
How much has it shrunk?
Only a couple of centimetres, so I'm told.
All the same, I don't like the sound of it.
What do you propose I do about it?
I didn't answer. I took his question to be rhetorical. He broke of a piece off the spinach roll and fed it to a most appreciative Jeremy.
And how are things with you? he asked.
So so.
A little bird, I hear, tipped you off about our family history.
You mean Frances?
Right on. She grassed. Can't trust anyone anymore.
Look, Ray. I saw a lot of it for myself. First hand.
So now you know why we both fled to this neck of the woods.
I don't know the whole story. Care to fill me in?
I think you've got the guts of it.
He paused.
Anyway, he said, it didn't work out for either of us. The clown just followed us here.
His exasperated eyes drifted upwards in the direction of the overcast sky. I waited. I had the feeling he had more to say, so I allowed him time.
He lowered his eyes.
Look, princess, he said. If I could only get out of here, I'd kill the bugger.
… I decided on this occasion to let the 'princess' bit pass …
He's your father, for pity's sake, I said.
… that sacred cow again, invoked this time by me …
I'd kill him just the same, he said.
Once again, I felt it was politic to say nothing. When he spoke

again, he changed the subject, something – as I have noted before – he was adept at doing.

Thank you, he said, for the support you've been giving Frances.

It's my pleasure.

That's what I hear.

He slurped disgracefully on the dregs of his milkshake. The insinuation in his voice and tone had been clear. So what? I thought. Doubtless, my relationship with Frances was common knowledge by now, and most people around the traps seemed to accept it without batting an eyelid.

That's when he reached through the frame and placed his hand on mine, just as he had the last time I had spoken to him across this interface. I felt as if I ought to repel the gesture but, hey, my day had been quite ordinary, and who was I to deny myself this simple pleasure? He squeezed my fingers ever so gently with a touch exuding warmth which, coursing through my veins, then transferred itself as if by magic to the extremities of my frame. I realized I still felt for this man. What did he feel?

I rose. He followed my example.

She comes off duty in an hour or so, I said. Better be on my way.

Cool, he said. I'll send the skip back with deliveries for you.

I waited at my end of the dolly track while Ray returned to his hut to collect the orders he had fulfilled. For a moment, the only sounds were the distant calls of currawongs as they rode the alpine updrafts, and the gentle susurrations of the snow-gums, as silken breezes played games with compliant leaves. This was a tranquil moment for me on a day that had up to this point proved harrowing. Not even the mountain, glowering at the world from beneath the heavy but high cloud which even its eminence failed to reach, could put the kybosh on this, my special moment.

Ray emerged from his hut carrying a stack of finished product. He loaded these items – framed pictures with attached delivery instructions – into the skip, wound it up, and pressed the button.

The skip hurtled between two incongruent worlds. This routine was very familiar to me. Having transferred the items from skip to van at my end, I gave Ray the thumbs up. He smiled back at me, a warm smile gladdening my heart.

On my way back, I stopped off at the small supermarket on the corner of The Roundelle and Labour Stem. Here I bought crisps and Coke, snacks to comfort me on a trying day. Walking back to my vehicle, I saw a young girl, maybe six years old, skipping rope down the footpath towards me, oblivious of all around her. This might, I reflected, have been me some decades earlier, in the country town of my guileless youth.

Suddenly, a few metres from me, she hesitated. She had seen, on the path directly in front of her, a hopscotch grid sketched in chalk, and was pondering how she might negotiate it whilst maintaining her skipping routine. She rose to the challenge. For the first three squares she managed to hop to the beat of the rope. On one foot. But then, when the grid required her to put both feet down and wide apart, she came undone, her feet snared in her rope. She tried to restart, but the moment had been lost. The hopscotch had defeated her. Within the confines of its chalk outlines, she was unable to reboot her rhythm.

She looked up. Our eyes met. At first, she showed embarrassment. But I smiled back and, leaving the hopscotch to its fate, she grinned in reply, skipping on past me with vigour, pleased to have an audience to which she could show off her prowess with the rope.

Back in my apartment, blissing out on crisps and Coke whilst looking out over an undulating expanse of olive-green snow-gums, a thought came to me. Was it a mistake to take on two aspirations simultaneously when they might prove incompatible with each other? In the case of the young girl, skipping and hopscotch. In my case, brother and sister.

Another rethink perchance?

An old fart leads the Conroy natives a merry dance

On my next visit to Conroy, not quite a week later, we – Frances and I – found ourselves in a familiar situation, one as innate to the scheme of things as was the fall of ripened fruit in spring. It was evening. We were in bed. It was in my bedroom, the one that still remained an option for us. The one we imagined was free from the intrusion of a certain unwelcome party.

How mistaken we were.

The loud knock of knuckles on glass awakened us rudely from our state of bliss. I sat up abruptly, thrown into momentary confusion. The rant from outside my window left us in no doubt as to the identity of its perpetrator.

I know, said the rant, the pair of you are in there carrying on like the fucking bitches you are.

Dad, yelled Frances, go home.

Not until you start behaving like a respectable young woman should.

What do you mean?

What you're up to is a bloody crime against nature and the law of God.

Enough's enough, I said in an aside to Frances. I'm calling the police.

We were both out of bed now, she trying frantically to restrain me.

Please don't, Frances pleaded. He's my father.

Sheba, I said, it's *my* apartment.

The number of the police station in Admin Stem was on my phone, in Contacts. Fighting her off, I managed the necessary keystrokes, swipes, and terse words to stir the authorities into action on our behalf. Frances yelled again to her father.

Dad, were her words, clear out while the going's good. The cops are coming.

There was no further sound from outside the window, so we dared to hope the nutjob who happened to be my lover's father had taken this advice. Regretfully, and with sighs of disappointment, we dressed. Dressed quickly. Now we had the constabulary to field.

They were at my front door before we had straightened our clothes. Two of them, both men. Behind their backs, one hundred metres away, and parked in the Stem, was a Lecky police van, sporting a flashing blue light.

What's the problem, ladies? asked the older (so I judged) of the two.

There's been an intruder at our window, I said.

A male intruder?

But his younger counterpart interrupted him with an expletive, loudly voiced.

Shit! was his expletive.

And I saw why. Out in the Stem, a furtive and familiar figure, resplendent in tatty chenille, was busy carjacking the police van. The two coppers, gobsmacked, dashed down the path to stop him, but were too late. With tyres squealing, and with the back wheels drifting, the vehicle did a U-turn and hurtled down the Stem at speed towards The Roundelle.

Leckies modified for police use had no speed monitor. And they had sirens. The old fart knew how to put his foot down and to make the sound show happen. That brought our neighbours out, but mostly all they saw was dust.

I was not present to see what transpired next. I must defer to accounts I was given later, variously by Ray, Gabby, and several police persons, who were privileged to be on the scene at one stage or other of the unfolding drama. None were in possession of the whole story. I, witness to none of it, shall now piece together their accounts for your benefit.

He, the renegade senior citizen, and supposedly blind at that, headed straight for The Space. On the road giving access to it, travelling at breakneck speed, he came across a Lecky headed the other way. Towards him. It was John Coffee coming off duty for the day. The unlucky guard, who never quite understood why everybody took him for a joke, failed to see the humour in this development either. His very survival at sake, he didn't hesitate to drive himself off the road, his vehicle sideswiped but nobody injured.

Crashing through and shattering the toy boom-gate, the elderly fugitive from justice reached the annular clearing round The Space, screeching to a halt adjacent to the conversation post. I'm pretty certain he would have disturbed Ray and Gabby in a very private moment, though Gabby wouldn't admit to this. As he emerged from the Lecky, flaunting his chenille and bellowing crude invective, he drew a loud response from his ropable and doubtless naked son.

Get out of here, you revolting old fossil, was Ray's response.

Nice welcome there, son, his father replied. I'm only the bastard spent a lifetime putting bread on your table.

These days, squire, I put my own fucking bread on the table.

Making picture frames, I hear. What sort of girly trade is that?

The sound of approaching sirens now reached them. Even Paul Cromwell, serial intruder, heard it. The noise prompted Ray's next remark.

Clear out, old man, he said. They're coming to take you off to the funny farm.

Father decided on balance to take son's advice. Scrambling back into the Lecky, he shouted his rejoinder.

Fucking glad to quit this den of iniquity.

Police vans – three of them – surged into the clearing, sirens screaming. When he figured the way was clear, Cromwell senior chose his moment. He made a break, heading out at high speed the way he had come in. The police, outmanoeuvred, could only look on in disbelief.

He made it out to The Roundelle again. By now, as some

would later put it to me, an irrational fury had gripped his brain, finessing any fear he might have felt. He may have lost the plot big time but, despite Frances' earlier hint, I doubt dementia played any part in it.

From this point it was unadulterated rampage. He gate-crashed an unlicensed gambling operation in Labour Stem, before being unceremoniously evicted. Moving on to Corrections, he hurled abuse at the clientele of *The Tight Spot* before being set upon by a brace of burly bouncers and hurled into the gutter. Finally, he was cornered by police at the poker machine venue in Admin, and dragged off kicking and screaming to the slammer.

Frances bailed him next morning. He had been charged with close to a dozen separate offences but, apparently, was not considered a flight risk. Frances took him to the hospital where he had a number of minor injuries attended to, a broken nose among them.

That night, I found her near enough to inconsolable which, I guess, was only to be expected.

It will pass, I said.

Don't you dare bullshit me, she said between tears.

Shocked by her force of conviction, I hadn't the courage to defy her. I mixed her a drink. Then I tried to put my arm round her, but she flung it aside. We slept with our backs to each other, each on opposite edges of the bed.

When I left for Melbourne the next morning, I'm not sure whose distress was the more profound or whose turmoil the less manageable.

An alarming missive comes my way from cyberspace

On return to Melbourne, a mental wreck, I was dismayed to discover that, in my absence, an imposing number of orders requiring my attention – some *demanding* it – had accumulated at

In The Frame. Evidently business was booming. To get on top of it, I would clearly need to lock myself in my workshop at the rear of the shop, and keep nose down bum up for an extended period. At first, I welcomed the prospect of some sort of break from what I deemed my relationship crisis.

I talked things over with Graham, the smart young guy with the pimply face who managed the front counter. Between us, we divvied up the work load between me and Ray. Even so, we figured my 'extended period' would be in excess of ten days.

Halifax, I thought. Frances badly needed my support right now, and – God knows – I itched to give it to her, but wouldn't be free to make it back to Conroy to deliver such support for quite some time. I rang her with this daunting news and with tidings of my deathless love. Predictably, she said it couldn't be helped and that she'd manage alright. I was doubtful. I urged her to join me in Melbourne where I could organize a camp-bed for her in my workshop. She declined. So, I said I'd ring her every day.

I rang Ray. He seemed deeply concerned, wracked with anxiety even, something unusual for him. But we both knew concern and anxiety weren't going to cut the mustard. He said he'd step up to the plate as best he could while I was out of town, adding the obvious corollary that his options were limited. What sort of bum offer was that? I thought ruefully. He expressed his appreciation for what I was doing then suggested I try Marius. I had no option but to resign myself to the reality of his impotence. And to pity him for it.

I rang Marius. He said his plan was to house Frances in a secure compound in the precincts of the hospital, a compound set aside for on-site medical staff. I thanked him. Then he told me the investigations into my role in the death of Harvey Eanis had been dropped, adding that he wasn't at all surprised. But, he warned, it was far from certain Ray was off the hook.

I asked him how his wife was faring.

She's gone, he said.

What do you mean 'gone'? I asked.

Left town.

For how long?

For good, I believe.

I'm sorry.

Don't be. Our marriage was a sham. I'm sorry to have to disabuse a starry-eyed young woman like you of any illusions she might choose to entertain about marriage.

What makes you think I have illusions?

You don't?

Not about marriage.

Then bully for you. I only took up with June for the image of solid respectability I thought it would cede me in the eyes of people like John Shepherd. It was a career move. It's no longer necessary. If it ever was. Here in Conroy, I've achieved the sort of position I've coveted all my life.

Really?

And truly. In Conroy I'm not obliged to lie in a bed prepared by others. I make my own.

What about her?

My wife? She married me because she saw me as a high flier. But she never settled into Conroy. Canberra should suit her better. By repute, the corridors of power. Gallery of sharp knives.

I've heard.

And vulnerable shoulder-blades. It should suit her to a tee.

We signed off at this point. I was flattered an interesting man like Marius would let me into such details of his private life. And, Sheba, the stuff within was worth pondering.

I had done the rounds by phone. Now it was time to settle into my work routine. The long haul. Work days twelve to fourteen hours long faced me. With Graham of the pimply face handling the front counter, I anticipated few interruptions. The routine that had evolved over the years – Graham holding the fort up front and me getting down and dirty out back – worked well. We were a proven team.

Late in each evening, having worked myself to a standstill, I would retire to my little upstairs room, where I would relax with junk food, while looking down on the pleasure seekers in Glenhuntly Road, feeling ever more envious of their lot, and ever more resentful re mine.

Next day, I rang to check on Frances. Her phone rang out, so I left a message. She didn't get back to me.

The day after, I rang her again, but the outcome was the same. Halifax. Even had I felt myself free to do so, I couldn't just get in the van and drive to Conroy. The van was in the custody of grease monkeys. Having its clutch fixed.

The day after, I was getting really anxious. I rang Ray who, though frantic, knew nothing. I rang Marius, who said he would check.

One more day on top of yet one more day. Still no news. I was frantic. And that's when the email dropped into my inbox.

This wasn't Frances' preferred mode of communication. Something was up. But what? I read the email. My heart was pounding in my chest as I did so.

It was long.

Dearest Tania

My greetings to you, and with them an abundance of love and kisses. I trust you are well. I wish I could tell you *I* was. I have been in hospital, in intensive care.

I'm tired. Tired of this whole situation. My father operates on a gross physical level only. It is pure, simple, and vile, untempered by reason. I can't take any more of it. I didn't see any way out of the situation except to take leave of my earthly life. I didn't see I had any other choice.

It was not an impulsive act. I had everything thought out to the last detail. I am well versed in pharmacology because I have a medical education. I had a quantity of a potent drug for lowering blood pressure, left over from a prescription my mother had had filled when she was alive. Her blood pressure had been exacerbating her renal insufficiency. But, unexpectedly, the renal problems got better, so she didn't need the drug. I still have it. Or had it, I should say.

There were 50 tablets all up. They had not yet reached their expiration date. The lethal dosage was 30 to 40 tablets for an adult male weighing 75 kg to 80 kg. I am only 70 kg, so I figured 50 tablets should be enough to make my heart stop.

The new real-estate man in town is a Mr Salmond, a nice guy. What fun, darling. His name rhymes with yours.

Through him, I booked a hotel room for one night. The hotel room was in Admin Stem. A quite superior room. The day before the event I ate nothing but, just to make sure, I injected myself with an anti-emetic. I arrived at the hotel at 8 p.m. I made myself up, did my hair beautifully, and put on my favourite dress. As you know, I am an aesthete. I wrote a farewell note to my brother. And another to my aunt Jane and her daughter Tess. And one to you, of course.

At 9 p.m. I gave myself three intramuscular injections of tranquilizer, opened a bottle of vodka, and washed down all 50 tablets. According to my calculations, the staff would find my body at 12 noon or thereabouts the next day. I expected to be re-united with my mother, but instead I woke up in the toxicological intensive care unit three days later. The doctors said it was a miracle. They hadn't expected me to pull through.

I don't remember anything after the tablets took effect. But here is another miracle. People tell me I did things in my unconscious state that really cannot be done in such a state. Before I was rushed to emergency, I had talked, walked from the hotel, and actually returned the key to Mr Salmond with thanks. Only when I arrived at ICU did I, timing things to perfection, lapse into a coma. I remember nothing of these strange happenings.

Darling, can you explain it?

When I went into ICU, my heart was beating with a frequency of less than 30 per minute. Doctors administered injections of atropine nine times a day. So, I survived, but I was not particularly happy about it. My soul is empty.

I've been discharged from my hospital bed, but Marius has me ensconced in the place reserved for live-in staff. But what to do next? The Problem remains. Besides I now have health issues. I have cardiomyopathy. But what of it? It's all a sick joke really.

Come see me when you can. You are so precious to me. You are what I have in the world. I love you.

Frances Cromwell.

In a trice I was testing the limits of a rental car, punishing the highway, and eating up kilometre after kilometre of bitumen.

I ask myself searching questions re the durability of love

Her tiny room in the compound for residential staff was neat to the point of desolation. There was no semblance of clutter. It comprised a single bed, a wardrobe, and seating furniture for two. Compact bathroom and kitchen were to be found in discrete annexes. A single window gave onto a view over the traffic in Heath Stem.

She lay on the bed. I sat on it, cradling her head. This was, and was not, the Frances I knew. Yes, the regal frame was there, and the hazel eyes, and the beautiful clothes. But there was a flippancy about her, a contrived casualness, seemingly designed to distract me and perhaps herself as well, from the real issues at play. Issues such as where she stood right now, physically and mentally, consequent on the attempt she had made to top herself.

Reflecting on her email, I saw evidence there of further contrivance. Of ploys intended to distract. Her use of technical jargon supported by numbers to describe a life-threatening situation when her emotional health is what I really wanted to know about. Renal insufficiency. Adult male weighing 75 to 80 kilos. Frequency of less than 30 per minute. Cardiomyopathy. What had all this boffinry got to do with anything of importance?

I was a silly duffer, I know, she said. It's amazing what life can throw up.

Frances, I asked, what is cardiomyopathy?

It's a cross I have to bear.

Frances!

Permanent injury to muscle tissue. That's what they tell me. The heart is one big muscle, you know.

Is it bad?

Mine is.

On a scale from one to ten?

Nine, say.

What's the treatment?

There is none.

You seem pleased.

Oh, I could get a transplant.

And if you don't.

One day it'll kill me.

Frances. You may be happy with that, but I'm not.

It's life, darling. Life I didn't ask for.

I looked down at her. There was no longer any joy in her, no vitality, no oomph. Just a frail frame, getting more and more frail by the minute. Where was the sparkle in her eyes, the encryption of her love for me? I wanted to shake her but this would have been so so insensitive and would have achieved nothing. Her love, the love I so much wanted to receive was ebbing away. My love, the love I so much wanted to give, could no longer find its object. Had love so little capacity to endure? The foam of the pounding sea was so much more durable.

I thought of gentle physical lovemaking, titillating the ocelot and the like, but gave the fleeting idea the short shrift it deserved. Had I followed through, she – I felt certain – would have feigned enthusiasm, faked it so to speak. But I didn't want dutiful compliance. I wanted love, love that had always been uppermost on our agenda, love that had all but been snuffed out by events.

I stayed the course. At dawn the next day I was still by her side. But then, with heart heavy, and feeling my impotence like never before in my life, I kissed her on the lips, and headed back to Melbourne.

The worst comes to pass, and I struggle to handle it

She was dead. Marius conveyed the news to me. I said, Thank you. And ended the call.

I dismissed Graham. I shut up shop. Then I went upstairs, flung myself on my bed, and howled, from the depths of my lungs and then deeper, confident those down in Glenhuntly Road couldn't hear me. Not that I gave a damn if they *did* hear me, but I certainly hadn't any appetite for a kindly knock on the door, a good Samaritan coming to check if I was alright.

After howling like this for an hour that seemed more like a day, I had no more howl left in me. For the moment. I fell back in a stupor redolent of menace. I shut my eyes, hopeful of some form of release. It was not to be. On the blank slate at the forefront of my vision's maw, an uninvited image of Frances appeared. Dressed in her finest, her demeanour solemn, she taunted me with a song. It was from an album called Cold Fact by Sixto Rodriguez. Frances had often played the CD for me in her apartment, in those happy days before said apartment had been turned upside down by a senior citizen whose name shall not pass my lips.

> Soon you know I'll leave you
> and I'll never look behind

> 'cause I was born for the purpose
> that crucifies your mind.

I sat upright as a stanchion. The words I uttered, *Frances darling, why ever did you leave me behind?*, were more like sobs than words.

What *was* it to be now that would see me through? Drugs or alcohol? Because it sure as hell wasn't sex.

I washed down some valium pills with Coke. How many? Too bloody many. I waited.

Next thing I remember, it was the wee hours of the morning. Which morning, I wasn't sure. I felt as if I had woken from a drug-induced sleep which, of course, I had.

I knew it was time for more howling.

Over the next hour alone, I howled to an extent adequate to fill an entire tormented night. A nightful of howls in a single hour. Get it right, please. Howls, not owls. Owls are awesome birds. Howls, on the other hand, are what wolves do. Wolves are harbingers of death, and in this instance they are too late. The death they foretell has already happened.

On my return, I find Ray in no mood to take prisoners

After a few days – I'm not exactly sure how many – I came downstairs. I needed therapy and, since no therapist had put up his/her hand, self-administered prophylaxis was called for. I found the perfect formula. Work. Soon the old team was back in action: Graham out front and me hunkered down in the back room.

To fend off the dreadful emptiness in my heart, and which was always there ready to pounce, I toiled sixteen to twenty hours each day. The backlog was large enough to allow me this privilege but, even if it hadn't, I swear I would have pulled things apart and put them together again just to keep the black dog at bay. I snacked constantly on my beloved crisps washed down with Coke, special treat for a desperately unhappy soul. In the wee hours of each day, hours as dark as my spirits, I crept back upstairs and fell exhausted into my bed. If it hadn't been for this self-induced exhaustion, I'm sure I would have had to resort to valium in ever increasing doses to the point of unshakeable addiction.

The funeral, in Conroy of course, happened in my absence. I really *couldn't* have put in an appearance. It would have finished me off. Besides, my grief wasn't the sort to be hung out there for all the world to see. I'm sure Frances would have felt exactly the same way had our positions been reversed.

It took me a couple of weeks before I felt mentally ready to make my way along the lonely road to Conroy to pay my respects in my own private way. Even then I was prone, at times and without warning, to fall victim to bouts of anguish difficult to bear.

I travelled overnight, the darkness a form of cover for my grief.

When I visited the cemetery next morning, I fancied she, well and truly in the ground by then, would have sensed my lone presence. There were four plots now, each with a gravestone. All the gravestones were plain, with the bare minimum of information engraved thereon, this being the preferred style of the artisan in Labour Stem who enjoyed a monopoly providing this service. I guess he was hoping privately for more deaths in town, so he could continue to ply his trade. I felt sure he wouldn't be kept waiting long.

I was mortified to find Frances' plot abutted that of Harvey Eanis. The horror, the horror. Imagine having that sleazebag as a neighbour in the next world. I was irate, but pleased at the same time to discover I was able to entertain emotions other than just those of grief and longing.

The bush telegraph works in unfathomable ways. I had been hoping to be left in peace but somehow Gabby found out I was in town and paid me a visit.

Welcome back, stranger, she said.

I …, was all I could blurt out.

So sorry about it, kid. Is there a way I can help?

The sympathy I sensed in her tone was a liability for me, fertile ground in which remembered images of Frances could sprout to torment my soul and threaten my connection to reality. I felt my anchor to the corporeal world dragging dangerously. Seemingly of its own volition, a small tear formed in the corner of my eye. I wiped it away.

Pour me something, I said. Campari and soda.

While she was busy doing this, and I was busy getting my shit back together, I reflected that maybe I'd prejudged this woman. She seemed seriously concerned, not just chasing another story. In a hard-nosed way, she was capable of simpatico.

How's Ray taking it? I asked.

She handed me the drink she had prepared for me and, not one to let a chance go by, settled back with one she had prepared for herself.

Inscrutably, she said. But I wouldn't be surprised to learn he's plotting patricide.

Good thing he's trapped in his bubble.

That might not do the trick. If he can't get to the victim, maybe he'll get the victim to come to him.

Seriously?

I'd put nothing past our Spaceman.

I'll check him out.

Keep me posted.

She had me worried now. Ray might do something precipitate. So, I high-tailed it over to The Space the instant Gabby was out the door. I caught my quarry jogging round the ski-pole perimeter. I pointed a finger at the conversation post indicating I wanted to talk.

But for fully five minutes we *didn't* talk. We – both of us – just sat with eyes cast down, holding hands across the interface, wordless moments of comfort and consolation we – both of us – sorely needed. It was pure magic, pure balm, and the last thing I would have expected from him. Nothing else I had experienced since the tragedy of Frances' death had exerted such a restorative influence on me as had these five minutes.

When Ray eventually broke the silence, I felt mildly vexed by the interruption.

I'm sorry, he muttered into his beard.

I'm the one who should be sorry, I said.

Why so?

I promised you I'd look after her.

I should never have put you in that position. It was a devil of a thing to ask.

I loved her, Ray, I said.

… and, at this juncture, it was inevitable I should burst into tears, which I did in spades …

I know, he said.

I looked up at him through tears, hoping and even expecting to see new-found tenderness in his eyes. I was in for a shock. The Cromwell features I had come to love were there in his face, but they were alloyed with a steely resolve and a frightful hatred. I froze.

Don't do it, Ray, I said.

His reply was predictable, as was his mock innocence.

Don't do what? he asked.

Don't come the cherub with me. You know exactly what I mean. Just don't do it.

Why not?

He's your fucking father.

He is *not* my father. He's not anybody's father. I disown him. I divorce him. I spit on him. And I swear to you, princess, he'll pay in kind.

And how might you propose to deliver on that?

You're asking me to spell out the future?

If you will. You're the oracle.

We must speak to each other only …

Can it, Ray. Give it to me without that absurd rigmarole. How do you propose to carry out your threat?

Too easy. I just wait for him to come.

Why the fuck should he oblige?

Your *language*, princess.

Don't fucking call me princess.

Admin has evicted him. That's why.

Who told you that?

Impeccable sources.

Who?

Marius. Twenty minutes ago. The news is as fresh as a newly-dropped turd. It's too early even for Gabrielle's eager nose to have picked up on this one. So, congrats. You've out-scooped our shit-hot journo.

I sensed he was wound up now. His reticence and his riddles, default strategies for him, had been finessed by his inner fury. He would talk, I felt sure. He would tell me everything I wanted to know.

This is the situation, he said. They've condemned my sister's apartment. Declared it a health risk. Boarded the whole show up. Dumped all his junk in the tip. He has no roof over his head. These nights it's cold as a witch's tit. And there's nobody fool enough to take him in.

There's you.

I'm fool enough?

No. But you'll do it.

And I shall. I'm his only option. I've got the bastard by the short and curlies.

Ray, what are you plotting?

Plotting?

What are you cooking up?

Want to know?

Sure.

Shoelace soup.

Run that again.

Shoelace soup. Want to know how it's made?

… you can take the man out of the riddle, I thought ruefully, but you can never take the riddle out of the man …

Give it to me, I said.

O.K. You take a couple of handfuls of fresh shoelaces, remove all the aglets, and beat …

Aglets?

An aglet, princess, is the metal bit on the tip of the shoelace. Seriously bad for the digestion and the integrity of your dental work. So, you snip off all those pesky aglets and beat the crap out of the laces with a meat tenderizer. Add herbs and spices to taste, and any other flavour you fancy, and boil till *al dente*. Then serve up.

You're taking the piss.

I'm not. I promise you I'll have the bastard eating shoelace soup. And choking on it.

Ray, I've no appetite for this nonsense.

I'm not offering *you* any. You can go cook your own.

I mean, I'm tired. Really tired. Fragile. My emotions are up the kazoo. I think I'll call it a day. Will you excuse me?

I rose.

Fine, he said. You must look after yourself.

It's you I'm worried about. I'm afraid you're planning to do something you'll regret forever.

There'll be no regrets, princess. That I promise you.

Tears, always pressing, now overwhelmed me. I bent down and gave him a daring kiss across the interface, a kiss much more dangerous than any of the tomfoolery I had seen him and Gabby enjoying on that moonlit evening. Then, amazed to an extent at finding I was still alive, I fled.

At the guard post, I waved to John Coffee. Then, before I even had a chance to start up my Lecky, Marius pulled up. Parking his vehicle beside mine, then alighting, he came to my driver's window. I wound it down. He looked worried, and I thought I knew why.

Glad to have you back, he said, but I do regret the circumstances. My sympathies. How are you coping?

Like Gabby's earlier, his words – and especially their tone – exuded sympathy, but I found myself wishing they'd never been spoken. They brought everything back, complete with a vivid mental picture of my late beloved, and with an alarming incipiency of tears. *Frances, Frances, I want to travel to the reaches of whatever distant realm you find yourself in. Let me come.* I tried to quell the gathering storm of tears and to quiet my quivering lip, but I'm sure Marius noticed.

I'll manage, I said.

Anything at all I can do …

I appreciate your concern but, as the saying goes, I need to get on top of this one by myself.

You've seen Ray?

I nodded.

How is *he* coping?

Not sure. He believes his father will descend on him now he has no home.

My guess is he's right on that score.

Can you head the old guy off?

I can try. But the law says he has every right.

That same law can't touch Ray. And he threatens to murder the bastard.

You think he could be serious?

No telling. He talks nonsense as usual.

What sort of nonsense?

Shoelace soup.

Come again?

Shoelace soup.

For a while, the Administrator of Conroy was at a loss for

words. I heard a magpie warble nearby. Still closer, I imagined I heard the mechanism of Marius' mind in action.

O.K., he said. Let me speak to him. In the meantime, my advice to you is to give him a wide berth for now. I wouldn't like to see you implicated in his plans. As happened once before.

Please, Marius. I've never been privy to his plans.

He made no reply. Giving a wave to John Coffee, he headed off on foot past the Mickey Mouse boom-gate – repaired now – and off to The Space.

Back in my apartment, I rang Gabby, whom I had promised to keep up to speed.

Shoelace soup? was her incredulous response.

Don't ask me to explain, I replied.

The Space is breached, and Marius grounds me

It happened in the dead of that very night. The Space now had two Spacemen. So much Gabby told me the next morning.

Despite Marius' warning to me, I resolved to see things for myself. My excuse was I had a van-load of undelivered framing paraphernalia. Soon I was transferring this stuff into the skip, while waiting to see some action from inside The Space. I couldn't imagine how two souls at such loggerheads would manage to co-exist inside Conroy's tiny hut.

I finished my unloading, sent the skip on its way across the interface, and then decided to stay around for a bit just to see if anything eventuated or seemed likely to. So, I stood by my end of the dolly track imbibing the restorative draught of natural sights, sounds, and smells the alpine ambience had to offer. I had all but decided to leave when suddenly there was action. Action, moreover, with a musical accompaniment.

J S Bach on the organ began at high volume from inside the hut. A few minutes later, Cromwell senior emerged from the front door of the hut, in his trademark dressing gown, effecting a backwards stagger. He had evidently been shoved out by Ray. Who slammed the door shut behind him.

The old man hammered on the door, shouting words I could barely decipher over the loud music. Some of it was invective. Between the invective were a few phrases I could just make out, such as '… treat the frail and elderly …' '… bird gets better attention …' '… hack the bloody music …' '… own flesh and blood …' '… answer on judgment day …' the last of these surprising me somewhat because, from what Ray and Frances had told me, I hadn't come away with the impression the old fogey was especially religious.

Then he turned around and saw me. That really set him going.

Hey son, he shouted, that lesbian floozy has come to see you.

This remark flushed Ray out. The door opened. He stood there in the doorway as angry as I had ever seen him.

What the fuck was that you just said? he shouted.

The slut responsible for your sister's death is here.

It wasn't mere anger now. It was blind rage, and it scared me witless. Ray flew at the old guy, the father he had disowned, flinging him down, picking him up again, flinging him down again, etc., none of it any too gentle. I was gripping the ski-poles now, my knuckles white.

Christ, Ray, stop it, I shouted.

When Ray pinned his father to the trunk of a snow-gum with a hand on his stubbled throat, I decided it was time to call Marius. Which I did. Cromwell senior was gasping for breath. For a mad moment, I had visions of Ray, in vindication of his own forecast, garrotting his father with a shoelace.

Finally, Ray let up, releasing his grip, leaving his father to slither to his knees at the base of the snow-gum. I was relieved to see Ray retire in pique to the hut, closing the door behind him. But, barely a minute later, the door opened again, and a battered suitcase flew out, its contents scattering in all directions as it did so. Clothing, scruffy and dirty, hung briefly in the air. Treasured tools of a once-practised trade, rusty and much-used, fell like stones. And magazines with photos of women, naked and near-naked, took wing like birds, before falling open at the most salacious pages. These were presumably the only possessions the sad old man had been able to salvage from Frances' apartment before his horded treasures had been cleared away unceremoniously by unfeeling authorities. His last hurrah of private ownership.

Ray emerged again, thumbs in pockets, cocky.

I was moved to compassion when I saw the pornography. As prurient and as disrespectful of women as it was, it spoke to me of a life not short of aspiration but devoid of realization. Here was evidence the man could truly claim membership of the human race. The magazines were a sleazy form of identity card or passport. Then I checked myself. Nothing could validate him. This man had driven the woman I loved first to devalue and then to forgo her life.

Marius arrived, with two female police in tow.

Turn the music off, he said.

His voice was not raised, but its authority was sufficient for it to carry to whomever it was intended, in this case Ray. The command it conveyed allowed of no breach. Ray went back inside. The music ceased. Ray re-emerged.

Marius' actions from this point were firm, forthright, to the point, and driven by single-minded determination. I had never seen him take charge quite like this. With an unequivocal finger, he directed Ray to the conversation post. Then he turned to me.

These two constables, he said, will escort you to your apartment, where I expect you to stay put. For your own protection. I'll not have you compromise your own position any further, as you seem fully determined to do.

The female constables duly took charge of me, one at each arm, and lead me away. I felt deeply humiliated, and resentful of the person who had served this humiliation on me. All my life, I had been a law-abiding citizen, even down to the smallest trifles. And here I was being manhandled (womanhandled?) by this same ungrateful law. When all was said and done, I guess I should have been glad I wasn't cuffed. As it was, they let me drive myself in my own van, with their police Lecky hot on my tail.

The last thing I saw of the scene was Marius sitting himself down opposite Ray at the conversation post. Only later, in my apartment under house arrest with a police guard stationed outside, did I get an account of what transpired next by … guess who? No prize. Gabby. Gabby of the green eyes, blonde hair, swank gear, and assertive mien.

Sitting opposite me on my *chaise*, her drink of choice – a dirty martini – in hand, Gabby told me how Marius, at the conversation post, had sought to bring about truce. First, he had talked to Ray and then separately to his father. Not surprisingly, the process had been a difficult one, but some form of consensus had eventually been achieved. Marius had been forthcoming when passing on this information to Gabby, and Gabby was equally forthcoming now when relaying it to me.

Bells of hell, girl, said Gabby, it's the Wild West out there.

So how is our gentleman sheriff planning to restore order? I asked.

Marius? Gentleman? When it comes to his own backside, he's the meanest gunslinger in the game. He was absolutely ruthless in his dealings round the negotiating table. The way he thumped it, you'd think he was bent on its demolition.

I wish I'd been there.

Don't even think about it, precious. You're grounded.

So why did Marius chuck a maddy?

He views these latest events as an existential crisis for Conroy.

Why so?

A harmonious Space, he would argue, is crucial to the prosperity of Conroy. And, *ergo*, to his tenure.

She thrust her empty glass in my general direction, so I went out to the kitchen to make her another. She shouted directions.

Don't spare the olives, were her words.

… faced with people like Gabby, compliance is the safest option. People like her have the knack of making you feel there is no alternative should you value your life …

I returned with a very dirty martini, and a question to pose.

What was the agreement reached? I asked.

Gabby spelt out its gist.

Ray and his father had no legal option but to coexist in The Space. So separate patches of turf would be set aside as *Lebensraume* for each of the antagonists. Ray's would be the existing hut. His father's would be quarters yet to be built. It would fall to Ray, as the only able-bodied person available on site, to construct it. In the meantime, Admin would provide temporary accommodation in the form of a glamping tent with all conveniences for Cromwell senior.

Sounds hunky-dory, I said, but what about the demands father has on son?

What sort of demands might you have in mind? she asked.

You mean, what does *he* have in mind?

O.K. He.

Filial duty. For 'duty', read services on call.

Marius has promised they'll take care of this over at The Depot.

Do they know what they're letting themselves in for?

Admin?

Yes.

They have no choice.

I suddenly realized I had taken over the role of interrogator, a role rightfully belonging to her. She was the professional. I felt pleased I could take control of the information flow in this way when dealing with such an experienced operator.

When it comes down to the line, I asked, what chance is there the warring parties will deign to behave?

Gabby, perplexed, raised her hands palm upwards. I watched her as she gathered her thoughts.

Marius thinks he's got the father covered, she said. It's the son he's worried about.

Attaboy, I thought (apropos of Ray). But I asked, Why?

He doesn't like his silent acquiescence. Or the hatred he sees in his eyes. Or the defiant curl of his lips. He thinks our Spaceman might have his own agenda.

Let me guess. Shoelace soup?

Shoelace soup.

That night in my lone bed, my thoughts turned naturally to Frances, a turn they had not taken all day. Distractions, plenty of them, had taken over the space in my head grief had previously colonized. Suddenly I felt guilty. Did Frances matter so little to me that, given no more than a week since her death, she should be out of mind to me?

Tears came then. Her image, a poignant reminiscence now captive in the aspic of the irretrievable past, was before me once again.

My guilt was assuaged.

First snow of the year, and shoelace soup is served

Mid-morning of the next day, Gabby called by phone to let me know Cromwell senior was now out of The Space. The news came as no surprise to me. My response was ingenuous.

Dead or alive? I asked.

Now what would you think? was her question in reply.

Dead?

No other way to get out of that fucking hole.

When did this happen?

Earlier this morning.

How did it happen?

Depends who you ask.

There was a pause on the line, a pause as cogent as any words might be.

Listen, she asked. Have you had breakfast?

No, I replied. I slept in.

Good. I'm on my way. Have some olives at the ready. And some of that moonshine for them to swim around in.

Soon, dressed somewhat inelegantly in a nondescript dressing gown, I sat across from her. She adopted a pose to which she gave every appearance of having been born, her frame free and easy on my *chaise*, her fingers wound round the stem of a charged cocktail glass. I assumed from her power dressing she had come in off the beat. An early riser responsive to the call of duty.

A heavy neck-scarf she had been wearing when she came in my front door supported her head and shoulders as she settled back. The thick weave of that garment told me it must be cold outside.

His body, she said, when they came for it, was lying face down in the snow. Clad in that dreadful dressing gown.

Snow? I asked.

Look outside, you dozy bugger. The first snow of the year.

I'm not allowed outside, you know. Those goons in the Lecky are watching me.

Get real, girl. Their brief is to prevent you going near The Space. You're free to go wherever you like in the Stems.

I shrugged.

He didn't come out in the skip? I asked.

The stiff? she asked.

I nodded.

Not this time, she said. Looks like he just walked out. Perhaps with a tad of physical persuasion.

You mean he was pushed?

That *is* a possibility.

What do the authorities say?

Well, that's quite interesting. There's lots of speculation. One moment they say he was pushed. The next they say it was a trip-wire. Made out of shoelaces, perhaps, to give some credence to the 'shoelace soup' meme. But the truth is they know nothing. They weren't there when it happened.

She paused to chew on an olive, returning the pip to her glass. When she spoke again, her tone was conspiratorial.

You know, she said, John Shepherd is in town. He's not impressed. Two deaths in a matter of days. Three in a matter of weeks. On his watch. How *could* he be? Freaking Midsomer Murders.

What's he planning to do about it? I asked.

Liberate some heads from bodies. Be warned. He'll want to talk to you.

I took in the implications for a moment, while my fingers tightened on the arms of my lounge chair.

Where does Marius stand? I asked.

Worried about his neck, I'd imagine.

Have you spoken to Ray?

Her entire posture changed. She sat up straight in the *chaise*, her eyes green rivets as they engaged with mine. The delight in those eyes said, I thought you'd never ask. She wanted her answer to be seen as significant investigative reportage. I would be the first to hear.

Of course, she replied. I was on the spot quicker than a fish off the hook.

I'm all ears, I said.

Allow me to set the scene, she said. Ray was …

Please do.

Ray was out and about when the event in question happened. Nobody else was. Except a man who is now dead. Who'll tell no tales. Ray's version has to be seen either as gospel truth or as clever lies. Or maybe a bit of both. Make your own judgment on that. But one thing Ray's version is not. It's not speculation.

O.K., I said. His version. Please.

She settled back, her face reflecting a degree of satisfaction. She was proud to be the purveyor of the good oil.

O.K., she said. Ray emerges from his hut early this morning and shakes the tent to wake the old man. Who emerges grumpy, not happy at all about the snow on the ground. Ray tells him he needs his opinion re the site where his permanent domicile will eventually be.

A request made in good faith? I asked.

And received with grudging compliance, it would appear, she said. Anyway, they set off. Ray leads. The old guy stumbles behind I imagine. Cursing, because profanity is what he does. When they reach the dolly track, Ray waits for his charge to catch up, and says 'You go on ahead. I need to tie up my shoelace.' 'Which way?' asks Cromwell senior.

My jaw dropped. Sheba, I said.

So Ray grips the old fellow by the shoulders, and turns him to face the direction of the gap in the ski-poles. 'Straight ahead,' he says. 'I'll be right behind you.' And he bends down to tie his shoelace.

My gasp was one of admiration. I felt like applauding. Instead, a hybrid of delight and incredulity spread silently across my features. I felt it spread as one might feel a shower of warm rain on the face.

Admit it, I said. Our Spaceman is a class act.

No argument there, she said. Can I leave you to imagine the rest?

I clapped my hands together, a single clap but one with much vigour. My gesture of wholesale approval, came from the heart. The monster who had terrorized Ray and Frances, ostensibly from childhood, was no more.

As Ray had foretold, he had fallen victim to cuisine whose theme was footwear. Soup whose prime ingredient, its very fibre, was normally found just south of the ankles.

My accusers sink the boot in, and prevent me leaving town

A single occurrence might be put down to accident, said John Shepherd, but two of them smacks of carelessness …

I blanched.

… or more to the point, should I say, complicity.

John had borrowed Marius' chair on this occasion. Marius and I, cowed, looked at him across the desk. *Gros Bonnets* peered down from over John's shoulder, the gormless grins of the petty town officials cold comfort to us.

The evidence implicating Ms Chalmond is flimsy, said Marius.

As it was on the last occasion, I do recollect, said the Lord our Shepherd.

I was not about to say anything, and I believe Marius was not yet ready to accept the verbal baton passed to him. The pulpit was John's and he was determined to use it to effect. Indeed, the white polo-neck of the knitted sweater he wore added a clerical touch to his presence.

I'll level with you, said John. The politics at play here are diabolical. There are forces out there baying for blood. It could be my blood.

So, John, said Marius, you're looking for a papoose to throw under the wagon.

John hesitated for a millisecond to get his head around the implications of Marius' rejoinder. Papoose? Wagon? Then, the penny dropping, and barely able to control his anger, he responded. The words from his mouth were venomous spit-balls taking on the form of discrete syllables at high volume.

You! – turd! – What! – the! – fuck! – would! – you! – know?! were the syllables.

I could see his embarrassment now as he tried to collect himself after this outburst. So his next words were so softly spoken they might have served as lyrics for a lullaby. But they were chill lyrics.

No butter would have melted in *that* mouth. And no baby would have been soothed.

I'm looking for due process, he said. And for that very reason, I shall insist Ms Chalmond stay around. She shall not leave town until inquiries are complete.

Do you intend to enforce that? asked Marius.

Don't doubt it, replied John.

There was nothing more either of us could say to that. Meeting over. Rolling his eyes, Marius took himself off to nurse wounds. I took myself back to my apartment, to serve out what – on the strength of things – was an open-ended term of house arrest.

My minders, airhead lackeys snug in their Lecky, were there of course. I chanced them a cheeky wave. But when I was inside, I realized the extent of my fury. I was riled up big time. John bloody Shepherd had allowed me no say, and I was stuffed if I was just going to roll over. I would not comply.

So, after treating myself to a stiff drink, I decided to put the matter to the test. I jumped into my van and made for The Roundelle as if I were off to the supermarket or some such. My minders were on my tail, of course, as they would inevitably be when I embarked on these innocent errands. But, on this occasion, my quest was not so innocent.

I turned into Homeland Security Stem, and made for Checkpoint Charlie. Ordinarily, the duty guard just raised the boom-gate as I approached and waved me through. But, on this occasion, the boom-gate was down, so I was required to stop. Hello, I thought, what gives? I stopped, alighted from my van, and headed for the checkpoint on foot. I could see my shadows parked just fifty metres back. Waiting on the outcome.

Then, before I could even produce my ID, the guard stepped forward from his post, wagged a finger at me, and followed up with an emphatic thumb-jerk to indicate I should return from whence I had come.

Fuck.

I went back.

So, I thought as I settled myself on my *chaise* with another stiff drink, *that* was their game. It was time for Plan B. Oh yes, you'd better believe it. I *had* a Plan B.

'What took you so long, princess?'

Next morning I checked the lie of the land through my window. The early snow of the last few days had turned to slush. Magpies warbled wondrously, as if striving to reinforce my resolve as of yesterday.

I showered, dressed, made a pot of strong hot coffee, poured a mug for myself, and left the pot simmering. I sat down and drank, glad of the warmth my hands derived from the mug. I was relaxed. Cool headed. I savoured every sip. I knew what I had to do. It felt like I had already done it. Plan B.

My caffeine fix accomplished, I poured some of the good stuff into polystyrene mugs, one for each of my two minders. I put lids on the mugs, and took them out to the police Lecky van, parked as ever opposite my apartment. I heard the occupants murmuring inside. They seemed resentful, as if demeaned by their assignment.

I rapped on their window with my knuckles, and brandished the steaming mugs before their startled eyes. They hesitated for a moment, conferring with each other. But then they wound the window down. The offer of a hot coffee on a cold morning, even from their quarry, was welcome, and to accept was surely no dereliction of duty.

I passed the mugs to them through the open window, gave a cheery thumbs-up, and then turned for home.

From that point I moved quickly. I headed as if for my front door but, although I had nothing packed, made for my van instead. I wouldn't need anything where I was going. I started the beast up, gunned the accelerator and – tyres squealing, engine at top revs – steered into Visitors and then down it at high speed. I imagined my stunned minders gaping, springing to action, spilling scalding coffee into their laps in confusion.

Left now into The Roundelle, then a high speed dash clockwise to the junction it made with the road giving access to The Space. As I turned right into this road, I glanced in my rear-vision. No sign of my minders. I had the drop on them.

Next, I smashed through the boom-gate – wham! – leaving behind me a despairing John Coffee waving frantic hands. He put me in mind of the scarecrow from The Wizard of Oz. I felt sorry for the poor guy. He had endured all this before. And much else, I suspected.

I saw my destination ahead. The Space. I brought my van to a shuddering halt near the conversation post, its back wheels skidding sideways, throwing up mud. Those of the white-coat brigade on duty scattered in alarm, like ducks at the first sound of a shotgun. And there was Ray. He was out and about setting things up for the day's anti-infective session. My arrival stopped him in his tracks.

I leapt from the van. There was no time to waste on second thoughts. Plan B. Do it. Just do it. Reaching the gap in the ski-poles that allowed passage of the skip as required, I allowed myself the briefest of backwards glances. There, of course, was the mountain, sinister witness to all the action. Not missing a trick. And, closer at hand, my minders were just pulling up behind my van. They were too late, of course. Losers.

I dashed through the gap, …

… and, *voila*, claimed The Space as my territory.

Ray was dumbfounded. I approached him, first at a run then, more tentatively, at a shuffle. Was I even welcome here? Only when I stopped dead a metre or so in front of him, hands on hips, defying him to respond, did he utter those words I'll never forget.

What took you so long, princess? were the words.

I heard their echo in my head.

What took you so long, princess?

He wore that strange lop-sided smile as he took a hesitant step or two towards me.

I didn't hesitate. Suppressing my instinct to chastise him for the 'princess' bit, I flung myself into his arms. It felt comfy. Sheba, it felt like home.

Book the Third

as told by

Marius Strangio

I must create a system, or be enslaved by another man's.

Blake

The Vanity of Hats

The framed lithograph skulked in a corner on the back wall of the sorting room of my tender years, relegated to obscurity by row upon row of pigeon-holes reaching to the heavens and bulging with mail. Even back then I could read the French title at the bottom of the print. *Les Gros Bonnets du Village.* Not so much different from the Italian. Nor from the English. As I was to learn much later, *Gros Bonnets* was the creation of 19th century caricaturist, Edmond Lavrate, whose signature I could only just decipher.

In sardonic depiction was a group of village identities, all male, each puffed up with an exaggerated sense of his own importance, each recognizable from his headwear. Two rotund luminaries, in top hats, one of them the mayor perhaps and the other the banker, seemed hell-bent on upstaging the rest. Nearby, the fire chief in brass helmet struck a Wagnerian pose. A couple of military types strutted, one with scabbarded sword prodding all within its reach, and with a hat suggestive perhaps of the foreign legion. The other, with bicorne hat, opted for a more Napoleonic stance. A labourer, or artisan perhaps, flaunted his flat cap. Town baker, priest, and joker wore hats flagging their identities. An elderly town patriarch, refusing to die, boasted a night-cap from an earlier more somnolent hour. And, *sans* hat, a goose stood in their midst.

Gift to your mother from her sister in *Milano*, papa had said.

But all I had eyes for was the mail seemingly bent on toppling from pigeon-holes into our space, threatening to envelop us both in an avalanche of envelopes.

Mail, I had said.

The cross I have to bear.

But so *much* mail.

More letters here, *ragazzo mio*, than in a Welsh railway station.

My father, Giuseppi Strangio, was postmaster in the provincial town of V– in Basilicata. I won't identify my town with any more precision than this short-form because papa, whose privacy I respect, lives there to this day, serving out his career as one might a life sentence. Perhaps I shall allow you one tiny bit of additional information about V– at the risk of giving the game away. It was high up in the Apennines. It was as pretty as a picture. And, in winter, as frigid as an icicle.

What I liked about my father was he had a face that spoke. His mobile mouth and eyes said as much as did the words he uttered. His full suite of facial features was rimmed by irrepressible black, the black of coarse stubble, bushy eyebrows, and thick hair. Sometimes, he came across to me as the sad clown and at other times as the placid stoic. I was startled when I looked in the mirror to find papa's visage looking back at me, *sans* the stubble and weathered skin.

Gros Bonnets had acquired a special significance for papa. It spoke to him in full colour of the inverted snobbery he had endured and would continue to endure every day of his life in this town. He was despised by most of the local peasantry with whom he came into contact. Because they worked the land, this peasantry deemed themselves more worthy than the likes of my father. Any activity not connected with the land they viewed with disdain on the grounds it was non-productive if not downright parasitic. Failing to see any point in pursuits that didn't get down to earth in the strictly literal sense, they concluded such pursuits must be some sort of swindle. They never sent mail themselves – most were barely literate – and what they received was almost always a bill, on receipt of which they would hurl abuse at papa. They would then take the offending piece of paper back to their abode and impale it on a spike reserved for such items, items destined from the start to be despised and forgotten.

Their disdain was not reserved for the postmaster alone. The peasantry viewed all petty officialdom in V– with similar contempt. The mayor, the fire chief, etc. So, papa came to view *Gros Bonnets* as a graphic encapsulation of their attitude towards those not able or willing to till the soil and/or husband animals. *All* town officials were subject to derision, were figures of fun, were putting on dog. With the exception of the Big Men. They were rumoured to carry instruments of torture or worse in their flash cars. Such as thumb-screws and bolt-cutters. So, the worthy soil-tillers never spiked a request from the Big Men. They paid up pronto.

Who was my mother?

Poor mama. Francesca Strangio, nee Leonetti. My memory of her inevitably turned on her health. Shortly after I was born, she developed multiple sclerosis and, soon after that, early-onset dementia. Whenever we visited her in the hospice at Como, she would greet us with language so foul it would have brought a blush to the face of the late Silvio Berlusconi. This from a woman whose language, prior to the dementia, would have flattered a nun. What unfeeling deity had visited such cruel indignity on her? Mercifully, she died young.

Fortunately for me, there was a replacement. Her sister, Claudia, married only to her career, took me under her wing. I found myself making the long journey on a regular basis between my humble southern town of V– in Basilicata to the great northern city of *Milano* in Lombardy, which is where my aunt lived and worked. I grew to love her as much as I did my father and (while she lived) my biological mother. She actually chose my name, Marius, preferring it to Mario or Marco, on the grounds that it reeked less of *le parti meridionale.* Auntie was, I regret to say, a bit of a snob.

From the observations I have shared with you so far, you shall have gathered the sisters were very different in temperament. For this reason, their physical resemblance was all the more striking. Both had faces that might have been moulded out of a fine olive-tinted clay. A clay with plenty of capacity to flex when the emotion called for it. Both sisters had the same lean countenance, faintly triangular, with prominent bones of brow, cheek, and chin. Both had the same dark glossy hair – thick and straight – features I found most becoming – alluring I could say – atop their heads – and then repeated again where eyebrows and lashes were wanted.

I gleaned mama's features partly from faded memory and partly from the framed head-shot gracing the mantel shelf in our living room. Auntie's I could glean without photo. I saw her so very frequently in those days.

At my *scuola elementare* in V–, I was introduced to 'proper' Italian (as opposed to dialect) and to English. I spent school holidays with my aunt who, plotting a future for me, emphasized the importance of these languages, and introduced me to French as well. On reaching an age where a secondary education was deemed necessary for me, I found myself, for the first couple of years, travelling daily to Potenza, a delightful bus ride through neatly cultivated fields slathering their fecund verdure over well-rounded hilltops sprinkled with snow when the season so decreed. But then my aunt intervened, deciding that her nephew – her Marius – deserved better. She insisted I continue my education at a prestigious *liceo* in *Milano*, returning to V– only for school holidays. I felt really sorry for papa, who would be left on his own now, with nothing in his life anymore bar his postal duties and perpetual putdown.

What a contrast *Milano* was. In place of the squat solid dust-coloured obloids purporting to be cathedrals but looking more like bank premises or the like, there was this stunning white *Duomo*, whose delicate fingers aspired to heaven, and whose *totum corpus* boasted ornamentation of a quantity and quality sufficient to hold one's rapt attention until such time as that naked guy on the cross chose to pay us a visit for the second time. The arcades and covered walkways of the city oozed sophistication and conferred status. The people privileged to walk these arcades mouthed not an uncouth regional dialect, but a polyglot of important languages from Europe and still further afield. At night, these same people swarmed to the theatre, opera, restaurants, and bars that beckoned to all contenders in this lively city. And the not-so-distant mountains were a breed apart – alps, they called them – treacherous jagged things dressed out in black and white, with deep valleys between in which one could learn to ski. Which I did.

I could not deny, of course, that Aunt Claudia had groomed me for the upper-middle echelons of society in *Milano*. Without her benevolent hand, I would have been left floundering, an outsider in a big impersonal city, an outsider – moreover – bearing the taint of his southern origins. Even as it was, and much to my chagrin, I suffered ridicule and worse on the grounds of my accent and use of patois, until such time as all such monkey talk had been purged from my speech patterns.

I had always suspected my aunt had disapproved of my father. So when I became sufficiently aware of how things stacked up for me in my new milieu, and of the contrast it made with my old, I dared to ask her how it had come about that my mother, raised in *Milano*, had become the wife of a provincial postmaster in the deep south.

Life plays cruel tricks if one lets it, she had replied. But, *tesoro mio*, I am in a position to take life by the throat and put things right as regards *your* prospects.

At an age when I might have been expected to entertain thoughts of amorous adventures with young women, I found instead I preferred to liaise with those of my own gender when it came to the more intimate particulars of my life. In *Milano*, this was no problem. Happily, a goodly proportion of the male population was this way inclined. Plenty of men like me enjoyed relations with men like me. But had I still been living back in the town of my childhood, my life – I knew for a fact – would have been pure hell. On the occasions I *did* pay visits to V–, I kept my proclivities a secret. Even from papa, though I think he may have had his suspicions.

Life was sweet.

My aunt worked at a university, not as an academic but in

administration. Her place of employment was a semi-private institution specializing in aspects of business management. Her title was Director of Admissions and Accreditation. After school on most days, I joined her in her work precincts, before returning with her to the apartment where we both lived. I would attend to my homework in a corner of her office while she presided over a small clerical staff, a front desk to field student inquiries, and some high-end printing machines. Part of this backdrop, I was never so busy I couldn't keep a keen eye on the way my aunt fielded the pressing issues arising in her line of business.

As one might expect, my aunt was gently but firmly steering me in the direction of a tertiary education, an idea to which she – understandably – was wedded. But I was not on the same page she was. So, when I matriculated, I took an *anno sabbatico*, actually two of them in succession, while I wrestled with this disputed point.

My problem revolved around headdress. The surgeon's scrub hat. The lawyer's wig. The engineer's hard hat. The academic's mortarboard. Tertiary honours merely fitted out their favoured sons (and daughters) with a *Gros Bonnet*. And *Gros Bonnets* invited derision. I knew this for a fact. Hadn't I seen it all firsthand? Hadn't I seen it happen to my unfortunate father?

This was something I knew I would have difficulty explaining to my aunt.

For years I had been an accidental observer at a significant institutional coalface. I had seen the cavalier treatment meted out to students by the minions at the front desk of my aunt's empire. If this was the way mere flunkies at *Record degli Studenti* treated the undergraduate clientele, how might the same supplicants be appraised by the staff in their very own faculties? As pieces of shit, I surmised. And this was happening to them before they had even come by their coveted hats.

I wondered, too, about those esteemed faculty staff. They were charged with instructing their young protégées in the niceties of business administration and the like, protégés who could be expected to hang on every word. But if they were such shit-hot experts in their field, why were they not out there in the real world administering businesses of their own? Why, when it came to the crunch, did they shy away from the pointy end of life's contract? Something didn't compute.

This was the system before which my aunt was keen to have me bow and scrape. And she was right about one thing. The magical piece of paper, the *accreditamento*, made to appear like a document out of medieval parchment, complete with pretend-wax seal and luminous hand-painted lettering, with which students were presented ceremoniously after many years of hard slog, was the point of entry into an elite and potentially lucrative career path. Point of entry? Without a shadow of doubt. But assuredly *sans* compass and map for the slippery journey down that path. To my way of thinking, the scheme was all smoke and mirrors, designed to entrench the entitlement of the elite and to invite the scorn of the common herd.

So, I had no compunction when it came to bypassing a system to which I had privileged (albeit unsanctioned) access. My aunt's office was always open to me. In her office were the keys to the machines used to print the 'pieces of paper'. I knew where those keys were kept. And operating the machines was a walk in the park.

Illegal? That was an academic question. I didn't intend to be caught. I just had to choose my moment.

My moment came. It being after hours, all staff bar my aunt had knocked off for the day. And my aunt then decided to excuse herself for an hour or so to do shopping or some such thing. Would I mind being left all alone for a bit? Mind? Not a problem.

The deed was done in a jiffy. According to the powers that be, I was now a qualified person. I had my piece of paper to prove it.

To this day, I can't be certain how she did it. But my aunt rumbled me. Perhaps the special paper on which degrees were printed was under strict audit, like banknotes in a mint. I'll never know. So, about a month later, I had to field her wrath. A wrath that was mild-mannered, but no less devastating for it.

Tesoro mio, she said, you've been a naughty boy.

How so? I asked.

No point pretending. Now you have two choices. Two only. You give it back to me, or you go elsewhere to perpetuate your deceptive practices. Far enough away from here there'll be no repercussions for me.

How far is that?

Try the dark side of the moon.

Auntie!

Then I suggest … Australia. It's a tad more hospitable.

Having come this far, I had no intention of surrendering my cherished piece of paper. The lesson I learnt by negative example from my father was that my life was *mine* to validate, not some other person's. So, I did some research on this place called Australia. They spoke English there, a language with which I was by now quite fluent. It was tolerably civilized. It had a celebrated opera house. It had ski fields. And, by all reports, it rolled out the welcome mat for people like me prepared to re-invent themselves. The downside was it didn't appear to have much of a sense of its place in the world. It was a backwater.

Perhaps, I flattered myself, I could change that.

Job for an Autodidact

Who would have thought my forged piece of paper would eventually land me in the demesne of Conroy? As its freaking Administrator, no less? Running the whole show? With salary to match, clients to serve, and flunkies to dance attendance? Hell, Toto, this is not Kansas anymore.

But, before I proceed any further, let me spell out how I got there. To Conroy.

I bid *arrivederci* to my father and aunt. By way of a parting gift, papa presented me with a postal cylinder out of stiff cardboard. When I opened it, I was surprised to find his print, *Gros Bonnets*, object of his rancour, scrolled up inside.

Let it be a reminder to you, papa said.

What of? I asked in reply.

Take your choice. For me it's been a reminder of my failings. A reminder I could have very well done without. Which, *come vedi*, I *am* now doing without.

My aunt's gift was also a reminder: a handsome hard-covered glossy volume of photographs of *Milano*, the city I had come to love. Wedged inside, opposite the frontispiece, were a couple of sealed envelopes with names and their Sydney addresses in her handwriting.

References, she said. You may need them.

After such preliminaries, and with the arrogance of youth in full blush, I showed the middle finger to my past. I took the long haul flight to Sydney. And, sure enough, before I could say *cotoletta alla Milanese*, one of the contacts my aunt had been kind enough to put at my disposal landed me a job.

My career was off and running.

It began with a company trading in companies. That is to say, a company that bought and sold companies in trouble. Lazarus companies, as we dubbed them. Companies unable to keep their heads above water in the maelstrom we know as the marketplace. For the brief period my outfit actually had their grimy hands on a particular company, I got to overhaul the whole box and dice – business plan, methodology, infrastructure, and – where no other alternative presented itself – personnel. When this moribund company was back on its feet we on-sold it at a profit.

I was good at this. I was good at picking companies ripe for exploitation, and then licking them into shape. Had my piece of paper spoken of something more than just a fancy printing machine spitting out empty words, I could not have done better. I was rewarded with bonuses and was hounded by head-hunters.

One such head-hunter was an agency of the federal government charged with making emergency medical equipment available to clinics and hospitals at the time of the viral pandemic. I should say a little more about this pandemic. As pandemics are wont to do, it cowed the entire planet. Including Lombardy, where it was especially ferocious. I considered myself lucky, having fled *Milano* at the right time. My aunt was not so lucky. It took her out.

I was distressed. I had grown very fond of, and learnt a lot from her kindly no-nonsense demeanour. This was the woman who had given me my given name. As for forms of address, I would never again get to hear the affection in her voice as she called me *tesoro mio*. On the upside however, cold comfort though it was to me, the only person with knowledge of my felony was now no more. And it would be fair to say she needed never fear any personal repercussions arising from my fraudulent behaviour. Not where she was now billeted.

As penance, I decided to avoid dishonesty from this point on. I would bury beneath a mountain of scrupulous practice, the inaugural falsehood underpinning the progress of my career. From henceforth, my word would be my bond.

The aforesaid government agency, based in Canberra, offered me a generous six-figure salary I could scarcely refuse. I signed up with them. Soon, I found myself identifying appropriate manufacturing operations and then persuading them to re-tool in order to churn out vital medical equipment. By the time the pandemic had run its course, in the process making my position redundant, I was well known in government circles. My fame had spread.

Now, in the Capital of my adoptive nation, that dreary excuse for a city, I found myself on the doorstep of what was known as The Alps. Which meant I could stretch my ski legs at weekends. Fields, with names like Thredbo and Perisher, offered both downhill and cross-country opportunities. They sounded their siren calls in my receptive ear. I found a regular skiing companion in one Klaus Anders. He was straight, more's the pity, as regards his sexual predilections, but his skiing credentials could not be faulted. He harked originally from the vicinity of Kitzbühel in Austria, a neck of the woods where everyone emerged from the womb with skis strapped to their ankles.

A second adversity followed on the heels of the pandemic. Humanity, it would appear, was about to be gobbled up by a malign force manifesting itself as 'The Space' (or – God forbid – as 'The Spaces' plural) from which no living creature could escape alive. Yes, a tad hard to get one's head around perhaps. But, the evidence on the ground was inescapable, except for those inured to denial. The government of the day, spooked big time, actually created a Directorate to deal with the emergency.

A high-level *apparatchik*, named John Shepherd, headed up this Directorate. Impressed with my record, he asked me to deal with the problem on the ground. I was to build – from nothing more than an alpine wilderness – a special-purpose township – or 'demesne' as he insisted on calling it – centred on the one active Space known to date. Then I was to administer this demesne. Conroy, as the demesne would be known, was to be my baby. I would be subject to no outward interference, provided I honoured the mission statement of the Directorate, adhered to John's rather loose guidelines, and made no waves that might disturb him.

So, I was given *carte blanche*, a handsome stipend for my pains, and very generous funding for running the show. For someone like me, an autodidact habituated to doing things my way, this appointment was a dream. I was convinced I was just the right person for the job. I don't believe some dude who had achieved his piece of paper the hard way, as well as – concomitantly – an innate tendency to doff the obsequious cap, could have handled it, or – indeed – would have wanted to.

I had been living in this, my adopted country, long enough to have twigged that it was an essential courtesy to consult the First Nations' people before embarking on a project of this nature.

They had nominal custody over the landscape I was charged with administering. No such consultation would have been required back in Lombardy, where the people on the ground were *themselves* the first (and only) Nation, and had to my knowledge been so for millennia. But here, in what the locals affectionately call Oz, the original sin – *peccato originale* no less – of colonization had plagued successive generations and, with justification, those colonized were not about to let them forget it.

So, consultation being deemed politic, consultation it was. There was no problem. When I put the issue to the elders in whose traditional lands my proposed development resided, they could only agree action was necessary. One of them observed cryptically, That old feller in the mountain, he's playing up alright. But beyond comment of this nature, they offered me no advice on how to handle the situation. They signed off on my project.

The Space, a constant reminder to all and sundry of Conroy's monstrous *raison d'etre*, was central to my ground plan for the demesne. A bearded guru, who fancied himself as a clairvoyant, and whose day job was picture framing, was prisoner inside The Space, which fact didn't seem to worry him overly much. His name was Ray Cromwell. For a time, he lived out a solitary existence in accommodation, well appointed by all reports and certainly exclusive, known eponymously as Conroy's hut. His assistant, one Tania Chalmond, ferried framing jobs from Melbourne to Conroy, and ferried the completed work back. Then, after just a few years as Ray's errand girl, she – in a moment of insanity triggered to all appearances by romantic love – joined him inside The Space. They settled there together, so I understand, in a state of connubial bliss.

My ground plan for Conroy – the demesne not the hut – consisted of nine 'Stems' radiating out from The Space. Six of the Stems housed Divisions from the six Government Departments that had vied successfully for representation. The other three Stems I gave over to Divisions providing essential services: Administration, Labour, and Visitors. With input from John, I appointed a Head for each of the nine Divisions. From the start, I enjoyed harmonious relations with my Division Heads. With one exception. More on this later.

Marius, John had said, a warning.

You have my ear, had been my reply.

Bullying, he had said, is in the DNA of Homeland Security. The bastards muscled their way into Conroy in the first instance and then, without even pausing for breath, went hell for leather in pursuit of total control. My advice? Don't give them an inch.

I won't, John.

But that mob didn't wait to be given. Their style was to take. Which, in due course, they did. But let's not concede the territory to them quite yet. The distant future may be theirs but the foreseeable is mine. The tenure I enjoyed was to hold sway for a significant period, more than six years in fact, and would even involve two bites at the cherry.

May I indulge in a tad of hubris here, in the interests of calling a spade a spade? In consultation with my panel of Division Heads, I managed to implement, without making too many waves for John, what I judge were some noteworthy innovations. These included, among many others, my repurposing of common-and-garden Quonset huts to address the problem of mass accommodation, my implementation of a fleet of free-for-use electric vehicles to serve as internal transport, and my disinterested allocation of recreational facilities between the Divisions competing for them. I like to think Conroy, under my watch, became a vibrant, functional, and socially cohesive community.

The Head of the Division of Homeland Security, a dour balding man, going by the name of Alain Valery, attended all my panel meetings, but said nothing. To say he kept a low profile would be a failure to plumb the depths of 'low'. He didn't even take notes, but I imagine he was wired. I suspect he saw his role purely as one of intelligence gathering for his superiors. He even looked like a spy.

His immediate superior, the Minister of Homeland Security no less, led by example. He also liked to keep a low profile. I had only ever met him once, at the official opening of Conroy, when he unveiled the brass plaque on its outskirts. He was a man, I recall, of pursed lips, dark countenance, unbending frame, intimidating stance, and steely handshake. I can't imagine he had, or even wanted, many friends. I wondered how he got his jollies. I was to find this out in time.

While on the subject of malign influences, I must not fail to mention the mountain. Which mountain? Mt Redoubt, of course. There was no other within cooee.

Local lore, corroborated by the stories of aboriginal elders, had it that this mountain was responsible for all the ills The Space visited on our uppity species from the moment said Space claimed its first human captive. I could believe that. The mountain was, indubitably, a physical presence. More than that. I could not look at it without suppressing a shudder. To my mind, it exuded menace and epitomized all that was sinister. To put a pantheistic spin on things, it seemed to possess a barbaric consciousness eager to exercise perverse action for its own unfathomable ends. If the mountain had not existed, I'm sure none of what I was hired to build, and then to oversee, would have been here. I'm sure *I* would not have been here. This was a mountain determined to hijack both human and natural agency.

According to local lore, then, the mountain wielded The Space like a lethal weapon. Or, more accurately, like a death trap. Its *modus operandi* was to strike all flora and fauna dead as it departed this Space. That's the reason I had to organize a detail to sweep up the corpses round its perimeter each day. Common presumption was the mountain was itching to strike down any human inhabitant of The Space the moment he/she chose to quit its precincts.

In the beginning, there was only one lamb scheduled for slaughter. Ray Cromwell. Later Tania Chalmond, impelled apparently by love, joined him. Accepting reality, the pair stayed put.

I liked them both, though Ray could be tricky at times. He liked to play recordings of J S Bach at high volume almost any time of day or night as the spirit moved him. Once Tania joined him in The Space, he modified this behaviour to some degree. We would still hear the J S Bach on occasion, but it was frequently supplanted by the gentler strains of Debussy or Dylan, played at a more civilized volume.

Two other less than circumspect visitors to The Space, in unrelated incidents, dared – once inside – to test the threshold. They became the first human casualties. Their demise sent a tsunami of waves in John's direction, caused me much grief as a consequence, and set in train a series of challenging investigations. The passings of these two recalcitrants – Harvey Eanis and Ray's father Paul Cromwell – were lamented by few, and marked by the third and fifth gravestones respectively to grace Conroy's (as yet) small cemetery.

I should put you in the picture apropos my private life. Even high-flying careerists are entitled to such. I was no exception.

Early in the piece I acquired a wife. In the business circles I frequented, a wife was considered an essential accessory. It conferred respectability. *Ergo*, I had to have one. I concede from the outset my reason for marrying was not love. It was cold-blooded calculation. But then, I believe, so was hers. She, June Cartwright before she became June Strangio, was the daughter of a CEO I had co-opted for the resurrected version of one of my Lazarus companies. She saw me as a rising star and decided to hitch a ride. We, each of us, kept our *amore vita* separate from our marriage. This was not dishonest behaviour, not by me, not by her. I hadn't exploited or deceived her any more than she had exploited or deceived me. She was no fool. She had gone into this with her eyes wide open.

But it's biology, not human expediency, that insists one have a sex life. So how did mine develop in these formative years of my career? On my arrival in Australia, I had resigned myself for such purposes to the rough trade, but clearly such clandestine (and risky) activity became less tenable as an option when I began to take on responsible, respectable, and publicly conspicuous roles. I had a problem.

Luckily, around this time, I met Max Baldock at a gym in Canberra. My darling Max. As is common in gay circles, we were both there pumping iron in pursuit of the body beautiful. Max was a public servant of low to middle rank who, in addition to the beautiful body, had an interesting hobby. He was an artist of sorts, whose chosen genre aped the elements of street art. Art of the stripe made popular, say, by that celebrated Brit going by the name of Banksy.

Once Max and I had become a shacked-up item, I persuaded him to follow me to Conroy and serve as my assistant. His role in the demesne turned out to be a useful decoy for him. Not only was he able to indulge with me – and accordingly I with him – the exquisite peccadilloes part and parcel of the territory of ardent lovers but, also, he found he could maintain the position of anonymity he craved apropos the exercise of his art. More of this later.

My relationship with Max was important to me in so many different ways. It was a resplendent, highly-charged, sexual thing. It was the cement that held together all the other aspects of my life. It was a validation of everything I had become. And I'm sure it held similar significance for him. From early in our relationship, I remember a verbal exchange between us, following the throes of consummated physical passion, that – in its simple brevity – encapsulated all this.

That was something else again, Max had said.

Ditto, I had replied.

Let's do it again soon.

How soon is soon?

Never soon enough.

So, by the time I made my way from Canberra to where Conroy – not yet so much as a dot on the map – was about to put down its roots under my direction, I had set things up entirely to my satisfaction. Here I could get to play God. Here I could create and then rule a living, breathing universe. Here I could mould the social order to my heart's desire, with benevolence tempering impunity. The people I wanted to keep at a distance, like John Shepherd, I had left behind. The people I needed to keep close, like my wife and lover, I had brought with me. Where, I ask you, is the downside to that?

My wife, June, didn't stay the course. Only a few years into her sojourn in Conroy, she suffered an accidental humiliation – none of my doing – which unfortunately she took to heart. She returned to Canberra, which – all said and done – was her true comfort zone. For me, she'd served the purpose I'd had in mind when I'd married her, so why should I have regretted her moving on? But I could have done without the bitterness towards me that she, from that point, nurtured in her bosom, a bitterness that would come back to bite me.

Three Futures Foretold

Who's responsible for all the great art work around Conroy? she asked.

Which art work, ducks? I asked in return.

The mock-ups of street art. Emulating Banksy.

I'm glad you like it. But I'm not at liberty to reveal its source.

You too?

Who else?

Basil Shirley for one.

Mr. Pig's Ears?

That's the dude. And your assistant for another.

Max?

I could barely suppress my amusement at the accidental irony here but managed to maintain both a straight face and my silence.

It was early in winter when Tania had taken up residence in The Space with such a spectacular display of abandon. And it was during the spring following this winter when we indulged in this particular exchange. We faced each other across the double-sided frame of the conversation post as had become our habit on so many occasions around this time. Invariably the encounters we had on these occasions were fruitful as regards both the information gleaned and the pleasure derived. Be assured the pleasure was mutual and the exchange of information worked in both our favours.

Tania, to my mind, had settled into her new circumstances much better than one might have expected. She seemed singularly content with her new domicile, despite the geographical limitations. And she seemed more than happy with her new partner. I think she loved Ray. In retrospect, I am inclined to think she always had.

As for Frances, Ray's late sister, I'm certain she was not forgotten, not by Ray, not by Tania. What was there about the Cromwell family that inspired other mere mortals to fall so comprehensively in love with them? I knew a thing or two about thwarted love, and I assert confidently that, following a significant loss from such an adventure, pain lingers in one's cognitive apparatus for the duration. Frances was Ray's beloved sister. Frances was Tania's beloved partner. Ergo, I suspect there were actually *three* residents of The Space, not just two, with one wielding a lasting influence over the headspace of the two with a claim to flesh and blood. Tania had mentioned to me – and, frankly, I would have suspected as much anyway – that a photograph of Frances – framed in house of course – occupied its own cherished nook in the hut, a nook that drew the eye at every turn.

Women, if you'll permit me a gross generalization, are governed more by their emotions, and men more by their egos. Look at

Tania when she first put in an appearance at Conroy. She was a tightly wound spring, ready to unwind explosively at the first opportunity. Frequently, as we in Conroy went about our everyday business, we were witness to a convulsive release of her emotions, if not the direct object of it. But happily, I am obliged to add, once women have had their emotional needs satisfied, they – by and large – put all that behind them, happy to settle back into a humdrum and quotidian routine. This, I would venture to suggest, is where Tania is at right now. The dead calm after the cyclonic storm. I trust it's not just the eye of the storm.

As for men and their egos, look no further than Ray.

When I look back on the punitive measures against Tania that I had endorsed back in the days when she had been free to roam the world outside The Space, I feel guilt and regret. Whatever shenanigans that rascally Ray had been up to, and there were a few, I don't believe Tania had been in any way complicit. I am not proud of my behaviour as John Shepherd's side-kick, or of the 'good cop, bad cop' routine we practised at that time. I have since acknowledged my sins before my panel of Heads and have, of course, apologized to Tania herself. My subservient actions back then were unbecoming in a man who prides himself on beating his own path through life to the extent he would rather falsify his qualifications than submit to another's regime.

Tania didn't believe my apology was necessary and, consistent with the air of calm currently holding sway over her, had insisted all that should be put behind us. According to her way of thinking, everything had turned out for the good, except perhaps for the events that had brought Frances to such an unfortunate end. She didn't speculate on how things might have turned out had Frances survived.

… as for falsifying my qualifications, I have confessed this to nobody. Come now. Do you take me for a complete klutz? …

Something's brewing, she said.

Are you offering me a cuppa? I asked.

Don't play the fool. I'm hearing stories.

From whom?

The natives. Science and Labour. They're up to something.

I shrugged.

Not necesselery, I said.

… it was a point of pride with me that I was so much at home with my second language I could fracture it whenever I liked in the manner of Spooner, Malaprop, and similar …

My flippancy, however, cut no ice with Tania, because at that point I got a lashing from her sharp tongue.

Fuck you, squire, were her terse words. Don't you think I keep my eyes open?

Oh dear, I said, I appear to have underestimated you once again, and …

That you have.

… on consideration, I guess you have a right to know.

That *I* have.

So, I'll give it to you straight.

Thanks heaps.

They're planning to move the ski-poles.

Where to?

Move them. Not *re*move them.

She looked blank.

They're taking up the slack, I said. Two centimetres of slack.

You've lost me.

The Space is shrinking.

She appeared stymied now. I watched her to see how she would receive the news. I imagined I could see the implications taking on tangible form as they flashed across her brow. It was some time before, collecting herself, she sighed first and then spoke. It turned out she knew all along about the possibility of The Space shrinking.

I know what happens next, she said.

Tell me.

It closes in on us fast. Like time was its enemy.

Who told you that?

It's common knowledge.

… so, I thought, not only had she known about the shrinkage. She even knew it changed from a walk to a gallop in the final stages. She was a smart cookie who kept her ear to the ground, not the sort of cookie at all to allow information on the loose to go un-corralled for long …

So, I asked after some moments, what's your plan?

No plan, she replied. We're cactus.

You can do better than that.

Should I take the cyanide pill perhaps?

Over Tania's shoulder, I spotted Ray emerging from the door of the hut, carrying the cage with Jeremy inside. He was headed in our direction.

Ray, I said. Coming this way.

There's a man without a plan, she said. Perfectly happy with his situation. No intention of moving house.

What about you? You having regrets?

About crossing the line?

I nodded.

None, she replied. Life has never been so intense for me since my grip on it came to hang in the balance. I can recommend the experience.

Quality of life. As opposed to mere quantity.

You've nailed it.

I'm happy for you.

You should try it.

Her eyes and voice spoke of the half-joke, but it was the half-serious bit that had me wondering.

I think I'll pass, I said.

We'd find room for you, she said.

Ray was with us now. He hung an enthusiastic Jeremy in the

tree, then stood behind Tania with a proprietorial hand on her shoulder.

What's it cost to join the club? he asked.

You could predict my future, I said. I believe you're good at that.

Only if I can do it from *my* seat.

Tania rolled her eyes. She rose. Tania and Ray changed places. Jeremy squawked by way of objection. Ray was now seated opposite me. Tania stood behind him, her proprietorial hand now on *his* shoulder.

He said, *We must speak to each other only …*

Take it as read, Ray, I said.

He feigned umbrage, but stopped his incantation, for which I was grateful.

You have enemies? he asked.

A few, I replied.

They'll come for you …

That's what enemies do.

… and they'll get you.

And what shall they do with me?

They'll send you down.

Down where?

On a very long journey to where your future gives the nod to your past.

That's it?

That's it.

I gave a short sharp laugh.

But Ray, I said, there's no riddle.

Riddle? he asked.

No spotted cats, no shoelace soup.

Christ, man. You wanted your future and I gave it to you. You want a riddle, you pay extra.

I rose, my face hostage to amusement.

Don't suppose you tell your *own* future by any chance? I asked.

I do indeed, he replied.

Well, I'd be very interested to hear when it is you propose to leave The Space.

Alive?

No joy in the alternative.

Ray gripped Tania's hand, the one resting on his shoulder.

We'll both come out together, he said. And we'll stand shoulder to shoulder with you on the other side.

Deal?

Deal.

I await you.

I turned to go. But as I did, Tania detached herself from Ray, moved to me, and addressed me conspiratorially through the ski-poles.

I *do* have a plan, she said.

Clever girl, I said. Of course you do.

I could tell she was waiting for me to ask what her plan might be but, deviously, I figured she would likely be more forthcoming if I stalled for time. I looked at my watch.

Raincheck. I have things to do, I said. Those enemies of mine are riding high in the saddle, and I hope to head them off at the pass.

Dream Team

The boardroom was located, together with my office and other vital administrative apparatus, in that four-story block in Admin Stem dubbed The Depot by some wag whose identity has been lost to memory. The name had stuck, and we have had to live with it ever since. So be it. It might have been worse.

I entered this boardroom, with Max and Gabrielle in tow. That's Gabrielle Zanders, of course, the TV anchor and journalist, for some time now on semi-permanent assignment in Conroy. Both Max and Gabby had laptops tucked under their arms, indicating they anticipated serious business. It pleased me to see both my sidekicks ready for action.

The style of the boardroom was brute Stalinist. My office next door, spacious as it was, could have served as lobby for this behemoth. It was an austere oblong high-ceilinged job in humdrum beige eschewing the slightest hint of adornment. The main entrance was through a massive oak door in one of the short sides of the oblong but we were privileged to slip in through an inconspicuous private door wedged into a corner on the opposite wall. Our immediate view, as we braved the expanse, was of a huge polished oval table, in cedar and with seats for twelve, caught up in the perspective of the long sides of the room. Ersatz lighting – cold, intense, and from a concealed source – fell on the scene from who-knows-where in the ceiling. Supplementing this artificial wellspring of illumination, light of a warmer hue intruded from two unshaded panorama windows overlooking Admin Stem, windows collectively taking up the greater portion of one of the long sides of the room.

Max had expressed his desire to decorate this room with murals of his inclination, but I had insisted the room remain free of such distractions to encourage the businesslike posture for which it was intended. I was not against Max's artistic predilections in general. Hadn't I given him *carte blanche* to indulge his inclinations almost everywhere else in Conroy? I just didn't want it here in this room.

This was the room in which, among other things I, with my panel of Division Heads, thrashed out a future direction for the demesne of Conroy.

Max's function on such occasions was much more plebeian than artistic, viz. to record formal minutes, a purpose for which I had groomed him. Gabby's was to invest proceedings with a public face, redolent of transparency and accuracy. Mine was to manage the Chair. We three had collaborated in this way many times before. Once each month, or as the need arose.

But, on this particular occasion, as I absorbed the ambience, it seemed to me things were different, at first in an indefinable way. Something was up. Against my better judgment, it seemed to me, I was about to be taken on a wild ride.

Let me try to explain.

There seemed to be two distinct personas of me, Marius Strangio, in play here: 'me' the *dreamer* and 'me' the *dreamt-of*. Me, dreamer, was an out-of-body critter experiencing remotely and vicariously the antics of me, dreamt-of, who in turn took the part of the high kai of twai of the demesne of Conroy. Accompanying my dreamt-of persona, there were two others of similar ilk: his assistant-cum-lover, Max, and his putative press-secretary, Gabby.

All three dreamt-of personas came across to me, dreamer, as oddly ephemeral, like intruders from another world.

Moreover, the in-your-face solidity of the surroundings was – to the captive mind of my dreaming persona – overlaid with an unfamiliar ghostliness, epitomized by atlantes (aka Atlases) and caryatids (female versions of such) lining the walls, and apparently providing stoic support to a chunky, and strictly functional, cornice. The atlantes, in accord with convention, bore the burden on their stooped backs. The caryatids bore it on their heads, all the better to flaunt the outthrust of their ample bosoms.

I, dreamer, swear these evanescent support staff had never been there before. They were new kids on the block. Interlopers. Nevertheless, here they were on *this* occasion, backdrop to events I dreamt of, quite a deal larger than life, as still as sculptures, as translucent as frosted window-glass, their garments and body hair diaphanous, their mien that of Greek deities. I, dreamer, could not dispel the pervasive suspicion that I knew them.

The presence of these shimmering apparitions, was evidence enough – should evidence be needed – that I, dreamer, was not dealing with reality here. I was in the thrall of a dream of which these chimeras were part.

There were nine of these apparitions. The long side of the room containing the windows housed three. The other long side housed five. One of the short sides, the one containing my private entrance, housed the ninth. As regards gender, the three on the windowed side were female. All the others were male.

Are they late? asked Gabby.

… it was, of course, the dreamt-of Gabby speaking …

We're early, I believe, was my dreamt-of reply.

We, dreamt-ofs, took our seats at the end of the table near the grand entrance, I at the head of the table with Max to my right and Gabby to my left. I poured water for each, and then for myself, from one of several decanters on the table. We waited.

My back was, of course, turned to the big main door, so I anticipated I would be unable to see 'them' as they arrived. I was mistaken. As my dream dictated, 'they' would contrive to enter through a more enchanted portal.

One of the caryatids on the windowed side seemed to blur before my eyes, its ghostly outline quivering as if presenting through a heat haze. A moment later, one of the atlantes on the opposite side did likewise. Then they both stepped forth, leaving unsupported the lengths of cornice for which they could be presumed responsible. As they did so, their outlines became fleshed out with substance and colour. They were no longer wraiths with the constitution of a clear gel. They were people. People all three of us knew and were expecting.

Hi, Desley, I said to the former caryatid.

Desley Longstreet, Head of Admin, sat herself down next to Max.

Hi, Corey, Gabby said to the former Atlas.

Corey Salmond, Head of Visitors, sat himself down next to Gabby.

You winning the game? Desley asked me with sass.

No prizes for losing, I replied.

How's our drop-dead journo? Corey asked Gabby, also with sass.

Beating them off with a stick, replied Gabby.

Desley, in her mid-forties, was at the height of her powers and a force to be reckoned with. She boasted a background in local government somewhere in the wider world. Corey, of similar age, was a genial fellow, who had cultivated a brand of camaraderie spiced with gentle flattery that stood him in good stead in the real estate game. He was Harvey Eanis' replacement in Conroy after Harvey had – ignominiously – gone to God.

Small-talk over, Desley decided to challenge me, off the cuff, with a line of business, a line dear to both our hearts.

That ski-run proposal, Marius, she asked. Any joy yet?

Before I could answer, three more support staff, one caryatid from the windowed side and two atlantes from the side opposite, began to quiver. By dint of their singular *modus operandi*, they transformed themselves from transparent spectres to real people in the flesh. We knew them, of course. They were Col. Karen Wilkinson (Head of Defence), Dr Magnus Christophersen (Head of Agriculture), and Daryl Coleman (Head of Corrections).

As they deserted their posts, I imagined I saw the portions of cornice they left unsupported begin to sag perceptibly.

We have a quorum, said Max.

He opened his laptop and began making entries. Good lad, I thought. He may have had the instincts of an artist but, when the occasion required, he could make the switch to dedicated desk jockey.

Here come the living dead, said Desley.

To the uninitiated, Desley's remark might have been construed as reference to the latest arrivals' former existence as wraiths, but all of us seated at the table knew better. That was only half the story. The Divisions they headed up were widely referred to as 'zombies', because they performed no identifiable function. They were sustained only by the hope that Science might come up with some skerrick of intelligence apropos The Space, such skerrick giving their briefs relevance and propelling them into the limelight they craved.

And, even before they took their seats at the table, they made known their gripes. Magnus, who struck me as a graceless knucklehead, wanted a designated daily timeslot for his Division, so his minions could pass vegies back and forth across the interface in an effort to disinfect them. Daryl, a colourless functionary, sought authority to train his personnel in the processes of incarceration and release using a pretend Space somewhere within cooee of the real Space. And Karen, the Colonel no less, with her hubris and her military mind-set, was hell bent on deploying troops to the vicinity of Mount Scornful, where they would engage in tactical manoeuvres – for whatever arcane purpose – using the extinct Spaces available to them there.

While the zombie Heads made their petitions, Desley was making a show of her disdain, apathy, and boredom. Totally exasperated with Karen's pleading with its overtones of entitlement, she interrupted the Colonel mid-sentence, addressing her question to the panel as a whole.

Where's Bert Tuesday? she asked.

You mean Mundey, was my response.

I mean Tuesday. The sod's never on time.

Speak of the devil. An Atlas on the side without windows quivered, lurched, and then morphed into a flesh-and-blood presence. The cornice sagged still further where he had vacated it. This new arrival was Bert Mundey, Head of Labour Division.

Greetings, comrades and fellow wankers, he said to the assembly.

Bert, jovial fellow, took his seat, and immediately launched into negotiations with Desley apropos the proposed ski-run, during which class warfare was not long raising its ugly head. Bert and Desley, made for each other, loved playing this game. Karen rolled her eyes.

Point of order, said Daryl.

… Daryl could always be relied upon to make points of order

willy-nilly and, in equally reliable fashion, he was destined to be ignored by all …

At which moment, yet more cornice-wallahs chose to appear. This time it was the last caryatid on the windowed side, and the last Atlas on the side opposite. The cornices on both these sides, now completely lacking in obvious means of support, looked to be on the point of collapse. Somehow, the ceiling above them, though sagging dangerously, held together for the moment.

The new arrivals were Dr Beverley Bancroft, Head of Health Division, and Dr Brian Collyer, Head of Science Division. We acknowledged their arrival with perfunctory waves.

… I should explain things here. That smart-aleck Brian Collyer had recently replaced Steve Crisp as Head of Science. If I'd had any say in it, Steve would have stayed on as Head but Canberra had decided to tempt him with a post outside Conroy. As for Brian taking over Steve's job, my choice would have been for Dr Li Wen to assume the position but I guess the boy's club, by all reports alive and well in Canberra, had had their own thoughts on that matter …

Beverley, though appearing unaware of or perhaps unperturbed by the sagging ceiling, ventured a comment that, to me, was full of unintended portent.

All staying safe, I hope, is what she said.

If you can't be good, said Brian, better be safe.

Regrettably, that was the strength of it. Wisecracks were the order of the day. That's how it was in my dream. Nobody seated at the table, not a single soul, showed the slightest concern about the integrity of what hovered above us. The room's cornice. The room's ceiling. With a mind to head catastrophically south.

I knew better. The fear inhabiting all dreams of such ghastly stripe as this one began to take hold of me. It was *my* fear, and mine alone. Holy Mother of Christ, where was *their* fear? *I* felt it. Why not *them*?

My gut wanted to do what guts do when panic struts the stage.

My spine wanted to do what spines do. And, as for my headspace, it was suddenly invaded by the lyrics of a popular song of recent times. Lyrics of such songs, it goes without saying, are open to interpretation. I saw the words as questionable advice to those stalked by fear. From the stalker.

> Don't you shiver.
> Don't you shiver.
> Sing it loud and clear.
> I'll always be waiting for you.

But life, I told myself, had to go on whether fear lurked or not. I was Chair of this panel. It was incumbent on me to get a grip on myself. Gut, settle down. Spine, stop shivering. Lungs, take in deep breaths please.

Beverley and Brian seated themselves.

The meeting moved on to progress reports – as dry as the terrain of Atacama itself – from the only two Heads who were in any real position to deliver such. Brian first, and then Beverley. And just as eyes round the table were beginning to glaze and heads to nod, the last member of my panel decided to put in a late appearance, to quit his phantasmal role beneath his patch of cornice, that is to say the patch on the short side toward which I faced, the side owning my private entrance. He, last of the wraiths, had decided it was time to take on a more carnal role, a human semblance.

There he stood. Alain Valery. Head of the Conroy Division of Homeland Security.

We have a full house, said Magnus in his booming schoolmasterly voice.

There was nothing of the *joie de vivre* about Alain that his name, by virtue of its resonance, might suggest. No Gallic good cheer had ever, even fleetingly, crossed his path. No French insouciance. Without a word, he planted his miserable backside in the only vacant seat available at the table and appeared to stare blankly at nothing.

We were now one short of the number required for a last

supper. And, if not supper, then something else with the distinct essence of finality was on the menu. Above us, the ceiling was swaying like a tipsy trollop on a high-wire. I was the only person in the room showing any concern. The others didn't appear to have noticed.

But when Alain had quit his post, a tipping point had been reached. The straw had broken the camel's back.

And so the whole lot came down in an almighty rush like the deluge of water in a lavatory. The sound was appalling. We were in the temple of Dagon when Sampson crushed the pillar to his manly chest. We, the unwary, playing out our petty games beneath the avalanche of masonry, were gone guys.

Ahhhggg …

Me, both dreamer and dreamt-of, now pulled off, in the nick of time, an impressive feat of encapsulation, proving 1+1=1. The 'me' emerging from this timely consolidation was the *everyday* me, the 'me' of the undreamt world, a world that affirmed reality.

Eschewing dream, I, of the everyday, found myself in my bed in my penthouse apartment, which is – to my considerable relief – where I had been all along. I propped myself up on a creaky elbow. Max, beside me, was sleeping soundly, exuding gentle snores. There was an animal beauty about him I found most becoming. Beneath his hazel eyes was an insistent shadow of darkest stubble, terrain for his prominent nose and well-upholstered lips. Above them, scraggy and dark, were motile brows and an enchantment of scalloped curls. The gentle arc of his body beneath the sheets was a reminder to me of past pleasures.

Let him sleep on, I thought. He looks so peaceful, and he's not needed on deck for some hours yet.

I rose to my feet. Above the bed hung the mud-map of Conroy, painted for me by our talented Tania, replacement for the inimitable *Gros Bonnets* that now graced my office. It was early in winter. Flooding through the window, the dazzling light spoke of a substantial dump of overnight snow. I moved across and looked out. Sheets of white reached out to the mountain, pale pillow against a headboard of blue. It might have been created afresh just for me that very morning.

But the mountain was no newborn. And it did nobody's bidding. It was a fiendish miscreation, bent perhaps on consuming all who dared to draw breath.

It said, *I'll always be waiting for you.*

Portrait of the Artist

I can think of no better adjective to describe Max Baldock than 'protean'. Not only was he my tender lover, but he filled to perfection the role I had pressed on him, viz. that of administrative assistant. Additionally, he contrived somehow to maintain his passion for the practical aspects of what might, in a limited sense, be termed community art. One might be hard pressed to decide which of these three guises was his preferred role.

How did he pursue the practice of his art? What was his *modus operandi*?

Because I was – and still am – his lover, and *ergo* he confided in me – and still does – I am able to satisfy your curiosity re this matter. First and foremost, he demanded obscurity. He despised publicity. His art was the point, not the artist. I agreed that, if secrecy were his goal, I would help him maintain it insofar as I was able, warning him that insatiable curiosity in the face of mystery was a ubiquitous human foible.

His anonymity established within such limits, he would identify a target in the demesne, e.g. a shop-front, following which he would press me to negotiate on his behalf with the proprietor. Then, negotiation successful, he would 'case the joint', sitting outside in his Lecky trying to look as inconspicuous as possible, making sketches. After which, in the privacy of his studio, part of the quarters I had wangled for him in the same block as my apartment, he would prepare in advance as much of the *materiel* as possible. This included, among others, the use of offset printing, the embrace of lithography, the cutting of stencils, etc. These processes came to define the essence of his art form.

But sooner or later, his moment of truth having arrived, it was imperative he put in an appearance *in situ*. He would choose his time carefully. Speed and cover – to his mind – were of the essence. He didn't want to hang around any longer than necessary. He didn't want to be sprung by some interfering Charlie. Typically, this would mean a 3 a.m. assignment on a dark and frigid morning when nobody was likely to venture out. Dressed like an Eskimo against the alpine chill, he would erect scaffold, clamber aboard, juggle his stencils, spray-cans of acrylic, etc., and be in and out in thirty minutes max. Job done. Signed off with a cryptic letter B. Later that morning, his finished work would astound passers-by, left wondering who the good fairy might have been, or what the B signified.

His work would always have a twist. He had no truck with 'straight', a boring concept of no interest at all to him, manifest only in the sides of rectangles, the edges of cubes, and the like. But 'twist' was cool. 'Twist' was the kink in the devil's tail. Usually, the twist would take the form of a private joke, an inbuilt irony for the discerning, a dog whistle to the elect.

Nothing epitomized this elitist signalling more than his design of the DETA logo, adorning – among other things – every Lecky in Conroy. A vague niggle in the brain told punters that something about the logo didn't feel right. Something didn't scan.

But only the most astute of punters would get to put their finger on this niggle. The logo took the form of a heraldic shield with diagonal band. And the band was a forward slash, not the conventional backslash. The bastardly bend sinister.

This was vintage Baldock.

Max's cover *was* blown, but on only a handful of occasions. I considered it my job to deal with these infractions as they arose. Basil Shirley, *maitre d'* at the Pig's Ears, was one person who stumbled on the identity of the phantom artist. I didn't bother asking Basil how he managed to do this, but I did bring pressure to bear that I hoped would impel him to seal his lips. One of my privileges as Administrator of Conroy is the power to do such things.

Max was grateful, and said so.

I'm obliged, captain, he said.

Don't mention it, I said.

I promise I'll return the favour.

I kissed him with a gentle passion.

You haven't exactly been indifferent to my needs, I said.

Before too long, much of the landscape of low-set blunt-ended semicircular prisms comprising the majority of the residential and recreational premises in Conroy had been made over in colourful and quirky fashion. An observatory and planetarium in Science Stem, called *Star Trek*, offering – for a price – telescopic views of the night sky and other cosmological treats, was graced – courtesy of an artist unwilling to be known – with a frontage suggestive of the man in the moon, complete with cratered face, monocle, and lewd wink. A *patisserie* in Agriculture Stem, called *Tarte au Citron*, boasted a facade in the form of a half lemon slice, its bright yellow segments (bizarrely) adorned with a grasshopper in lime green and an ant in rust red.

By such means, Max had, in splendid obscurity, transformed many of the presenting surfaces of our demesne into outdoor works of art.

I'd like to recount to you a special moment I was privileged to share with him. It was a couple of years after the occasion of my portentous dream, around the high point of my incumbency. I happened to suggest to Max late one fine afternoon late in autumn that we put in an appearance that evening at *The Tight Spot*. We were a well-established item at the time, an item known to all and sundry.

What the freak for? he asked.

Just for the hell of it.

Conservative suits were *de rigueur* for us when on duty. There, we had an image to uphold. But suit and necktie would not cut the mustard for a visit to a gay bar. *The* gay bar of Conroy. A place for hooking up, for flaunting one's private proclivities, and for sampling all manner of forbidden fruit.

The gear I chose for the occasion was pale grey slacks, tailored light-tan leather shoes from my distant homeland, pale blue cashmere jumper, and rainbow cravat. Max, much more daring, decided on gear too flamboyant for my taste. Suffice to say its least outrageous items included boots in lollipop-pink, jeans skinny tatty and embroidered, singlet with horizontal grey stripes, glasses dark brand-named and horn-rimmed, and baseball cap in pink bearing the message, My Finger Salutes You. Oh dear. And this from a man whom, I had been lead to believe, liked to keep a low profile.

Max, darling, I asked, what *are* you thinking?

His reply came by way of a croon.

I do it my way, were its words.

So, come the night, we entered through the *faux* Stonewall Inn arches. The facade was not one of Max's creations. He would never have had truck with anything so blatantly derivative.

Once inside, we were faced with a scene of unabashed gaud, a scene in which Max's clobber was par for the course. In these traps, I found myself underdressed. The place was swinging, mostly with men who must be presumed gay, but with a sprinkling too of women who preferred an intimacy with those of their own gender. Its ample width, enabled by the merger of two Quonsets, allowed for a long bar to the right of the entrance and for the consequent swarm of patrons in its orbit. Behind the bar, were row upon row of bottles, their multicoloured iridescence seeking to advertise the moonshine they contained. Here it was all bright lights, but should one press deeper into the premises, there were plenty of secluded crannies wrapped in darkness, offering the sort of privacy some of the clientele might, in the course of events, crave.

We were, of course, acknowledged by present company, and we acknowledged many of these rabid ragers in return. In the evening's crowd there were innumerable faces we were accustomed to seeing by day in white coats, blue coats, or other varieties of uniform. Some showed their appreciation of our unannounced presence by dint of cheers, foot stamping, and wolf whistles. We were royalty of a kind. Since taking up residence in Conroy, I had never made any secret re my sexual preference, and the upshot was that hereabouts we were totally among friends.

Max and I watched the progress of the meat market with, we dared to hope, not too much overt condescension, grateful we no longer felt pressed to be part of it. And, talking of meat markets, there, as large as life, was none other than Magnus Christopherson – in leather, the old stager – his arm around the waist of a likely lad from Labour who, in deference to the night's festivities, had swapped his Hi-Vis for tank-top and shorts. The former stopped well short of the navel, and the latter were skimpy, tight-fitting, and – to seriously understate the case – short. I caught Magnus' attention and fluttered my fingers in his direction, a non-verbal Hello. He, jovial fellow, grinned broadly by way of reply. Max and I hadn't realized until now that Magnus was part of the fraternity. Well, well, it just goes to show one never can tell, can one?

Leather's so very *not* in vogue, Max confided to me.

I joined the melee at the bar to secure us drinks.

Driving By

Later that evening, as we enjoyed a post-coital snuggle in bed, my mind turned nostalgically to matters of comparable bliss from my past. Sportive moments back in *Milano* with earlier lovers. Athletic moments skiing the *Dolomiti di Brenta*. Operatic moments with Giuseppe Verdi in the *Teatro alla Scala*. Epicurean moments over pasta at *Ristorante Savini*. Conversational moments with my Aunt Claudia in her cosy *apartamento*.

I was on the point of succumbing to that strange drowsy

interlude typically presenting just prior to full-blown sleep, the interlude when one's short-term memory decides to shut down for the foreseeable. True to form, it left me scrambling to recall the fragment of thought so vivid in my mind just a second or two ago. Fragment of thought? What fragment of thought?

Just before I drifted off into total oblivion, the real world reasserted itself with a vengeance. The air crackled with a repetitive chatter bringing to my mind the distant sound of automatic gunfire. One burst only. I waited for more, but there *were* no more. I sat up in bed. My mind asked the usual questions. Did I *really* hear something? Was it the backfire of an internal combustion engine? Was it fireworks?

When the sirens sounded down in Admin Stem, I suspected the worst. Perhaps it *had* been gunfire. The insistent shrieking of these non-verbal calls to action now demanded my full attention. One by one, their sound faded in volume and in pitch as the emergency vehicles that owned them headed off towards The Roundelle. I leapt from my bed and, hurriedly sliding on trousers shirt and shoes, made myself passably decent. I was Administrator, and duty was calling.

Max, dazed, sat up in bed.

Go back to sleep, ducks, I said. I'll handle this one.

Seizing myself a Lecky, I made for The Roundelle and, following the sirens, turned left onto that grand circle. Said sirens were now doing their thing off to the right, down the road giving access to The Space, which fact made my heart sink. I asked myself anxiously, Were Ray and Tania alright?

Turning down this road, I came across the emergency vehicles stopped dead before the retrofitted boom-gate, sturdy and fully automated now to discourage impulsive *blitzkrieg*. Just as I pulled up behind them, John Coffee emerged from his guard post to open it. Strange, I thought. What was he doing on duty at this ungodly hour?

He didn't look like he'd been wrenched brutally from slumber just this very minute as I assuredly had. His grooming was shipshape. This was not somebody who had only now been caught up in a frantic struggle to find the correct sleeve for his arm, the correct trouser for his leg. This was somebody who had had ample time to put a comb through his hair. And to tick the boxes of that irreverent genuflexion, the routine check for spectacles, testicles, watch, and wallet.

When the convoy of vehicles screeched to a ragged halt outside The Space to which Mr Coffee had d-d-deigned to grant them access, I was relieved to see Ray and Tania, both unharmed, standing by the conversation post in their nightwear, illuminated by a galaxy of headlights. Tania's garb was rendered transparent by the ferocious lights, and it crossed my mind she had a most passable body for a short-arse. Jeremy, the gang-gang, his cage dangling in the usual tree, was making a screeching noise suggestive of a multiplicity of fingernails across sandpaper.

All of our police force were new hands at the game. When they emerged from the convoy, dragging their grotesque shadows behind them, they hung around in a state of confusion, not at all sure how they should proceed, waiting perhaps for Godot to tell them. Minutes earlier, they had flung on their uniforms in a tearing hurry, and it showed. Caps were askew and shirt tails were hanging loose. They had never before had to deal with anything of this nature.

Some had decided to examine the wheel tracks in the slush for clues, but quickly concluded this was a pointless exercise. The tracks of their own vehicles had muddied the waters, figuratively and literally. The crime scene was – to use words John Shepherd might have used – corrupted to buggery.

One of these rookie coppers, a young woman whose eager approach belied her lack of experience, had taken it on herself to approach the conversation post with the intention of plying Ray and Tania with a series of inane questions.

What happened? was her first question.

The adrenalin rush was evident in the eyes of the Space-dwelling couple.

God said 'Let there be bullets', replied Tania. And lo. Bullets were not in short supply.

A drive-by, said rationalist Ray by way of contradiction. Aimed one quick burst at our hut. Then they were out of here before you could say Kalashnikov.

Like shooting fish in a barrel, said Tania. We were the fish.

And what was your response? was the rookie's next question.

We hit the deck, replied Ray. Pissed in our daks. As you would.

No injuries?

Only fallen arches, but I think that was pre-existing.

What damage was done?

The fuckers took out a window. And otherwise improved the hut's ventilation.

Other contenders were beginning to arrive. Several Heads of Division put in an early appearance, including Karen Wilkinson and Cory Salmond. And Gabby Zanders came, of course, but given the assiduity for which she was renowned, I found it surprising she hadn't been first on the scene for this most newsworthy shindig.

As the various parties shuffled around, their elongated shadows slashed the floodlit scene like scissor blades. Voices reverberated in the clear night air under a canopy of stars whose clarity was scarcely believable. The night was staging a theatrical subplot of some cogency, and my mind was in thrall to it.

Col. Karen, putative expert on military matters, was examining empty shell casings retrieved from the scene by the police.

Not one of ours, said Karen.

Whose then? asked Gabby.

Class of weapon favoured by the gangs.

Organized crime?

Precisely.

In Conroy?

You'd better believe it.

But Gabby, pricking up her ears, was onto a more interesting conversation. She was hearing snippets of a promising exchange between Cory and one of the male cops. Leaving Karen to muse further on the criminal community's hardware of preference, she moved off in that direction.

… they get in? Cory was asking.

Same way we did, replied the cop.

Wasn't the boom-gate down?

Apparently not.

John Coffee not in charge?

I assume he was.

We need to speak to him.

We'll follow that up.

Could we do that now?

Now?

Like now.

The cop was spurred to action by Cory's insistence. Apparently able to lay claim to a modicum of seniority, perhaps on account of his gender, he ordered the young rookie, who had earlier interviewed Ray and Tania, to seek out John Coffee. The stuttering giant, courtesy of Cory, was now flagged by the law as a person of interest.

Gabby followed the enthusiastic young rookie off in the direction of the guard post in search of a story.

How had I, Marius Strangio, been conducting myself all the time the wheels of forensic investigation had been turning? An excellent question, I grant you, and I shall give you the answer it deserves. My instincts are non-interventionist. I prefer to sit back, taking everything in, nodding my head occasionally, and refraining from interfering until asked. Certainly, there can be no doubt I am the boss. But those in my charge are the experts in their field, at least nominally. If I were to tell them how to suck eggs, they would legitimately take umbrage. Umbrage is their right even when they don't really know what the hell they are doing. The more incompetent they are, believe me, the more umbrage they shall take.

So, what is the point of my being here at all? Is my position logically justified? It is all a matter of perception which, in this game, is everything. One thing I gleaned from my studies at the *liceo* back in my mother country, the *liceo* to which my late aunt had sent me, was a philosophical point made over a thousand years ago by a Chinese gentleman whom I recollect went by the name of Lao Tzu.

This ancient luminary had given some thought to the issue of leadership. A person may properly assume the stamp of great leader – so Lao maintained – when and if, in the aftermath of some significant accomplishment, those in his charge felt moved to say to each other, What a superb job *we* did that day.

I believe this to be a truth valid to this day. Valid across all space and time. And across all cultural divides.

Gabby and the young rookie returned. The young rookie, downcast now, reported to her putative superior that John Coffee was nowhere to be found. Gabby reported the same to me.

I asked myself, Where did this leave us? Mr Coffee, if he could be found, was an employee of the Division of Homeland Security. So, could I assume his suspect behaviour was a response to orders from his employer? Was the drive-by, then, orchestrated by Homeland Security? And, if so, what could be their motive? And did this event, and any similar events the future might hold, signal a challenge to my leadership?

What might have been Lao Tzu's take on these matters? How might he have recommended the situation be handled?

So many questions.

A Ski Jaunt and Its Aftermath

For weeks following the drive-by, many of us were of unhinged mind. Certainly, *I* was spooked. Walking the streets, I flinched each time a Lecky passed me from behind, as one flinches at a sudden flash of lightning during a storm. At night, I lay awake waiting for a burst of gunfire, as one waits for the roll of thunder.

When, a week or so after the event, the panel of Division Heads gathered in the boardroom according to schedule, the drive-by was – predictably – the main topic for discussion. Alain Valery, who might have been expected to know more than the rest of us, didn't bat an eyelid. Or so we assumed. We couldn't see his actual eyelids because his gaze was cast down obdurately as if he were examining the fine grain in the cedar table.

A motion, proposed by the Colonel, seconded by Daryl Coleman, and passed unanimously with one abstention, demanded the requisition of records from Checkpoint Charlie on the eve of the event and for the few days following.

I'm not sure what we expected these records would tell us when and if we got our hands on them. In the first instance, they would certainly have been redacted comprehensively by Homeland Security before they reached us. And in the second, we had Buckley's chance of identifying the culprits from a bald list of names. How could we? None of us could lay claim to any familiarity with the Who's Who of the criminal community.

Our demand for release of these records was not the only business arising that day in respect of the drive-by. A further motion, proposed Salmond, seconded Christopherson, and once again passed unanimously with one abstention, authorized a reward of $10,000 for information leading to the arrest of the perpetrators.

The records from Checkpoint Charlie, when they were eventually released with great reluctance by Homeland Security, told us nothing of significance. Nor did anybody claim the reward.

As the weeks passed without further display of criminal firepower, our anxiety – and the vigilance consequent on it – subsided gradually until it merged with the background of everyday stressors always at play in a place like Conroy. Even our

Spacepersons began to relax their guard, repair their bullet-ridden hut, and put their reminiscences to bed.

Did I say, A place like Conroy? OMG. There *was* no place in this wide world like Conroy, except Conroy.

Then winter arrived, bringing clear blue skies and an abundance of powder snow. Some of us, the aficionados, now turned our minds to pleasures appropriate to the season. The drive-by was history. We had done what we could and let no man/woman say it wasn't enough.

One vice I *didn't* share with Max was cross-country skiing, such indulgence the upshot of my background in Lombardy where ski fields are plentiful and, more recently, of my sorties with Klaus into the Australian Alps. Nordic skiing, as it is also known, is not so popular with the punters as is downhill skiing, where gravity does all the work, and the aforesaid punter only needs parade his/her skill or lack thereof while hanging out for the delights of *après-ski*. To tell the truth, I am a fan of both modes of skiing. I am no purist. I like to see people enjoying themselves. But the accoutrements necessary for the downhill variety – ski-lifts, chalets, and Harvey Wallbangers – were pipedreams only, still in the early planning stages in Conroy.

Not so for cross-country. No need to dream. No accoutrements were needed bar those provided by nature, supplemented by a frugal attitude and a free spirit.

So, one fine winter's afternoon, when things were quiet at The Depot, I left my estimable assistant in charge of the fort while I took to the lower slopes of the mountain. At the rear of my office, I strapped on my skis and set to it. What a rare luxury it was to move so seamlessly, and in a trice, from a work environment to one of leisure.

Travelling solo, I glided lightly over the flat stretches and tacked across the pull of gravity on any slopes that might present. I planned one day when I had plenty of time at my disposal to circumnavigate the mountain, but today I intended nothing more than a brief sally within cooee of the southern Stems. The exercise was both a release from the stresses of my professional duties and an affirmation of the freedom granted me courtesy of these duties. I was my own man on the slopes as I was in my office. How good is that?

But as I zigzagged down the slopes just north of Admin Stem, I saw Gabby and a camera crew standing near the court at the end of the *cul de sac*. Obviously, I was their target. At first, I was miffed by this invasion of my private moment. Then I remembered I had given Gabby the O.K. to organize a shoot about contemporary life in Conroy, and that I hadn't specifically forbidden her to video me. Quelling my initial anger, I waved to them with one of my stocks and resolved to give her a benign roasting when we next talked.

This incident brought to my mind some rancorous memories.

Specifically, I recalled the shit-storm with which I had been obliged to deal when the media had first descended on Conroy in the early days. Obsessed with their mission, each of them itching to be the first dude to break the news, and each armed with state-of-the-art audio-visual recording technology, these jumped-up envoys of the fourth estate had arrived uninvited, showing scant consideration for – and constantly getting under the feet of – Conroy permanents just going about their legitimate business.

They had treated Ray – then the sole resident of The Space – with the disdain typically reserved for a zoo animal. Ray, outraged, had retreated to his hut, refusing to co-operate with them. Their reaction had been to stake out the hut, keeping well clear of the diabolic interface of course, waiting for their prey to emerge, salivating at the prospect of a photo scoop. An avalanche of complaints had soon reached me, and not just from Ray.

I had acted.

Proper respect must be shown, I had insisted, by *all* visitors and ergo by the press. To this end, I had demanded these notebook-wallahs and their hangers-on obtain advance approval through my office for any future ventures they might contemplate. They had screamed about their rights. But freedom of the press be buggered. I had determined to take a hard line. Those refuseniks not complying with my directives, I would ban.

When the dust had settled, only one journalist was left standing. Gabrielle. She had shown Ray the proper respect, and – Holy Mother of Christ – a little more besides. But, for the most part, the blackguards I had blackballed hadn't gone quietly. A few returned, chastened, prepared to abide by my rules. The majority, though, wouldn't do the decent thing. They continued to cover the Conroy story *in absentia* and from a contrarian point-of-view.

They had swallowed, or had at least pretended to swallow, the line put out by the Minister of Homeland Security, never a great fan of my administration. Nor of John Shepherd's. And the line advanced by said Minister and his cronies, had been a shrill version of the justifiable alarm the general public was feeling apropos of The (people-eating) Space. Shrill? And as raucous, I might add, as a bash of off-key bagpipes. Their message was that something most certainly needed to be done – exactly what they conveniently forgot to say – and was decidedly *not* being done by my administration.

I had made new enemies. Whatever. Absolutely just an unintended consequence of my exercise of power.

I put these memories aside.

It was time to quit the slopes. I had plans for the remainder of the afternoon. Crossing the small snowbound cemetery, I reached The Roundelle where – skis offering no advantage here – I struggled across the bitumen like an enlarged version (so I imagined) of some demented praying mantis. There I gained the track leading to The Space. I was forced to pause here to give way for a Hertz van making its exit. This, I presumed, was the fortnightly run from Melbourne, just finished delivering framing jobs for Ray and Tania. An expensive operation, I figured, but one about which the pair were adamant. It allowed them to keep their hand in while confined, so to speak, at pain of death.

Working my stocks with vigour, I glided to the boom-gate. Here, executing a sideways slew, I braked to a halt. John Coffee's replacement pressed the necessary buttons, the gate opened, and I continued on through to the black hole at the centre of our penny-ante universe.

... yes. You heard right. John Coffee was gone. He had not been seen, nor had his stutter been heard, since the night of the drive-by. It was as if, in some seamless operation carried out under cover of darkness, he had been spirited away and a replacement installed ...

All scheduled activities at The Space were finished for the day. Tania, whom I had alerted by text, was expecting me. She was pottering around near the boundary of ski-poles, bent over some wentesters she had apparently snaffled from Science, something I couldn't imagine Ray ever feeling inclined to do. I detached my skis and moved across to my side of the conversation post. She moved to hers.

What are you finding? I asked.

The boundary's still as lethal as ever, she replied.

Would you expect otherwise?

I live in hope.

Why not leave this to the scientists?

My hunches don't scan with their evidence base.

Tell me about your hunches.

Let me cut to the chase at this juncture, giving you – my presumed reader – the gist in *précis* form. Tania's hunches seemed not unreasonable. One of them, her hunch that the mountain was responsible for all the grief – dare I say a mountain of grief – was something I certainly could relate to. Another of her hunches, somewhat anthropomorphic in nature, proposed that said mountain had occasional lapses in concentration and that, during one of these moments, moments when its guard was down, the interface might turn out to be temporarily benign. When first she aired this hunch, I wondered if it might not be a case of wishful thinking.

You trying to second guess the beast? I asked.

Just keeping my ear to the ground, she replied.

So, you think a moment might come when you could make a dash for it? A window of opportunity?

I'm not ready to stake my life on it …

I raised my eyebrows.

… quite yet.

She made it clear she was not about to do anything hasty. She was trying to figure if, apropos of these presumed lapses on the part of the renegade mountain, there was some sort of pattern, a method in its madness. Were these lapses more prone to happen at specific times of day? For certain phases of the moon, mayhap? When dozing, did the peak inadvertently give out any observable indications, dare I suggest leonine snores? Were there any clues to be found by sifting through the daily accumulation of animal corpses? Could some variety of human intervention, yet to be identified, serve to distract the mountain thereby causing it to drop the ball? Might not the first peoples, worthy custodians of the land, throw some light on the subject? Everything was on Tania's metaphoric table.

And Ray's involvement? Stressing that she loved the guy dearly, she went on to say his commitment was strictly to the here and now. Hadn't I noticed his eyes light up when called upon to play the role of guru, either as an oracle, or (more controversially) as enabler of the anti-infective treatment? Didn't I not see how wedded he was to his daily routine? Yes, I affirmed, I *had* noticed that was how he got his jollies. How could I not? Well then, she pleaded, it would surely be cruel to deny him such simple pleasures. Please, she went on, won't you accept there is a division of labour here? *He* predicts the future, and *I* make it happen.

Perfectly reasonable, I said. Now I've a favour to ask of *you*.

What is it? she asked.

If the time comes to activate your escape plan …

When, not if.

This stopped me in my tracks.

I'm impressed, I said.

The impressive I do on a daily basis, she said. Spectacular may take a little longer.

O.K., Wonder Woman. When the time comes for your spectacle, I want to be there to see it happen. Do you think you can arrange that?

Not a problem. I'd insist you be there in any case for such a hysterical moment.

… a tiny brainfart sounded in my head. It was accompanied by the reverberant thought, *Santo sgombro*, this woman is taking the piss …

You mean 'historical'? I asked.

Can't we have both? she asked.

Not necesselery.

She smiled. I pointed towards the hut, which I assumed was where Ray was currently cooling his heels.

Will he come out with you? I asked.

I'm not leaving him behind, she replied.

He won't look back?

What if he does?

Pillar of salt?

He won't look back.

Moon, Mountain, and Megaphone

That evening, I was alone with a glass of cognac in the living area of my apartment. Max was busy in his studio close by, wrestling with pre-production of his next masterpiece, the facade for a popular fashion house in Agriculture Stem.

Presently, the only light in the room was from the standard lamp behind me. As a consequence, my eyes were drawn to the picture window beside me, dominated by a choice view of Mt

Redoubt. Its shape was that of a big cat, but its complexion – as determined by a near full-moon – reminded me of a pearly white – and improbably gigantic – line of cocaine.

Max burst in. Crossing to me, he kissed me on the lips.

Cognac? I asked.

Raincheck, he replied. I'm out of here as soon as I find my lino cutter. Seen it?

Try the drinks cabinet.

He clicked his fingers.

Where else? he said.

While he rummaged in the semi-darkness, I took the opportunity to seek his opinion on a matter currently in my thoughts.

You spoken to Ms Chalmond recently? I asked.

Tania? he replied.

We know another Chalmond?

His reply was evasive.

Maybe I have.

What do you think she's up to?

Nookie?

24/7?

Found the beast.

He brandished the lino cutter triumphantly.

What else is she up to? I asked. Spill it.

I think she's trying to talk to the fucking mountain.

He dashed out the door without further comment. I shrugged.

I took a sip of cognac. So, I mused, Tania regards the mountain as a sentient being with whom she can hold conversations. Or so Max would have it. Turning towards my privileged view of the mountain, I wondered what I might say to the beast, should dialogue be a possibility, and should I feel moved to participate in such. In that moment, I fancied Mt Redoubt was actually inviting me to communicate. I took another sip of cognac and used my tongue to spread its soporific warmth around my mouth.

What is your agenda? was the query I imagined I put to the moon-blessed monolith, in response to its putative overture.

I fancied I could hear a muffled reply from the mountain in the form of a deep-throated whisper, a signal carried on the back of a reverberating Ooommm. Hardly the most cogent answer to my question. But, of course, one could not expect, even in the wilds of one's imagination, the mountain to be fluent in English. Indeed, the fact it could reply at all was surely an eventuality of no small significance. Now all that was needed was a decent translator …

… or a reality check. Get your shit together, I told myself. Mt Redoubt was assuredly *not* a sentient being. It was only a hunk of inert rock. Consequently, it was incapable of speaking to me, except in my excessively fertile fantasies.

But I was unable to suppress completely my notion that the mountain was sentient. And maybe, just maybe, it had been speaking to Tania. To Tania, specimen of humanity, recipient of sentiency, denizen of The Space, hostage of said mountain.

Once again, I gave my imagination free rein. I pictured Tania this very instant, sitting at the conversation post, drenched in ambient moonlight, engaging the mountain in discourse, pressing the mountain for answers just as I had done in my small way. To stay warm, she had wrapped a blanket over her flimsy nightwear, the same garment she had been wearing on the occasion of the drive-by. The dialogue was passing through Ray's double-sided picture frame, which – in deference to its intended function – was amplifying the discourse in both directions. Tania spoke to the mountain as if through a megaphone. The mountain spoke back to her as if through a megaphone.

And, in the scenario my imagination wove, both parties understood each other *sans* language barrier, with a clarity brooking neither denial nor excuse.

Why are you doing this to us? Tania asked the mountain.

The mountain's reply, conveyed on the back of a thunderous

Ooommm, seemed to come from all directions at once, as if leaking out of the air itself.

Who might 'us' be? asked the mountain by way of reply.

Ray Cromwell and I.

I am just playing my allotted part.

Who does the allotting?

You don't know?

No.

You really *don't know?*

I told you. No.

It is Magna Mater.

Magna who?

Magna Mater. Call her Gaia if you will.

I'll play your game. Let her be Gaia. So why is Gaia doing this to us?

The mountain elaborated at length, or so I imagined. And this is the spiel I fancied Tania heard:

Gaia is doing this in order to let you know, by way of a lesson, that you and your melange of upstart apes cannot presume to be masters of the universe. That is just an arrogant delusion on your part. It is an insult to Magna Mater and to the natural scheme of things.

Ray and I have no such presumption.

Prove it.

Let us out of here first …

Oh ho. You wish.

… and I *shall* prove it.

Prove it first, and then *I shall let you out.*

My reverie was interrupted. Max came charging back. He settled on the arm of my lounge chair, his face eager, and his arm around my shoulder.

I'm ready for that cognac, he said.

Profitable evening's work? I asked.

My art is ready for launch.

What does that mean?

It'll either charm or offend. No middle ground.

Shit, it *must* be good.

His eyes narrowed in response to my flippancy, but there was mirth in them. He rose, moved to the drink cabinet, and raided it once again, this time for its fare of alcoholic sustenance. When he had poured himself a generous measure, he settled back again on the lounge chair with me. For a while we took sips from our glasses and exchanged cognac-charged kisses. A moment arrived when we came up for air and it was then I ventured my question.

What did you mean just now, I asked, when you told me Tania talks to the mountain?

He explained:

Rendezvous in the Wee Hours

Some weeks earlier, Max had been adding the finishing touches to yet another clandestine assignment. This time, it was the facade of a popular wine bar, known as *The Top Tipple*, in Corrections Stem. The hour was 3 a.m. or thereabouts.

Contained in, and restrained by, the semi-circular front face of the Quonset was, in sardonic depiction, a man hanging from the minute hand of a town-hall clock, his trousered legs dangling in a fearsome space some hundreds of metres above traffic. In his free hand, the one not hanging on for dear life, he clutched a flute of champagne. On his face, he wore inebriation, and an exaggerated look of drunken anticipation.

Max's creation was, of course, based loosely on an iconic image from the days of silent movies early in the 20th century. The champagne flute and the smashed expression on the man's face, were Max's unique take on events. As was the style in which the entire box and dice was delivered. Not just a bald photographic image in black and white, but a pastiche of colour, stencilling, and lithography.

Max was in a hurry, lest he should be sprung. He didn't even stop for a quick overview of his finished work. He was itching to be out of here. Hastily, he dismantled his scaffolding, and stacked it together with his other gear in the back of a Lecky van. He drove off accompanied by a sense of relief. He had pulled it off unobserved yet again.

Free as a breeze, purely for pleasure, and motivated by justifiable pride, he treated himself to a tour of his established repertoire scattered throughout the Stems. That is to say, throughout eight out of nine of the Stems. The Stem not graced by his work was Homeland Security, fixed in its determination to maintain an aspect as dreary as a moonscape.

Sufficiently gratified, Max, on a whim, turned into the road giving access to The Space. He couldn't rightly say what impelled him to make this detour. None of his *oeuvre* was to be found here. Pulling up in front of the boom gate, he continued on foot, finding his tentative way with the help of torchlight.

There was no moon.

… it was different in the living area of my cognac-fuelled present, a present where Max was in the process of delivering to me his account of these events. The moon outside my picture window at that time and in that place was bright enough to snuff out the panoply of stars and to lay bare a multitude of earthly sins …

A female voice, alarmed and disembodied, carried on the still air of the moonless night.

Who is it? the voice asked.

Just me, he replied. Max.

Now he saw her or – more accurately – he saw – from whence the voice came – her deep dark diminutive shape in relief against a slightly less dark background. Tania. Who else could it be? She was sitting still, in a meditative pose, at the conversation post. Given Max's description, I pictured her facing off with the outline, dim and blurred, of Mt Redoubt captured for her in the double-sided frame.

What are you doing here? she asked.

What are *you* doing here? he asked.

Sex. And Matters of Similar Moment

When it comes to matters of a sexual nature, I have found women much more willing to confide in a man who is openly gay than in a man who is straight. And when – on top of it all – the particular woman is inclined – by her gregarious nature – to be enthusiastically forthcoming, the confidences shall pour out of her like vomit. So it was with Gabby that day in my office when I dared venture a personal question.

Do you feel miffed that your man was taken from you? I asked.

Ray? she asked in reply.

I nodded.

Why should I feel miffed?

Well, I think *I* might.

Get real. *I* wasn't prepared to move into The Space with him. Not with any man. But *she* was. She deserves him.

No hard feelings?

Give me a break, squire. Do I seem like the jealous type? It was all recreational for me. With the added thrill of flirting with death with each thrust of the pelvis. That's what ...

So graphically put.

... we were in it for. Never for keeps. Unlike a certain novice I know who – can you believe it? – took to spying on us ...

Spying?

On at least one occasion. Wanted to know ...

A knock sounded on my door.

... how it was done, I expect.

Come in, I shouted.

In came the Tweedledum and Tweedledee of Conroy. Desley Longstreet of Admin and Bert Mundey of Labour. They had come to thrash out some dog's breakfast of an agreement on projects slated for completion this financial year, including the downhill ski facility. Gabrielle was here as an interested bystander. Could it be, mayhap, she was dedicated to duty? Or inclined to masochism? Or both?

I organized coffee for the new arrivals. Then, without further ado, they were at each other's throats.

Bert's line mimicked that of union organizer. Desley's beef was fiscal responsibility. They were never going to see eye to eye. But they wouldn't have missed the opportunity to shake each other down, not for quids. This was their chosen sport. A blood sport. I settled back for a torrid session. Gabby, pencil poised, opened her notebook.

Peanuts for monkeys, said Bert. You expect an adequate job, then you bloody well better fork out the lolly for it.

Desley thumped my desk.

Bull-crap, she said. Taxpayers are fed up with paying through the nose for Conroy. It's accountability, you turd. They want to see some half-decent results.

Giddy-up, Neddy, urged Gabby.

And, shazam, they were off at a gallop. While the inimitable pair tore shreds off each other in time-honoured manner – and I knew from experience they were only just getting warmed up – I drifted off into a world inhabited by my own musings.

In a sense Desley was right. Fatigue had accreted – had become rife – in the ranks of the voting public since the early days when DETA and Conroy were spirited into existence by a panicked government. Now the punters wanted an end to it. They had had enough. They were no longer prepared to pay any price. There were rumblings a government conspiracy was afoot. Some Charlies were out there spreading the notion that The Space was an elaborate hoax. John Shepherd himself had warned me of disquiet such as this among the natives.

I was worried. Should such sentiments gather momentum, then maybe the writing was on the wall for my pet hobby. My discretionary venture into social engineering. My junket. My Conroy. Best go softy softly, was the current drift of my thinking.

That's when my desk phone rang. Its strident tones jolted me out of my reverie. Then I asked myself, What's the problem? Shouldn't I view this as a welcome blessing? A break from the brouhaha I – against the odds – was expected to adjudicate.

Excuse me, I said to those assembled.

I took the call. It was from John Shepherd. My heart sank. Calls from John never brought welcome news. They only brought trouble. And, on this occasion, his voice sounded especially terse.

Marius, said John, I'd like you in my office tomorrow morning. Sharp. Take the early morning chopper.

… I ask you. Does that sound like trouble or does that sound like trouble? …

A Toast to Cactus

Next morning. Canberra. John Shepherd's office.

John plugged a memory stick into the USB port, selected 'Start', and then settled back. I was on the edge of my seat. The audio began. We heard the interplay of two voices, first his and then mine. To and fro. We listened in silence. Awed silence.

… won't last forever. Closure is our goal. Our mission statement says as much. So, when the present emergency is done with, when we've slain the giant, when DETA is wound up, when the future of the demesne hangs in the balance, what would you like to do with the freaking thing? Let your imagination run riot.

(A silence. Then it was my voice.)

The demesne?

The demesne.

Well, for starters, I'd drop that word. Demesne, for Christ's sake. Who chose that dreadful word?

I did.

Well, you're welcome to it.

O.K. Call it what you like. Call it a fucking town if you must. The town of Conroy. But remember this. You're *the fucking mayor. And a despot to boot.*

And who might you be? God almighty?

Try 'godfather'?

You want me to spell out a future for our town?

That's the idea.

How about a ski resort?

Follow the money, man.

A casino?

Good boy. Now you're talking. And we want to make a killing, so what sort of client should we cultivate?

High rollers?

You're right on the lolly. We sit back. They rock and roll. We launder their shekels for them. At a price.

(The pause was pregnant with danger, now as it was then. John's voice broke it.)

Our *price.*

John, what you're proposing is unethical. And possibly illegal.

Fuck the ethics.

A faint hiss from the equipment signalled the end of the recording, though not however – or so I recalled – of our conversation from that earlier time. Those last words – 'fuck the ethics' – damning words that were unmistakeably John's, echoed in my head. John reached forward, selected 'Stop', settled back again, and then spoke.

Focuses the mind, wouldn't you say? were his words.

Who organized this abomination? I asked.

The memory stick?

The memory stick. With our freaking words on it.

Homeland Security.

How did they get it?

They commissioned Basil Shirley …

That turd.

… and your ex.

You joke.

No joke.

The bitch.

John raised his hands, palms upwards.

The pressure is on me to resign, he said.

John, they can't mean it.

Never fear. I'm fighting it. My legal team is making a submission to the Tribunal.

What's your case?

My case is I was just taking the piss. Alcohol fuelled. Anybody who bothers listening to the whole fucking conversation, and not just to selected portions of it, shall get the true picture. You know that. You were there.

So they've set you up?

John nodded.

And when we force the buggers to surrender the recording in its entirety, the full fucking transcript from woe to go, that'll become as obvious as balls on a dog, he said.

I'm sorry, John. But rest assured. You can count on my support.

John crossed one leg over the other.

Marius, he said. There's something more.

Yes?

The Prime Minister's asked me to secure your resignation.

Mine?

John nodded.

He wants me gone?

John nodded.

Why? I asked.

Some irregularities have turned up.

What irregularities?

Relating to your qualifications.

Silence was the only suitable response, and silence there was. I imagined I heard my deceased aunt speak from beyond the grave.

Her words were, Oh, *tesoro mio, tesoro mio*, bite you on your cute little bottom, did it?

Eventually John spoke.

It's true then? were his words.

What exactly?

That you faked your qualifications.

It is true.

Why did you do it?

Because I could.

I'm so sorry. Those fucking ferrets find all the deepest holes.

So, …

My single conjunction quivered in the air for a moment.

… are you going to sack me?

I have no choice, Marius.

Come on, John. You protest your innocence. But you'd hang me out to dry.

There's a difference.

Which is?

You have no case.

I felt my jaw drop. The cold-blooded nature of his response took away my breath. I could not believe what I was hearing. My future, such as it was, hung on the moment. The moment duly passed, and my future was cactus.

John rose and crossed to the drinks cabinet.

What's your poison? he asked.

… my world was collapsing around me and – Mother of Jesus – all he could think of was to offer me a drink …

Come now, he said. Let's toast the occasion. Single malt Scotch I think.

He poured shots for two.

John, I said, what the fuck is there to toast?

He passed a drink to my shaking hand. He raised his.

To a singular partnership, he said. Ours. Over many many years.

He tossed his shot back in one.

No bastard, he said, can take *that* away from us.

I slammed my glass down on the table in front of us. Slammed it so hard its contents erupted from it. It was him I should have slammed.

Fuck the partnership, I said. Fuck the toast. And fuck you.

I left.

Last Drinks

I chose the venue carefully. My silent prayer was *che Dio ci auti* and, cognizant of the grace for which He is legendary, I asked that He allow no more bugs to come our way. The scheduled time was mid-afternoon, and therefore not the peak hour. This suited my purpose nicely. And I chose my company carefully. My two most trusted lieutenants. Max delivered the invitations to them personally under the guise of routine memos from The Depot. I didn't want to arouse suspicions. Profiles must be kept low. Heads must be kept down.

So, we met up in a private room at *The Top Tipple*, the bar whose facade Max had recently blessed with his creative efforts. As we entered, I imagined the fellow dangling from the clock was channelling my current perilous situation. Max must have sensed my anxiety because I felt his reassuring hand squeeze mine.

There were four of us. Me, Max, Beverley Bancroft from Health, and Cory Salmond from Visitors. I had often wondered if Beverly and Cory were an item. Slipping on my matchmaker hat, I figured if they weren't an item, then perhaps they should consider becoming one. Such liaisons came with benefits, a particular for which I would vouch.

On my instructions, Max had brought with him a bulging plastic carry-bag. I could see Beverley and Cory were curious about its contents. As a further deliberation, I had insisted Max not take minutes of this meeting. There must be no paper trails.

Cursorily, I glanced round the room for hidden cameras or

mikes. There didn't appear to be any. I had no option but to take the chance. When the other three had taken seats around the table, I – still standing – opened the meeting. As I did so, I sensed the mood change from modestly festive to deadly earnest.

As from tomorrow, were my words, I shall no longer be Administrator of Conroy. Those duties, I am told, shall be assumed forthwith by Basil Shirley.

I took my seat.

Sycophantic sleazebag, said Cory.

Will Max be staying on? asked Beverley.

I shall, said Max.

Beverley chanced a sly smile in his direction.

What fun for you, she said.

An oversight, mayhap, by the new brooms? asked Cory.

And one we shall take full advantage of, I said.

So, what are your plans? asked Beverley.

I shall lay low in Canberra, I replied, until the moment is ripe.

Ripe for what?

My return. I have unfinished business.

I turned to Max.

Show them, Max, I said.

There was an almighty clatter as Max emptied the contents of the carry-bag onto the table. We, all four, were treated to the sight of a cascade of cell phones. Several dozen of them. None would have been classed as recent models.

Burners, I said. Single use. Strictly one per call. Divvy them up.

Security, said Max. Your sole means of communication with Marius in his absence. No exceptions. I'll drill you on the necessary protocol.

How do we dispose of used phones? asked Cory.

Burn, bash, and bury, I replied.

Ex-ter-min-ate, said Max in the monotone of a Dalek.

Is anybody else in on this adventure? asked Beverley.

Only the Space wallahs, I replied. Ray and Tania.

They have burners?

Oh, yes.

Beverley and Cory each scooped up their complement of cell phones, stashing them out of sight in carry-bags provided by Max. I rose to my feet.

Meeting closed, I said. Will you join me at the bar for drinks?

Days of Exile

Canberra, I have said before, is not the most exciting of locales. It is as dull as the proverbial ditchwater, and that's its most biddable aspect. The pollies, wedded to it, make a passable pretence of actually loving it. Otherwise, the city is, to my mind, the ideal place for an addict with a mind to detox. It's a bland precinct, striving to be free of pretentions, distractions, or temptations.

I missed Max. My unrequitable passion for him was a desperate ache. It had occurred to me I could resort to the rough trade for physical gratification, and in fact I knew exactly where to go to follow up this chance, but I resisted. It might be months before I saw him again but I knew Max was doggedly loyal. I tried, with limited success, to console myself with thoughts such as this.

I mostly hung out in the somewhat faded but very central Civic precinct of the city because this was where I crashed at night. The open colonnades abutting the streets there pretended to confer a sense of importance on those who frequented them, but I had lived in *Milano* and I knew the real deal. These were shabby and unconvincing fakes.

My loneliness presented itself to me as a tangible threat to existence. I coped by persuading myself repeatedly that, come *l'inferno* and its full complement of diabolic retinue, I would nevertheless manage to survive. I ate at a solo table each evening, envious of the life swarming around me. I visited my old gym, pumping iron and treading mills in solitary silence. I drank alone in shadowy bars with my demons cavorting all around me. But I would, I would, I would pull through.

Calls to me arrived on my burner phone, usually from Beverley or Cory, sometimes from Max. It was great to hear their voices, especially Max's, but invariably such calls were of little practical consequence. Stripped of its *simpatico*, the stuff they told me I could have guessed, e.g. no-one was enjoying life under Basil Shirley. I told them not to waste time and risk a breach of security on social calls and the like.

… oh, I tell a lie. I *did* glean one item of consequence I hadn't guessed. Tania was *in stato interessante*. Pregnant …

But the call I was really hanging out for was the one from Tania herself, letting me know she and Ray were ready to break out of The Space. I guess, in view of Tania's newly acquired condition, action would now be a top priority. Otherwise, Ray would soon get to play obstetrician, gynaecologist, and midwife, roles he would, I'm sure, prefer to leave to the experts.

I began thinking about whom of my former associates in Canberra I might call on. John Shepherd, of course, was a non starter. If I had come across him by accident in the street, I'm sure I would have decked him. There were business associates out there somewhere from the days I spent resurrecting Lazarus companies for a living. Most, like me, had moved on. There was Klaus Anders, with whom I had tested the slopes in my leisure days at Perisher and such places. Was he still in play?

In the end, I made the worst choice possible. Indicative of how desperate for company I had become, I visited June, my former wife.

She had reverted to her former name of Cartwright. After the false start she had made with me, she now moved in circles more appropriate to her aberrant talents. She had risen to a position on the staff of the Minister for Homeland Security no less, a position with the obfuscatory title, Manager Administrative Services. I found this out, and more besides, one balmy autumn evening at a classy restaurant in the suburb of Manuka. Crisp golden leaves fell silently around us as we ate *al fresco*.

The grapevine has it, she said, you are no longer flavour of the month.

I poked dispiritedly at my pork belly with my fork. She continued to stick the knife into my vulnerable flesh.

Your mistake was to put all your faith in science. Boffins here. Boffins there. Boffins for breakfast, lunch, and dinner. Boffins for bedtime.

What's your problem with boffins? I asked.

Boffins don't count. The laws of physics won't solve the problems of Conroy. What matters are the laws enacted here in our Capital by our elected representatives.

I didn't react. So, she tried another tack.

As for your friend, John Shepherd, he seems …

No friend of mine, I said.

… he seems to think we have more of him on record than we actually have. He wants to acquire by subpoena something he asserts is out there but which in reality doesn't exist. That is a losing strategy.

Not my concern.

So, you're not of a mind to support him?

Hell no.

Wise move. No point flying the flag for a nogoodnik.

May I suggest we change the subject?

More than happy to, pumpkin. Where does your career go from here?

Bit of this. Bit of that.

Best get some qualifications first.

Even by the standards to which she aspired that remark was low. But I didn't take the bait. I stuck things out despite the cards she held. In truth, she held every last one of them and was eager to table them. To play each with a flourish just to watch me squirm. I couldn't take a trick. In the present circumstances, she would have derived satisfaction even had I risen from my seat, upended the table, and stormed out on her, leaving her to deal with the shambles. I asked myself why, in the holy name of Christ, I had set myself up for this humiliation. Clearly, the spiteful bitch was bent on destroying every last vestige of my self esteem.

I repeat, I stuck things out. Eventually, the evening's benign ambience bore witness to a parting of ways as much a relief to me as it was bitter.

Bitter?

Nothing is bitterer than a Canberra winter. And, within days, one such arrived to inflict its pitiless chill on the dreary streets. Is it perhaps nature's way of chastising those with the temerity to maintain a human presence on those mournful plains? Even in the *Dolomiti*, even in Conroy, it hadn't ever felt as miserable as this.

I, prisoner, hunkered down in my studio apartment, my loneliness closing in round me. I looked out my frost-glazed window over roads slick with ice, trees skint of leaves, air sour with fumes, curbs slave to blizzard winds, gutters subject to glacial eddies, work-bound wage-wallahs swaddled in winter woollies, feckless footsloggers sapped of soul, scenes categorically short on hope. I began to envy those I saw outside because I imagined they had more purpose to their lives than me. For pity's sake, I was comparing myself to such a low base.

What was my mission? Only recently I *had* owned one, one redolent of promise. It had been a mission that redeemed my existence, challenged my imagination, and fostered my ingenuity. I had left it behind in Conroy. Now, here in Canberra, my only mission was to survive this winter season without succumbing to the siren call of alcoholic oblivion or otherwise surrendering to abject loneliness.

What had I to help me achieve this modest goal?

For disdainful space, I owned an empty room with four walls, a ceiling, a floor, and a depressing view. For implacable time, I owned empty minutes, hours, days, and months. For conscious mindset, I owned a confusion of memories, regrets, resentments, longings, obsessions, desperate hopes, thwarted ambition, fiery demons, the turn of a hamster wheel, and the tightness of a coffin. For forlorn distractions, I owned frigid streets in which to stretch aimless legs, wretched saloons in which to drown resilient sorrows, solitary dining purely for the sake of sustenance, darkened movie halls selling tinsel town to teenyboppers, and glitzy shopping malls providing retail therapy for mums. Is that a recipe for survival or for the nurture of any remnants of sanity?

The light at the end of the tunnel was nothing but a cruel fiction. My inner scream, worthy of Munch, said, Ahhhggg …

But relief *did* come, God be praised, at which time I crawled out from under the carcass of the black dog to resume an existence. The experience of exile had been a ghastly price to pay for the glory of that moment, and one I hope I shall never have to pay again.

What form did this relief take?

With springtime round the corner, the message I had been waiting for, the message I feared might never happen, the message that finally saved my bacon, arrived. The SMS from Tania, soon to be a mother, was refreshingly brief and to the point. It said:

Come ASAP. We are ready to break out. We shall wait for you as promised. Regards, Tania, Ray, and Jeremy.

Shazam.

I hit the ground running.

Sealed Train and Broken Glass

In truth, it was the snow fields I hit. Launching ourselves from a trailhead south of the city, we set out. Never have I been so glad to leave a neighbourhood behind. *Sia benedetta la liberazione!* With light heart, I showed the finger to Canberra.

We?

My travelling companion was Klaus Anders. I had tracked him down. I figured it would not have been prudent for me to undertake the journey solo. To bring us within reach of the Stems would necessitate a two-day trek across uncharted alpine terrain. Klaus, with his superior skills, was just the right person to serve as my guide and, as for him, he was only too happy for any excuse at all to strap on the skis.

I imagined we really looked the part. Our provisions and gear straddled our backs, secure and dry in bulging slim-line frame-packs. Gore-Tex covered us from head to toe. Wrap-around goggles, as flat as fried eggs, protected our eyes from ambient glare. The music of our motion spoke of our athleticism. Did I say we looked the part? Holy crap, we *were* the part.

At first, we glided lightly, Klaus gracefully and me a shade less gracefully, over the freshly fallen snow. The terrain was flat or gently uphill so our action was akin to skating. When reception and battery life allowed, Klaus used GPS and the compass app on his cell phone to find a path for us through virgin territory. When they *didn't* allow, he resorted to a paper contour-map and physical compass.

The going was easy. The sky was clear and blue. When the gently folding surfaces over which we slithered were sundrenched, their bleached brilliance seared our eyes. When in shade, the uncanny blue they exuded played tricks on our minds. We weaved our way between snow-gums whose olive-green aspect was attenuated by heavy burdens of frozen snow. Rocky outcrops, partly hidden beneath icy overhangs and – I imagine – suggestive to the superstitious of entry points to hell, declared themselves every so often, forcing us to divert from the route our navigation decreed.

Silence hung in the air like an intangible fragrance, forbidding distraction from and adding vigour to our movements. The only sound, music to ears assailed over the weeks and months by urban clamour, was the gentle swish of our ski strokes.

At one of the rocky outcrops, our skis and stocks wedged upright in the snow, we lunched, feeding our faces on sticks of carrot and celery dipped in humus. I began now to piece together fragments from my memory of our past association to help me construct a picture of this person I knew as Klaus Anders.

He was endowed with traits conforming to the classic Aryan myth: fair skin, blond hair, blue eyes, and athletic mien. As I recall, he was a retainer on the advisory staff of our lack-lustre Prime Minister who – God help the man – was surely in need of decent advice. Somehow Klaus had secured for himself the rare luxury of setting his own timetable, by which means he was able to come and go as he pleased. Ergo, he was able, at a moment's notice to drop everything and come with me on this skiing jaunt.

Like most people who moved in Government circles, he had developed over time an innate cynicism that stayed with him even as he moved outside these circles. So, he had difficulty seeing any value in my quest to return to Conroy, dubbing it a futile exercise in subversion which he went along with anyway because he found it diverting.

The way you're coming in, he asked. It's a back door, isn't it?

I wouldn't be welcome at the front door, I replied.

You *will* be at the back door?

Well, there'll be nobody there to stop me.

Are you, perchance, a student of history?

Try me.

Vladimir Ilyich Ulanov. Alias Lenin. He took a sealed train from Zurich to St Petersburg, arriving at Finland Station in said city. That was *his* back door. The welcome he received there was tumultuous. The city changed its name to honour him, and the Bolshevik revolution was launched.

My aims are much more humble.

Our hunger appeased, we set off again. From this point, the going was mostly uphill, and so much more taxing. Klaus seemed not to feel the effort, but for me it was an act of will to keep up. We were no longer skating. Each stride involved placing a ski at an angle to our intended course, with weight on the ball of the foot, so that the body of the ski gripped the snow and held, as it was intended to do. The constant repetition of this action was sapping my reserves by degrees, but my pride would not let me fall behind.

Every so often, there was a moment of relief while Klaus stopped to check our bearing. We hardly talked during these moments. To do so would have had no point and been a waste of much needed energy.

The sun was low in the sky when we scouted around for a camp site. There was no rocky outcrop now against which we could shelter, so we had to settle for a patch of weather-hardened snow to which we could anchor our one-man bubble tents. Using spirit stoves, we cooked up some dehydrated vegetables and ate them with bread. Hardly a gourmet choice, but we were not in the restaurant strip out here.

The bright night of stars hovering above confirmed our experience of the day past and our expectations for the day to come, viz. clear skies. So, grateful for the hand nature had dealt us, we slithered into our tiny tents, and zipped ourselves into our thermal sleeping bags. I fell asleep instantly, such blissful release consequential on my total exhaustion. The months of my exile in Canberra had evidently left me very much out of physical condition.

Morning found me with clear head, new energy, and knackered muscles. After we had broken camp, it was back to the hard uphill slog again. I threw myself into it. Looking ahead of me, I would imagine the horizon of snow against sky signalled the top of a ridge and, ergo, an end to this uphill ordeal but, on reaching said horizon, I saw more, and then more again, of rising terrain to endure. Would it never end?

The afternoon saw me on automatic pilot, body straining, mind disengaged, and soul dispirited. Time and space, our axiomatic inheritance from birth, ceased to have meaning for me. And then, with aspiration all but extinguished, I reached the top of a ridge and saw this one was no illusion. It really was the top this time.

I believe we're here, said Klaus.

Where? I asked.

Finland Station.

Looming above us, to our right and at a distance, was Mt Redoubt. I had never seen it before from this angle, but it was unmistakeable. It was indeed 'The Mountain', the embodiment of supreme unconcern, the arbiter of its alpine domain. Nestling beneath it in a shallow basin were the factorials of human settlement. At this remove, the telltale Quonsets appeared similar to and no bigger than our bubble tents. Yes, this was the demesne of Conroy. Our destination, and my destiny.

Closest to us, down a gentle slope, was the court at the end of one of the Stems. Corrections Stem, by my estimation. A small number of people had gathered in this court, presumably to receive us. At this distance we couldn't make out who they were but the joyful expectation invaded my mind that one of them was likely to be Max.

When it comes time for introductions, said Klaus, I am *not* Klaus Anders.

Who would you like to be? I asked.

You choose.

All that remained for us was to slalom down at our leisure, our tortured muscles readily finding new energy for the purpose. When we reached the point where faces were more than mere flecks, I was able to confirm that Max was indeed one of the group, as were Beverley Bancroft and Cory Salmond. Gabrielle Zanders was also there, having apparently got wind somehow of my imminent return. The remainder of those assembled in the court were sundry administrative personnel I had worked with over the years of my tenure.

My delight was as palpable as the stocks guiding my descent. Our skis throwing up snow, we slid to a halt beside them. In the manner of groupies, they surprised me by breaking into spontaneous applause. There were hugs all round for me, the last and most cherished being from Max. Klaus, having stood back through all this display of camaraderie, needed to be introduced, and this I did.

Folks, I said. Meet Eddie.

Then, while enjoying the glow of our moment in the sun, we busied ourselves detaching our skis.

The rest of the gang are waiting for you, said Beverley.

Where? I asked.

At The Depot. Where else?

Does Basil Shirley approve?

Basil's in the slammer.

How …

Were my ears deceiving me? Was the voice impacting my brain the product of my exhaustion? Was I perhaps delirious? I couldn't quite believe the information I was being fed, and I'm sure it showed.

… did this happen?

It has a name, said Klaus. Revolution.

A good fairy broke the glass, said Cory.

The flood of events, exacerbated by my fatigue, was a blight on my ability to process information.

Glass? I asked.

Set off the emergency evacuation alarm, said Cory. Flushed the scum out. Then we took possession of the vacant premises.

Bloodless, said Klaus. One for the textbooks.

Their enthusiasm trumped my bewilderment. Skis and all, Klaus and I were bundled into a Lecky van and driven, as part of the very first motorcade Conroy had ever seen, to The Roundelle, and thence to Admin Stem. Braving the cold, residents lined the streets all the way to cheer and clap. On arrival at The Depot, with Cory leading the way, we took the lift to the fourth floor, and burst through the oak door into the boardroom.

And there they all were swarming round the cedar table like excitable insects. Most of my former Division Heads were there.

My entire panel in fact bar one. Was Alain Valery also behind bars? Cooling his heels with Basil? Later, when I put this question to Cory, I was told they hadn't been able to nab him. The weasel had gone to ground.

But right now, it was colourful balloons festoons and streamers for the eye, applause and cat-calls for the ear, backslaps and handshakes for all touchy-feely nerve-endings, and the choice of champagne or beer for all palates. Many worthy citizens of Conroy had joined the party, some spies I suspect among them. Most of them – perhaps not so much the spies – quickly forgot the intended purpose of the occasion, a fete for my return, preferring instead to embrace the festivities, particularly the booze, as ends in themselves. For them, the night promised to be a wipe-out.

Gabby's camera was letting off spit-ball after fiery spit-ball of flash.

And Klaus, alias Eddie, camouflaged in ski-goggles beanie and thick scarf, was intent on blending studiously into the background, seeking an incognito role. He was happy to take in all the flap-doodle, to see local history being made, to enjoy the moment vicariously but, when the chips were down, his career took priority for him. A trusted *apparatchik* of Government should not be seen to be fraternizing with such subversive elements nor condoning such behaviour.

I could see his point. Despite my state of exhaustion, any delusions of grandeur I might have been tempted to entertain evaporated forthwith. A rebellion of this stripe had no chance of success when pitted against the force of a nation-state, with resources measured in billions of dollars at its disposal. Although, at this moment, the cheap tinsel and raucous hullaballoo was plying its seductive horseplay for all it was worth, I could only conclude this venture, of which I had become unwitting front and centre, was doomed. For ventures such as this, the only paths forward from this point were bad ones.

In the throng before me, I saw my beautiful Max studying me

fondly, reading the air between us. Bless him. I was certain he was aware of and in sympathy with the turmoil going through my head at this time. I found myself thinking, I shall keep this guy.

Brian Collyer of Science took me aside from the brouhaha for a few private words apropos The Space. His manner was uncharacteristically serious. His news was not pretty.

The beast's collapsing in on itself big time, he said. Eating itself alive. Imploding.

Give me some figures, I said.

Gripping me by the shoulder, he launched into his doomsday spiel.

Well, on the ground, were his words, the interface now is a good metre closer to the centre point of the whole thingummy than when you last saw it. We've crunched the numbers and figure this brainchild of hell shall have shrunk to nothing in three weeks max. What remains of it won't be enough to fit on the point of a pin. It goes without saying those people inside must come out, and that means now.

Thank you for the reality check, I said.

That night, bedded down with Max in his quarters, we teased to fever pitch the desire for each other we had kept on hold for months, and then assuaged it by customary means. In the process, my aching muscles found relief at last, my exhausted frame recovered some of its bounce, and my tortured mind edged closer to karma. Surrounding us, propped against walls and benches, and filling the air with their aromatic fragrance, were samples of Max's art in its incipiency. They would, should events favour them, go on to become peerless creations strewn across the landscape of Conroy.

In these congenial and life-affirming circumstances, I sought clarification from Max on a moot point.

Who set the ball rolling? I asked.

I'm guilty, he said. I was the one broke the glass.

Nobody's guilty, I said. It was a telling move.

Sure. Events have done the telling.

Don't be hard on yourself. Let *me* deal with the unintended consequences.

Best of British.

We left things at that. Tomorrow we would see what we would see. We embraced yet again. Right now, in the gentle ambience night deals out to lovers, we had a different row to hoe. The moment was too precious to be squandered on vulgar thought and facile word.

The Great Escape

That's something I'm not at liberty to divulge right now, said Tania.

There was mockery in her tone, foil to the wild excitement in her eyes. The excitement in turn was foil to a quiet inner glow consequent – I surmised – on her pregnancy. She had parroted, almost verbatim, my own words, the words I had uttered in response to her request, some time back, re the identity of Conroy's clandestine artist, the wannabe Banksy from Antipodean climes. Now the boot was on the other foot. The request was now mine, the response hers. *She* was the one in a position to say yea or nay.

She saw, with satisfaction, that I had made the connection. With this in mind, she took the initiative.

I know who it is, she said. It's Max.

I tried to bluff.

Who? I asked.

She, not inclined to take any nonsense, snapped back at me.

Your assistant, were her terse words.

In saying this, she turned slightly sidewards and I caught her profile. She was quite a few months gone and it showed. Clearly, she was one of those women who, when the time comes round for her to deliver the goods, shall have taken on the shape of a round ball, almost as wide as high. A force to be reckoned with, nonetheless.

I spread my hands, palm upwards, before her.

So, I said, it's *quid pro quo* time. You know my secret. You tell me yours.

You'd like to know, she asked, how I managed to negotiate this escape?

Hold your horses, said Ray. We haven't escaped yet.

It's as good as done, Tania said. We're free to leave right now.

How do you know? I asked.

Dr Li's tests don't lie.

So how did you manage to wangle an amnesty?

Casting a quick glance over my shoulder – at Mt Redoubt I assumed – she held up her hands, fingers spread, palms vertical, as if to halt my physical advance.

Raincheck please, she said. This is a precarious moment. I don't want to tempt the fates. To offend the gods. To challenge the runes. To piss on my own parade.

You'll tell me afterwards?

The very moment we're out of here.

Shit, let's just do it, said Ray.

This exchange took place the day after my triumphant reception in the boardroom, the reception celebrating my return to Conroy. You are entitled, of course, to draw your own conclusions, but I insist the main reason I returned at all was not to enjoy accolades or foment revolution. I came back because I wanted to be physically present to witness the moment Tania and Ray escaped alive from The Space, something Tania had promised would happen pending my arrival.

And, *voila*, here I was.

We had gathered around the conversation post, I on one side of the interface, Tania, Ray, and Jeremy on the other. We were all standing, humans on the snow-covered earth and bird on perch, as if poised for action. In addition to the bird cage with its avian resident, Ray had brought with him the sketch map – large and unwieldy now it was framed – of the demesne Tania had made for him many years prior. Tania, intended, on the strength of it, to travel light. She had brought nothing at all with her bar the clothes she stood up in.

She had requested a limited audience for the event, on the grounds, once again, that she didn't want to try the patience of whatever higher power – read the mountain – might conceivably have a stake in this adventure. Even Max had not been invited to this particular party. I couldn't help feeling Gabby, a lesser power but certainly not negligible, might be lurking somewhere out of plain sight. And I guess we need not count any who might be travelling *in utero*.

This was the time of day when, ordinarily, personnel from Health would be thick on the ground, organizing anti-infective treatment for those seeking it. But given the way The Space had been shrinking lately, Basil had deemed such activity too risky, and had postponed it indefinitely. Quite possibly permanently.

I was shocked to see how much The Space *had* shrunk in my absence. As Brian had warned, its radius was at least a metre shorter now. To accommodate this shrinkage, to take up the slack so to speak, the ski-poles together with the conversation post had been moved, leaving an annulus of dead snow-gums where the deadly interface had swept over them like a plague. The tree from which Jeremy's cage had hung in earlier more settled days was now outside The Space, a grey lifeless shrivelled-up presence, a wake-up call for all denialists.

It was clear The (ever shrinking) Space was now doing its final dash to oblivion, prepared to take all its live hostages with it. A truly monstrous prospect. How much time was left? Brian had said three weeks.

And, to precisely this point and in this very setting, Ray – man of action – had proposed we get a hurry-on. The time for talk was over. I remind you of the precise words he had used to make his proposal. I repeat for your benefit:

Let's just do it, he had said.

Point of order, was my response. What does the oracle think the outcome of such action might be?

Ray stroked his beard. I suspect there was a moment when he considered launching into his usual tiresome spiel. Mercifully, he thought better of it.

Oh, there'll be a glitch, he said.

What sort of glitch?

It involves my family.

My sympathies, Ray, but I understand your family are all dead.

But not their DNA, captain.

I imagined I saw Tania casting a nervous glance in the direction of the mountain behind me. Then she spoke.

Not the time for riddles, she said. Time to quit the premises.

I concur, said Ray.

Jeremy first. He's our canary.

Stone the freaking crows. What have I been thinking all this time? I was under the illusion he was a gang-gang.

He lifted the cage gently from the ground where it presently stood, setting it down on his side of the conversation post, on his side of the double-sided frame. He sat facing cage and bird and, further back, the mountain. Jeremy knew things were afoot. Unnaturally silent, but wide eyed, he tilted his head to one side. Something about him suggested to me a ventriloquist's doll waiting for the word from his master.

He got it. Ray opened the cage door, and said, Out.

Jeremy hesitated for a couple of seconds. Then, with a screech, he took a few stiff-legged steps to the cage door and was out in a bound. Still earthbound, he tested his wings. Then, by way of showing the middle finger, or should I say claw, to all those inclined to think he'd forgotten how to fly, he took off. We all held our breath. He landed on the branch of a snow-gum ...

... on the other side of the annular clearing. Outside of The Space.

Dumbfounded, I responded instinctively in my native language charged with peasant superstition.

Lode all'Onnipotente per questo miracolo! I said.

… then I wondered if, in this pagan neck of the woods, the omnipotent one might more properly have been the mountain …

It's time, said Ray.

He gathered up the awkward frame with one hand and threaded the other round Tania's waist. Together, the pair of them then made for the gap through which the dolly track was laid. In an instant, they were across the interface, standing shoulder to shoulder with me in the snow on the other side. Just as Ray had predicted they would.

The hugs I exchanged, first with Ray and then with Tania, were both prolonged and intense, as befitted the gravity of the moment. We were witness to and participants in history. The spell The Space exercised over all living creatures had finally been smashed.

To Ray I said, Welcome to the world. To Tania I said, You're a clever little number.

I'm not sure I like 'little number', she said, but I'll accept 'clever'.

Confirming my suspicions, Gabby with camera now arrived on the scene as if from nowhere. She wasted no time in stealing snaps of the escapees. Then she embraced Tania.

I'm at a loss for words, she said to Tania.

First time in recorded history, Tania replied.

Mind this for me, said Ray.

And, propping the framed mud-map against Tania's leg, he did the unthinkable. He dashed back across the interface and made for the hut while we, each of us in a state of shock, inhaled reflexively and watched gobsmacked.

No! Ray! Tania shouted.

But he was inside the hut, and we were as if rooted to the ground.

Soon he emerged. He had a small framed picture under his arm. As he headed for the interface, intending – what else? – to cross to safety for the second time, I chanced to look behind me at Mt Redoubt. A glint of sunshine, the merest of flashes, reached me from the granite embed where the eye of the lion might have been. The mountain had winked.

What we dreaded now happened. The glitch. Ray barrelled across the interface and promptly sprawled face down in the snow on the other side. The item he had evidently gone back to rescue – that fatal picture – slithered across the snow under its own momentum, coming to rest face up at my feet. None of us made a sound. Not a gasp, not a scream. All our screams were interior. Tania clapped a hand over her gaping mouth. Her eyes widened to the extent they seemed ready to burst from her face. We all knew what had happened.

We knew. The Spaceman was dead.

Tania was first to move. Wordlessly, she approached him, knelt beside him, gently turned his body over, cradled his head in her hands, and kissed his lips – surely still warm – with soft open mouth as she would have kissed them had he been living. We could not doubt this was tribute to an act of love she had enjoined with him countless times before. This, her *momento di pieta*, was paean to the world and rebuke to the mountain.

Gabby stood frozen to the spot, wordless once more, not venturing to photograph the breaking news to which she had just now come to enjoy exclusive access. That would have been an appalling violation of unspoken etiquette. Her camera, in reality an albatross, dangled from her left shoulder.

Jeremy looked down from the branch of the snow-gum that was just a paltry corner in the vast new territory he now owned. He seemed forlorn, his brilliant red plumage notwithstanding. But who knows what goes on in the head of a foreign species of critter? We can barely know what goes on in the head of our own.

I looked down at the picture that was the cause of our newly arrived agonies, crouching for a closer view. I figured the mitre joints of the frame, executed with obvious precision, were Ray's work. The head shot inside was of Frances, his late sister. I imagined she spoke to me through the frame that was in reality a megaphone.

She asked, Why?

The Minister *sans* Face

I never *did* get to learn Tania's secret despite her promise that day. The secret, that is, of how she had cajoled the mountain to drop its guard. In fact, as events transpired, I wasn't to see Tania ever again in this incarnation.

My job in Conroy was over. The Space had disgorged its human occupants, and was set to shrink to nothing in a matter of days. The special purpose for which Conroy was set up in the first instance was soon to be no more. Conroy would no longer be a demesne. It would doubtless take on a new identity, in essence no different from that of countless sleepy regional towns in Oz. As an exercise in democracy, its residents would vote in its own councillors and mayor. It would have no further need of an appointed administrator. It would run its own affairs *sans* me or, for that matter, Basil Shirley. That was as things should be.

So, I gathered up my bundles – physical and intellectual – and – with Klaus as guide – retraced my steps to the bush capital, where I set myself up in luxurious accommodation I was not sure I could afford. I waited. I knew full well 'they' would come for me.

Come they did.

I sat in the office of the Minister of Homeland Security. His office was not that of a desk jockey. It was the chamber of a grand inquisitor. The desk before which I sat was devoid of all clerical paraphernalia. This desk was in no way reflective of the work ethic of its owner. Its gleaming and uncluttered surface was intended to intimidate.

The Minister sat behind this desk. Behind him was an unshaded window through which the brilliant sunshine of an early spring day poured its dazzling display. So, all I could see of the Minister was a dark blob traced out by a blinding halo of light. I'm sure this was his deliberate intention in the interests of more effective interrogation. He could see my face but I, not his.

Do you imagine, he asked, I'd allow free publicity for you and your fellow insurgents?

I'm not asking for it, I replied.

That's not the way *I* see it, pal. So, let's cut to the chase. You have two choices. Stay in Australia and I'll file a charge of sedition. The charge will stick and you'll do time. Plenty of time. Or you take advantage of your dual citizenship and go back without fuss to where you came from. In which case I won't pursue charges.

I was silent. Speaking would give him satisfaction, I thought, and why would I want to do him the favour? He who holds all the cards. So, let him speak.

After a few seconds, the back-lit fuehrer *did* speak.

And, by the by, who is Eddie? he asked.

I'll play your game, I replied. Who is he?

The Minister thumped the desk. Nothing bounced because there was nothing on it to bounce. Now he spat his words.

You want to do it the hard way? he asked rhetorically. I can oblige.

Edmond Lavrate.

That's Eddie?

Yes.

He opened a desk draw, extracting from it a pad of paper and a pen. He slid them across the desk to me with vehemence.

Write it, was his demand.

I wrote it and slid the pad and pen back to him.

Where can we find this low-life? he asked.

In Chamonix, I expect, was my answer.

Chamonix, France?

That's where the guy hangs out.

We'll check it out. Don't doubt it.

I sat still, hands on thighs, my eyes averted. For more than just one reason, looking at him was proving arduous for me.

O.K., he said. You're out of here. I won't have you wasting any more of my valuable time. Get your arse out of this country and don't bring it back. You have two weeks to be gone.

I left, shocked by his ultimatum. The shock was heightened by my feeling that I was being singled out. Neither Max nor my former Division Heads had incurred the wrath of the Minister. Bully for them, I thought, but couldn't help wondering, Why me? Max would be waiting for me back in the plush apartment that was eating my last reserves of funds, so I thought I might put the direct question to him when I returned, hoping he wouldn't see it as unbecoming acrimony on my part.

Why? I asked.

I'd tell you, he replied, if I could read the Minister's mind. They had every opportunity to nab me at Checkpoint Charlie, but they waved me through. For which I am grateful. I'm here with you which is exactly where I want to be.

I poured cognac for two.

For the next two weeks only, I said.

After which I'll come with you.

Though I felt a touch of the warm fuzzies at his proposal, I could see some problems with it. I chose not to raise them with him at this precise moment. I wanted time and a clear head to think things through.

And, I said, I hear my former Division Heads are carrying on as usual, despite Basil Shirley being in charge.

Basil's out of custody? he asked.

That's what I hear.

I didn't add it was from Beverley Bancroft I had heard this news. And he declined to comment further, preferring just to raise his hands in the air, palms upward.

Things suck, I thought. I needed answers. If I couldn't get them from my beloved Max, I would have to go for a jog.

Yes, reader, I did say 'jog'.

This is how I arranged things. In my Nikes, I set off at a moderate pace around Lake Burley Griffin. Spring was putting on quite a show and so the fraternity of pavement-pounders were out and about, indulging their crazed obsession, many running on sprains and stress fractures. Just as one of them drew level with me, I feigned a stumble. He stopped to see if I was O.K. and, afterwards, we carried on jogging side by side. To the casual observer, perhaps one lurking with telephoto lens behind the weeping willows, it was meant to look like we had met each other for the first time. But it was staged.

The other jogger was Klaus, whom I had contacted an hour earlier by burner phone.

Thanks so much for covering for me, he said.

Not a problem, I said.

I'm mortified by what's happened to you. It's a terrible thing. I only wish there was some way I could return your favour.

I drilled him. He was happy to be drilled.

As I expected, the circles he moved in proved valuable sources of information. I learnt that the Minister had decided punishing the personnel in Conroy as things stood would make too many waves. So, for the present, they retained their former positions. The lucky devils had a free pass. There was no place to which they, as opposed to me, could be deported. And because he didn't want them going public so soon after the event, it was politic to keep them sweet until such time as everything had blown over. He would bide his time. He was not done with them yet. No siree. Their arses would keep.

You know of course, he said, The Space is no more?

I expected as much, I replied.

So, the demesne of Conroy has run its course.

And the Directorate?

Not so.

Why not?

His pause was telling. As I listened to the slap of our runners on concrete, I was certain he was about to reveal to me something of great moment.

So, what I am about to tell you, he said, must go no further.

O.K., was my response. Spill it.

Two new Spaces have cropped up.

Where?

One is in a wilderness area in Tasmania near Mt Ossa. The other is more of a worry. It's at the base of Mt Bellenden Ker in North Queensland. There's significant human habitation nearby.

Ri-i-ight.

So DETA shall stay.

Who'll head it up? John Shepherd?

No way. He's yesterday's man.

So, who?

Your ex. June Cartwright.

I stopped dead in my tracks. Out there in the middle of the Lake, a single spurt of water rose promisingly, before dispersing as fine spray. It was Canberra's premier water feature. Behind it, across the Lake to its furthermost bank, Black Mountain, with its iconic tower, dominated the landscape of the city. Perhaps this prominence too would one day get to sponsor a Space.

Let's have coffee, Klaus said.

We sat at an outdoor table, part of a small bistro where fellow joggers rewarded themselves for having done their penance to the god of wellness. Klaus chose the table, making sure nobody was within earshot. While we waited for our coffee, he took it upon himself to fill me in, keeping his voice low, re the machinations of our current Government as he saw them. Flashes of his innate cynicism, more than just an edge, came through as he expounded. I wondered whether this emblematic attitude of his could be attributed more to nature or to nurture.

He set the conversational ball rolling by posing a question, *sotto voce*, to me. I found myself answering, through subconscious mimicry, in a whisper.

Have you ever stopped to ask yourself what makes the Minister tick? was his question.

You mean my nemesis? I asked in return.

He nodded.

I mean the Minister for Homeland Security, he said.

I guess it's all about power.

Then why doesn't he covet the Prime Minister's position?

I raised my hands, palm upwards. He certainly loved posing questions. Our coffees arrived, and we began stirring in sugar.

Let me enlighten you, he said. You're right about power, of course. But there's power and there's power. The power the Prime Minister claims as his own is ceremonial in nature. Our Minister of Homeland Security is not interested in that sort.

There's a division of labour, I ventured.

You're onto it. The Prime Minister wields spin not substance. He woos the voters with his rhetoric. He wins the elections. He's in his third term now, going for a fourth. But once in the top job, he hasn't a clue what to do. You must have noticed.

I nodded.

On the other hand, Klaus continued, our friend from Homeland Security can't do spin. He's not sufficiently popular with the electorate to pull it off. But he *can* do substance. Oh, yes. He knows what to *do* alright. His forte is action. So, what do you suppose we're dealing with here?

Horses for courses, I replied.

Unquestionably. But you've missed the point.

What *is* the point?

A symbiosis made in heaven.

So, you're saying one man acquires power, and the other wields it?

I am.

Which makes each dependent on the other.

And ensures neither covets the other's job.

I took a sip of my coffee to give myself time to take his thesis in. When he spoke again, it was to pose another question to me.

And, he asked, whom do you suppose is the more dangerous?

The Minister for Homeland Security, was my emphatic reply.

Right. And that's why we must never meet like this again.

I looked into his steel blue eyes and realized with regret I was seeing Klaus Anders for the very last time.

Return of the Prodigal

I was home. At the Post Office, in V–, Basilicata, Italy. In my own small bedroom above the shop, watching out of my tiny window at the gloomy day, a day that insisted autumn leaves shall drop.

Since returning, I had taken to wearing a hat, though this had never before been my habit. I guess after all these years of pointed resistance, I was surrendering to the inevitable. My choice was a bucket hat in soft tweed. I wore it most times, even when (as now) I lay at rest on my bed.

Alone in the semi-darkness, I could just make out my reflection in the oval mirror opposite. I was seeing this image, barely identifiable as me, through an oily veil, a dark palette that would have done Rembrandt proud. And sometimes what I saw in that mirror was not me at all. It was variously Tania, Ray, Klaus, and Max. Ray's image might have been on loan from some depository of the dead. Max's might have been there to deliver me a bitter reprove.

I had left them all behind in Oz.

> So, I am a loser, and I live with papa,
> where we work at the postal trade.
> And every single time that I look into his eyes,
> I'm reminded of my masquerade.

Gros Bonnets had been restored to its former position downstairs in our workspace atop the pigeonholes that housed the town's mail. The hook that had supported it in my childhood days was still there as if it had been waiting all this time to be reunited with the scurrilous tableau it had historically held aloft. Papa naturally saw this as a bad omen. So, one day it happened that, with a petulant cry, he flung his postmaster's hat, a soft flat-topped job in navy blue with a sloping peak in front, onto the pan of one of the post office scales.

My fate never lets me forget, he said.

It's my destiny too, I said.

By reason of association?

With the Post Office. Not with you.

I *am* the Post Office.

So now am I.

Ragazzo mio. You're talents shall be in high demand. Before too long headhunters shall beat a path to our front door.

Looking for me?

Certainly not for me.

I understood why he had made this prediction, but was not convinced. His rationale was in the news each day. Replicas of The Space had cropped up around the world, though not yet in Italy. First in Indonesia, at the base of Mt Agung. Then in Japan, in the Kirishima National Park. Then in California, at Mt Lassen. Then in Germany, at Der Brocken. An epidemic was underway. A pandemic. The earlier one had killed my aunt Claudia. This one would surely be the death of us all.

And China, spared exposure for the present, was demanding a comprehensive inquiry into the source of this new scourge.

We shall see it here soon enough, said my father. In our own backyard.

How I missed Max. Our separation at this intercontinental remove was scarcely bearable to me. I was beset constantly by physical desire I could neither contain nor consummate. I had asked him to write to me frequently, which he did, sometimes by email and sometimes by handwritten snail-mail. The latter delighted me. Its cursive strokes – a natural choice for the artistically inclined – contained within its flowing whorls and calligraphic verticals a hint of the personal not to be found in cyberspace. I replied, of course, but always electronically.

In this way, we compared notes. And our passions, their full sway not amenable to expression in mere words, were bound to be found lurking in the subtext of these notes by minds receptive to such.

The problem with snail-mail was that, when it arrived in V-, its handler was my father. Papa could put two and two together. So, one day, to my astonishment, he put a question to me.

Why don't you invite your Max here? he asked.

I picked myself up off the floor.

You know about him? I asked stupidly.

He waved Max's latest letter under my nose.

To this parochial backwater? was my response. Without language? He'd go bananas.

No problem. He's a smart guy. He'd pick up the dialect. We'd teach him Italian. Find a good Italian name for him. How does Massimiliano Baldacchino grab you?

He winked. *Mio Dio.* The old scoundrel was having a proper lend of me. I snatched the letter from him and retired to my room to read it.

It ran to several pages.

My darling Max, bless his cotton socks, had been in touch with Tania. She was living in country Victoria with her former schoolmate, Christine. Having given birth to a boy about a month back, she had – predictably – named him Ray. Had it been a girl, there would have been no prizes for guessing what name she would have chosen. The child would go on to be custodian of the Cromwell DNA, whose twin helixes were very much in working order, spinning like tops, just as his late father had foretold.

I speculated on a suitable epitaph for Ray. The Spaceman could be, and had been, variously described as an enigma, an embarrassment, a guru, a shill, an asset, a living treasure, a wellspring of showmanship. Not to mention a lover. But all punters would agree on one thing. He was one of a kind. It was not certain the lottery known as human heredity would turn up one of his breed again anytime soon, but in order such a possibility be given every chance, it was imperative his genes were perpetuated. As was now happening.

Back to Max's latest letter and his news re Tania:

Incredibly, Tania had received a phone call from the Minister of Homeland Security. He had wanted to know the secret behind her escape from The Space. She had told him emphatically she was not about to divulge this sort of information, and especially not to some Charlie with a track record of putting people's life in danger. When asked by the Minister to clarify this point, she cited the drive-by shooting that had happened while she was still living back in The Space.

The Minister, of course, had promptly denied any involvement.

The word around town, Max went on to say, was that the Minister planned to make good use of The Spaces cropping up all over the shop – the latest examples of which were at Mt Kaputar in New South Wales and at the iconic Hanging Rock in Victoria – to accommodate immigration detainees. Ergo he sought means to release said detainees should they agree to go back where they came from. That would explain why he had contacted Tania. Alas, without success.

The Minister set a new course. It didn't matter much in the scheme of things that Tania was not prepared to be forthcoming. That was on *her* conscience.

So Max, pursuing further the subject of sidelined consciences, explained that the Minister went on to pressure the Prime Minister into using his marketing skills to groom the electorate re his plans for refugee detention. Just as soon as the voting public were brought on board – or, more plausibly, found to be profoundly indifferent – Homeland Security would spring into action. The unsolved issue of release from detention – slated for some later date or perhaps never – was immaterial. That particular can could readily be kicked further down the road.

If the plight of the unfortunate refugees tore at my heart, the next paragraph of Max's letter ripped atrium from ventricle. His need to join me was urgent. He pleaded with me to let him do so. Did this dear man imagine for an instant I didn't wish also for this outcome? Did he imagine the upshot he longed for wasn't the same as that for which I pined? I wanted him beside me day and night, to feel my blood pumping in tandem with his, to experience the congruent arcs of our mutual passion, to follow with him the loci of our desires.

I reflected on our life together so far. Beyond the inevitable niggles part and parcel of any relationship, we had no gripe with each other. On examination of the big picture, I could find only harmony and love in place.

But I couldn't now be party to the destruction of his soul. The constraints of living in V- would surely have precipitated such an outcome. He was an artist lacking both a day job and the local lingo. I was a blotted copybook.

It had occurred we might perhaps move together to *Milano*. He would enjoy free rein there. But that was out of the question. *Milano* was the scene of my crime.

In *Milano*, I had sought by illicit means to become my own man, a man *sans* hat, beholden to nobody but myself. Instead, I had become everybody's chattel, a utensil at the service of all.

> I'm a little teapot, short and stout.
> Here is my handle. Here is my spout.
> When I get all steamed up, hear me shout:
> Tip me over and pour me out.

I put Max's letter aside. When night fell, I sought refuge in sleep. But in sleep, there are dreams, over which one has no control.

The Minister for Homeland Security, his face as always nothing more than an inky void, was standing proprietorily beside one of the newly-formed Spaces. As would become apparent to my dreaming self in the course of this dream, the man of the moment was determined to turn the Space from liability to asset.

To keep the *hoi polloi* at bay for their own protection, and to keep his furtive secrets banged up and hidden from the curious, he had organized a steel-plate fence, topped with razor-wire and security cameras, around its perimeter.

The Prime Minister, hapless puppet on strings, stood beside him.

A fork-lift arrived, loaded up front with roughly a dozen sealed cardboard cartons. The Minister charged with keeping the Oz homeland safe and secure, pressed a button on a hand-held remote control. *Voila.* A gap opened in the steel fence. The driver of the fork-lift manoeuvred his load through the gap while he and his cabin remained outside where things were more conducive to life. It was never clear in my dream how the cartons unloaded themselves. But they surely did. Inside The Space.

What have we here? asked the Prime Minister.
Documents, replied the Minister for Homeland Security.
What sort of documents?
The sensitive variety.
How long shall they stay here?
Until The Space implodes.
And then?
The Statute of Limitations shall kick in.
And my job is ...?
Sell the fucker, Prime Minister. Sell it hard. That's what you're good for.

He pressed a button on the remote. The gap closed up.

My dream, as it turned out, was of the repeating kind. It had re-runs. In its next run, an Armaguard van pulled up. Two armed men in grey overalls unloaded obloid steel boxes with handles. The gap opened as before, but my dream never bothered to made clear to me how the boxes managed to get themselves inside The Space. Yet they did.

What have we here? asked the Prime Minister.

Cash, replied the Minister for Homeland Security.

What sort of cash?

The unwashed variety,

How long shall it stay here?

Until The Space collapses.

And then?

It shall be clean.

And my job is …?

Sell the fucker, Prime Minister. Sell it hard. That's what you're good for.

The gap closed up. The next run started. A truck carrying a huge shipping container, pulled up. The gap opened. Once again, I was not privy to how the container ended up inside The Space.

What have we here? asked the Prime Minister.

Bodies, replied the Minister for Homeland Security.

What sort of bodies?

The dead variety.

How long shall they stay here?

Until The Space runs its course.

And then?

There'll be nothing but bones.

And my job is …?

Sell the fucker, Prime Minister. Sell it hard. That's what you're good for.

That was the last run. I woke and found myself back in V-.

The day was clear and crisp, the ideal autumn day. I felt cheered. I was not in Australia as my dream would have it. I was in Italy, the land of my birth.

And suddenly, optimism – rare for me these days – ambushed my mind. The future, though vague, looked bright. I even began to feel it might be possible to invite Max over here to join me, without triggering the intractable problems I had been dreading. I felt he and I might be able to make a go of it after all. Joy filled my heart at the prospect.

There was news. My father announced it from the front counter of the Post Office, while I stacked parcels in the back room. There was a gap, a small unglazed window, through which he could speak to me.

Ragazzo mio, he said. We can, with pride, take our place in the big bad world. We now have our very own Space. A people-eater to rival Godzilla.

Where? I asked.

Not here in Basilicata. Not yet. Further north. In Abruzzo. In the Gran Sasso.

He passed the newspaper to me through the window. Black on white confirmed what papa had said. Supporting the story was a photo purporting to be of the location. It could have been anywhere in Italy: cultivated fields of green in the foreground and a peak – possibly the Corno Grande – in the background tipped with what might have been the first snow of the season. I'm sure the evil was lurking somewhere, but there was no sign of such in this benign picture.

Any people inside? I asked.

Give it time, he replied. May it eat the hatless people first.

I'll second that.

He was interrupted by a customer of this hatless variety. Normally, his interaction with such a person would have been brief, brusque, and confined to business, but today their take on the breaking news would have its out, and they rattled on with animation for a full minute or two. After which my father turned back to me.

It's very bad news indeed, he said, that's bad for all. I expect you're due for a visit sometime soon.

It came that very afternoon. Two visitors emerged from their chauffeured vehicle, wearing smart contemporary business suits with fedoras to match. They looked at ease. Nothing like the Big Men, strutting in their zoot suits as they burst from their mobile torture chamber. Minus their hats, this pair might have been career public servants transplanted from Canberra.

Unobserved, I watched through my window as they approached papa at the front counter. They were on a mission. On reaching my father, they removed their hats before speaking. That's the thing about hats. If one wears a hat, one can always choose to take it off.

We're looking for Marius Strangio, they said.

Acknowledgements

Without the inputs of those parties I acknowledge below, this book in its present form would not have happened.

At unsung sacrifice to herself, my life partner, Janet Ward, has allotted me the substantial amount of time and space essential to me apropos the creation of The Spaceman. For this, I really cannot thank her enough.

John Timlin has done a superb editing job, and has brought The Spaceman to the attention of main-stream publishers. Sylvie Blair, of Bookpod, who eventually took it on, has – in tandem with Ingram Spark – produced the handsome job you now have the privilege to see and hold. To these people, I am grateful – perhaps not eternally – but certainly for my lifespan on this good earth.

Greg Carroll was the artist responsible for the concept behind the wonderful map of Conroy contained herein, and Terry Sykes was the artist who subsequently took it through to completion. Both these people have skills I can only envy. To them, I extend my sincerest thanks.

The Hotel Monterey in Sendai, Japan, whose décor and motifs flaunt an unlikely 19th Century European theme, owns – in all likelihood – the most extensive collection of antique prints by Edmond Lavrate to be found anywhere in the world. Lavrate's *Les Gros Bonnets du Village*, a photographic copy of which I have appropriated for the back cover of my book, tells a story – nay, several stories – that a thousand words cannot. When international travel becomes practicable again, I swear I shall be off like a shot to the Monterey and to the vibrant city of Sendai.

About the Author

The author's main paper qualification is a PhD in photonuclear physics, i.e. nuclear reactions induced by photons, from the University of Melbourne. He has necessarily written a number of scientific papers in this field.

In the 1970s, he wrote a review paper on the subject of Global Atmospheric Consequences of the Combustion of Fossil Fuels, which (as might be imagined) was ground breaking at the time.

His literary accomplishments are a short story published in the Australian literary journal *Tabloid Story* in the 1970s, a screenplay funded by Film Victoria in the 1980s but never produced, and a novel *Where Pademelons Play* published in 2018.

The Spaceman is his second novel.

* 9 780648 428725 *